A GILDED CAGE

Tempest Rising Book 3

Elliott VanDruff

Belle Rose Press

Books by Elliott VanDruff

TEMPEST RISING SERIES

Beyond the Shroud

The Last Dusk

A Gilded Cage

Empire of Dust

The Tempest Queen

Dedication

To my sisters, Hannah and Olivia, who were comrades in arms in our exploration and delight of all things fantasy.

Map of Lyrica

Chapter 1

I HAD NEVER LOOKED more beautiful.

I had never felt more trapped.

I left Morgania with nothing but the clothes on my back, which Duke Agramon tossed into the sea the moment we'd boarded the ship. I stared at the mirror, scarcely able to recognize myself. My hair had been curled and primped until it flowed over my shoulders and down my back in voluminous black ringlets that stood out in stark contrast to the milky-white gown.

The cosmetics were another thing altogether. Kohl had been rubbed over my eyes, and a feather was used to line my lids. Rouge on my cheeks made me look flushed.

My tattoos were the only part of me I recognized. The black imorets, marking me as a Morganite, winged out from the corners of my eyes. The necklines of the dresses Duke Agramon ordered me into were all scandalously low, each one revealing the ten-pointed star with a sideways crescent on my chest that was supposed to mark me as Imor's chosen one, but now I saw it as a curse. Morganian rose blossoms, the symbol of my mother's family and the lost line of the Morgans, curled around my neck. What would my royal ancestors say if they could see me now, painted and fussed over to look like a Lyrican puppet?

Staring into the mirror, I noted how all the paints and finery dulled the colors of my stone. I preferred myself clean-faced, allowing the gem to give my features the color they lacked. The gem, or gems, rather, as I alone bore three, marked me as the most powerful sorcerer in the realm. Yet, I'd never felt so powerless.

I'd left a part of myself on the shores of Morgania. Now I was listless, tethered to nothing as I headed to the eastern shore. My family, my clan, had sold me. They'd made it clear I would never be welcomed back. I had no home.

So what if I were the lost heir to the Morgans? What good would it do me without a single ally?

During my night at Darkport, as the hours trudged toward morning, I'd waited for someone to rescue me, for Destrian to see that I was simply trying to save his life, for my family to reclaim me and take me back to the shelter of their home, but the only person who'd emerged in the morning light was my handmaid, Ena. I'd tried to send her away. I'd tried to tell her it wouldn't be safe, but she refused to listen. Though I worried for her, it had been a welcome gift upon my dismal departure. At least I had one friend.

I had no one but Ena.

Ena, and a shadow of a family.

"Echo?" I whispered, looking into the corners of the cabin. I saw the shadow soul better at night in the flickering candlelight dancing along the walls. It was then that she preferred to appear, an ancestor who had followed me from the Nightlands.

Echo had initially communicated by repeating what I said, as though she'd forgotten speech in the centuries she'd been trapped in the Nightlands with the rest of the lost tribe. She'd begun to pick up more words throughout the voyage, as if being around me and the shipmates jolted her memory. Echo couldn't drift far. She was bound to the Nightlands and now tied to me through the stones embedded in my brow and hands. I didn't know why she followed me out of the darkness. I only knew I was grateful. Echo was the only family I had left.

"*I'm here,*" she hissed in my ear, her voice so faint that the lightest of breezes could carry it away.

"We're nearly at the capital," I whispered, looking through the porthole to the eastern shore.

"Keep strength," Echo murmured back. "There are troubles ahead."

Echo was right. I had to stay strong. Though I'd always feared what fate would bring if I was taken to the capital, it was becoming increasingly clear that it was the only place

A GILDED CAGE

I had left.

I had to make a home somewhere.

I had to make do.

The unknown.

A chance for a new beginning.

A new beginning with the most feared man in the entire realm. I peered out the small window of my cabin. The Gilded Portal stretched across the mouth of the inland sea that led to the capital of Somme. The bridge rose high above the water, allowing ships to pass between the gates covered in hammered gold that was near blinding in the sunlight.

Farther away from our ship, a pod of dolphins leaped out of the water, their sleek, gray bodies disappearing into the crystal-clear waters of the Ballerian Sea before reappearing above the waves. I wished my friend Fin were there to see them with me. How she would've marveled at their dance.

The memory of Fin nearly sent tears running down my cheeks, so I tore my eyes away from the dolphins and instead studied the shoreline. Massive homes with the golden domes Somme was famous for rose above the water. Little figures ran along the sandy beaches or used sticks to poke through mounds of seaweed that had washed ashore.

As we sailed closer to the golden city, the houses

multiplied along the shore, shrinking in size but increasing in number as if the city itself were growing before me. Fishing boats trolled through the waters beside us, the shirtless men on board shouting at each other as they pulled in nets and tossed sea creatures overboard that wouldn't sell at market.

"I think we're nearing the harbor, Echo," I murmured. My long journey across the sea was coming to an end, and I was all the more dismal for it.

The door to my small cabin creaked open, and Duke Agramon, the most dangerous sorcerer in the empire, stepped in, looking resplendent in white-and-gold robes. That was one thing I already disliked about Agramon; he never knocked.

Though Duke Agramon struck fear into anyone who uttered his name, his features were surprisingly unremarkable. His hair was a mousy brown to match his muddy eyes and weak chin, but he made up for his common face with an immaculate wardrobe. I'd mostly seen him in spotless white robes made of the finest silk. He'd shaved recently, revealing his poor bone structure, but eyes would be drawn to the soft pink gem at the center of his brow, marking him as a sorcerer. His ability to read others' thoughts, to make them bend to his wishes, was legendary, even in the wilds of Morgania where I grew up.

His eyes flitted around the cabin before coming to rest

on me.

"Talking to yourself again?" he asked, his staff hitting the ground with a thump. Though I was the only sorcerer to bear three gems, Duke Agramon's staff held a second gem welded to the tip, a mirror to his own.

I wondered about its purpose, but Duke Agramon had scarcely spoken to me on the voyage. After the first day at sea, when the duke insisted on me changing into a dress, he'd left me with Ena and my thoughts.

By the way Duke Agramon approached, his staff thumping against the floor with every step, I could tell that my time of solitude was at an end. Turning to face him, I clasped the folds of my gown, trying to wipe the sweat from my hands.

Duke Agramon rested a hand on my shoulder. My nerves sparked and my body tensed. "Let me see you, my dear." I stilled as he circled me. His fingers reached out, adjusting a comb holding back my black curls. "The rouge is too much," he said with a frown. "I'd thought to give your cheeks some color, but it makes you look like a common whore, and we can't have that."

My temper got the better of me. I hated nothing more than being afraid of a man. "Better an expensive one, my lord?"

Duke Agramon slapped me soundly. My head jerked to the side, ears ringing as I instinctively grabbed my cheek.

"Rub the rouge off," Duke Agramon said smoothly, his voice unnervingly steady as he pulled a handkerchief from a hidden pocket in his robe and flicked it toward me, letting the air catch it as it fell. I grabbed it before it dropped to the floor. "Your spirit is one of your charms," the duke said. "A charm I've enjoyed in ladies I've sponsored in the past, but I will not abide rudeness, nor disrespect." The rose gem at the end of his staff glinted ominously. "Apologize."

I thought to say nothing. I didn't feel him in my mind like I had with Vianne, which meant I had my thoughts to myself. The Girdle of Ephema, a gift from some unnamed savior, was one grace of my imprisonment. I felt it even then, nestled on my waist under my expensive gown.

Agramon's eyes narrowed, glinting dangerously. It was probably unwise to test his anger so soon.

"Apologies, my lord," I said begrudgingly, bowing my head. "I meant no offense."

"Very good," the duke said. "Gillius thought it hopeless to bridle you, but I assured him all that was needed was a firm hand."

The duke's mention of Gillius sent bile rising to my throat. To think I'd trusted the man. That he'd had my best interests at heart. If my uncle sold me out, Gillius stamped the bill of sale, feeding information to Agramon while I'd attended to my studies at Solridge.

"We'll dock in Somme in a few hours' time, but there are matters we must attend to before we reach the city," Duke Agramon said, motioning to my bed. I went and sat on the pallet, smoothing my skirts across my lap instead of meeting his eye.

I'd been waiting for this moment ever since we'd boarded the ship. What did the duke expect of me? What would my life look like now that I was with my true sponsor? Now that I was a slave to the empire I loathed.

Duke Agramon swept his robes beneath him and took a seat at my looking glass. He regarded me thoughtfully. "I've heard so much about you already, I feel as though I already know you quite well, my dear."

I raised my brows, recalling the scrap of letter I'd found in Gillius's room at Solridge. "What did they tell you?"

"That you are headstrong and speak your mind, both traits I prefer in moderation."

Of course I could be myself, but on his terms. "How many other students have you had?"

"Many."

"Were they all girls?"

The duke's eyes narrowed. "Yes, though I fail to see why that matters."

But it did matter. The whispers of the duke's lascivious ways were not unknown to me. "Were you involved with them?"

"Of course, I was their sponsor. It's common for sponsors to be involved in their students' daily lives. It would be deficient of me if I were not."

I let out a gust of frustration. "That's not what I meant. Were you involved with them . . . romantically?"

Duke Agramon's eyebrows rose. "It's not something I require of them, if that's what you're implying."

I emitted a sigh of relief.

"You've probably already guessed that your mind is closed to me, which is . . . uncommon, but not unheard of."

Hmph, I gave another silent thanks to whoever ensured the girdle found its way to me.

Duke Agramon twisted the staff in his hand. "There was a hint in young Lord Destrian's mind that you were closer than I'd gleaned from the letters I received before your journey. Tell me truthfully, and know there will be consequences if I find out you're lying. Were you lovers?"

I froze, gooseflesh prickling over my skin as a chill swept through me. I tried to keep my voice steady and opened my mouth, ready to lie.

"If you deny it, I will have you inspected to make sure."

My lips drew tight. Heat burning my cheeks, I nodded and looked down at my hands.

"There, that wasn't so hard, was it?" Duke Agramon said, leaning back into his seat.

"Why do you want to know?"

"I'm your guardian. I have to know if I receive a proposal of marriage for you, of which, I'm sure there will be many."

My nose wrinkled in disgust. The corner of Agramon's mouth twitched at my reaction. Destrian had said there would be marriage offers. I hadn't believed him at the time, but hearing Duke Agramon say it didn't feel like the warning it was with Destrian. It felt like a promise. Given how the noblemen at Solridge reacted to me, I bet I could put off any unwanted suitors if I put my mind to it.

Duke Agramon went on, "You must keep in mind, though I have sponsored many young sorcerers, you're the first whom I've been given complete guardianship of."

"How does that change things?"

"Many things will remain the same. I will take care of your schooling. I will clothe you, feed you, ensure that you have the best the court has to offer, but I do not give these things freely. You will be required to work your power to the betterment of the empire, just like any other sorcerer schooled by a Lyrican purse."

I glanced at Iranoct hanging beside the door. Duke Agramon's gaze flickered to it.

"Will I be allowed to continue my weapons training?" I asked.

Duke Agramon twisted the staff with light fingers.

"They claimed you were a great fighter, given your Morganite upbringing. Those skills served you well in the Nightlands, as I see you are all in one piece, though I don't know how useful it will be for you at the capital." He looked back at Iranoct. "Continuing your weapons training will depend on you."

"What must I do?" I asked, my voice growing stronger. My father and clan had always been proud of my skill with the sword, but perhaps I was a fool for thinking that others would find it a valued trait. Solridge was merely a taste of what was to come.

"From what I've been told, you're already quite proficient in the fighting arts, while your other areas of instruction remain woefully inadequate."

Duke Agramon's comment rankled me. I'd done the best I could at Solridge. I'd even enlisted the help of Fin with mathematics and Araceli for my deportment. I'd never considered the possibility that I wouldn't be allowed to continue weapons training at the capital. Fighting was the one activity that I took pride in—my outlet. I should've known it would be taken away, but it still came as a shock.

"I have a reputation to uphold," Duke Agramon went on. "The court has heard many rumors about you already. There is quite a bit of excitement surrounding your arrival, and I'll require you to live up to that excitement." A smile tugged at the corners of his lips. "Since I am your guardian, not merely a sponsor, I will be much more demanding of you than I have been with previous students. After all, it is only I who can claim kinship to you now. As you are bound to me, I am bound to you. Your mistakes at court are my mistakes. Though I value unique traits in my students, you are so unlike the others that I'm inclined to be cautious. If you can impress at court, if you conduct yourself in a way that brings pride to my name, if you follow my rules and comply with every demand I make of you, then I may reconsider."

I nodded. He expected me to play his courtly games if I hoped to get what I wanted. My mind went back to the people of Helena and how they greeted Destrian and me on our return. The people of Somme seemed no different, if not more desperate. With three gems under my control, impressing the Lyricans should be simple enough. "So, what will you require of me at the capital?"

Duke Agramon leaned back in his chair, seemingly accustomed to conversations centered around the fate of young apprentices. "You are to follow my rules and honor all my requests. It's that simple."

"What are the rules?" I prodded. It couldn't be so simple, and while I didn't have much of a choice in the matter, I didn't like the assumption that the obedience expected of me was limitless, as if the tasks were of no consequence.

"I have enlisted the help of a tutor to educate you in the customs and courtesies of the Lyrican court. You will meet her when we reach the capital, and I expect you to treat her with the utmost respect, as she's doing me quite the favor by taking you under her wing. The rest of the time will be spent with me, training to use your power for the betterment of the realm. The emperor throws many court functions for the nobility, and you will attend those unless I deem otherwise. I'll have you know, my apprentices are quite popular at court. They are always dressed in the latest styles and behave with impeccable manners. In addition, they have all had a certain sense of . . . allure."

"Allure?"

Duke Agramon smiled as though I were a willful child and he a doting father. "They are all attractive, my dear, in their own way. I know it doesn't seem like it now, but you are a lucky girl. Most young ladies would give their right hand for a chance at wearing the most beautiful gowns, dining in the halls of Somme every night, and having goblets raised in their names. It's a coveted position, being my apprentice. I've had mothers and fathers begging on their knees for me to take their daughters under my tutelage."

I had to forcibly stop myself from rolling my eyes. I'd glimpsed what life was like for young noble ladies at Solridge. Their hands and virtues sold off to the highest bidder if it would benefit the family. Perhaps the parents thought they were ever so lucky to send their daughters to Agramon, but did the girls feel the same way? "Since it *is* such a popular position, as you claim, why don't you select a girl who is willing? Granted you could find one, of course."

"Because, you will be one of the most coveted sorcerers in the whole of the empire, and I have a reputation to uphold. I suggest you stop being ungrateful and start counting the blessings that you have. Though I understand that you've lost your family and that you come to me unwillingly, your feelings are foolhardy, and my patience will only stretch so far."

I ignored his underlying threat and instead asked something that had been bothering me for a long time now. "How did you even find out about me? How did you come to be my sponsor?"

"I am seated on the Council of Five, and part of our job is to monitor those practicing magic in the realm. We heard about you in the same way we hear about most unclaimed sorcerers, through the whispers of others."

The duke's answer surprised me. I'd figured the council would've heard of me from the seer, Chassandre, who'd sent her monster to assassinate me. If it wasn't Chassandre, then who? I met Gillius soon after leaving the shroud, so what "others" would have known of me if not a seer?

Regardless, I didn't have time to dwell on it. The golden

gates of the capital were approaching, and I had very little time to steel myself for the tests to come. I looked up, meeting the duke's eyes. "You haven't spoken of the university. I thought . . . Somme has a great university. Would I not attend there?"

"I would never allow a student of mine to attend with those . . . radicals . . . let alone a child under my guardianship," Duke Agramon sneered. "No, if you can read, which I've been assured that you can, then you can use the library and study whatever you please in your rooms."

I took a deep breath. "How long?"

Duke Agramon raised his brows. "Pardon me?"

I suppressed the bubble of fear in my throat. "How long must I stay under your guardianship?"

Duke Agramon tilted his head. "My dear, I don't think you understand your position. You are under my guardianship until it is relinquished to another, which I assure you, I won't do without proper diligence and care."

"I propose a deal," I said, straightening and looking him in the eye.

"A deal," Duke Agramon repeated with a condescending smile. "I'm afraid you're not in the position to make deals, my dear. I already have what I want."

"You may have me in your grips, but you also want me to behave," I said, rising. I fully intended to grasp my freedom once again, and I refused to give in to the duke despite my growing fear of him. "I'm sure it would be much easier for you if you could force me to do as you wish, but as it stands, my mind remains my own. As you said before, I can be *very* strong-willed. I imagine you will want me to call my power whenever you wish. You may even want me to charm others. How much easier would it be for you if I was willing?" It was a gamble, but I prayed to Imor that the duke would take the bait.

Agramon rose from his seat. The tight line of his mouth hinted at suppressed laughter. "I would remind you that I've been at this game of deals far longer than you. Do not push me."

Duke Agramon stepped to the door but paused at the threshold. "Remember, Rowyn, I can be a powerful ally to those I deem my friends." He then swept the door shut behind him, leaving me to my thoughts and sinking hopes.

You would be a powerful ally and an unholy enemy. They were Destrian's words, murmured to me on the beach at Solridge. It seemed so long ago. I'd give anything to go back.

I looked in the mirror, reevaluating myself. I was trapped in the capital, but I was the direct descendant of the two greatest Morganites to ever live, Helen, the first queen of my people, and Morius the Black, the sorcerer who ensured Morgania flourished for a generation. I would not be cowed by Duke Agramon, nor anyone at the capital. I was going into battle, but unlike the Nightlands,

I would need my wits over my sword.

I would do my damned best to make him regret dragging me from my homeland to the gilded city. Without control of my mind, he would find it very difficult to tame me.

It was decided. I would be the biggest nuisance he'd ever come across. And I wouldn't stop until he sent me home.

I would be a new Rowyn. A girl with all the power in the world, and nothing to live for.

Chapter 2

DUKE AGRAMON LED ENA and me out onto the deck of the galley. Seeing the enormity of the city, I balked, my mouth agape as I took in the towers and walls of Somme, the capital of Lyrica, a place where I'd vowed never to set foot.

The entire city seemed altogether too full, as though the gods were making a stew and the people were nearly bubbling over the top of the pot. There was no color: no green nor plants, nor trees that I could see. White clay made up the structures of the buildings, and the gold rooftops caused the city to appear too bright to be believed. Sitting atop it all, perched on the rising ground at the city center, was the sprawling imperial palace. White flags with the golden sunburst of the emperor fluttered over the bridges and turrets against the clear blue sky. A flock of gulls flapped over the harbor, their ringing calls filling the air as they followed the fishing boats preparing to dock. I couldn't help but admire the beauty of it.

Ena began to tremble beside me. I grabbed her hand, squeezing it. Despite my relief at her joining me, I couldn't help but view her presence with apprehension. Though neither of us belonged at the capital, Ena was only there for me. I wasn't sure I deserved such loyalty, but I hoped one day I might.

"It's not too late to send you back," I whispered, eying the busy wharf. It seemed word spread quickly in the empire, for a crowd of people was gathered near the dock, pointing at our ship. I looked up and noticed a white flag bearing Duke Agramon's eagle of Solin flapping above us, announcing his arrival.

Ena shook her head. "No, my place is here, Rowyn. What use am I at home?"

I looked over at Ena. I'd noticed the imorets around her eyes had been redyed in the time she'd spent at home. Her dark hair was plaited and wrapped in a loop at the base of her neck, and the linen dress she wore was pressed within an inch of its life. In Ena's way, she'd prepared for the golden city.

"If anyone gives you trouble here, any lord or servant steps out of line, you *will* tell me," I said, holding her gaze.

Ena nodded.

Agramon strode over to us. I clutched Ena's hand tighter.

He didn't even spare my handmaid a glance. "Are you ready to depart?"

I nodded, my mouth dry as the sailors slung a gangplank between the ship and the dock. Agramon went first, stepping gingerly onto the other side, breathing deeply as he surveyed the bustling dock before us.

A sailor grabbed my hand to help me up onto the board. When his fingers brushed my gem, he drew his hand back sharply.

"Your horses will be ready in a moment," the sailor said hurriedly, then scurried off, leaving me to step off the ship unaided.

"What do you think of the golden city?" Duke Agramon asked as I stood beside him, my feet relishing the steadiness of land.

I eyed the fortifications that wound in a spiral throughout the city. "There are far too many walls for my taste."

"The city has never been breached," Duke Agramon said. "Not even lifelong denizens of Somme know all of its secrets."

"Of course, everyone has been too busy fleeing Lyrica's conquests to attack the capital itself," I said.

Agramon turned to me, his brows furrowed.

I grinned, palming Iranoct at my side, knowing that Agramon might eventually take even that small freedom.

Thankfully, our horses arrived before he answered. Agramon mounted, then called a guardsman to assist me, but I refused to wait. I lifted my foot to the stirrup and pulled myself into the saddle, dragging the voluminous white skirt over. Before Agramon could say anything, I reached down and dragged Ena up behind me, then readjusted my neckline that had fallen askew and revealed my corset beneath.

Duke Agramon turned his horse with a scowl, speaking to the lead guardsman who'd accompanied him on the journey west. The other guards had all donned their white tunics once more, the stitched golden sunburst in the center marking them as men of the emperor. They mounted their own horses, shouting their excitement at arriving home.

I looked out over the city. Could I ever call it home? Would there be a time when I would feel relief at seeing the white walls of Somme? I brushed those thoughts aside when the guardsmen shouted at me to hurry up, and I followed our party toward the city.

THE WHARF WAS BEDLAM as we rode through, our horses kicking up great clouds of dust in our wake. Screams of "The Morganite!" rang out through the crowd. Some women even cried, muscling their way through the masses to grab my hands. Ena was clutching me so tightly, I struggled to breathe. It took a moment for me to realize a man had managed to grab hold of her skirt and was doing his level best to pull her out of the saddle. I pushed the man away with my foot, realizing that if the crowd grew any more unruly, we'd soon be overrun.

"Is this because of the Nightlands?" I shouted to Agramon over the cacophony, remembering how I was greeted at Helena when Destrian and I had returned. Still, Helena was nothing to Somme. The desperate crowd of people before us seemed unending, and they pressed ever closer, now blocking the street. My eyes were drawn to the children's faces. Their thin cheeks were coated with dirt as they raised empty cups toward me. Just one look at the clouds of dust billowing up from the streets told me Somme was dry as bone.

Agramon shook his head. "It's for what's to come," he shouted back, his eyes on a particularly unruly group. I couldn't ignore the creases of worry on his face, even as a few people close to Agramon seemed to turn as one and disperse into the crowd. Another group turned away, and another, but each group Agramon sent on their way was replaced by others, their eyes verging on madness as they screamed at us.

Ena's grip on my waist tightened.

Our escort was losing patience with the mob. We hadn't even made it out of the wharves and into the city proper. The guardsmen drew their swords as our procession came to a standstill, the way through the streets blocked by a crush of people.

"Can't you do anything for them?" Ena said into my ear.

Arda the Seer's words swam into my mind. "If all you seek is freedom and happiness, then you must fulfill the task Imor put you on this earth to do. You have a duty and a choice. Using your gift to help others is the only road to freedom now."

In front of us, one of the guards raised his sword, aiming at those pushing against his horse. I kicked my steed forward, unsheathing Iranoct as I went. I made it to the guard just in time, my blade meeting his with a resounding clang.

"Get back, my lady!" the guard shouted, trying to shove me aside. "They'll be merciless if they get ahold of you."

I gritted my teeth and held my place. Agramon hadn't said I couldn't use my powers whenever I pleased; he merely stated that I must use them when he requests. I let the stones warm within my hands, and a host of clouds started forming above us.

When the guard tried to lash out at the townspeople again, I raised Iranoct to the sky and unleashed a bolt of lightning. My ears rang at the deafening noise, but I pushed more power to the sky, unleashing a deluge that blanketed the wharves, soaking the people in the streets as well as our party.

"Stop that display at once!" Agramon yelled. "The

emperor wished to be the first to witness your skills."

"Look at them!" I shouted back, shielding my eyes from the raindrops. "Sating people's thirst should be our first priority."

Agramon rode up beside me and grabbed my wrist. "You overstep your place," he growled.

I met him glare for glare, unable to disguise my hatred for the man.

"Your Grace, look," Ena said, pointing over my shoulder. Agramon turned, his eyes on the street. As we argued, the crowd had thinned as many found cover from the rain, their faces streaked with rivulets of dirt and mud. The people who stayed were shrieking and lifting their cups to the sky or dancing in the street, their dirty clothes soaked through. The heavy scent of rain and mud filled the air, mixed with the briny sweat of the masses.

Horns sounded in the distance, and people scrambled to get out of the way as dozens of soldiers splashed past. I could barely make out the dark figure of a man on horseback, shouting orders as soldiers lined the street, locking their staffs together and pushing the crowd back.

The man giving orders rode toward us, his hand gripping the hilt of a large sword hanging at his side. He didn't look like any of the Lyricans I'd known during my time at Solridge, nor was he dressed like one of the soldiers. He'd cropped his dark hair close to the scalp on the sides, while the top looked tousled, as if fingers frequently ran through them. Though most Lyricans were known to be clean-shaven, heavy stubble blanketed his face, promising to morph into a full beard within a day. He wore a black tunic underneath a leather jerkin and cloak that shielded him from the onslaught of rain. Though he bore no helmet, nor insignia, the soldiers followed his every command.

Agramon scowled at the man's approach and straightened in his saddle as though trying to look intimidating. I wouldn't say he pulled it off, considering he was soaked through, his limp, mousy hair plastered to his head and the once-white robes now splattered with mud, but he faced the man with such an air of contempt that I wondered about Agramon's anger.

"I told you it was madness to think a single squadron of men would be enough to quell the crowd upon your return," the man said, leaning onto his saddle. "If you'd sent word and waited to dock, we could've secured your passage easily." His hooded eyes fell on me, crawling from the top of my soaked head down to my dripping toes. The man nudged his horse forward and pulled off his cloak. "You certainly have the look of a Morganite," he muttered, draping the cloak over my shoulders. I couldn't help but notice how startlingly green his eyes were.

The man turned to one of the white-cloaked guards-men who had accompanied us from the harbor and nodded toward Ena. "Can't you see they're soaked to the bone? Give the other lady your cloak."

The guardsman scowled. "But she's not even a la—"

The green-eyed man backhanded the guardsman right out of his saddle, grabbing his cloak as he fell. The man landed in a great puddle of mud, which spoiled his snow-white tunic. The remaining guards seemed visibly affronted, while the soldiers lining the streets laughed, nudging each other and shaking their heads at the guardsman's foolishness.

The green-eyed man draped the white cloak over Ena's shoulders, then dismounted. "Now the lady gets use of your horse as well," he said, stepping over the fallen guardsman. He lifted Ena from behind me and onto the saddle of the other horse. The green-eyed man mounted again and rode forward, shouting at the other guards to flank us as we continued making our way to the palace, leaving the fallen guardsman to the jeers of the soldiers.

Though I sent the rain clouds behind our party, the damage had been done. Agramon scowled the entire way to the palace, seemingly affronted at his perceived loss of dignity, though the green-eyed man didn't seem to mind, even without his cloak. The leather was heavy on my shoulders and stank of bear grease and sweat, but it was welcomed considering the cool air that was brought on by the storm.

The soldiers controlled the mob well, even with the rain hampering their jobs. The people who chose to greet us in the rain were held back from the road without any threats of violence. After a while I ceased the rain altogether, letting the eye of Sol shine down onto the city once more, this time reflecting on the glistening puddles and slick cobblestones that made up the street.

IT WAS LATE IN THE DAY when we finally made it to the golden gates of the palace. I'd never seen a place so heavily guarded. I eyed the soldiers stationed along the battlements as we passed through the decorative gate and beneath the iron portcullis raised above us. A wide expanse of green fields sprawled beyond, containing gardens almost overrun with blooming flowers whose scent wafted toward us even at a distance. Within those gardens were women, dressed much the same as I was, lounging on stone benches as young girls in short linen tunics waved palm fronds to fan them.

Within a short hedge of greenery, a group of children dressed in silk was playing some sort of game, running between bushes trying to grab each other. An older woman in a short linen dress was with them, her voice carrying over to the drive as she scolded one of the boys who'd tripped and ripped his embroidered tunic on a rose bush. My heart skipped a beat at the inconsistency. It appeared the emperor employed sorcerers or other methods to ensure that his fields and gardens remained verdant, while letting the masses outside the palace grow half-crazy with thirst.

I clenched my teeth, turning my eyes to the massive palace. It was a mountain of a place carved from white marble. Arched colonnades ran along the bottom and on several of the half dozen stories that made up the main building. Each turret, rising higher than the main palace, was topped with an arched roof of pure, gleaming gold.

Presented with such magnificence, I felt like an imposter in every sense of the word. I was still soaking wet, smelling of musty leather, with my hair a snarled mess. Agramon didn't look much better, and he seemed to know it. I must've ruined the grand entrance he'd planned for us, and though I was a bit sorry for it, it was too late to do anything except pray that we didn't run into anyone Agramon knew.

The green-eyed man led us up the road that curved around the back of the palace, near a large outbuilding that gave off the appearance of a grand stable. Agramon dismounted as soon as we stopped, practically throwing himself off his horse and barking orders at the flurry of servants that appeared at our arrival.

The green-eyed man dismounted and called a guard over before striding toward my horse. He grabbed the reins and handed them to a young stableboy before gripping my waist and lifting me out of the saddle while the guard did the same for Ena.

Seeing the green-eyed man up close, I noticed that, though he was still taller than me, it wasn't by much. He made up for his lack of height with the most muscled arms I'd ever seen on a man at least a dozen years my senior.

"Thank you," I said as he pulled away. "What you did for Ena, it was very noble of you."

The man raised his brows. "No thanks necessary, as long as you stop calling me noble."

A surprised smile broke over my face. I reached up and undid the cloak's pin, about to slide the heavy leathers from my shoulders, but the green-eyed man was already turning away. "Your cloak, sir!"

"Return it later," the man replied before ruffling the hair of the stable boy who'd begun to lead our horses away. "Ladies as pretty as you two shouldn't be walking through the halls half-naked and soaking wet, no matter what your lord says."

I had to stop myself from going after him as he walked away, nodding to the saluting guards at the doors before striding into the palace.

Chapter 3

THE HALLS AGRAMON LED us through were made of the purest white rock, with gold veins inlaid throughout. Great columns rose on one side of the massive colonnade. Sheer white curtains floated in the breeze, beckoning me to gaze at the sprawl of the city beyond. We passed women with golden armbands and heavy skirts, whose faces were delicately painted. Men in ornate robes nodded at Agramon when he greeted them.

All those we passed stared at our bedraggled state, given that we were leaving a dripping trail behind us. I noticed a large group of young women, about my age, pass with their hands over their mouths, the hiss of whispers echoing in the hall. I looked away, trying to ignore them. I couldn't escape the heat rising to my cheeks.

Finally, we stopped outside a heavy set of doors. Agramon pulled a key from the pocket of his robe and swung open the door with a flourish, revealing an ornately gilded receiving room.

He turned to me as the servants swept inside. "This will be your home during your time at the palace."

The receiving room was overdone with tapestries, rugs, and gold furnishings. Red velvet curtains did their best to block out the afternoon sun from the line of open windows along the back wall. Finely crafted couches and chairs were positioned with care over a massive, intricately woven rug that had been laid out over the white marble floors. Beyond the sitting area was a large table and chairs, exotic fruit in various states of decay filling a bowl on the table.

"I don't have regular servants," Agramon said. "If I need something done, the palace staff does it, but always with my supervision. So, I expect you to be tidy and clean up after yourself. Under no circumstances should you or Ena enter my sleeping chambers when I'm not present, or without express invitation." Agramon pointed to a door on the right that a servant had just opened. I glimpsed a massive bed draped with a white coverlet. The servant began pulling back the gauzy white curtains on the long row of arched windows, their embroidered golden sunbursts glinting in the light.

"I'm a lover of the light," Duke Agramon went on, "and I confess, there is nothing I enjoy more than decorating."

He motioned me to a door on the left side of the receiving area. Inside was a much smaller bedroom painted a deep indigo. The tapestry on the far wall was a scene of a hunt at dusk, a buck flying through the forest as dogs and hunters chased it. Similar curtains to Agramon's donned the windows, though they were a deep blue with silver crescent moons and ten-pointed stars stitched into them.

"Thank you, my lord, it's beautiful," I admitted, hating myself for liking it. Everything about the room reminded me of home, from the dark colors to the crescent moons, the symbol of Espiria. But in the next moment, the sight saddened me. I didn't want to be reminded of home anymore. I wanted to forget it. My people had betrayed me. They'd delivered me into the hands of the enemy.

"I thought it fitting that I should have the sun room and you the moon room." Agramon flicked his hand toward the large bureau that took up almost an entire wall. "As you found on our journey, I've taken the liberty to furnish a wardrobe for you. There are gowns for all manner of occasions there," the duke said casually before turning to Ena. "If you have questions about the appropriate cleaning procedures, please direct them to Shivi Abuya in the Fiber Market."

Ena nodded, her eyes on the floor. The duke turned back to me. "Get dry, and presentable. People will find out we're here and may come calling instead of waiting for your presentation at the banquet tonight." Agramon paused at the door, then turned back to me. "And no more using your powers today." He shut the door, leaving Ena and me blessedly alone. I let out a sigh of relief and pulled the leather cloak off, hanging it on a nearby hook.

I walked to the ebony wardrobe and opened it. Hanging inside were dresses of all colors, from the deepest reds to the palest blues, most heavily adorned with embroidery or jewels. The fabrics were as varied as the colors, with buttery velvets and clouds of gauze. I flipped through the dresses, marveling at their beauty. I remembered a time, not so long ago, that I'd caught myself admiring the lovely dresses the other ladies at Solridge wore. They would've grown green with envy seeing the wardrobe Agramon had prepared for me, but I couldn't seem to dredge up much happiness about it.

I shut the wardrobe on the most expensive gowns I would ever wear and turned to find Ena at the dressing table. She had pulled out kohl, rouge, paints, and powders that shimmered like fish scales, glass bottles filled with scented waters, along with brushes and feathers. Another drawer held an array of ribbons and elaborately decorated combs, some carved into gold or silver filigree of the smallest size, others embedded with soft pearls or rows of sparkling diamonds. She handed me an exquisite comb inlaid with green stones.

"I didn't expect him to be so generous with me," I muttered begrudgingly. His generous nature toward fashion was hinted at on our journey, but I never expected to see such a multitude of pieces. I lifted another comb, this one with a milky pearl shaped as a crescent inlaid within. Beneath the crescent were three small diamonds. I recognized it as the Espirian sigil, the old symbol of Morgania. Perhaps there was a kindness to the duke.

"This isn't generosity," Ena said, placing everything carefully back into the drawers. "You heard what he said: 'There's nothing I love more than decorating.' He's treating you like a doll. You're to grace his arm at the capital, so he's making sure you look the part."

I frowned. "I didn't think of it that way, but you may be right." Still, I held the comb, unable to stop myself from admiring it. It was obvious that Agramon knew me far better than I knew him. The thought frightened me more than a little, no matter his seemingly generous nature.

"I know I'm right, otherwise he would have waited to furnish your wardrobe till you were with him and able to make some choices yourself. It will be a miracle from Imor if you can make it through the day without embarrassing yourself in one of those dresses. They barely cover your chest!"

I set the comb down, clenching my fists. "Ena," I said quietly, "please don't think of these things in his presence. Don't give him cause to question or even harm you."

Ena shrugged. "Why would the duke care about my thoughts? I'm a mere servant, and a Morganite at that. The only way I could be lower is if I were one of their Ylirian slaves."

I took a steadying breath. "But he can't read my mind, so I'm positive he'll read yours just to make sure I'm not planning anything, or maybe to find out more about me. Who knows what he could pull from you to use against me. Please, just be careful."

"I'll be sure to think vapid thoughts in his presence, my lady, I promise." Ena helped me peel off the ruined gown. "Have strength, Rowyn," Ena said as she worked. "You will endure this trial, as you have endured the others. The rise of the Morganites is at hand."

"You sound like Conal," I said as Ena pulled off the corset and held out a midnight-blue gown made of silk. I slipped it on, tying the sash tightly around my waist while Ena uncoiled my wet hair and toweled it off. "That's what he always used to say, before he sold me to our enemies."

Ena sighed as she untangled my hair. "Your hair needs to dry, and I need to change. I'll take your gown to soak and find my quarters, but as soon as I'm presentable, we'll find you something new to wear."

"Thank you for everything, Ena," I said, grabbing her hand.

"The Espirians might have sold you out," Ena said softly, her dark eyes urgent, "but there are other Morganites who still believe in you. The last time we had a hero like you was at the rise of our empire, and given your stones, you're far more powerful than he. Know that we still have faith in you, even if you don't have faith in yourself."

I smiled tightly as Ena slipped from the room. Her words hardly had the comforting effect she intended—quite the opposite, in fact. I wished everyone would stop expecting things from me.

I CONTINUED EXPLORING MY ROOM when Ena left. The furniture was all carved ebony, the intricate designs filled with fantastical beasts of legend. I ran my fingers over the frame of the vanity mirror, tracing the shape of a dragon, its wings folded against its back.

I couldn't help but wonder what Destrian was doing at the moment. Had his sisters joined him in Helena for his father's funeral rites? Were the Espirians giving him trouble in the valley they claimed in exchange for my freedom? Had he forgiven me?

I knew our time in the Nightlands would be short-lived. I hadn't known how much it would hurt now that it was over. How could Destrian feel anything but hate for me now? By all the gods, I hated myself. It was only right that he'd feel the same. It was all too familiar a feeling. I felt it when my betrothed, Luc, was taken from my clan so many years ago. And I felt it when I left Destrian behind.

I sniffed back the tears. If Destrian forgave me at all, it wouldn't be so soon. I didn't have a chance to tell Destrian I left to save him. I couldn't be the one to curse his reign in Helena before it even began . . . and what of Destrian's father? Though I'd loathed the man, every discussion Destrian and I had about Consul Colman indicated that Destrian loved him, despite his many faults, and it was because of me that his father was dead. I couldn't predict how Destrian would process that memory, but I was fooling myself if I thought it wouldn't have any effect on Destrian's feelings for me. Still, I felt the loss of his love like an arrow to the heart.

My one comfort was that neither Agramon nor the empire would have the best pieces of me, for they remained in Morgania.

When I found a small stack of parchment, a quill, and an inkpot, my hands trembled. I wished I knew Agramon's motives for placing them in the drawers. Did he expect me to send missives to other nobles at the palace? Or was he hoping that I would send revealing information to those I cared about? Surely, he would read any communication I sent.

I stood and grabbed Iranoct, unsheathing the sword and running my hand over the blade. Gripping the hilt, I closed my eyes and thought of its twin, Destrian's golden sword, Phyranox. The blade responded by pulling my arm down, then pointing out the window, toward the north-west, and home.

I doubted Agramon would allow any letter to be sent to Morgania, and there was nothing I had to say to Destrian that I wanted others to read. No, I couldn't write to him.

My fingers brushed against the leather cord I'd worn in the Nightlands, now wrapped around the hilt of the sword for safekeeping. Dangling from it was Fin's timepiece, Araceli's key, and Pedr's chess queen. They had been gifts for my quest, bits of good luck to keep close in the darkness. Destrian wasn't the only person I loved who I'd left in the western land.

I sat at the table, carefully opened the inkpot, and began to write.

"I TRUST EVERYTHING IS to your liking," a voice said from behind me as I carefully blew on the parchment to help the ink dry.

"It seems you've thought of everything I could possibly need," I said, turning in the chair and rising with my letters.

Since Ena hadn't returned, I still wore the silk dressing gown. Agramon didn't pay it any mind. If the rumors were to be believed, he'd witnessed ladies in all manner of undress. "I was hoping to send these letters to Solridge, to let my friends know that I made it safely to Somme." I tried to keep my voice light, but the tone rang false.

Agramon, wearing lavender robes, held out his hand for the papers. I hadn't stuffed them into an envelope yet, figuring it would be a fruitless exercise. My intuition was correct, as Agramon began reading right there in front of me. After a moment, he glanced up. "I will see that these are sent. It pleases me that you seek to keep friendships with the students at Solridge. The Count of Calla is well-liked at court, and though the Tores aren't known here in the East, Livian is still a prominent holding in The Fens. I'll make sure any responses find their way to you."

"I appreciate that," I said, then added, "If you show me how to send and check for letters myself, I could save you the trouble."

Agramon smiled, though the expression failed to reach his eyes. "It's no trouble at all, my dear, as I send numerous correspondence myself. Now, can you please do your best to dress since I'm expecting a guest who will want to meet you?"

"Of course," I said, gritting my teeth. "I haven't always had a lady's maid, you know."

A GILDED CAGE

I made sure the door was completely shut before opening the wardrobe and pulling out a red dress that laced in front. I ran a brush through my hair and slipped on a pair of soft leather slippers, touching nothing inside the vanity. Agramon was sure to be disappointed in the lack of paint on my face, but I was happy I at least looked like myself.

I heard the door to the hall open, and voices reached me from the receiving room. I sheathed Iranoct with a sigh, running my fingers over my tokens again before hanging the sword on the wall over the leather cloak that the green-eyed man had let me borrow. Taking a deep breath, I opened the door.

Chapter 4

AN ELEGANT WOMAN was perched on the couch beside Agramon. She looked older, about the duke's age, and appeared as though she'd emptied her entire jewelry box to wear. Her flaxen hair was roped around a small crown winking with gems. Gold chains and medallions hung from her neck, and rings of various sizes filled her fingers, each band bearing at least one large gem. Her sky-blue eyes narrowed as they studied me.

"So, this is your new protégé?" she asked, her voice sharp and clear. Vianne would've admired her poise. The woman was looking down her nose at me, despite the fact that she was seated and I was standing.

The duke rose, beckoning me forward. "Indeed, Princess Willene, may I present Rowyn the Morganite. Rowyn, this is High Princess Willene of Lyrica, the emperor's sister."

I curtsied.

"Princess Willene has agreed to assist you in the manners and customs of Lyrican court. You're very blessed to be under her tutelage."

"She certainly is a fair creature," Princess Willene said, wrinkling her nose, "but she has that wild look in her eye that I see in the war dogs. If you ask me, they should all be put down."

I bit my cheek. She seemed to think us no better than an infestation of rodents. I supposed remarks such as those were to be expected, being one of Agramon's baubles.

The duke shrugged. "She's known for far more than her beauty."

Princess Willene raised an eyebrow at Agramon before standing and stepping toward me. Reaching out, she grabbed my hands, her silken glove like butter against my skin until the sensation disappeared, her fingers meeting my gems. Her eyes strayed to the opal on my brow. "Strange, I have never before seen three gems on a sorcerer. How did you come of these?" Though she was finally addressing me, her tone left everything to be desired.

"The Nightlands, Your Highness. All three called to me. I'd learned that Morius the Black, my predecessor, had opals buried in his hands, so I figured I must do that as well."

Princess Willene nodded. "I'd heard that you had some great ancestor, but to think, three stones. You must be very powerful indeed."

"One has to be if they're to control the heavens," Agramon said, placing his hand on my shoulder. Though he may have wanted it to appear as a fatherly gesture, I still shrugged his hand away.

Princess Willene's eyes flicked to mine, studying me as she let my hands go. "These marks are so . . . exotic." Her fingers rose as if to trace my imorets but then lowered again at the last moment, presumably with the realization that it would be neither polite nor wise to touch me in such a manner. "I've seen them on war dogs, of course, but never a woman."

Agramon gave me the slightest nod, which I took as an invitation to speak. "My clan follows the old ways. Most of my marks were earned through blood." I let the princess's imagination fill in the information I failed to deliver.

Princess Willene's eyebrows shot up. "My brother will enjoy this one," she said, turning to Agramon. "He may even demand her guardianship back for himself."

Agramon frowned. "The emperor knows not to interfere with my students, especially with one so valuable. Despite her other . . . attractions . . . she will still need to be fully trained if she is to benefit the empire. He can't very well do that himself."

Princess Willene pursed her lips, then turned back to me.

"You will come to my rooms every morning and take lady's tea with me. There you will remain until lunch, where we will eat with the empress and other ladies of court in the gardens, as is the custom." Princess Willene rose from her seat. "You're lucky in your guardian, Rowyn. No man in the empire holds as much power or prestige as Duke Agramon." Princess Willene took a sip from the goblet on the table. "Save my brother, of course," she added, as though it were a mere afterthought.

I bowed my head. The casual mention of the emperor didn't escape my notice, and I wondered if it was a reminder for her sake or for the duke's.

When Princess Willene took her leave, Duke Agramon turned on me, his eyes flashing. "Make sure you treat her with respect during your lessons. She has a fearsome temper and will lash out if provoked."

"She doesn't seem to hold much respect for the emperor," I commented, tossing myself on the couch and lounging against the armrest.

The duke straightened. "Be wary of your tongue, girl," he snapped. "Men in this empire have lost their heads for less."

"Of course, Your Grace. My utmost apologies," I gushed, clasping my chest. "I wouldn't want my slights against Lyrica's most beloved emperor to cause me to lose my head, or worse, embarrass you."

Duke Agramon glared at me a moment longer, probably trying once more to needle his way into my thoughts. Finally, he strode to a table in the corner where a small stack of scrolls and parchment sat.

"The banquet will be soon," he said, glancing at the door. "I've called Ena to help you dress."

That was as clear a dismissal as any. It took a moment, but I decided not to try his patience. There would be plenty of time for that later. "Thank you, Your Grace," I said, without a hint of sass, before rising and dropping into my best curtsy.

The duke waved me away, so I left him to nose through my letters.

"I AM TO ATTEND a banquet tonight," I said to Ena when she came in later.

She nodded. "My lord asked that you be highly presentable; the emperor will be there, after all." I noticed the quiver in Ena's voice.

"Are you afraid?"

"I am a bit. I've been asking about Duke Agramon in the servants' quarters, and they say to be wary of his temper. For the most part, he is a congenial man, but when his temper is aroused, they say he can be downright barbaric. Be cautious of him, my lady. He shows kindness now, but . . ." Ena trailed off, her hands fluttering down to her sides.

I nodded. "I'd thought as much." I went back to the wardrobe and glanced through it. "What shall I wear to this banquet?"

Ena joined me, flipping through the dresses before pulling out a gown. "His Grace requested you wear this one." It was the deep blue of a starless dusk. I ran my hands down the plush fabric, my heart skipping a beat at the intensity of the color. It skipped another when my gaze fell to the plunging neckline.

The corset Ena stuffed me into was cut into a deep V supported by stiff boning. Ena grabbed my hands and stopped me from trying to stuff my chest in further before she tied the laces tightly behind me.

Then came the dress. I was right in thinking it was far too low in front. The neckline plunged nearly to my belly, the sleeves mere strips of fabric that fell off my shoulders. I balked at the dress and its lurid exposure. My gaze was drawn to the tattoo of the star with a sideways crescent on my chest. My eyes narrowed. Blessed by Imor, my foot.

"Does he really expect me to meet the emperor wearing this?" I asked, glaring at myself in the looking glass.

"Yes," Ena said simply, adjusting the skirt until she deemed me presentable.

I insisted on wearing the necklace holding Fin's time-piece, Pedr's queen, and Araceli's key. For good measure, I strapped Iranoct to my side and began to feel more like myself. Ena *tsked* at the weapon, but she began darkening the lids of my eyes without further comment, sweeping black kohl along my lashes and lightly feathering rouge over my cheeks.

Agramon came in as Ena started on my hair.

"Leave it loose," Agramon said, leaning against his staff.

"The neck is too low. I will surely disgrace myself, my lord," I insisted.

"Nonsense, you shall dazzle all with your charms," Agramon countered, flashing a devilish grin as his eyes devoured all the parts I wished were hidden.

"I look like a whore," I said matter-of-factly.

Duke Agramon's gaze continued to crawl over me like insects I couldn't brush off. "Ah, but an expensive one." I sighed, unsure how I felt that he used my earlier sarcasm on me now.

Ena stepped back, and Agramon circled me, inspecting each fold of fabric and fussing with every curl. He stopped in front and swept the loose hair off my shoulder.

"You did well, Ena. You may go now," he ordered, not even glancing in her direction as she ducked out of the room. The duke's muddy eyes met mine. "You look magnificent," he murmured, his fingers skimming down my jaw. There was no ignoring the predatory glint in his eyes. It was a possessive look, as if he owned me.

I suppressed a shudder as his touch drifted lower, featherlight over my collarbone, until he paused at my necklace.

"Tokens from your lovers?" he asked, almost to himself.

"They were gifts from my friends," I said, leaning away.

Duke Agramon leaned in, untying the necklace. "You're not the girl who left the shores of Morgania, Rowyn." His hot breath over my ear raised the hair on my neck. I recoiled within as the smell of vanilla and mint swept over me. "You must shrug off the past," Agramon went on, pulling away with the necklace in his fist. "It will only hold you back."

"Please," I said, catching his hand in mine. "I can hide it. Just don't take it away."

Agramon hesitated, but he let me pull the tokens from his hand. His gaze trailed down my side to where Iranoct was belted.

"It fits with the image," I said, my voice hopeful, "of the girl who conquered the Nightlands."

The duke's eyes hardened. "Most men aren't allowed swords at the emperor's banquets, and certainly none of the ladies. Do you not think I will keep you safe?"

I unbelted Iranoct, knowing that if I pushed him hard enough, he would take away the sword altogether. I refused to take that risk. I wrapped the leather necklace around the hilt of the sword and hung it back on the wall.

I felt even more exposed without my weapons. I had half a thought to hide them, but concealment was nigh impossible with this dress. I couldn't tell if Agramon intended to cripple me, but it certainly felt that way.

Still, most ladies walked around without weapons, and there were guards posted all throughout the palace. Somme gave every indication of being heavily fortified, and I was a valuable commodity. They wouldn't go to all the trouble of shipping me across the sea if they didn't value my life. Besides, if all else failed, I still had my powers. I'd used them to defend myself before, though it was still such a new skill, I was loath to depend on it.

I took Agramon's arm and allowed him to lead me down the darkening corridor. More people in short linen tunics or dresses, their arms bearing a branded sun, lit the torches along the hall. I stared at them as we passed, finally recognizing them for what they were—Ylirian slaves. Most were young, their whole lives ahead of them, yet they were tied permanently to the palace. How had they come to Lyrica? They had to have been prisoners of war, brought back by the armies. Perhaps the people serving the palace didn't even have homes anymore after the emperor's pet commander, the Butcher of Bruin, razed a thousand villages to the ground. Each of the slaves' eyes were haunted, and I shuddered to imagine what they'd seen in their lifetime, or who they had lost. It made my suffering seem small in comparison.

"When we enter the throne room," Agramon said, interrupting my thoughts, "make sure you grace the emperor with a deep curtsy, and don't raise your eyes to him until he speaks to you."

I nodded, trying to control the nervous hum that was building within my blood. We passed more slaves hurrying about with an air of purpose, but I couldn't let myself get distracted, for the greatest trial of the day was still to come.

We stopped outside an open set of doors where the duke had words with a man in royal livery. The man nodded, then stepped into the room beyond where the thundering of voices echoed off the walls.

"Presenting to His Imperial Majesty, Agramon the Divine, the Duke of Solin, Grand Sage of the Guild of Mystics, and lord of His Imperial Majesty's High Council. His ward, Rowyn the Morganite of the North and Wielder of the Black Opals of Iriset, Conqueror of the Nightlands, and the Bringer of Rain."

I was going to kill Agramon. Just before entering the ornate room, I spared one malice-filled glint to the duke for, I assumed, providing the ridiculous monikers, then I turned my attention to the throne before me.

Chapter 5

A HUSH DESCENDED OVER the hall as the courtiers craned their necks to get a better view. Their faces, all painted and rouged, seemed to blend together as I tried to take everything in. Gold glinted at every corner, from the chains of the chandeliers to the plates along the banquet table. Many of the courtiers sported golden gowns and robes, or held gold staffs similar to Agramon's, their necks and wrists dripping with the metal.

I'd thought my gown was excessive, but other ladies had taken the style to the extreme. Some skirts were made up of mere strips, revealing the sun-darkened legs and skin the Lyricans were known for. Others wore a mere rope of fabric from their front to their back, their more intimate bits concealed by gilded necklaces and collars chained together. All of the women held their hands to their faces, their whispers like the hissing of snakes, their eyes filled with judgment. One woman laughed, her voice carrying over the others, followed by another snorting to herself.

Duke Agramon pulled me toward the white marble dais that stood at the rear of the large hall where Emperor Arthello and Empress Lesedi sat.

The emperor was younger than I expected, and far

more handsome. He had Willene's coloring: tan skin, blond hair, and clear-blue eyes. The large crown on his head was molded into a golden sunburst, matching the white flags that fluttered throughout the grand hall. On his fingers were enough rings that his hands appeared to be anchored to his lap. While Princess Willene sat with regal poise, the emperor slouched in his chair, as though bored with the fawning courtiers around him.

Someone offered him a goblet of what I could only presume was wine, and he took it willingly, downing a long sip.

Next to him, the empress couldn't have been more different. Lesedi the Peerless, known as the most beautiful woman in Lyrica, leaned toward the herald, smiling at me. She'd been a princess of Ember Innes, offered as part of an alliance. Gold dust had been brushed over her rich brown skin. Tight black curls were piled atop her head in an intricate style with gold beads and rings wound throughout. Her golden headdress framed high cheekbones and black, almond-shaped eyes so lively, it was as though she were smiling at every individual in the room at once.

"Duke Agramon," the emperor said, sitting up in his chair and flashing a genuine smile that would make the ladies swoon. "You've brought her, as you promised."

The empress flinched at her husband's words before

turning to me. "We here on the eastern shore welcome you and look forward to hearing more of your story."

Both the emperor and empress were flanked by body-guards. The emperor's was a man in a Lyrican tunic bearing the sun sigil, but with a golden crown above it. At his side was a sword with a golden hilt and ornate scabbard. He stood erect, his hands clasped behind his back, his eyes on me as though I were liable to take a running leap at the emperor and sink a blade into his chest. His dark hair was longer, the length of most of the noblemen rather than the many guards posted around the room. It tumbled over his brow, adding a debonair look that would leave many a lady flushed if his sultry eyes landed on them.

On the other side of the dais, the empress's bodyguard took the meaning of the word *vigilant* to heart. She was also from Ember Innes, her skin so dark that it appeared nearly blue. The female guard paid no attention to introductions. Instead, her eyes flitted about the room as though an attack were likely to come from the nobility, and there was no mistaking the strength of her grip on the hilt of two curved blades hanging at her waist.

"Indeed, Your Excellencies," Agramon said smoothly, sweeping his hand out to me. "My student has returned from the Nightlands, bearing the jewels of the north. She has quite the tale to tell, I assure you."

The armed woman behind the empress gave me a

quick, appreciative glance before her eyes darted away.

The emperor leaned forward, his hands on his knees as he studied me from the top of my head to the tips of my toes.

"The story the bard sang yesterday made it seem like you would be taller. Tell me, what of the monsters up there—were they as fearsome as everyone says?"

The empress placed her hand on her husband's arm. "Now is not the time for stories, Your Excellency. There are still many introductions to be made, and it would be unkind to the others who have traveled so far." She turned to me, her black eyes sparkling with intrigue. "I look forward to hearing more about you, Rowyn the Morganite."

The emperor pulled his arm out of his wife's grasp and slouched moodily. "I suppose it can wait. Duke, you know the routine. Please take refreshment with us this evening, and make sure to greet the councils. They've been restless in your absence."

Duke Agramon pulled me away from the emperor's dais and into the crowd of nobles. Music played faintly as others conversed, holding goblets of wine and tasting delicacies being delivered by an army of Ylirian slaves.

I watched one girl skirt around a group of particularly rowdy-looking young men who laughed as she twisted away from their grasping hands.

"Duke Agramon, you've returned!" a melodic voice

sang out. A young woman swept in front of us. Agramon took the woman's hand and bowed, gracing her with the first true smile I'd seen on him.

"Delise, you look ravishing, as always," Agramon said to the sorceress with a chocolate gem embedded in her brow. She tossed her thick, wavy hair over her shoulders, her freckles, uncommon on such dark skin, dancing as she laughed.

"There's no need for such pleasantries with us, is there, Duke?" Delise asked, swatting his arm in an oddly playful gesture. The duke didn't seem to mind it. In truth, Delise's wide smile was infectious. I felt a tug at the corners of my mouth, like I wanted to smile and laugh along with her. "I'm so glad you've returned. The court has been positively boring lately."

Agramon put his hand on my lower back and nudged me forward. "Rowyn, may I present Delise of Marion. Delise is an accomplished sorceress, and one of my former students."

Delise turned her mischievous amber eyes to me. I held my hand out to greet her, but Delise grabbed my arm and threaded it through her own, pulling me close. "You can call me Del. You're all anyone's been talking about for the past week. The court has been positively pining for a new face to stare at."

When Del's fingers ran over the gem in my hand, her

eyes grew wide, and she brought my hand up to look closer. "By Sol above," she breathed. "Aren't you full of surprises? This will be the most exciting season since Lord Ramin decided he was a gifted actor."

Agramon chuckled, and Del leaned toward me conspiratorially. "Miyu was positively beside herself when he insisted on performing his one-man show about the shepherd who fell in love with one of his sheep. He made the entire court watch. I thought the emperor would behead him right there for his atrocious singing voice." She straightened, smiling at Agramon. "Now *that* is a man's mind I wouldn't want to dwell long in."

"I wouldn't wish that depravity on you," Agramon said. Then, he looked down at me. "If you're not busy, Del, would you do me the favor of introducing Rowyn around?"

Del's eyes lit up. "Of course, Your Grace. It would be my pleasure." She grinned as she pulled me away.

"Who is Miyu?" I whispered.

"She's the emperor's master of ceremonies and a sorceress as well," Del whispered, pointing to a woman who directed a team of slaves holding trays filled with roasted meats, decadent cakes dripping with sugar icing, and large bowls of the most colorful fruit I'd ever seen.

"A sorceress?" I asked, not seeing a gem on her brow.

Del nodded. "She's from Lu Shen, northeast of the

Ylirian Desert. They embed the gem in their chests."

I craned my head and managed to see a gem winking out from her collarbone. "I knew the Morganites used their hands, but I didn't realize there would be other variations."

"That sorcerer you see with her, there"—she pointed to a man with tattoos running up his neck like a collar and a clear gem on his brow—"that's Owain. He's on the Council of Five with Agramon. He's a warder."

"So, he protects the emperor?"

Del nodded. "He can ward others from more than physical harm too. If he had a mind to it, he could make all the sorcerers in this room powerless for a time. It's a *very* coveted skill."

"Even Duke Agramon?" I asked, shooting a glance to my guardian, who spoke with a nobleman on the other side of the room.

"Especially Duke Agramon," Del murmured. "Owain's presence is the only thing that makes the others easy around the duke. Nobody likes their mind tampered with."

We drew up short in front of two formidable-looking sorcerers. The first was an older man, reed-thin, with his face covered in scars. His hair was stark white, oiled back to reveal a yellow gem in his brow. The second was a woman with a deep red gem that brought out the reddish-brown hue of her skin. Both sorcerers stopped speaking when we stepped in front of them, the woman's golden eyes seeming to pierce through me as I shifted my feet, wishing my dress had more fabric to it.

Del's grip on my arm tightened as she turned to me, her smile disappearing. "Rowyn, let me introduce you to Elgar the Swift and Pythia. Elgar is on the Council of Five with Agramon. Pythia is the court's resident necro-mancer."

The two sorcerers merely studied me.

"What does a necromancer do?" I asked.

"I speak to the dead," Pythia answered, her voice like a wisp in the wind. "I can also help those living join them."

"You speak to the dead? How?" I was unsuccessful in keeping my voice from trembling.

Pythia looked over my shoulder. "Sometimes, after the dead pass, their spirits remain as shadows in this world. I'm able to speak to those shadows, at least for a time."

Gooseflesh prickled over my skin. "Is the presence of spirits very common?"

"You mean, besides the one that follows you?" I shrank inwardly as she assessed my reaction. She raised a single brow, her golden eyes sharpening "Yes, there are some, though they aren't as tied to the world as your lady."

Del frowned at me. I wished to all the gods that Echo had stayed away from the banquet hall. Then again, I couldn't really blame her, as I wasn't sure how far she could wander. I would have to work very hard to distract the others in case Agramon read their minds to see how my evening went. I didn't want to consider what he'd do if he tripped over that tidbit of information.

"You're a league leaper?" I asked Elgar the Swift. Lord Obi had claimed to be a league leaper when he'd randomly appeared in my room in Helena. He'd left as quickly as he arrived after speaking in riddles and gifting me the Girdle of Ephema.

The older sorcerer merely nodded.

"Do you know Lord Obi?" I asked.

Elgar took a sip of his drink and regarded me thoughtfully. "We've met," he said finally, "though in passing. He's well-known to those of my guild. No man has traveled farther in the world than Obi. Of course, reaching for such renown has its own limitations."

"Are there many of your kind?"

Elgar shrugged. "There are a fair few. It takes a strong gem to travel a great distance at one time, which is rarer, but there are many who can jump short distances in succession. Mostly we are used as messengers."

Del nudged my arm. "Well, we should continue our rounds of introductions. I'm sure Rowyn will see you again during a council meeting."

Pythia nodded. I felt her golden eyes watching me as I turned away. Elgar didn't even bother to respond.

A GILDED CAGE

I was more than thankful when Del tugged me into a crowd. "Do they frighten everyone, or was that just me?" I asked, hoping she wouldn't relay any part of our conversation to Agramon.

"That's everyone," Del whispered. "Elgar isn't so bad, even though most of his contacts outside of court are thieves and cutthroats. He has deep ties to the crime lords of Lyrica. They use Elgar to drip wishes into the emperor's ear, while the emperor uses them to do jobs that would otherwise sully the crown."

"What of Pythia?" I asked.

"Pythia scares the pants off everyone except Tristam and Elgar. Even Agramon avoids her. My advice? Stay away from her."

Del was speaking to my instincts. I hoped that Pythia and I would have few chances to meet. I sent a silent prayer to Imor to keep Echo from her sight.

"Everyone is so excited to meet you," Del rattled on. She pulled me to a group of younger courtiers and sorcerers sitting on couches and chairs in a corner of the grand hall. All held goblets as they leaned on one another and laughed uproariously despite the glares from older nobles. In their center was a man a bit older than the others, with brown curls and gray eyes. I kept glancing in his direction, sure that I'd seen him before.

Del introduced the group as university students. I

immediately forgot most of their names as she rattled them off until she came to the gray-eyed man in the center of the group.

"And of course, you know the Lyons. This is Mellan, the Hero of Ayastaren."

Chapter 6

MY STOMACH DROPPED to my knees as the young man rose from his seat, his eyes on my gems and markings. It was as though my life were woven through the Lyons', and I couldn't be rid of them, no matter how many times I swatted them away.

Mellan remained standing after his introduction while Del took his seat and engaged in conversation centered around one of the school masters and his affair with a student. Since it held no interest for me, I turned to Mellan, who was watching me out of the corner of his eye.

"So, the fabled Mellan Lyon," I said, recognizing the telltale curve of his nose that all the brothers had. I tried to mask the ice creeping down my spine and cocked an eyebrow.

Fin had told me of the young man who'd left for the Ylirian War, leaving his betrothed, Aureliana, behind. In Mellan's absence, his father's wife had died, and Roland Lyon had taken Aureliana to wife for himself. Mellan had yet to return to the western shore.

"It's been so long since I enjoyed the comforts of your father's hall." I sighed, accepting a goblet of wine from one of the slaves meandering past. I murmured a thank you under my breath. "But of course, I was given the opportunity to pay his hospitality back in kind upon my return from the Nightlands."

A slow smile crept over Mellan's face. "I am, of course, the most dastardly of my brothers, at least according to my father. That may be because I'm not perpetually licking his ass like the rest of them."

"Have you heard from your father? Or the rest of your family?"

Mellan's eyes sparkled. "You mean, from what's left of them after you had your merry way?"

I choked on the wine and began coughing and spluttering. Mellan raised his hand and whacked my back a touch too hard to be deemed helpful.

"I must say, I've imagined murdering my brothers myself, but you do it with such cunning efficiency, I fear I may be half in love with you already, and that's without my father's demand that I court you."

"Your father sent word to court me? *Me*?" I asked, incredulous.

"Oh yes," Mellan said over his goblet. "I received a *very* demanding letter. I was to find a way to woo you and bring you to Ayastaren at all costs." I was surprised a Lyon was even talking to a woman given the behavior I'd seen in his father's court, so it shocked me when he held his hands out and actually bowed. "So here I am, ready to woo. I've not much to offer as the third son, but I'm damned good with my sword, *both* of them, in fact." Mellan wagged his eyebrows, but I refused to take his bait. I would match Mellan with a sword or with words.

"There's no one on earth I would be less likely to tie myself to than a Lyon," I lamented. "Given the dealings I've had with your family over the past year, it's my indelible understanding that you all are the worst of men."

Mellan laughed as he took another swig from his goblet. "Quite right you are, Rowyn, quite right. I assure you, an acquaintance with me would not diminish that sentiment. I'm merely the more fun of the lot, but I'm a cad, same as the rest of them."

"It's true that your courtship is doomed from the start, but I would think I'm not a proper enough maid to tempt a noble Lyon."

"To be sure, I'd bed you in a heartbeat." His eyes strayed to my chest. "But you're too skinny, and your breasts are too small to keep me tempted for as long as marriage, or, for as long as my father decided to keep you alive."

"To be sure. Were we to be engaged, it's far more likely your father would bed me himself," I quipped, glancing at a group of nobles next to us.

When Mellan didn't respond, I turned back to find him frozen, the goblet trembling halfway to his mouth.

Heat rose to my cheeks with the realization that I'd gone too far. What rankled was why I would even care. The silence could only be characterized as fraught.

I took a deep breath. "I'm sorry. That was unkind."

"You have a keen choice of weapons," Mellan said, his voice suddenly gruff. "Befitting a woman of spite, I suppose."

"I've lost two loves," I said when he didn't move away. "I know what it's like to be betrayed by your family and lose the people you hold dear. I *do* understand how you feel."

Mellan shrugged, but the banter was broken. "So, your clan sold you out?" he asked, his voice subdued.

I nodded, then let out a biting, cold laugh. "For a parcel of land. I've been told I'm not welcome back, so I've no home now save for the one the emperor and my keeper demand of me."

Mellan's expression softened. Elias was handsome, but Mellan's eyes held a kindness to them that was absent from the rest of his brothers. He was by far the most attractive of the bunch with his strong, square jaw and untamed hair. "He wants me back," he said, his eyes on the crowd. "But how could I stand it? Watching him, with her?"

"Why would he expect you to return, after what he did?"

Mellan shook his head. "The man's incapable of deep

feelings for anyone. As a result, he doesn't think others have them. He's wondering why I haven't gotten over it already. He thought the war would've beat the thought of her out of me. Mind you, it's not for lack of trying that my feelings aren't gone. I've had plenty of women here, keeping my bed warm, but such is love, I suppose. Not that you would know, according to the tales."

I frowned. "What are you talking about? What tales?"

Mellan glanced back at me. The twinkling in his eyes returned. "The bards say that you seduced the young heir of Helena so that he would usher you through the Night-lands and fight against his overlord to protect your clan. The minute you'd gotten what you wanted from him, you slew his father and turned Lord Destrian away for the chance of glory and riches in Lyrica."

I was stunned. "They said *what?*"

Mellan held up his hands in mock surrender. "I'm only telling you what was sung, nothing more. You have quite the reputation to live up to now, you little seductress, you—especially with that last verse."

"Settle a bet between us, hero," Del called to Mellan, though I scarcely heard her.

Mellan's words filled me with anger and dread. I suddenly understood the sneers and whispers that had followed me through the hall. A buzzing filled my ears as I faced the room. The drone of whispers seemed to intensify. One of the students nearby let out a piercing laugh, and I stepped away from the sound. The hall was suffocating with all the courtiers milling about, staring at the marking on my chest. The women's eyes were filled with judgment, the men's with lust. I could only guess what evil thoughts entered their minds. I watched them feed off each other, their eyes bright and wary, my gaze wandering from each noble to the next as they inspected me. I felt like an animal in a cage, put on display for the others to gawk at.

I pushed my way through the crowd, seeking an escape from the accusatory thoughts that chased me through the hall. To the right of the great hall was a large pair of glass doors. I threw them open and nearly ran onto the balcony where twinkling lanterns illuminated the enormous garden below. Taking deep breaths, I stepped to the railing.

Jasmine climbed along the balustrade, the white flowers filling the air with their scent. I breathed in the fragrance, closing my eyes and letting my mind wander back to the Nightlands, to those long moments by Destrian's fire. But those memories were fleeting, and now our story was being tainted by Lyrica. Could the nobles inside see me breaking? Their whispers and stories poisoned the love that we'd had, that I still had for Destrian. Would he believe them?

"Don't let them see your fear," a brusque voice said

from the shadows.

I sucked in my breath and whirled. The green-eyed man who'd escorted us to the palace was sitting in the shadows, leaning back into a chair with his feet propped on the balustrade. One hand rested on the hilt of his large sword. The other held a glass filled with amber liquid.

"I'm not afraid," I said, "and I didn't realize anyone was out here, otherwise I would never dream of infringing on your solitude." I turned, embarrassed that he'd witnessed a moment of weakness.

"The fear will pass," the man said, his voice gruff, despite his easy manner. "But if you let them see it, they'll eat you alive."

Gooseflesh prickled over my skin. "I'm not afraid," I insisted, more to myself. The man shook his head, his full lips taking a sip from his glass. I gripped the handle of the glass door. "I apologize for disturbing you."

"You do not disturb me," the man replied. "But when you let them see how they affect you, it gives them bloated heads, and they're already unbearable."

Gazing back into the great hall through the crystal panes, seeing all the primped faces and silk gowns, I realized the man was right. I attempted to muster the courage to face the stares within. It felt too much like Espiria with the whispers and the dark thoughts, but these were strangers. They'd only heard of the terrible things I'd done.

Somehow, that made it so much worse.

"You don't need to leave, if you've no wish to," the man said, his voice softening. "Somme is a lot to take in. Trust me, I know."

I let out a breath I didn't realize I'd held. "It was just so stifling in there," I said, though the tension in my shoulders eased as I faced him. "What are you doing out here in the darkness, anyway? Shouldn't you be enjoying the festivities with the rest of them?"

"I don't care for the company of nobles," the man admitted, palming his sword hilt.

"So why come out at all?"

"I'm forced to attend the royal festivities in order to enjoy my favorite descent into oblivion." The green-eyed man took another long sip from his glass, then turned his gaze to the city beyond. "But, if you want to know the truth of it, I came for the same reason as everyone else."

"What reason is that?" I asked, keeping the distance between us as I stepped back to the edge of the balcony.

"To see the lady from the mist," he said. "She's all anyone's been talking about for months."

Heat surged to my cheeks. I cast my eyes down, running my fingers over the cool marble. "No doubt you've heard the stories." My mind lingered on the whispered lies. Of how Destrian had practically thrown me over his shoulder and carried me through the Nightlands. How romantic it was that he risked his life to save me, over and over again. Of me, murdering Destrian's father in cold blood and abandoning the heir to Helena as soon as I'd gotten what I'd wanted. It was a charming picture they painted.

The man's brows furrowed. "I ignore the wagging tongues of fools. Even the most hardened warriors have perished in the Nightlands, yet you spent an entire summer there and walked free."

"But the way the bards sing it . . ."

The man took another sip from his glass, his sharp eyes on my tattoos, which were clearly visible given what little fabric made up the bodice of my dress. "Unlike the doughy nobles inside, I've fought alongside Morganites. You all breed some of the empire's best warriors." His eyes broke from mine as he shrugged. "But what do I know? I'm just a soldier."

"I didn't realize Lyrican soldiers held the war dogs of Morgania in high esteem," I said, a sick twist of guilt forming in my gut, but I ignored it. The Morganites sold me out. I held no allegiance to them anymore. "What is your name, sir?"

The man swirled the liquid in his glass. "Call me Sam," he said, tipping his glass in greeting.

"Rowyn," I replied. Belatedly, I remembered to drop in a curtsy.

"Don't," Sam said, rising. "It doesn't become you to defer to anyone, least of all me."

I straightened, not knowing what to say next. Duke Agramon was sure to wonder where I was. No doubt he wasn't finished parading me about.

Sam saw the direction of my gaze. "You don't need to return just yet. I would appreciate hearing of your travels myself . . . the truth of it, anyway."

"The duke will want me back," I said, hating the fear creeping into my voice. "Do you know him?"

"Everyone knows him."

I nodded, but that hadn't been my true question. How did Sam know Duke Agramon? The duke's behavior during our meeting in the city made me assume that he didn't like the soldier very much. Sam had introduced himself as a mere soldier, yet he was welcome at court where I hadn't seen any other soldiers save the guards at the doors. Given the way he'd behaved in the city, it seemed he was a man of some note for all the guardsmen and soldiers to defer to him in such a way, but I pushed those thoughts aside.

"So, what were you doing out here, besides enjoying your drink?" I asked, curious why he was all alone.

"Watching you," Sam said, his eyes still studying me with that maddening intensity.

"Why?"

"Because you looked like a fox cornered by the hunting

dogs, already defeated and trying to figure out which will strike first."

"Is it that obvious?" I muttered. I hated the idea of people knowing what I was thinking.

"Your lord may be able to read minds, but I've become an expert at reading fear. You give those you fear power over you, and if they know that, they will use you."

"I don't understand how you can read me so well, having barely met me."

Sam lifted an eyebrow. "What I don't understand is how you fear them, yet do not shy away from me."

I nodded to the large sword at his side. "I know the sword. I have little to fear from strength and steel. I've trained my entire life in battle against such foes. But I don't know wit and intrigue. I don't know the whispers behind closed doors, and those who make deals in shadows. The fact that I know nothing of that way of fighting terrifies me."

"And I don't?"

"Don't what?" I asked when he didn't continue. Sam's eyes glittered in the darkness.

"Terrify you?"

I shrugged. "What do I have to fear from you?"

"What indeed?" Sam replied, his eyes traveling down my length. "For such a little thing, you frighten me more than I do you, no doubt."

"Do you frighten so easily, sir? I am but a woman," I challenged.

Sam tilted his head. "No, you are a little fiend, come to turn the capital on its end. I'm convinced nothing less would've survived the Nightlands."

I couldn't help but chuckle. "You speak nonsense, sir."

"What is there to speak but nonsense when one is surrounded by all manner of fools?"

I laughed, startled by his wit. Out of everyone I'd met at the capital so far, Sam seemed the least affected by the pomp of court. "So how does one mask fear?" I asked. "If I were, in fact, afraid?"

Sam set his drink on the marble balustrade and stepped toward me, reaching out a hand before pausing. "May I?" he asked. I glanced at his hand. He was the first person in the capital to ask my permission before touching me.

I nodded.

"Stand tall," he said, flattening his hand against my lower back, straightening it, while the other went to my shoulder. When he was satisfied with my posture, his fingers tilted my chin up, forcing my eyes to meet his. "Meet them stare for stare. They are nothing more than the dirt under your shoe. The minute you allow them to be something more is the minute you lose the battle to be had in this damnable place. Stand tall, and make them see that it is you who should be feared."

Thrill jolted me at his words. "Much of this goes against everything I learned from deportment," I admitted. The posture was the same, but Lady Vianne insisted on demurely lowered eyes.

Sam snorted, releasing me for inspection. I stood tall and met his gaze. "Good," Sam said, his hand falling to rest on his sword hilt. "And stop curtsying to everyone. Save it for the royal family, but no one else."

A clock struck somewhere in the city, and I looked at the party. "I really must return," I said, the deep reverberations of the hourly bell reminding me of the tenuous position I was in with Duke Agramon.

Sam bowed. "Of course. I can't claim the attention of such a renowned lady for the entire evening, as much as I may wish to. I hope to see more of you, Rowyn the Morganite. I anticipate hearing your story from your own lips."

"Thank you for the kindness," I said. Self-conscious, I turned and stepped back into the hall.

Shoulders back.

Stand tall.

Meet their gaze.

I ran through his directions in my mind as I made my way through the crowd. I glanced over my shoulder, meeting Sam's eyes as he watched me through the panes, saluting me with the glass back in his hands.

Chapter 7

ECHO HADN'T INVADED my dreams since that terrible night waiting for the dawn in Darkport. I'd learned enough about the shadow souls to know that the dreams they sent me rang true to life as memories they had witnessed. That first night in Somme, Echo came to me again as I drifted into a hazy sleep.

The memory was from the emperor's hall. I glimpsed a courtier I remembered who had worn a particularly revealing outfit. Echo watched me as I made my way to the glass doors of the balcony. Pythia appeared at the edges of Echo's vision, so she turned away, rushing back into the crowd until she came upon Agramon standing with a group of sorcerers in the corner of the room.

"Was there trouble getting her?" an old man asked, his translucent gem reflecting the candlelight. I'd never seen so many wrinkles on one person before. Wizened dark eyes followed Agramon's movements as he perched himself on a chair beside Elgar the Swift.

"The Morganites accepted the land deed with no fuss. We may have issues with the new lord of Morgania though."

"I don't think any of us were under the delusion that

they would give up their most valuable asset without a fight," Owain said, crossing his arms over his chest as he leaned against one of the marble columns. Instead of wearing robes, like most of the noblemen in the room, he wore a short tunic and breeches.

"There is an emotional attachment to consider," Agramon said, clearing his throat. "Though his thoughts were a tangle, that much was made clear. How those feelings may change with her absence and in light of other events, time will tell."

"What of Ayastaren?" the old man asked, leaning forward with his hands on his knees.

"The emperor has been wanting to bring the Lyons to heel for some time now," Agramon said. "Given Rowyn's protected status and our new alliance with the Morganites, he's willing to overlook the lord of Morgania's involvement with the battle. If Duke Roland wants to bring the issue to court, the emperor is prepared to question why he would take such drastic steps without court approval. His foolishness cost the lives of two loyal nobles and a host of men. The emperor does not take such losses lightly."

"We still have the issue of Chassandre though," Elgar said, his voice as sharp as the daggers strapped to his side. "Despite her failed portents of the past, she's convinced that the Morganite will be the doom of the empire. She's already managed to convince others. I fear the golgeman was just the beginning."

"Keep us posted on what your spies hear," the old man said. "I think the sooner we send Rowyn on the road, the better off we will be. Once the people see what she can do, they will be loath to lose her."

"*We* still haven't seen what she can do," Elgar said. "You said Gillius's letters made it seem as though she had no control, yet no one has seen a sorcerer with three gems. We need to test her."

Agramon nodded. "I was planning to take her out to the fields tomorrow afternoon to test her skill and range."

The old man shook his head. "The emperor will want to see her power for himself, as well as the rest of us."

Agramon frowned. "She may not perform well with such an audience."

The old man met Agramon's eye. "We must all see what she is capable of instead of relying on the reports of others. The emperor was very clear on this. There is far too much at stake to allow anything to be kept secret."

Agramon rose. "Very well, if you wish to risk the safety of everyone here, then she can perform at the palace to-morrow afternoon."

The old man rose as well, his eyes narrowed. "She's a gift to be shared, Agramon. It's best to remember that. We'll all be invested in her welfare, guardianship or not."

Agramon didn't bother to answer. Instead, he turned

and disappeared into the crowd, his staff thumping beside him.

I WOKE UP, STARING at the ceiling. Echo's presence was proving to be quite useful in the grand scheme of things. At the capital, knowledge was power, and I was one of the few people in Somme whose mind was immune to Agramon. If they insisted on keeping me in the capital, I couldn't spend my time sulking. Pedr had once said the court at Somme was the ultimate game of chess. I'd been terrible at chess, but it wasn't too late to learn. In the capital, you were either a chess piece or a chess player.

"Did you hear what Pythia said about you?" I asked the darkness.

I felt something weigh down the bed near my feet, as though Echo had perched herself on the side. "*Yes*," she whispered.

"Stay away from her," I cautioned. "I don't know the extent of her power, but I would hate if something happened to you because of me. I certainly wouldn't want Agramon to find out."

"*Secret*," Echo agreed.

I hadn't even told Ena about Echo, for fear that

Agramon would find it while shuffling through her mind.

"That was smart of you, to follow him and everything," I said, mulling over what I should do next. "As long as you can keep yourself safe and hidden, keep doing it. I want to know what the others say about me, what their plans are. Knowing Agramon, he probably won't reveal all his plans to me, but I'm betting he'll let it slip to someone else."

"*Yes*," Echo said, the indentation on the bed rising. "*I listen. I watch.*"

Agramon made it seem like I was his and his alone. Given his conversation with the other sorcerers, that didn't appear to be the case. He'd probably hoped to keep me ignorant to their attentions. Still, nobody in Somme really knew me. They probably thought me to be the ignorant heathen that everyone assumed I was at Solridge. It wouldn't take much to play into that ideal. The less of a threat I appeared to be, the safer I would make myself and the more likely I could escape.

I would also need more allies, at least more than a silent shadow and Ena. I ran through my memories of the night before. My first thought was Del, but I immediately dismissed it. Though Del had been friendly, she seemed far too close to Agramon to be of any use to me. Mellan Lyon was tossed aside in much the same manner. Though I liked him completely against my will, he was a Lyon, and therefore would forever be regarded as an enemy. Sam had intrigued me, and out of everyone at court, he seemed to be the most like me, but I didn't know how useful a soldier would be for my needs. After all, I was perfectly capable of fighting my own battles with weapons, and Sam admitted that he hated the intrigues of court. No, I needed someone better versed in court politics on my side.

That left the other sorcerers. The old man from my dream seemed to have my better interests in mind, and he appeared to distrust Agramon, which immediately raised him in my esteem, but the other sorcerers were far harder to read. I would have to wait, and watch, and see who didn't trust Agramon. Surely a man of his renown had enemies. I endeavored to find out who they were.

What a fool I had been to trust the sorcerers at Solridge. What a fool I had been to think I could sway my clan into letting me stay. I was no one. I held more power in my gems than most sorcerers could even dream of, and for what?

I'd trusted Lyricans, and this was where it got me.

I'd trusted Morganites, and this was where it got me.

Chained to one of the most feared men in the empire.

No one held loyalty to me, so I would hold loyalty to no one. I was done trying to appease those around me.

To act the part.

To behave.

ENA SLIPPED IN AS THE morning light peeked through the curtains. I'd already risen and stood at the washbasin splashing the cool water over my face.

"You have a big day today," Ena said, walking to my window and throwing the curtains open, the early morning sun illuminating a halo behind her. "Did you sleep well?"

"The bed was comfortable," I said, patting my face dry with a woven cloth beside the basin. "How were your quarters? I hope you're not too far."

Ena shook her head as she flipped through the gowns in my wardrobe. "The servants' quarters are on the lower level of the palace. I and several other handmaids share a room. It's better than the slaves' quarters, at least."

"Did they feed you well?" I asked. When I'd arrived in my room the previous evening to find Ena waiting to attend to me before bed, I scolded myself for not thinking to bring her a few delicious refreshments from the party. I endeavored to remember the next time.

Ena was nodding as she flipped through the gowns. "Yes, the servants eat in shifts so there is always somebody to attend to the nobility. I just picked a shift, and we had a lovely meat stew with good crusty bread. There were a few jokesters who kept me distracted for a time."

She turned, smiling as she drew down a light green dress made of gauzy fabric. I obediently let her pull the gown over me and sat at the dressing table for her to paint my face. In the corner of my eye, I noticed a flutter by the window, a flash blocking out the sun for a moment, followed by a soft scratching. Ena and I both turned at the noise.

There, standing on the stone sill of the window, was a large bird ruffling its feathers.

"A shadow falcon," Ena gasped, dropping my hairbrush with a clatter.

The falcon tilted its head to the side, studying the brush on the floor before looking about the room with a studious air.

"What is a shadow falcon doing in Somme?" I asked, trying to keep my voice low. The birds were from northern Morgania, in the mountains where I'd grown up. Some were even raised as pets. But I'd never heard of shadow falcons in the Eastern Empire.

"Don't you see, my lady?" Ena said, placing her hand on my shoulder. "It's a sign from Imor. You must keep faith, for he's watching over us."

I felt immediately guilty that my faith was in poor spirits next to Ena's, but the presence of the shadow falcon gave me pause. Suddenly, the bird let out a squawk and leaped from the window. Ena and I hurried to watch the falcon rise in the sky and soar over the city.

"It's a sign," Ena breathed, more to herself than me. "It's a sign that he will take care of us."

I watched Ena leave, not feeling the swell of hope that she clearly had at the shadow falcon's arrival. But I wanted to feel hope.

I went to the wall and pulled Iranoct down. Closing my eyes, I thought of its twin, Phyranox, and let the sword point lead me to the window that faced the northwest. It was only then that I felt comforted. It was as though there were a string at the tip of the sword leading me back to Destrian. It felt like a cruelty and a mercy, to be tied so closely with him. To always have his memory lingering at the back of my mind. Did he ever think of me? Could he ever love me again?

"BY ALL THE GODS, I'M STARVED," I exclaimed as I entered the receiving room. The welcome sight of a low table covered in sweet breads and fruit greeted me, immediately boosting my mood. I grabbed a roll and collapsed onto the couch, stuffing the sweet pastry into my mouth and licking the sticky syrup from my fingers. When I looked up, Duke Agramon was watching me from an armchair across the table with revulsion. I smiled inwardly. I'd rather he viewed me with disgust than some girl he could trifle with. He'd become far too familiar with me the night before, and I was determined to keep him at a healthy distance.

"What?" I asked through a mouthful of bread. "Did Gillius not tell you? I had quite a horrible time at Solridge. The masters had *no idea* what to do with me." I reached for another piece of delicious bread but got caught up when my voluminous skirt twined itself around my legs. When I wrestled my feet free, I grabbed another roll and propped my feet onto the couch, lying back to enjoy the fruits of someone else's labors.

Agramon's nose wrinkled. "He mentioned you struggled, but I had no idea you were so . . . loathsome."

"It's true." I nodded wisely. "Lady Vianne would have fits over me. It was more than her tender heart could bear."

Agramon cleared his throat. "How is she?" he asked, slowly turning the staff in his hand, his eyes on the gem embedded at the end of the golden rod. "Is Vianne enjoying the western shore as much as she'd hoped?"

"I don't know," I said between bites, surprised by the sudden deviation from slinging insults to more passing pleasantries. "It's not like she took me into her confidence." She wouldn't have had time, what with trying to erase my mind to keep me in line and all.

"And Alexander, is he keeping her happy?"

I stopped chewing and really looked at Agramon. He was feigning interest in his stupid staff, but I could tell he was watching me from the corner of his eye, as though he were curious about my response. But of course, he had sponsored Lady Vianne himself. Thinking back on the fear in Vianne's eyes, I'd wondered then if there had been more to her story at the capital. Looking at Agramon now, it was becoming all too clear.

"You were in love with her."

Duke Agramon rolled his eyes. "Don't believe everything you hear. Out of all my students, she was the most like me. The most . . . promising. It's a pity she threw it all away to go traipsing off to the western shore in the name of love. I fear her power will wane there, and she will become a mere shadow of who she was meant to be."

"Well, that was a pretty speech," I said, staring at the ceiling as I stuffed another roll into my mouth. "But it's my experience that she uses her power quite a bit. It's not like she's wasting away."

Agramon tapped the arm of his chair. "I saw you had words with Mellan Lyon last night. What did you think of him?"

"He's a Lyon," I said, licking the syrup from my fingers. "I thought he looked remarkably similar to my closest enemies."

Agramon chuckled. "His father wrote to me, asking that I consider Mellan for your hand once your training is finished. His is the first offer I've received, though I anticipate many more to come."

I choked on the sweetbread and began coughing. Agramon tossed me a handkerchief with a look of distaste.

"You can't tell me you're considering marrying me off to Mellan Lyon," I said when I'd regained my breath.

"Why should I not? The Lyons are the most powerful family in the Western Empire. I'd be a fool not to consider an alliance with him."

"What alliance? Are you at war? I'll tell you now, I want no part of it," I declared.

"I've made no decision yet," Agramon said, using his staff to help him rise. "But if Mellan seeks to romance you, let him. I want him to give his father a good report for the time being. Spend some time with him, dance with him at parties, laugh at his foolish jokes—whatever you women do to ensnare men's attentions."

"So, you want me to flirt?" I groaned. "Now I know you've lost your mind because I'm an abysmal flirt. I've never been good at it."

Agramon glowered. "I must say, I'm becoming more and more disappointed with the number of things you do poorly, Rowyn."

I grinned up at him. "You wouldn't be the first."

"By Sol above, get up! It's past time you were to be at Princess Willene's. Clean those crumbs off you and attempt to make yourself presentable. I'll show you the way this morning, but afterward you will make the journey on your own."

"Aren't you afraid I'll run off?" I asked, then kicked myself. If I'd shut my mouth, I might have actually been able to run off. Then again, I couldn't imagine that Agramon would give me any semblance of freedom without the proper safeguards in place.

"No," Agramon said. "The palace guards and crime lords of Somme have instructions that if they see you trying to escape, they are to stop you immediately at all costs, and that is just the beginning. Know that if you make any attempt to escape, what few freedoms I bestow on you will end the minute you think of sneaking away."

I glared at him. "It's not like I have anywhere to escape to, anyway," I mumbled before rising and brushing the crumbs from my skirt.

Agramon led me through the palace to an ornate set of doors engraved with golden-winged spirits. I knocked, and the door swept open, revealing a room richly decorated with pastels and gold.

Princess Willene rose as we entered, and the slave holding the door bowed low. "Ah, Rowyn," the princess said, "we were waiting for you before we began."

A GILDED CAGE

Princess Willene waved me over. A girl was sitting on the couch, her black hair woven into a wealth of tiny braids with gold beads and other rich-looking ornaments twined in. Her eyes were a sparkling clear blue, a shadow of the emperor's. They met mine with remarkable solemnity for one so young.

"I'll expect you in our receiving room after lunch," Agramon said before turning to Willene. "Thank you again for granting me this favor. It won't be forgotten."

Willene gave a slight nod before Agramon swept out of the room.

"Rowyn," Willene said, her voice hard, "I would like to introduce you to Princess Lesedi the Younger, firstborn of the Empress of Lyrica."

I swept into a curtsy. Princess Willene watched me with a sharp eye while the corner of the young princess's mouth twitched.

I rose, heat rising to my cheeks.

"Well," said Princess Willene, "I suppose that is where we will begin."

I spent the morning practicing the different curtsies befitting the titles of nobility. It was quite like drills in weapons training. I had to lower myself farther for a duke than for a baron. The emperor received the lowest curtsy, of course, with my knees nearly to the floor. I practiced over and over, trying to memorize the feeling of the different curtsies, while the young princess walked around the room balancing a large tome on her head. Though she was far younger than me, perhaps ten years old, she was already much more experienced with posture.

When lady's tea was brought in, we moved to the table where Princess Willene motioned me to sit in the oddest chair I'd ever seen.

"What is that?" I asked, eying the leather straps.

"Your posture is atrocious. This will help you practice."

"If you think I'm going to let you strap me in . . . whatever that thing is . . . you must've lost your mind," I said, not caring that Princess Lesedi's eyes had bugged out of her head at my rudeness.

"Do you want me to send a bad report to the duke?" Princess Willene asked, her eyes narrowed.

"What do you think he'll do? Bend me over his knee? Take a strap to me? Refuse to let me practice my 'gift' for everyone's benefit?"

Willene's eyebrows rose nearly to her golden hair. "Oh, my dear, you think those are the worst things the duke could do? I would've thought you'd have more imagination than that. I assure you, *he* does."

"If you're insinuating that he would hurt someone I care about, then I'm sorry to tell you, those closest to me are across the sea, far from the duke's grasp."

"Oh," Willene said, "just as *you* were. Yet here you are,

exactly as the duke wished it."

I clenched my teeth. Princess Lesedi was looking from me to Willene, her eyes wide.

I sat down, and Willene began to strap me into the chair, starting with my torso, then up to my neck, and finally, to my forehead.

When I was fully strapped in, Princess Willene stepped away to have words with the slave about tea service. Princess Lesedi leaned in and whispered, "If you clench your body while she's tightening the leathers, they won't end up cutting into your skin. It took me weeks to figure that one out."

I couldn't turn my head toward her, but I managed to raise my brows a bit.

"She put *you* in this? You should've clapped her in the chair herself, Princess."

Princess Lesedi shook her head. "No, having Willene instruct me in courtly manners was my father's idea. He thought Mother was teaching me to be too willful. It was a compromise."

"So, they hope to reform you?"

"I suppose. Father thinks I should be more Lyrican in my ways and less like my mother's people. After all, we live in Lyrica—it's who we rule—so we should seek to be more like them."

I scoffed. "Typical of a Lyrican to think their way is

best. Take it from me. I'm living proof that reformation won't work. No matter how many uncomfortable chairs they strap me into."

Princess Lesedi giggled but quickly hushed as Willene returned to the table. She didn't speak to me again for the rest of the service but glanced at me from the corners of her eyes, sneaking little smiles my way. I wondered about the poor girl, stuck in Willene's chambers all morning instead of playing with children her age. I felt for her, for in the depths of her words, I noticed a little girl trying to live up to the expectations of her father, and constantly falling short.

Chapter 8

THE EMPRESS'S LUNCH was everything I envisioned Somme to be. It was held out in the gardens, surrounded by fragrant, late summer blooms of hibiscus and roses. The ladies of court filled the open space, laughing and gossiping from table to table, their jewel-colored dresses and perfectly decorated faces making the scene look like the most exquisite painting I'd ever beheld.

Among the largesse, the image was tainted by the figures of slaves weaving in and out of the droves of women, offering a golden drink that bubbled up from the bottom of the glass. One slave girl was sporting a black eye, and it took everything I had not to make a scene and ask her who had lain their hands on her. I glanced at the princesses beside me to see if they noticed. Willene looked as though she'd sniffed something awful, her nose wrinkling as she surveyed the scene. Lesedi the Younger was craning to see around the large groups of women. Neither paid the slaves any mind.

I gritted my teeth, wishing there was more I could do for the poor people's plight. Would I eventually become like the nobles, looking past the slaves as though they didn't exist outside of serving my needs? I didn't think I'd ever get used to their presence. They reminded me too much of the war dogs taken from my homeland. Every slave boy could've been my childhood love, Luc, who'd become lost in the empire's wars. I tore my gaze away from the ragged Ylirians and instead studied the heavily painted noblewomen.

The youngest courtiers seemed to try to place themselves close to the empress. A group of older women was clustered by a set of couches, fanning away the heat of midday beneath large umbrellas held by shirtless Ylirians. The tables were filled with large dishes brimming with exotic fruits, breads, and cold meats that a few women had scooped onto crusts of bread.

In the middle of it all was the empress, Lesedi the Peerless, her smile brightening the gathering as she laughed and talked with the women around her. The intimidating bodyguard I'd marked at the banquet the night before stood behind the empress, holding a staff with a sickening curved blade at the end, her gaze just as sharp as her weapon as she studied the surroundings.

Though Lesedi the Younger had accompanied Willene and me to the luncheon, she slipped into the crowd, winding through women until she sank down at her mother's side. Empress Lesedi didn't look away from the richly dressed lady she was speaking to, but she grabbed her daughter's hand, her fingers stroking the princess's palm.

The young girl smiled up at her mother before accepting a small piece of fruit from a nearby slave.

"The empress insists on holding lunch every day for the ladies of court. It gives them a chance to bond as females without the company and influence of men," Princess Willene said, her eyes darting around the women. "It's mostly just simpering know-nothings trying to weasel their way closer to the royal family, but Her Eminence wouldn't be dissuaded from her new *tradition*."

I looked around at the chattering women, the different groups taking each other into their confidences, but there were no other sorcerers save for Del.

"Everyone seems to be having a good time," I said, making my way to the table of food. I grabbed a plate and began loading it down with meats, cheeses, and pickled fruits. I'd been near starving in the Nightlands and was keen to build my muscle back up to its former strength. Once my plate was full, I evaded Willene's reproachful look and went to Del, who waved me to a seat beside her on a couch.

"How were your lessons with the grand shrew?" Del whispered as I took a bite.

I choked on the bread, trying to stifle a laugh. "It was awful, made worse by the fact that I've never been adept at courtesy to begin with."

Del shrugged. "Perhaps I can kidnap you one of these

mornings to show off the new project I've been working on."

"Would Agramon let you?" I asked, my heart rising. After all, he seemed to have a bit of a soft spot for Del, and I fully intended to capitalize on those feelings for my own benefit. Namely, escaping Willene's lessons as often as possible. "I would love to see the city and meet more of the sorcerers here."

Del squeezed my arm. "Don't worry, I'll break you out and show you a good time."

Suddenly, ringing filled the garden. All the ladies stopped their chatter and turned to the center of the circle, where Empress Lesedi stood from her couch.

"Ladies," the empress began, holding her hands out to the crowd. "I wanted to take this opportunity to congratulate Lady Johane on the birth of her firstborn."

A scattered applause spread throughout the crowd. The empress smiled, beckoning forward a young woman who blushed as she went to stand by the empress. Empress Lesedi turned to the slave holding a pillow beside her, lifted a small woven chain studded with gems, and clasped it around the woman's wrist. The applause was greater now, and I noticed other women in the crowd wearing the same bracelet.

The empress continued, "With Lady Johane's joy, I ask that we all remember who we strive to better the empire for. The children are our future, and for them we would toil to achieve all ends. Let this bracelet, then, be a symbol of the future to come, where all those who hunger shall be fed, where all those shivering will find shelter, where all our stories are shared to a greater understanding, and where all children are born equal under the light of Sol."

"As the mother wills it, so may it be," the ladies said, speaking as one.

"Was that a sermon?" I whispered to Del.

Del rolled her eyes. "The bracelet is just a symbol of the empress's grace. She gifts it to women upon a successful birth, or if they provide a great service to the city, or a variety of other tasks that she deems worthy." I heard a tinge of anger in Del's voice.

"Have you not received a bracelet yet?" I asked. There was no mistaking it. Del was not meeting my eye.

"The empress can be very choosy as to who is brought into her inner circle, and she doesn't trust sorcerers."

"Pity," I said, settling back down with my plate. "I kind of like her."

Del wrinkled her nose, but I ignored her, focusing instead on my food.

The ladies' luncheon lasted for an hour before the others began making their way back into the palace. I rose with them, about to ask Del to lead me back to my chambers, when the empress approached us.

"I'm glad to see you made it to my luncheon, Rowyn the Morganite," the empress said as she took in my empty plate. "I worried that the duke wouldn't share you but am delighted to be proven wrong."

I couldn't help but grin back at her. "I had a lovely time this afternoon, Your Eminence, and look forward to dining with you and your ladies regularly while I remain at the palace."

The empress nodded, but the look she shot her towering guardian seemed pointed. "I was curious to hear of your adventures in the land of darkness. Would you mind accompanying me to my chambers and regaling me with the story? I found the bard's tale not as thrilling as I hoped it would be."

"I was told to meet Duke Agramon after the luncheon." I glanced at Del. "I would surely get in trouble if I kept him waiting."

The empress smiled brighter, revealing perfect white teeth. "Luckily for me, the will of an empress outweighs the wishes of a duke. Lady Delise can inform the duke where you've been detained, and that you will return after I've been sufficiently diverted."

Del scowled at the clear dismissal, but she could only curtsy low to the empress, then turn and scurry back into the palace with the others, shooting glances at me from over her shoulder.

The empress led me through the halls of the palace, holding the hand of Lesedi the Younger as she went. We passed noblemen who bowed low, their eyes on their feet. I didn't know what to do, or how to act when accompanying the empress, so I merely followed behind her at a stroll and amused myself by watching the nobility trip over themselves in her presence.

"Rowyn, I don't think I've introduced you to Mem, my guard," Empress Lesedi said, motioning to the warrior woman striding behind her. Mem nodded stiffly before turning her attention back to the windows.

The empress paused outside a set of golden doors. The guards posted outside quickly opened them, and the empress led me inside.

Arched windows ran the entire length of the stone wall in the massive receiving room. Low couches and large cushioned seats sat upon massive rugs woven with geometric designs I didn't recognize as Lyrican. Palm plants and exotic flowers grew in large pots near the windows. Dozens upon dozens of gilt cages were scattered throughout the space, hanging from the walls, sitting on tables, and placed artfully on the floor. Jewel-colored birds flitted behind the golden bars, the melody of their songs and the soft rustling of wings making the entire room feel as though it were a living, breathing entity. Shuffling among them was a wizened old woman, her skin dark like the empress's, carrying a large golden bowl of seeds. She whistled and clucked at the birds, moving from cage to cage and filling the dishes within while greeting the feathered occupants by name.

On one of the rugs crouched two small children playing with a set of stacking stones. One was a little girl, a mirror of Princess Lesedi, with her hair combed out till it surrounded her head in a dark halo. The younger child was a boy, his eyes blue like his oldest sister, bearing the royal crest on a ring, heavy on his small finger.

"Please have a seat," the empress said. "I hope you don't mind, but I wish to change into something more comfortable."

"By all means," I said, curious that she'd even asked my permission. The empress disappeared through a side door, and Lesedi the Younger lowered herself to the ground to play with the other children. I sank on a chair and watched them. I couldn't help but notice that both the empress and the oldest princess bore a twin of the jeweled bracelet that the empress had gifted earlier.

Mem stood outside the empress's door, her eyes on me as she gripped her odd-looking staff. "What weapon is that?" I asked, pointing.

"It's a ukilite," she said in stilted Lyrican. I wondered if she had many occasions to speak to anyone other than the empress.

"You're the only woman I've seen carry weapons at the capital," I said, unable to keep the envy from my voice.

Mem's black eyes gave me an appraising look. "I was surprised that you did not. Aren't you supposed to be some great warrior?"

I shrugged. "My sponsor doesn't think it's necessary."

Mem raised an eyebrow. "And are you always so obedient to what the lords tell you?"

"No," I said, "but carrying a sword would be a pretty obvious refusal of his wishes."

Mem nodded, her eyes shooting to the windows and doors before coming back to rest upon me. "Where are you from that they let the girls fight? I understood that they thought you too delicate for such tasks here."

"Morgania," I replied. "It's far to the north, in the Western Empire."

Mem nodded. "We haven't seen any girl Morganites in the years I've been waiting on my lady. I've seen plenty of your men though."

"Yes, the doghunters raid the bigger cities for fighters—ever since the war in Yliria began."

Mem didn't say anything.

"Is it rare for women to fight where you are from?" I asked, shifting my weight.

Mem shook her head. "Our seat is passed down through the eldest's line, no matter the gender. My lady,

Lesedi, is a younger daughter of High Queen Ishtari. Her elder sister, Morana, will take the throne when her mother dies."

I nodded in acknowledgment. I'd heard that there were lands ruled by women over the southern sea but hadn't made the connection that the empress fared from them. "Do they teach all women to fight?"

"No." Mem laughed. "Do all men here learn the fighting arts?"

I shook my head. "Only those who choose or are forced to through war."

Mem nodded. "We have far fewer wars, so there isn't as much need to fight as there is here. Diplomacy is the ruling force in Ember Innes. Mainly, we learn fighting skills to protect the royal family. I am bound to guard Lesedi through my birth. My father is guardian to the queen herself, my sister to the first princess."

"So, you do not protect the emperor too?" I wondered if there was a conflict with Mem protecting the empress and only the empress. Mem shook her head. "The emperor has the whole army to protect him and his interests. My empress has only me."

"It's a noble cause, to be sure," I said hurriedly.

"I asked if I could recruit some guards for the children of my empress, but the emperor said no," Mem added, and I could tell from her expression that she wasn't happy about it.

An awkward silence passed. I fiddled with my hands while the children whispered to each other nearby. The old lady was still busy feeding the birds at the far corner of the room, now communicating in a series of clicks.

"You are apprentice to the great sorcerer from what I hear," Mem said suddenly.

"I am." I couldn't help the note of warning and fear in my voice.

Mem narrowed her eyes. "A man who can manipulate minds is never to be trusted. I wonder at such a man at court."

I knew to be careful with what I said, but it had also been so long since I felt I could speak my mind that my mouth got the better of me. "If the emperor were wise, Agramon would be sent far from court. But I am not ruler here, nor is there any reason for him to listen to me."

"The great sorcerer has had the emperor's ear for a long time. Since before he and the empress were wed. It would be no small thing for him to end the false friendship of the sorcerer, or so my lady thinks."

"Does she feel she is in danger?" I asked.

Mem shrugged. Clearly, she was not going to answer me.

"There now," the empress said, appearing at the doorway in a different gown that didn't appear to be so tight.

"I see you've been getting to know Mem. Nini is my children's nursemaid," the empress said, gesturing to the wizened woman who was whistling now. She glanced at me with a toothless smile. "She's raised three generations of my family's children and knows more stories than the university library here at Somme. Isn't that right, children?"

The little girl giggled as she looked up at her mother, while the boy just ignored us, beating rocks together as he played.

"You met my eldest, Lesedi the Younger, while under the tutelage of my illustrious sister-in-law," the empress continued, sinking onto the couch and pulling her feet up beside her.

Princess Lesedi looked up from her toys and smiled. "You can just call me Ledi. It makes it so much easier."

"It was lovely to attend class with you, Ledi, though I'm sure I'm a terrible influence already."

The empress laughed as Ledi shook her head, turning back to her siblings.

"My other children, Princess Eledra and Prince Artian the Eighth, heir to the empire of Lyrica."

The little prince didn't look up. Instead, he knocked over his sister's tower with his little fist.

"Omri, you mustn't be rude," Nini said, shaking the little boy's shoulder and pointing at me. "Say hello to your blessed mother's friend."

The little boy looked up at me, wrinkling his brows together and twisting his lips into a pout. "Hello stranger," he said before returning to his game.

Nini shook her head at the empress and began speaking to her in the same language she'd spoken to the birds in. The empress nodded, saying something softly before turning back to me and smiling. Nini *tsked* and went to set down the bowl of seeds on one of the tables before lowering herself onto her haunches next to the children.

"Forgive my son," the empress said. "He is spoiled here at the palace and becoming unruly as he gets older. I hope to teach him better manners befitting an emperor in time."

I found myself surprised by her candor. Even more surprising was the fact that I was spending the afternoon in the Empress of Lyrica's receiving room surrounded by royalty, and I felt more relaxed than I'd been since leaving the shores of Darkport. "You're an asset to this empire, Your Excellency. We are lucky to have you here."

Lesedi dipped her head to the side, but Nini piped up again, this time speaking in the common Lyrican tongue that we all could understand.

"Rubydoo is mad since you left," the old woman said, addressing the empress. "He'll not eat and will die soon."

Lesedi sighed, then signaled to Mem, who disappeared into the maze of cages before returning holding a large cage with a red bird inside. The bird tweeted angrily at

Lesedi as she opened the hinged metal door and carefully lifted the bird, which perched atop her finger.

"Poor Rubydoo," the empress said. "His spirit is low because he's far from home, away from his old life and loved ones." The empress's eyes flicked to mine. "Without proper care, he will be lost to us forever."

"So, what do you do, to ensure that his spirits remain high?" I asked, the gooseflesh rising on my skin.

The empress grabbed some seed from a little dish on a side table and held it up to the little red bird. He chirped, as though defiant, before leaning down and pecking the seeds. "I feed him from my own hand. I make sure that he knows he's loved. I croon to him and tell him how special he is. He is new to my flock and the farthest from home. Soon he will make friends and gain allies among my other little birds, but I want him to always remember who gave him the strength to live on, who gave him purpose, the one to whom he should remain loyal, at all costs."

"What is it you want from me?" I asked, her meaning all too clear.

The empress set the bird beside her on the couch and turned to the others. "It is rest time," she told Nini.

The children sighed. Prince Artian opened his mouth but closed it quickly when the empress raised her brows threateningly. Princess Ledi picked up the stones and dropped them in a basket underneath a table before taking

little Princess Eledra's hand, kissing her mother, and disappearing through a nearby door into what I assumed was
their nursery. They were quickly followed by Nini and the
little prince, who rubbed his eyes as he laid his head on his
nursemaid's shoulder.

When only Mem remained, the empress turned back to
me, her dark eyes somber. "The duke is not able to read
your thoughts, is he?" she asked. "Which puts you in the
perfect position to spy on him for me."

I froze, my heart dropping to my knees. "How do you
know the duke can't read my thoughts?"

"Because I know what sits upon your waist," she said.

My eyes widened. "It was *you* who sent the girdle?"

The red bird hopped down from the couch and jumped
toward the open balcony door. Empress Lesedi sighed.
"See how they try to escape? Even with clipped wings,
they make bids for freedom."

Mem leaned down and scooped the bird back up, setting it beside the empress once more.

Empress Lesedi stroked the red bird, her fingers light
upon its feathers as it settled down beside her. "When I
first came to the capital, there was a girl here who arrived
around the same time I did. We were both foreigners in a
strange land, trying to survive in the most vicious and op-
ulent court in the world. We made another friend quickly,
a kind girl who taught us the ways of court and took us

under her wing. She was a distant cousin of the ruling family, so she knew her way around the nobility. It was lucky we all found each other. I don't know if I would have lasted those first couple of years without them."

"What happened?"

Lesedi smiled. "Lady Noemi, the kind girl who took us under her wing, was happily married soon after I was. Her husband, Captain Abelard, swept her away to The Fens after the wedding, and I haven't seen her since, though the captain still frequents court during wartime. Every time he comes, he brings letters, but she's been indisposed with several children over the years and was never a fan of court to begin with."

"I've never heard of this Lady Noemi, nor Captain Abelard," I admitted, hoping my lack of knowledge wouldn't anger the empress. She merely shook her head. "But what of the first girl?" I asked, thinking back to her story. "What ever happened to her?"

"The girl's mentor had become obsessed with her, but she fell for another man. A brother, in fact, to Lady Noemi, but the duke wouldn't even discuss releasing her from her bonds. So, I helped her escape."

I withheld a gasp, realizing of whom she was speaking. Who had actually ensured I received the Girdle of Ephema. "Lady Vianne," I murmured.

The bright glint in the empress's eyes was answer

enough. "She wrote to me of you, of your potential and wish to remain free of the empire, of your fear that you will fail to be everything everyone expects you to be. I know that you hold no loyalty to the duke, nor my husband, nor to the empire itself, but now that your clan has abandoned you to those you've always hated, you are floundering, with nothing to keep you moored to this world. What will become of you now, Rowyn?"

I shrugged. "I don't know. It seems that everyone I meet has some ideas for my future though."

Mem shifted her feet. I supposed I shouldn't have let my irritation with the empress show.

"The duke is scheming," the empress said, leaning back into the cushions on her couch. "He's been vying for more power ever since he was appointed to the emperor's council. You can bet that if he has a chance to seize the throne from the emperor, he will take it. I've been paying close attention to him for the past year, and he's shoring up loyalties with some of the emperor's most staunch supporters. He's planning something big, something that involves you. My husband's life, the lives of my children, depend on me knowing what that is, and preparing for it."

"So how can I help?" I asked, running my fingers through my skirt. I wished I hadn't let my emotions get the better of me. The empress seemed desperate to keep her family safe, and she was reaching out to someone who could very well tip the scale in her favor. It was what I would've done if I were her. "I'm new here and don't know the hidden schemes of others. Why trust me with something so serious? You don't even know me."

Lesedi's eyes flashed. "Because I don't have a choice. My husband won't listen to me because he's a simple-minded lecher who has been spoiled with the crown all his life and can't abide the fact that someone may know more about leadership than he does. The noblemen do not listen to me because I'm a woman and a foreigner to boot. I come to *you*, Rowyn, because whether you like it or not, you are the most powerful woman in the realm, and you are the greatest chance I have for my children's survival. The crown is weak with my husband as head. Duke Agramon sees that, and it is only a matter of time before he acts on it. So, I am here, doing you the courtesy of being honest and asking for a chance to show you that I am worthy of your loyalty."

I clenched my fists, totally unprepared for the conversation at hand. By all the gods, what was I getting dragged into?

"So, should you show me that you're worthy of my loyalty, what then?" I asked, trying to steady my voice.

"So far the duke doesn't suspect that your ability to block his magical influence is linked to an outside source. It made sense to gift *you* the girdle because there have been occasions, though they've been very few, that a person with a particular power, or someone who wields a large amount of it, deterred Agramon from getting into their minds. You're my lifeline. Agramon is infamous for not letting anyone close to him, but you are his ward. You share his quarters and accompany him when he travels. Because he values you so highly, he will keep you closer than most. You will see what he sees and hear his conversations. I want you to notice whose loyalty he's trying to buy and share what you learn."

"Won't he suspect something if we're constantly meeting?"

Lesedi nodded. "Indeed, which is why I've had to be candid so quickly. We cannot meet alone after this. Everything else will be done either in the open or through messages passed during your morning lessons. Nobody watches Ledi, so she's the perfect courier."

"You said you would show me you could be worthy of my loyalty," I said, meeting Lesedi's gaze. "I must see with my own eyes who to trust my freedom to."

Lesedi nodded, signaling to Mem. "A group of ladies accompanies me to the market twice a week. It would not be out of the ordinary for you to join us. There you will see how I seek to rule Lyrica."

Agramon would likely allow me to join the empress's group, considering he wanted me to behave like a noble lady. "I will see what I can do about meeting you in the market. I can give you this chance, but Your Majesty, I'm very weary of betrayal."

Empress Lesedi rose, her hand outstretched. "I've never failed those I hold in high regard. I can help you escape your gilded cage, Rowyn. All I ask is that you return the favor."

Chapter 9

"DEL SAID YOU WERE waylaid by the empress after lunch," Agramon said as I stepped into our receiving room after losing my way three times. Luckily, he merely glanced at me before turning back to the looking glass to adjust the drape of his robes.

"She wanted to hear my story of the Nightlands," I said as nonchalantly as I could. "I was certainly surprised by the honor."

Agramon rolled his eyes. "Don't be. She invites every lady new to court to her chambers to talk about children and gossip about gowns. It isn't really an honor when it's given so lightly."

I let out a breath of relief. "Well, we had a nice time. I got to meet the young prince, and the empress invited me to attend her when she goes to market, if that's all right with you."

Agramon waved his hand. "Yes, yes. Enjoy the cackling of the court's spinsters as they wallow in city rot for a few hours, see if I care, but after that, we must focus on your studies. Ena is on her way to ready you for the presentation of your skills to the court and council. It's time to show everyone what all the fuss is about."

I nodded before retreating to my room to await Ena. I went to the window, looking out over the city, bustling with all manner of people. My first thought had been to fail at my grand presentation—to show everyone that my presence was nothing and that I was hardly worth all the trouble—but my meeting with the empress had changed my mind. I'd told her I wished to see that she was worthy of my loyalty, but that ship could sail both ways. Shouldn't I endeavor to show her that my loyalty was worth something too? After all, I was in dire need of allies, and gaining the empress's trust was no small feat.

Everything about the empress seemed earnest, but something held me back from giving in to her wishes so quickly. Perhaps it was because she gave the information so freely, or because she seemed to assume that my answer would be yes, considering she sent the Girdle of Ephema *before* I'd agreed to her terms. In truth, I knew it was her self-proclaimed closeness with Vianne. Lady Vianne had spent my entire time at Solridge lying and forcing me to lose my memories. Perhaps the empress didn't know her friend as well as she thought she did. After all, I could've had my freedom much sooner had Vianne left me alone to make my own choices.

A shrill call sounded above, and I stepped back from the window as the shadow falcon landed on the sill. The falcon tilted its head to the side and looked at me before lifting its wing and preening its feathers. I took a tentative step forward.

"Where did you come from, friend?" It didn't answer, of course, and continued preening its feathers. I reached out to touch it just as Ena opened the door to my bedroom. With a loud squawk, the bird leaped back out the window and disappeared into the sky.

THE ENTIRE COURT WAS WAITING for us on a massive covered balcony overlooking the city and harbor beyond. I recognized a few other sorcerers sprinkled through the crowd. Miyu looked exquisite in robes embroidered with gold thread, the gem on her chest barely visible through the silk fabric. Del, standing next to Mellan Lyon, shot me a wink as I passed. The emperor and empress were seated on a raised dais, the empress's sharp eyes following me. Her husband sat at the edge of his seat, hands clasped together, his eyes on the sky.

I tore away from the crowd and focused on the end of the balcony where a group of sorcerers waited for us.

"Rowyn, may I present the Council of Five," Agramon said, extending his arm toward me. "I believe you met El-gar last night. This is Berinon, the court's alchemist, Owain the Warder, Tristam the Miraculous, and Edmund the Bright, whom I'm sure you've already heard of."

Elgar nodded as though acknowledging our recent acquaintance. Gillius had studied under Tristam, the court healer. Apparently, the man was somehow related to Lord Alexander and the emperor, and looked very much like them, with his blond hair and ruddy complexion.

"I don't like the idea of doing it so close to the palace," Owain said. Though we hadn't been formally introduced, I recognized him from the banquet the night before and the dream Echo had sent me. In person, the tattoo on his neck was more pronounced. It looked like a dark collar with spikes running up toward his chin.

"We didn't expect there to be quite this much audience," Edmund the Bright added, a hint of apology in his dark eyes. I recognized him as the old man from my dreams with the power to call pure light.

I looked back over my shoulder at the courtiers crowded together, their eyes on me.

"I heard she already called a small storm when she arrived yesterday. Perhaps we should give her the benefit of the doubt," said Berinon, a young man whose tanned skin and black hair made him look as though he hailed farther east, near Yliria. Despite his words of assurance, his fingers trembled as he adjusted his spectacles, his eyes on the sky. There was something about his appearance that looked off, and it took a moment for me to realize what it was. He had no eyebrows.

Duke Agramon had narrowed his eyes at Owain. "Surely you can protect the royal family and their court in so small a space."

Owain's nostrils flared. "The *court* will be protected, but what of them?" he asked, nodding toward the city.

My breath caught in my throat as I peered over the balcony. People of all classes and creed stood elbow to elbow, filling the streets of the capital, their faces raised to the balcony. When they saw me, a murmur rose through the crowd. Children scrambled up archways or hung from windows of shops, waving at me from their perches.

The blood drained from my face. "I can harness it," I said, thankful my voice didn't tremble. "I have control that I didn't have at Solridge."

"I won't wager the lives of innocents on your word," Owain replied. "Especially if it's just to put on a show." His eyes went to Agramon, as if he were challenging him.

Agramon bristled, but it was Tristam the Miraculous who spoke from his seat on a stone bench, his hair bright in the afternoon sun. "The street singers have been belting her story for the entire day. The people know the risk. If the girl claims to have control, let her show them what she can do."

"Quite right," Berinon agreed, clapping his hands

together. "It's not like we can order them all inside."

Edmund the Bright frowned, looking from Owain, who shrugged, to Agramon, who looked practically beside himself with frustration. I could almost read the duke's thoughts. He'd brought me out on the balcony, dressed and primped, ready to put on a show for all of Somme. He wasn't about to let another sorcerer take it away from him.

Edmund the Bright's eyes fell on me. "If you're sure," he said, backing away from the edge.

Agramon rested his hand on my bare shoulder. It took everything I had not to recoil. He leaned down to my ear and whispered, "I want the whole of Somme weeping at your power. Do not fail me in this."

The hair on the back of my neck rose. I nodded, my eyes to the clear sky overhead. I'd told myself on the journey to Somme that I would use my power to help the people, and that was precisely what I meant to do.

My gems were already warm and pulsing. The magic within the stones was giddy to be let out. I stepped to the edge of the balcony and held my hands out, letting the magic stream toward the sky. Clouds billowed above, tumbling over each other. I pushed out more power, the clouds unfurling over the heavens until the eye of Sol was blocked completely, casting a great shadow over the city and the commoners, who looked up at me with open-mouthed stares. I continued to let the mass of clouds build, layer upon layer, reaching as far as the eye could see, over the harbor and to the sea beyond. I sent more magic to the north where the farmlands sat.

Agramon had wanted me to put on a show, and a show they would get. With each pulse of power, my confidence grew. The wind picked up, sending my cerulean gown billowing around me, black curls whipping over my face.

Thunder pealed, echoing off the stone palace. Someone behind me squealed, and I couldn't help but smile. The clouds darkened until it seemed like night had fallen. Thunder rumbled and growled like a living beast galloping over the city, chasing the streaks of lightning that threaded through the sky. It was at the darkest moment, when the wind was at its peak and the lightning at its brightest, that I unleashed the torrent, letting my hands fall to my sides.

Rain streamed from the heavens, beating against the marble and pooling at my feet. My dress was soaked in seconds, but I didn't care. The people below had their hats in their hands, letting the rain pool in the folds and drawing it to their lips to drink. Children danced and splashed in puddles, chasing each other through the streets, but not even the voices of the people rose above the roar of my tempest.

I calmed the storm a bit so that no errant bolt of lightning found its way into the crowd. I'd put on a good show while still holding back. Agramon wouldn't ever see what

I was capable of or how varied my abilities were. No one in Somme would. The only person who would've seen most of what I could do was Destrian, and he was across the sea in Morgania. The empire would only know what I chose to show them.

I turned to the sound of clapping. My gown clutched my skin, soaked through with rain, my hair forming an ebony river down my bare back and shoulders. Agramon was at my side at once, lifting my hand. I played my part, curtsying to the applauding court. When I straightened, I noticed the emperor had risen from his seat, his blue eyes wide as he applauded the loudest.

"It was just as you said, Agramon," the emperor exclaimed as we passed. "Well done finding her. The drought is as good as over!"

The empress stood beside her husband, an eyebrow cocked as she watched me. I met her stare for stare, letting Agramon lead me back through the parting crowd. If I gleaned anything from her expression, it was that I'd pleased her.

"Your Grace," a nobleman said, stepping into our path. His wizened eyes watched me hungrily before they flickered back to Agramon. "What a gift she is, to the whole of the empire."

"Indeed, the emperor was quite insistent on hosting her here at Somme," Agramon said, his hand tightening on my shoulder.

"But surely," the nobleman said with a nervous chuckle, "you will allow others to host her as well. The whole of Lyrica should benefit from her skills."

Agramon's eyebrows rose. "That all depends, Count Grachan, but I'm sure we can come to some sort of agreement."

The nobleman's eyes fell. "Indeed, with the emperor's blessing."

"Why, of course!" Agramon exclaimed, his nails digging into my flesh. "Now, I would like to attend to my ward, who is sure to be exhausted after this ordeal."

Agramon sidestepped the count, pulling me with him as we made our way back to our quarters.

"You did much better than I anticipated," Duke Agramon said, turning to me as we entered the receiving room. "I wondered about your range, but it seems your reach is quite far."

"It's the gems," I said, holding up my hands. "When Master Gillius tested my range before, it wasn't nearly so far, but when I practiced in the Nightlands, I noticed a difference. Lord Destrian even remarked on it."

Duke Agramon's brows rose like they normally did whenever I mentioned Destrian's name. "You've certainly piqued everyone's interest, now that they've seen your powers aren't merely rumors."

I shivered, running my hands down my arms from the chill. Duke Agramon seemed to remember himself. "Of course, you must change into dry clothes. The council will want to speak to me, so I'll send Ena back in, and then I'll escort you to the emperor's banquet. He has already requested that you share your story of the Nightlands tonight, before the start of dinner."

Agramon paused at the door, turning to me with a smile. "You did quite well today, Rowyn. Quite well indeed."

"Can I hold you to your promise then?" I asked before he could slip through the door.

Agramon frowned. "What promise is that, dear girl?"

"You said that if I followed your orders and impressed at court, you would allow me to continue my weapons training."

Agramon closed the door slowly, his expression dropping to a frown. "And you think, after a day at the capital, that what you've done so far is sufficient for me to change my mind?"

I thrust my chin forward. "Gillius never saw a problem with me doing it," I snapped. Of course, that was a bald-faced lie. I wondered what was in the letters Gillius had sent to the duke during my stay at Solridge. My room, decorated perfectly to my tastes, dresses that fit like a second skin—it was as though the duke knew all too much about me. What other intimate details could he know?

Duke Agramon strode toward me, his muddy eyes snapping with tightly coiled anger. I darted into my room, rushing toward Iranoct hanging on the wall. Duke Agramon was faster. He wrapped his fingers around my wrist and yanked me toward him. I raised my other arm, my fist closed, ready to fight back.

"It is by the grace of Sol that I allow you to keep that sword," Duke Agramon snapped. "But the moment you threaten me with violence, I will take it to the smithy and have it melted down."

I left my hand raised a moment too long. Agramon made as if to grab Iranoct, but I lowered my hand. "No! I'll not fight, I swear," I stammered. Destrian had made Iranoct for me. For *me*, and no one else. I couldn't let him take the only thing I had left from my time in the Night-lands where I'd finally found happiness, even if it was for the briefest of moments. I would carry Iranoct with me always, for it was as precious to me as my own skin.

Duke Agramon's brow rose as a sinister smile crept over his face. "Well then, I suggest you listen. I will not have my charge making a fool of herself in front of the knights of the realm. Moreover, I have deals to make with some of those boys' fathers. I don't need you to spoil those plans by knocking one of their sons into the dirt, or worse, injuring them. I heard how most of the issues with

Ayastaren stemmed from your precious weapons training, and I do not wish to repeat that folly."

I took a deep breath. "Can I at least train by myself, when the others are gone?"

Duke Agramon rolled his eyes. "Finding someone to train you is not high on my priority list, but I'll think about it. Meanwhile, don't ask me about it again." Agramon turned and disappeared through the door, probably to discuss my future without my burdensome presence.

I gritted my teeth and trudged to Iranoct, angry that Agramon went back on his word. Pulling the sword from the wall, I'd half resolved to slash through those beautiful gossamer curtains but thought better of it. Instead, I closed my eyes and thought of Destrian's sword, Phyranox. Iranoct's blade lowered and turned toward Morgania. Destrian and I had used that trick more than once in the Nightlands to help each other escape from danger, and now it was as though I held a guide stone to Destrian in my hands. No matter where I went, I would be able to find my way back to him.

For now, I'd have to find contentment in knowing where to look.

Chapter 10

THAT EVENING, THE COURT at Somme bore witness to my appalling skills at storytelling. Even with the stone Miyu gave me to amplify the sound of my voice, the courtiers and nobles in the back still shouted at me to be louder. I didn't have Destrian's gift for knowing the right time to pause, or the way he would drop his voice lower at the exciting parts. I was too nervous to think of anything but relaying the next leg of my expedition, and it wasn't long before little conversations sprang up throughout the room.

The only person who noticed when my tale was finally over was Miyu. She sped toward me, taking the stone from my hand and patting me on the shoulder.

"I'm sorry it was so dull," I muttered as voices rose higher.

Miyu smiled, her dark eyes kind. "Don't worry. Your gifts lie elsewhere, and we're all thankful for them."

My first stop was at the table laden with food. I filled a plate with delicacies, slipping some into my pocket for Ena.

Del joined me there and plucked a slice of bread from my plate. "Well, you managed to impress today," she said, turning back to the crowd and leaning against the table. "The entire court is awed by your skills." It was impossible to miss the jealousy dripping from her voice.

I shrugged, not really caring what the court thought, and watched Owain approach Miyu and hand her a drink. He leaned down and murmured something in her ear. Miyu smiled.

"Are they . . ." I began.

"Lovers?" Del asked with a grin. "Oh yes. Ever since Miyu came to court several years ago, they've shared quarters. I saw you met the rest of the council earlier too," she went on. "My lover works with Berinon, so he's the one I know best, next to Agramon, of course."

"You have a lover?" I asked, intrigued at how casually she said it. Then again, I heard the eastern shores of Lyrica were far less conservative than the West, from the style of clothes down to the relationships. "Who are they?"

"She's a sorcerer from the academy who's been helping him with his alchemy and transmutation. Apparently, it's very serious business if the requests for funds are to be believed."

I noticed Berinon talking animatedly to another sorcerer in the corner. I couldn't help but gawk at his appearance. "What happened to Berinon's eyebrows?"

Del snorted. "The poor man's laboratory exploded the other day. It's the fifth one he's destroyed this year."

I raised my brows, which were mercifully intact.

"He's a brilliant mind though," Del went on. "Recently he's been investigating a mix of powder that can blast things, similar to battle sages, but without the need of a sorcerer. Sparks has been really excited about it."

"Sparks?" I asked, a grin tugging at the corner of my mouth. "How come she's not here, at the emperor's banquet?"

Del sighed. "Sadly, she isn't the social creature I am. Many days it's a chore just to drag her away from her desk, but I'm sure you will meet her in time."

Del spotted a gathering of university students and invited me to join her in their conversation, but I declined. Instead, I retreated to the alcove, watching the courtiers dance, eat, laugh, and make general merry. The emperor was already down in his cups. A scarlet stain had spread over his royal breeches where he'd slung some wine. The empress was nowhere to be seen, so I assumed she'd excused herself early, probably sometime during my horrid storytelling.

I spotted Mellan Lyon heading straight for me. I thought to escape another conversation with the man, but something held me to the spot. I attributed my hesitation to the fact that Mellan was an entertaining conversationalist, and nothing more.

"By Sol above, you could put a whole army to sleep

with your tales," Mellan said loudly as he slung his arm over my shoulder.

I stiffened as the scent of drink washed over me. It took everything I had not to throw his arm off and shove him into the crowd of noblemen nearby.

"But you stopped just as it was about to get interesting," he slurred, running his fingers over the gems in my hands. "Tell me more of the attack on Espiria."

"Teilo was a victim of a foolish campaign," I said, unwinding myself from his arm. "There is a reason that Espiria has never been conquered."

Mellan laughed. "Yes, it was a bad campaign on my father's part. He never was one for subtlety. I would've loved to see his face when he received the news that a wild band of heathens defeated the mighty Ayastaren forces."

"It was a close battle," I said, still unsure of Mellan's state of mind toward his family, but Agramon had ordered me to let him romance me, and I could feel him watching from across the room. I had to put up some pretense, no matter how much I loathed Mellan and his family. Especially when weapons training was still on the line.

"Come now, Lyon," a man said, stepping beside us. "You forget yourself in the company of the lady." I recognized him as the emperor's handsome bodyguard. He winked at me before turning to Mellan and shooting him an exaggerated frown.

Mellan harrumphed. "I don't need you to nanny me, Diardo. There was no love lost between Teilo and me anyhow."

"The girl doesn't know that you tease. Given her past dealings with your brothers, I'd be cautious to rile her anger."

"Have you met this handsome fool yet?" Mellan asked as I took a bite from my plate. "Captain Diardo, the legendary voice of wisdom on the emperor's council, has been reduced to nannying the capital hooligans." Mellan leaned closer to my ear. "He's in charge of the emperor's security and probably the best of men in this room."

"You honor me, Lyon," Captain Diardo said dryly before his eyes fell to me. "Are you all right with him? Mellan tends to be foolish when he's drunk, which is more often than anyone would like."

I shrugged, taking another bite from my plate. I'd proven time and again that I could best a Lyon. Where was the harm? Besides, Mellan appeared to be in a particularly playful mood, and as much as I disliked his family, I couldn't deny that their hero was the more entertaining of the lot.

"Alas, I'm striving to be an obedient son. My father asked me to romance the girl, so here I am, exploring mutual interests. We've found so much in common already." He held up a hand, ticking off his fingers. "We both grew up to be a disappointment to our families—both are uncommonly good at murder. I've always wanted to kill my brothers, and she's managed it. It's like love at first sight!"

"If you're sure you're all right, then I'll leave you two to your doomed romance," Captain Diardo said, though it was obvious he was suppressing laughter.

"If I have trouble with him, you'll find him with the rest of the Lyons who have crossed me," I quipped, taking another bite of food.

Mellan scowled while Diardo disappeared back into the crowd, chuckling. I caught Agramon's eye from his perch next to Edmund the Bright. He gave me the slightest nod before turning back to the other sorcerers, whispering their secrets.

Mellan drew his arm off my shoulder and leaned against a pillar, signaling to a slave. "Your power was impressive to behold today, my dove."

I let myself relax. "Have you seen much sorcery?"

Mellan shrugged, grabbing a drink from a nearby slave. "I saw enough during the war. Most of the sorcerers in the army are blasters, though we have one or two necromancers too. Pythia was there, scaring the pants off all who crossed her."

"We were lucky that Ayastaren didn't have any sorcerers on their side," I admitted. "We may not have been able to hold them off if Des . . . if I hadn't used my powers." I almost let slip that Destrian had gone against Ayastaren. It was probably common knowledge at this point, but Destrian didn't need me to go rubbing it in everyone's face that he committed treason.

"Normally sorcerers don't involve themselves with skirmishes between consulships and landholdings. The emperor prefers to keep them neutral unless he's the one starting the conflict."

"You don't think he'll punish Destrian, do you?" I asked, lowering my voice.

Mellan shook his head. "He can't very well punish him and not you, now could he. Besides, who would rule Morgania for him now that the old consul is dead? No, your love is safe, from the emperor at least."

"I can't imagine he loves me anymore," I admitted. "Not after what I did to him."

Mellan took a long drink. "You'd be surprised how long the feeling sticks around, even after all hope is gone," he said, wiping his mouth with his sleeve. "Now, tell me, are there more marks on you to be discovered? I fancy if we're married, I might get myself one or two. I always admired them on your war dog brethren." His eyes crawled from the tattoo on my neck, to the band on my arm, and finally to my chest, boldly staring at the curves of my breasts that peeked out from the scandalous neckline.

I met his eye. "You know I could never agree to marry

you, right? I'll let you romance me because Agramon wishes it, but I'd sooner die than let myself be bound to your family."

Mellan leaned against the pillar, sweat collecting on his brow. "I'm not interested, either, Rowyn, but I have to show I'm making an effort. My father will cut me off with nothing if I don't, and I won't have a choice but to return home."

"Maybe we can help each other," I offered. "We both agree that there will never be feelings between us, so what's the harm in putting on a show? You appease your father, I appease Agramon, and it might even keep some of my other potential suitors at bay."

A ghost of a smile lit Mellan's face. "That's not a terrible idea. Are you sure you'd be willing? We'd need to be seen together, not just at the emperor's dinner, but out in the city and whatnot. My father has many spies in the East."

I smiled. "You're welcome to whisk me away from Agramon any day."

Mellan grabbed my hand and kissed the gem. "Then, my dove, prepare to be duly romanced. I demand, as my first suitor's request, a dance."

I laughed as Mellan took my plate and tossed it on a table, then led me to the dance floor where a few other couples spun to a lively song played by a group of musicians from the city. He was a good dancer, even when drunk, leading me expertly through each step. He might've even made me look good.

The song ended, and I found the emperor shoving toward us. When another noble stepped into his path, he shouted, baring his fist. The nobleman scuttled out of the way, his ears pink. The emperor broke off into delighted laughter as he finished his drink with a swig and tossed his goblet onto a table before careening into me.

"I'm stealing the lady for the next dance," he slurred, grabbing Mellan's arm and pushing him away.

Mellan bowed. "Of course, Your Majesty." He shot me an apologetic look before backing into the crowd, leaving me to face the emperor on my own.

I curtsied as deep as I was able, trying to breathe calmly. Looking up again, I searched the crowd for the empress, but it seemed she'd truly retired for the rest of the night.

"Your Majesty," I said, realizing I had to say something. "You honor me greatly, but I am overtired."

"No, you will dance with me," the emperor insisted, grabbing my hand with his sweaty one and placing his other on my lower back, pulling me sharply against him.

The musicians, evil creatures that they were, began to play a slower song. The emperor stepped around the dance floor, crushing me against him all the while.

"She warned me about you, you know," the emperor

said suddenly, his blue eyes a bit glassy as he looked down on me. "I'm glad I didn't listen. She's always trying to tell me what to do."

My brows furrowed. "Of whom do you speak, Your Majesty?"

"That seer," the emperor said before tripping on his own feet. I gripped his arms, holding him up. Nearly the entire court was watching, leaning forward in their seats as the emperor danced with his new pet sorcerer.

"I want to show them," the emperor said, jerking his head to the crowd. "I want them to see that I honor you. You will serve me well, I think. With your help, I think the people will love me again."

"They do not already love you, Your Excellency?" I asked, not knowing what else to say and wishing to Imor that the dance would end already.

"Most do, probably," the emperor said, screwing up his face in what was probably him trying to be thoughtful, yet it only made him look childish and unsure. "Agramon says they do, anyway. I won the war in Yliria for them, but the drought spoiled it, I think."

The drought, the plague, the stealing of sons in the middle of the night to be butchered half a world away. I didn't have the courage to tell him that though. "The ending of the drought will ease some suffering," I offered instead. "I'm fully committed to the cause if it saves innocent lives."

"You owe me a debt, you know, saving you from squalor." The emperor gripped my hand far too hard in an effort to keep himself upright. His hand on my lower back tugged on my dress. If we danced for much longer, I was sure he would tear the damned thing off of me. He stumbled again, and I did my best to catch him.

"Your Majesty," Captain Diardo said, appearing out of nowhere to grip the emperor's arm. "You've overtired yourself."

"No, I haven't," the emperor snapped, trying to shove Diardo off of him.

During the awkward scuffle, I slipped out of the emperor's grasp. Diardo jerked his head, a silent order to disappear, which I followed willingly. I couldn't see Agramon or Del in the crowd, but I was close to the balcony doors. Since it proved the perfect hiding spot the night before, I slipped along the wall and out to the balcony. A wave of fresh air swept over me, scented with jasmine and damp earth from the rain I'd called earlier.

"Diardo will see to it the emperor finds his bed," grunted a voice from the shadows. "He's had enough practice with it over the years."

I stepped closer, recognizing Sam's silhouette in the darkness. "I was wondering if you were out here again tonight," I admitted.

"And I was wondering when you'd come looking for me," Sam replied.

I raised my brows. "You speak as though me looking for you was a sure thing."

Sam's eyes lingered on my rose tattoo. "It was a sure thing," he said. "Like always seeks out like."

"Are you always out here during the evening festivities?" I asked, intent on changing the subject.

"When I'm in the capital, yes," Sam said. He sat still as a statue. I wondered if he thought he would frighten me away with sudden movements. If he knew me better, he would know I was not so easily scared.

"Do you find solace in the darkness?"

Sam's brow quirked. "I've not found solace in a long time. The nobles cringe away from my presence, so I stay out here until my lord summons me."

"You said you're a soldier?" I asked, curious how so normal a man spoke such dark portents. "Were you involved with the war in Yliria?"

Sam dropped his eyes to his glass and nodded. "I was sure that campaign would be the death of me, yet here I am, for better or for worse."

"Surely you can find happiness in your life now that the war is over. I know most soldiers have wives waiting for them at home, and farms ready to be plowed. Do you not have such things that you can take pleasure in?"

Sam chuckled darkly. "I have a farm, but I take no pleasure in it. Nobody has with the drought gone on so long."

I waited for him to add how that all would change now that I was there, but he didn't.

"What of you?" Sam asked. "What do you take pleasure in?"

The answer fell so fast from my lips that I didn't even realize I'd said it until Sam frowned. "Weapons training."

"Does Duke Agramon not allow you to fight?"

I sighed. "He said I had to earn the right. Apparently, he would have to find someone to train me, and he thought it would take time away from my less developed skills work."

"But you do not agree?" Sam asked.

I gritted my teeth. "Even at Solridge, they let me do weapons training. A couple of my friends, Fin and Araceli, began training with me. It helped keep me focused. Everything about my life is now so different, so changed. The people I'm surrounded by, the land, trying to control my powers, but at least I had weapons training to relieve some stress. It was something I knew. It's one of the few things I'm good at."

I knew I should stop pouring my heart out to a stranger, but I hadn't been able to share my feelings with anyone.

"Now here I am, in the exact same situation,

surrounded by strangers in a land I don't know, thrust into a court I don't understand, and I have nothing to myself. I know ladies would cut their eyeteeth for an opportunity like this, to rub shoulders with the elites of the empire, to dress up in the most beautiful clothes and play at intrigue, but I've never wanted this for my life."

"So, weapons training would make you happy?" Sam asked, leaning back in his chair.

"Immensely," I said, but I began second-guessing my haste in confiding in Sam. What could he do for me? By all appearances he was an outsider at court, and Agramon would surely be angry if Sam attempted to interfere in his guardianship duties. It was no use.

"Are the nobles always lost to their own vices?" I asked, disgusted with Mellan's and the emperor's horrid display. Was everyone in the capital a drunk?

Sam shrugged. "They drink out of boredom, while the rest of us drink to forget."

"And what is it that you seek to forget?"

"Guilt, mostly," Sam admitted. He joined me at the railing, setting his glass down as we both watched the banquet through the glass doors.

"Was the war really so bad?" I asked, my eyes on the Ylirian slaves winding through the crowds, offering up drinks with lowered eyes and trying not to be noticed.

"I watched it turn the best of men into ghosts and

monsters," Sam said, not taking his eyes off the party. "Many a young lad, full of promise, found his end on those battlefields, and the empire will be all the worse for it."

I lowered my eyes, thinking of those who'd been taken and would never return home. "It doesn't seem fair, does it? Watching the nobles eat their rich foods and drink their fancy wines while the rest of us suffer for their foolishness?"

Agramon would be angry if he heard my words. He made his living at court. His position allowed me to have a room in the palace with a beautiful view, but I hadn't asked for any of it.

Sam looked at me. "I've heard some say the drought is the gods' punishment for our sins from Yliria. Though your presence will ease the suffering of the common folk, who have already suffered enough from the war, I don't think the folks inside have learned their lesson."

I let his statement hang in the air as we watched the revelers. Though it was late and the banquet guests had dwindled, the musicians still played their rollicking tunes, and couples still swung about the room in reckless abandon.

"I'd best return," I said with a sigh. "I've dallied too long."

Sam nodded, then took my hand and lifted it to his lips. Instead of kissing my gem, the way other noblemen were apt to do, he kissed my fingers. "I enjoyed your story ear-lier," he said without a hint of jest.

I blushed and went back to the door, casting one last glance over my shoulder before slipping back into the noisy hall. I still didn't know what to make of the man who sought solace within the shadows. He insisted we were the same, and in truth, he was right. If I had my way, I would've hidden out on the balcony as well, concealed from the gossip of court. Was he trapped as I was? Why didn't the man seek to free himself? At least it was a com-fort that I wasn't alone, that someone was indeed watching over me.

Chapter 11

A GRAMON BURST INTO MY room at the crack of dawn. "The emperor wishes to see us," he said loudly, slamming the door against the wall. "I can't imagine what it's about. He's given no warning, but he requires your presence as well. Did you displease him last night?"

I groaned, rolling over in bed. Echo had sent me terrible dreams of men scheming to get me to their lands and university students whispering about what it would be like to bed me. It was awful. Then again, when I had a moment to speak with her, I could direct Echo to listen on the empress's behalf as well, just in case I decided to take her up on her offer. Though my dance with the emperor had soured me against the royal family, I promised I'd give her a chance.

"I said nothing to rouse his anger, if that's what you're wondering," I said, sitting up and wrapping my arms around my knees. "If I had, I doubt he was even lucid enough to remember."

"Hurry up and get ready then," Agramon ordered. "You're supposed to be at Willene's in an hour, and I don't want you to be late."

Ena rushed in, and I dutifully dressed before following Agramon through the golden halls of the palace. His step was measured and calm. The only hint of worry was in the way his eyes darted through the halls. He stopped in front of a pair of soldiers who opened the doors behind them to reveal the chamber within.

The room was bright, with floor-to-ceiling windows that overlooked the city. The only furniture was a long, mahogany wooden table surrounded by matching chairs. It reminded me of the council room in Espiria, where the fates of men were decided.

The emperor sat at the head of the table, his head resting in his hands in a stance I'd seen in men who spent their nights drowning in drink. Behind him, against the wall, leaned Captain Diardo.

"Your Imperial Majesty," Agramon said, bowing deep. I lowered myself in a curtsy, fear coiling in my stomach at the unexpected summons.

"Rise," the emperor said, opening his bloodshot eyes and taking a drink from a steaming horned mug.

"I didn't realize there was a council meeting today," Agramon said. He flashed a look of annoyance at Captain Diardo, who met his eyes with boredom.

"There isn't." The emperor sighed. "I thought it appropriate to greet your new charge without the pomp of court."

Agramon's brows furrowed. "I apologize I didn't think of this before. I suppose it's because you haven't taken any interest in the welfare of my students prior to this."

Captain Diardo inspected his fingernails. "Remember that the girl's guardianship is to the emperor first, and you have merely been granted arbiter of her day-to-day welfare."

"What is this really about?" Agramon asked, his voice dripping with annoyance.

"It's been brought to our attention that you are not taking the pains necessary in Rowyn's education or her happiness," Captain Diardo said calmly, his eyes coming to rest on me. "Are you happy here, Rowyn? As you can see, the emperor himself is invested in your welfare. We understand that you've been taken from your home in less-than-ideal circumstances, but we aren't jailers."

Agramon scowled. "I would like to see someone do better. Her wardrobe rivals the empress herself. She's enjoyed the best the capital has to offer. I've even taken pains with making her maid comfortable. What more can I do?"

I was torn. I felt Agramon trying in vain to enter my mind, battering my thoughts to get me to say he was the most wondrous benefactor. If I told them how I really felt toward Agramon, would they take me away? Give me another guardian? Captain Diardo had kind eyes. Perhaps he was as good as he was handsome, but Agramon would seek revenge for my defection. Of this I was certain, and he wouldn't harm me to do it. He would use someone I loved. Perhaps Ena, or Destrian, though he was still so far away. No. I couldn't take the risk. I'd already lost so much. It was best to play along. To continue our tentative truce.

"I thank you for the inquiries to my welfare," I said, my voice wooden. "I'm quite happy here, I can assure you."

Captain Diardo's eyes shadowed, then he glanced down at the emperor, who'd slouched in his chair, his chin resting on his hand. "Allow her to speak for herself in our presence," the captain said sharply.

"Her mind is closed to me," Agramon confessed.

The emperor's eyes widened. "Is this true?" he asked, directing the question to me.

I nodded.

The emperor exchanged a pointed look with Captain Diardo. "Does this happen often?" the emperor asked.

Agramon shrugged. "Owain's effects are similar. The more power a person has, the more their mind is foggy, or unclear. The girl has three gems. It wasn't surprising when I realized I couldn't delve into her thoughts."

"That makes me feel better, at least," the captain said. "What are you doing to enhance her education? I was told she wouldn't be attending university."

Agramon scowled. "I thought it unwise for her to begin classes since we would be here for such a short time. I was under the impression that His Imperial Majesty wanted me to train her across the empire so the land could benefit from her skills. If I was incorrect in that directive, please let me know now."

The emperor sighed, rubbing his temples with his fingers. "You are correct, Agramon, but we don't want her mind to go to waste. What are you learning, girl?"

"I have the pleasure of studying with Grand Princess Willene in the mornings with your daughter, Princess Lesedi," I said, turning my thoughts away from the emperor's appearance and back to the issue at hand. "I am to attend the empress in a few days when she enters the city, but otherwise, Agramon has said I am to train with him."

"Seems well enough," the emperor said, "though I would agree that studying with my sister is its own form of torture. It seems he's taking the pains he's supposed to with the girl."

"What of weapons work?" the captain asked, his eyes narrowed like a blade. My heart skipped, but I retained my composure. "Someone so accomplished in the fighting arts should continue their training, especially if it's a routine she's used to."

The emperor frowned. "That's right. I was told she attended weapons training at Solridge. Why would you not continue that practice here?"

Agramon chanced a glance at me, his eyes filled with

warning. "I thought it wise to focus on her deficiencies."

"Come now, Duke Agramon," Captain Diardo said. "I completely disagree with your assessment of her skills. She's versed well enough for court. Don't let her more useful skills lie fallow while you fill her head with foppery."

"Do you wish to continue weapons training here?" the emperor asked me.

The door behind us opened and someone stepped in, but I was distracted by Agramon's pulsing enmity. I fought to ignore it. I needed an outlet. I needed something to keep me from going mad in the palace. "If I could work on weapons training, I believe I could find some happiness here," I said. "Though I've worked toward it all my life, and it is unrelated to my sorcery, it helps me clear my thoughts."

A muscle twitched in Agramon's cheek. "If you wish for Rowyn to continue training, I will take pains to find someone to tutor her."

"There's no need," a familiar voice said from behind me. I turned as Sam walked into view. He bowed to the emperor and took a seat at the emperor's left hand. "I will train her."

My eyes widened. What was Sam doing here? Though he'd described himself as a simple soldier, and I'd known his words were a half-truth, I'd not considered the possibility of him seated at the emperor's side.

Sam seemed to note the expression on my face. He glanced down, likely aware that he had quite a bit of explaining to do.

"I'm sure that's not necessary," Agramon said tightly. "I would think you'd have far more important things to do than waste your time training a novice girl."

"Though I appreciate your concerns for my time," Sam said, his gruff voice dripping with unspoken threats, "I alone get to choose how to fill it, save for the imperial majesty himself." Sam turned to the emperor. "The war is over, and the men have either returned home or been sent to the fields." He propped his boots on the table, leaning onto the back legs of his chair. "Though the end of the war was welcome, I have a bit too much free time on my hands, and I'm in need of a project."

"Perhaps you should train the squires and pages then," Agramon said through clenched teeth. "I'm sure Richard of Bekiwin would welcome your assistance."

"He has a point, Baron," the emperor said.

My eyes widened. Baron? Since when was Sam addressed as a noble?

Sam harrumphed. "What can I do that Richard of Bekiwin cannot? I refuse to waste my time training green noble lads to whack dummies with a stick."

"Yet you would waste your time with a young girl?" Agramon asked, his voice icy.

"A young *lady*," Sam corrected, "who battled all manner of monsters in the Nightlands. Name one knight or noble lord who could do the same."

"Lord Destrian," I said immediately, my eyes on Sam. Though he was the architect toward me gaining something I desperately wanted, I also hated being toyed with. It seemed that from the beginning, he'd been keeping something from me. I would have to rethink my estimation of Sam's abilities as an ally, as it appeared he carried far more power than I'd initially thought.

Sam froze. Captain Diardo's brows were raised in surprise. Even the emperor hid a laugh behind his hand.

"So be it," the emperor said. "She's your project, Baron, until I find you something more worthwhile to do." The emperor returned his attention to me. "You may leave us; though, Agramon, we have a bit more to discuss about your upcoming travels."

I stepped out, trying to calm my ragged breaths. Footsteps followed me. I whirled around when Sam shut the door, his expression guarded.

"What was that?" I seethed. "I told you those things in confidence. How could you betray me to Agramon like that? He will surely find a way to punish me."

"I would like to see him try," Sam said. "I did this for you, so you could find some semblance of happiness in this hellscape. I thought only of you in this."

I let out a gust of frustration. "You all play with my life as though I were merely a puppet."

"I just want the best for you," Sam said slowly.

"Who are you really," I demanded, "and don't lie to me this time."

"He's Baron Samael of Bruin, the imperial commander of the Lyrican forces," Agramon said from the doorway of the council room.

"By all the gods," I gasped, the blood draining from my face. "You're the Butcher of Bruin?" It was a question, but Sam couldn't escape the accusation hidden there. He'd said he was a mere soldier, and though I imagined he was probably more than that, I didn't think he'd be the highest military commander in the empire. The Butcher of Bruin, whose prowess on the battlefield and inhumane cruelty were known across the empire. If rebel clans feared one man, it was he, who wielded the blade of Lyrica mercilessly against any who protested the empire. He was the Espirians' worst nightmare.

I couldn't speak. I simply stared, horrified.

Sam glared at Agramon over his shoulder. "I was going to tell her myself."

"And why didn't you reveal your true person sooner?" Agramon said, approaching slowly. "Could it be because you knew she'd heard of the terrible things you've done? The war in Yliria was hard-won through spilled blood and terrors, lessons in fear, orchestrated by your deft hand. He really is something to behold, Rowyn." His icy glare made my stomach tight. "People whisper of my cruelty, but there have been moments I've seen within his mind, and Samael of Bruin has wrought such terror in Lyrica's enemies that it makes me look like a true novice."

Sam's eyes hardened as he gripped his sword hilt.

"You're a monster," I whispered, the color draining from my face.

"Should I tell her?" Agramon asked quietly. "Should I reveal the horrors in your thoughts? The memories of your victims screaming for mercy as you let your war dogs rip them to pieces?"

"Stop," I said, my hands clasped over my ears. "I don't want to see you anymore," I told Sam. "I don't want to speak to you. You're the worst of them."

Agramon glared at me. "It's too late for that, Rowyn. The emperor has ordered that you train with him. So, train you will, to your willful heart's content."

Sam glared at Agramon. "I will escort Rowyn to her training in the evenings, before dinner. That shouldn't interfere with any other lessons you had planned for her."

"So be it, seeing as we don't have a choice," Agramon snapped, grabbing my arm and pulling me down the hall.

I was practically running to keep pace with him as we turned a corner, headed to Princess Willene's chambers.

"You should've stayed away from him," Agramon said as we strode away.

"How was I to know who he was?" I fumed. "I'd think he'd be your type of fellow, considering his rank and the number of people who follow him."

Agramon whirled on me. "That is a man who can't be bought. Who's loyal to a fault. By Sol above, the entire army holds blind devotion to him. But know this about him, he doesn't ever question the emperor. I don't know what to do with a man like that. There have been times I've glimpsed the depravity in that man's mind. Woe to you if he chooses not to stay away from you."

Chapter 12

"NO LADY CAN BE TRULY accomplished without some musical skill," Princess Willene said as she stepped regally across the room, looking down her nose at Princess Ledi and me as we each strummed a lute.

Princess Ledi was already an accomplished musician, her fingers waltzing over the strings of her beautiful instrument. Since my mind was still reeling from the realization that my new confidant was the Butcher of Bruin, I contented myself with listening to Ledi play. She sang a popular ballad about two Lyrican royal brothers, Adonas and Rodan, and their love for a beautiful Adarite princess, Niathora. As with all tragic stories, neither of the princes won the hand of the beautiful Niathora, for both died on some battlefield long ago, forgiving each other's folly in their last moments of life. Niathora, upon hearing the demise of her lovers, flung herself off a waterfall near her Livian palace.

I dabbed my eyes, not because of the brothers' pointless rivalry, nor the princess's outrageous death, but because its tune brought me back to the scent of dusty books and candles, the sounds of Pedr's voice echoing off of stone walls as the sun set behind the leaden panes of the windows in the library at Solridge. I wondered how his summer at home had been. Had he returned to Solridge yet? Was Lord Obi back and convalescing over his adventure to Helena? What of Fin's quest? Did Araceli continue her weapons training? I thought of my letters and hoped that Agramon fulfilled his promise and sent them. I would give anything to receive word from my friends.

"You blundered far too many notes in the arpeggio, Lesedi," Willene snapped. "Remember that your future match will be royalty. As such, they'll know the difference between your ham-fisted bungling and a virtuoso."

"Yes, Aunt," Ledi said, her head hanging low. "I'll make sure to practice more."

Could the high princess and I have been listening to the same song? "I thought she played quite well," I said, setting my lute next to the poor excuse for embroidery that I'd tossed on the floor. "I have a friend who's very nearly a virtuoso, and he couldn't play the tune better, Ledi."

Ledi glanced at me and smiled. Princess Willene wheeled on her heels, her mouth puckering. "Stand," she ordered. I stayed seated a moment too long, my eyes moving from Ledi, who'd gone back to staring at her lap, to the high princess, who was approaching me with slow, measured steps. In the end, Agramon's orders of obedience won out over my stubbornness. I stood, albeit reluctantly.

"I would like to make one thing clear," Willene said, looming over me. Her voice dropped lower, her eyes filled with enmity. "I won't let a feral girl from the wild interfere with Princess Lesedi's progress toward acclimating to the expectations of Lyrican royalty. You may be the newest bauble of the emperor, some foreign girl to perform for the court, but I assure you that your time in the emperor's favor will eventually wane. I've only brought you on because Duke Agramon, my dear friend, has asked this favor of me, but if you cause difficulty between Princess Ledi and me, I will end this little experiment of the duke's. Do I make myself clear?"

I gritted my teeth, meeting Willene's stare. I dearly wanted to spit in her face, but my lessons with Princess Willene were my only chance to pass information to the empress, and my mind still wasn't made up regarding her offer.

Hating myself all the while, I bowed my head and nodded. "My apologies, Your Majesty. I meant no disrespect."

Princess Willene glared at me a moment longer, then turned toward Princess Ledi who feigned interest in adjusting her skirt.

"Come, niece, the tea will be served in a moment. Lady Rowyn, if you can rein in your natural tendencies toward barbarism and be civil, you may join us."

I bit my tongue and followed Willene to the table.

"DID YOU ATTEND UNIVERSITY HERE?" I asked Del as we sat beside each other at the empress's luncheon. I'd tried to meet the empress's eye more than once, but it turned out she was as good as her word when it came to her valuing secrecy. The woman didn't so much as glance in my direction.

"I did for my earlier years, before my Trial by Stone. Once I finished questing for my gem, Agramon had already agreed to take me under his wing."

I wondered what the university at the capital was like. The students seemed very much like the students I'd met at Solridge, a great mix of people with far-ranging talents who worked to learn from each other within the university walls. I hadn't missed my classes during my quest in the Nightlands, but I'd certainly missed my friends. Now that I'd returned to the realm of humankind, I found myself longing for the scholarly environment more than I thought I would.

"It was glorious at first. Mind you, I am the youngest of six children, so I didn't really receive much attention at home. The university was where I finally found friends who weren't siblings, who actually liked me for me and my talents. It was refreshing to get away from the shadows of others."

"If you liked it so much, why didn't you return after your quest?" I asked. In truth, I was suspicious of Agramon's keeping me from university. Was it simply a rule he enforced among all his students, or was he making sure that I formed no close relationships with anyone else?

"Agramon has always frowned upon the university here at Somme. He abides it for a time, but he can't stand most of the professors, and thinks that what they teach us is all theory and drivel. He feels that others learn best by doing and living, not by hiding behind stone walls and reading books."

"I find that assessment of him to be shocking, to be completely honest," I admitted. "I would've expected Agramon to be a great supporter of the school."

Del shook her head. "No, that's Edmund the Bright's job. He's headmaster at the university and the chief sorcerer on staff. Owain helps teach classes now and then, and Tristam is who trains all the healers in the realm, but Agramon refuses to take part in the university program because when he was younger and tried to get in himself, they denied him entry."

My mouth opened in surprise. "But he's one of the

most powerful sorcerers in the land. What reason or right did they have to bar him from studying his skills?"

"Mind readers haven't been well-regarded for a long time. Most don't trust them. Many outright fear them. Edmund said that at the time, he was afraid the other students would revolt if he allowed Agramon in."

Well, that was something to consider. I'd bet my entire wardrobe that Agramon was still pretty peeved at Edmund the Bright for that omission.

"What of you?" Del asked, her tone oddly nonchalant. "You had friends at Solridge, did you not? Isn't that where you and Lord Destrian fell in *love*?"

I hated how she dragged out the word *love*, as though our feelings were nothing more than young passing affection, the flame shining bright and strong, petering out as quickly as it came. I wondered about her question though. So far, no one had outright asked me about Destrian save for Agramon, and his questions were only related to whether I was still virtuous. I hesitated to answer, simply because I didn't know Del very well, and I wouldn't put it past Agramon to have the woman begin a friendship with me to give him an avenue into my thoughts and mindset. In fact, I was sure that was something he would do. I considered my approach.

If I'd still been at Solridge, the old me would've rebuffed her friendship altogether. I dismissed that thought.

I couldn't behave the way I did before, openly defying the will of Agramon and the empire without a second thought. No, I was playing a much different game now. What if I turned the tables on Agramon? What if I used Del to feed him information about me that I wanted him to find out? Could I use Del to make him think I was complacent?

For that to work, I would have to convince Del, and in turn, Agramon, that our friendship were true. If Del were Fin, I would have no problems sharing my thoughts about Destrian. Then again, what was there for me to say about Destrian that could bring me danger? No, if any topic were relatively safe, it would be Destrian. If I wanted Del to believe that I trusted her, then I would need to tell her about him.

"We didn't fall in love at Solridge," I said. Del's eyebrows rose with curiosity, likely wondering why it took me so long to come up with such a simple answer. "At least I didn't. It wasn't until we were alone in the Nightlands that I really saw who he was and began to admire him."

Del set her plate on the table beside us and leaned against the back of the couch, her head resting on her hand. "I'd seen your lord Destrian when he was returning from his quest to Yliria. He certainly is a handsome one. Then again, I've always had a thing for redheads."

I laughed. "He is handsome," I said, surprised how easy it was to speak of him. "I'd always thought him good-looking; it's just that I didn't like him at first. There's bad blood between his family and mine. He seemed to sweep it aside so easily, but with me, it took much longer." Of course, being enchanted to forget some of my more crucial moments with Destrian didn't help. Still, I was pleased that I could easily share with Del. Though I was intent on deceiving her, not one word I said was false.

"Is none of what the bards sang true?" Del asked, her eyes flashing mischievously.

I shrugged. "I haven't heard their song, but given what I've been told by others, I'd guess most of it is false. I didn't lure Destrian to the Nightlands. I actually didn't want him to go at all. I tried to convince him to stay after another student pointed out how dangerous it would be for Destrian, but he refused to be left behind. I didn't kill his father either—that was one of my clansmen."

I paused, unsure what to say next. On the one hand, I knew Del was close to Agramon, and she would either share what I said to him, or he would glean it from her mind. On the other hand, Agramon was there that day in the road, and if I lied to Del about what really happened, Agramon would become suspicious, and the ruse would be up before it even began. Given the two choices, I knew I had to remain honest.

"The only reason I left Destrian was because Agramon forced me to. He threatened to bring charges of treason against Destrian if I didn't go with him. I had no choice but to leave if I wanted to protect him."

"So, is he waiting for you now?" Del asked, leaning toward me to whisper. She didn't even look surprised by what I'd said against Agramon. "Do you two have some sort of understanding?"

That must be the information Agramon was looking for, I was sure. But I held no hope left.

"We don't," I said with a frown. "That day when I left, the look on his face . . ." I sighed, picking at the delicacies on my plate. "I don't think there's any way he would forgive how I left him, and there isn't a way to let him know that I had nothing to do with his father's death. If the bards are spreading the story over the entire empire, then it's only a matter of time until Destrian hears the story himself. How long will it take for him to actually believe their words? Especially since I'm not there to refute them?"

"Surely he knows you better than that," Del said, taking a sip from her glass.

Did he? I'd scarcely realized my feelings for Destrian before he was ripped away by circumstances. It almost seemed unreal, like a beautiful dream that I'd been cruelly woken from.

I shook my head. "The Nightlands were so different. After all, it was just he and I. Something was bound to happen, and as I fell in love with him, I doubted we would be able to last in the real world. Even if Agramon hadn't taken me away, the battle of Espiria made it obvious that I was right. Neither of our families would've accepted the union. But none of that matters now, of course. I doubt Agramon would let me return to the western shore, and even if he did, it wouldn't be to go to Destrian, who's merely a consul. It's no use, Del. My time with Destrian is over, and I've no cause to hope for him anymore. I simply dream of a time where we could've been together, in another life possibly, or if things had been different."

Del reached out and patted my hand. "You're so wise already, Rowyn. I wish I was so clear-headed about love."

"So, tell me about this sorcerer who works with Berinon," I ordered, hoping to change the subject.

I was already fighting back tears as I brought up all my painful memories and feelings about Destrian. It came so easily.

Del was happy to recount her meeting the young apprentice of the court alchemist. Apparently, the girl had a brilliant mind but could barely be torn away from the laboratory where she and Berinon worked. Del assured me that one day I'd meet her. I glanced at the empress as Del talked, but she still seemed to be avoiding my eye. I was due to venture to the market with her in two days' time, so perhaps we would have a moment to speak. Till then, I wanted to ensure that the empress knew that my infor-mation would be useful. After all, she was the clearest path I had toward escape.

Chapter 13

WHEN I RETURNED to my room, Agramon had been waiting for me. He stood next to me now, looking at the city over the balcony I'd performed on the day before.

"Just look at them," Agramon said, eying the city dwellers below. I peered over the edge of the balcony and admired the river of people pulsing through the streets, going about their daily lives. Though I was used to looking out over great heights at home in Espiria, the views were nothing compared to the golden-roofed city of Somme. I missed the smell of mist interwoven with Morwood pine, the evergreen treetops reaching to the heavens.

I chided myself. Espiria wasn't home anymore. My clansmen had been pretty clear about that.

"Do you think they will be happier now that they have rain?" I asked, my voice hopeful.

After my luncheon discussion with Del, I felt subdued. The act of bringing Destrian up to Del was oddly draining. I never had the chance to grieve for the lost hope of what might've been. Then again, I sometimes felt that I spent the whole of our trip in the Nightlands grieving for the young man I knew I was bound to lose.

"They will be happy for a time," Agramon said, leaning against the balustrade. "Until they begin to take us for granted, just like your clansmen at home. When we leave on our expedition, they will undoubtedly come to appreciate us again, and when we return, you can bet they won't take our presence lightly."

"Are you counting on that being the same for the nobles?" I asked, starkly aware that Agramon was giving me much more insight into his mind than perhaps he meant to. It also didn't escape my notice that he kept using the word *us* instead of me, as though he were also gifting them with rain, even though he practically had nothing to do with it other than ordering me about. "Do you think they will take me for granted as well?"

Agramon laughed. "Not as much as the commoners. Most noblemen are able to remain in power due to their adeptness at forward planning and seizing opportunities. Everyone here can see that our presence is a wonderful opportunity to shore up their strength among those within their borders. The nobles will take that opportunity and know exactly who to thank for it too."

"You speak of noblemen, but what of the ladies? Are they not also sensitive to opportunities to be found in the empire?"

Agramon rolled his eyes. "They only see so far as the gold in the man's purse, or the number of men who pledge loyalty to him. The ladies are most adept at sniffing out powerful men, but far less so at seeing opportunities that could make men so."

I raised my brows. "You seem to have very established opinions about my sex. No wonder you aren't married."

Agramon scowled. "Never forget I can read minds, Rowyn. I know of what I speak. Women's minds are droll and boring, save a few who have sought to expand themselves beyond the court dalliances and gossip. There is very little sense to be found in the mind of a woman."

I frowned as I looked back out over the city, hating Agramon's assessment. Granted, I'd thought the same thing of most of the girls at Solridge, save for Fin and Araceli, but at the same time, I felt that most common women were quite adept at seeing opportunity themselves, and seizing it when society let them. Looking at Agramon now, and thinking back to our voyage across the sea, I realized that perhaps Agramon's only experiences came from noblewomen, or at least, perhaps those were the only women he seemed to bother to know and understand. Throughout our trip over the sea, he'd barely paid Ena any notice, and when we rode through the market, his nose was held so far up that it was a wonder he could see the road in front of him. It appeared that Agramon had turned into a snob over the years.

"So did you just bring me out here to rail on women

and expound on your dreams for the future?" I asked, my tone dripping with irritation. After all, I had my weapons training session with Sam that evening, and I'd been half looking forward to taking a nap beforehand. "Why are we out here?"

"I wanted to see your range of skills for myself. I know you were putting on a show yesterday for the court and emperor, and everyone was pleased with your performance, but I want you to show me the parameters of your magic. How big can you make a storm? How small? Can you control certain elements better than others? Can you change the temperature? Make it snow?"

I called a small cloud that hovered above Agramon, letting loose a heavy rain that cascaded down onto him alone. In a moment he was soaking wet and shot me a glare.

"Stop that this instant," he said when he tried to move away, and I sent the rain cloud following him.

I giggled as he tried swatting at the cloud. It was far harder to keep such small, concentrated magic going than it was to call a great swath of weather. The clouds wanted to balloon, to get bigger and reach higher. I lost my grip on the magic amid my laughter, and the cloud dissipated into a burst of mist.

"That was a brat's trick," Agramon snapped, attempting to wring the water from his clothes. "Were you always so difficult at Solridge?"

"No, but I would've thought Gillius sent you plenty of warnings and advice on how to handle me best," I said, batting my eyelashes. Gillius's name was acrid on my tongue. I'd never fully trusted Vianne, so it wasn't a surprise when I realized she had erased several important memories to make me compliant, but Gillius had been false from the start. I'd given him what semblance of trust I could give in my mental state after being ostracized from my clan, and he'd lied the entire time.

It was Destrian who helped me realize that Gillius went to Morgania for the express purpose of finding me and bringing me to heel for the empire. How the empire had even known about me was anyone's guess. Destrian didn't think it was anything another sorcerer could merely sense, given that I was hidden by the shroud of Espiria, the layer of magical mist that surrounded the mountain where my clan dwelled. No, if they couldn't sense me, they must've been told of my whereabouts. I suspected it was my uncle, Baylin. He'd never wanted me to stay with the clan and tried his damnedest over the years to make me feel unnatural and unwelcome. It wouldn't surprise me if his deal with the empire was struck from the very beginning: my freedom for immunity and a chance to emerge behind the shroud and become farmers once more, instead of the raiders we'd grown into.

Then again, I had a perfect opportunity to find out how

they were able to tether me. I looked back at Agramon, who was still wringing water from his robes and letting it stream onto the balcony.

"How did you find out about me?" I asked, now wishing I hadn't angered him. "In the beginning, how did you come to find out about my existence?"

Agramon scowled as he inspected the fabric. I didn't know what he expected. He *did* drag me onto the balcony to make it rain. "Chassandre the seer prophesied about you over a year ago," he said grumpily, but I couldn't tell if that was the truth or not. I'd known there was a prophecy, but was that really the first they'd heard of me?

I ran my hand absentmindedly over the balcony rail. "I was given to understand that the shroud hid me from magical sight. I was still living behind the shroud over a year ago." There was no mistaking it. Agramon was *definitely* avoiding my eye, but I was pretty sure it would be a fruitless exercise to try to get more information from him. I sighed and leaned against the balcony, looking down at the mob of people surging through the market below us.

"Did you want me to make it rain again?" I asked, nodding to the city beyond.

Agramon glared at me. "There's no sense in ruining their day as you've ruined mine."

I let Agramon grab my arm and pull me back from the balcony and into the halls of the citadel. As we walked through the corridors, I let my mind race. Someone had given me away to the empire, and it was unlikely that I would find out from Agramon. He wasn't the only one who'd known about me though. The emperor and seer had also known, which meant it was likely that those on the emperor's council knew as well.

I ran through the figures I knew on the emperor's council. There was the handsome Captain Diardo who seemed nice enough, but he would have no loyalty to me to give me any extra information beyond day-to-day pleasantries and would certainly not give away protected information. I knew the infamous Bald Walden, captain of the city watch, was on the council, but I doubted he knew about me given that he would have no need to. The most likely candidates were those on the Council of Five. In fact, they'd outright spoken like my arrival had been planned for some time. They wouldn't likely give me more information. But I could send Echo after them, to see what she could dig up by listening to their conversations. Of course, there was one other person, an unlikely ally—Sam, the Butcher of Bruin.

I found myself puzzled at his interference on my behalf to the emperor. He seemed pleasant enough in our interactions during the emperor's banquets, but there was something hidden under those interactions. Something almost sinister. Why did he seek to put himself in my way?

Why did he interfere on my behalf? After all, I was no one to him. I might've looked like his comrades-in-arms, the Morganite war dogs, but they were practically enslaved to the Lyrican fighting force. No, it wasn't that. There was something else he was seeking. Something I couldn't quite put my finger on. But I was determined to find out what he wanted from me, and I would have an opportunity to pry that very evening.

I looked at Agramon as he strode grumpily next to me down the hall. I endeavored to take my nap after all so that I would be well-rested for the upcoming battles.

Chapter 14

A GRAMON WAS GONE when I awoke later. I ventured out into the receiving room and noticed the sun sitting low in the sky, casting its light onto the lute beside the couch. Since I'd woken up in plenty of time to await Sam's lesson, I grabbed the lute and sat on the couch to practice strumming the way Princess Ledi had taught me.

Though I'd always enjoyed music, I was never one to create it. Pedr had been born with the gift of song. I wished I could recall the verses to the beautiful ballads he'd sing to me in the library during those nights while we were studying, but the stories were so complicated and long that my memory proved hopeless. In fact, the only song I could remember was one I'd heard on the streets of Seaport, sung by a rowdy group of revelers. I began to pick up the tune on the strings and sang.

"The lady of Mulroney rode through on a pony.
She was selling her ribbons and bows.
When what did I see, when I asked for a peek,
And glimpsed the warm purse where she hid all her money."

I strummed some more, enjoying the tune, and sang the second verse even louder.

"Her daughter was fair, and plump as a pear,
I took her to bed and plucked her golden flower,
But when we awoke to her father she spoke,
And I could only bed her ever after."

"By Sol above!" a voice shouted behind me. "What is that drivel?"

I craned my neck over the back of the couch and noticed Duke Agramon standing at the doorway with Sam at his side. "Princess Willene says that no lady can be truly accomplished unless she's able to entertain others with her music. Am I not impressive?"

Sam's hand was covering his mouth, stifling laughter as Agramon turned almost purple. "I swear to the heavens above, if you sing that song to the high princess, I will never hear the end of it."

I shrugged. "It was the only song I knew."

Agramon's eyes nearly bugged out of his head. "That says more about you than you realize, girl. Now get up. The baron is here to take you to your lesson."

"I don't have anything to wear for my lesson," I said crossly, setting the lute on the couch.

"Well, luckily for you, your clothes from Solridge

arrived this morning while you were at Willene's. Ena has already put them away in your wardrobe."

"Really?" I asked, brightening as I rushed to the bedroom. I threw open the doors to the wardrobe and found all my old dresses, tunics, and breeches that I'd used while at school. Of course, they weren't really mine. They were technically Agramon's since he'd paid for them, but I'd picked out what they looked like, and my taste ran far more conservative than his. In a thrice I was changed into a tunic and breeches with Iranoct slung around my waist.

Sam led the way out of the palace, nodding at the guardsmen while being wholly ignored by the nobility. We passed through the gardens to a large field near the stables, split into several pens. In one were straw dummies painted with different colors to show strikes, another pen held a dirt arena, and another ran the length of the field with two lanes, I figured, to mimic jousting. I crossed my arms and faced Sam.

"What would you have me begin with, Butcher?" I asked as he pulled two wooden swords from a barrel next to a nearby outbuilding.

"Don't call me that," Sam said, holding the practice blade out to me, hilt first.

"But that's what everyone calls you," I countered, unbelting Iranoct and hanging it on the fence before taking the wooden sword from him. "You worked so hard to earn that reputation. I'd think you'd be proud of it."

"I'm a soldier, Rowyn," Sam said, leaping over the fence and into the pen. "What would you have me do?" He held his hand out, but I ignored it and climbed the fence unaided. Sam dropped his hand with a frown and went to stand at the end of the pen, his practice sword slung over his shoulders, his arms draped over the ends.

"You could've used your position to broker peace instead of quashing the other kingdoms under your feet," I said. "Since I've been alive, Lyrica has been involved in endless wars. First it was the western shore, then Ember Innes, then Yliria—what's next? Do you really think you honor your god by spilling blood all over the empire?"

Sam spit to the side, pulling the sword off his shoulders and swinging it before him in a couple of practice strikes. "There is no great creator, Rowyn, whether it be Sol or Imor. The only god I know that can transform the world is suffering."

I dropped into a fighting stance, rolling onto the balls of my feet so that I could move quickly. "Rumor had the Butcher out to be some great religious man, Sol's blade on Earth, or so the stories say."

"You of all people should know the fallacy of rumors," Sam said, swooping in with startling speed given the man's age and size. I'd nearly forgotten how muscular his arms were under the loose tunics he wore, but it was impossible to forget while fighting him. Each strike of the blade jarred my bones, and it took everything I had to hold my own against him.

"So, the only god you believe in is suffering," I gasped, fending off his blade and spinning away from his next attack. "I suppose that explains so much given your reputation. Is that all you believe, I wonder?"

Sam stepped back, barely breaking a sweat. At least it gave me a chance to wipe the moisture dripping from my head. He feinted once or twice but didn't seem to be in a rush to end the match. "No, but you're not going to like the rest of it either," he said, frowning as though he was irritated with how the conversation was going.

"Whether I would like it or not, I'm still curious," I admitted. "After all, you were the one who said we were alike." I leaped toward him, sweeping my blade in a blur of strikes. Though Sam was far stronger, I was quicker. He blocked each strike, but I surprised him when I kicked him on the back of the knee, sending him to the ground. Out of options, he rolled out of the way and rose with a smile.

"I was wondering when you were going to go rogue," he said, gripping his sword with both hands.

I rolled my eyes. "Here you go again, acting like you know me so well." My mind went back to my meeting with Agramon earlier. When we first met, had Sam known more about me than I realized? Had Gillius's letters been read by more than just Agramon? I narrowed my eyes. "Did you enjoy the letters Gillius sent? Did all you men pore over them together, sitting around your little council table, debating what my fate would be? How did you find out about me anyway?" I asked, angry now that I realized what I should've known all along. It wasn't just Agramon who was working to control my life. It seemed everyone at the capital was in on it.

Sam shook his head, a glower at the corner of his lips. "No, I answered your questions about my rumors—now it's your turn."

I glared, angry that he thought it was all a game. But if I was ever to survive long enough at the capital to escape, it was a game I would have to play. "Fine, what do you want to know?"

"Was it true, about the Everett boy?" he asked, his voice softening.

I froze. Sam, who claimed not to listen to the rumors, was actually asking if I'd entrapped Destrian. "You mean, did I cruelly pretend to be someone I wasn't so that he would trust me, only to deceive him in the end?" I spat. My knuckles whitened with the force of my grip, and the sword began to shake.

"No, that's not what I meant," Sam said. "Did you love him?"

I felt my anger fall away. Sam's eyes met mine, but I

couldn't answer him. It wasn't the same as telling Del, so I didn't speak at all. I just stood there, my sword point lowering.

"You don't have to answer," Sam said, spinning the wooden sword in his hand. He seemed to revive himself, crouching once more.

"It's still painful to talk about," I admitted, matching his stance.

Sam nodded, almost to himself, before striking forward. We parried for a bit, each of us trying to best the other. I got a lucky strike in early, smacking his ribs with my sword before he beat me back against the fence, his weight bearing down on mine.

"Yield," I gasped, sweat streaming down my cheeks. The weight lifted as Sam stepped back. At least he was somewhat winded, though I was embarrassingly out of sorts.

"You're quite good, Rowyn. Not the best I've fought against, but still quite good," Sam said.

I smiled. "I don't often lose my fights," I admitted. "At Solridge, there were only three swordsmen who could best me: Lord Alexander, Marc, and Destrian."

Sam's nostrils flared. "When you grew tired, you left your lower half open. Perhaps it's because of your height, but you will need to watch it."

I wiped my brow with my sleeve. "Thanks for the tip."

Sam tossed the sword into the bin with the others and headed to the archery pen.

I followed him to the field where several targets were set up across from us. Sam handed me a longbow and watched me string it. "In answer to your question, I believe that men like me, spilling blood into the earth, create opportunities for others to rise as heroes."

"I was given to understand that all men were heroes in their own stories," I said, holding up the bow and nocking an arrow. "You must have suffered greatly to believe in such things."

Sam was quiet as I aimed. It took merely a moment for me to shoot, hitting the target dead-center. My archery had always been better than my swordplay.

"What has amity ever done but create a fat people who grow indifferent?" Sam asked, handing me another arrow. This time, he kept talking while I lined the arrow up. "The beauties of life all come at a cost, Rowyn, and it's people like us that they send to their deaths so others can really live and be called good."

My arrow flew straight and true, whistling through the air as it hit the center once more, splitting the other arrow into pieces.

"You make odd excuses for committing evil," I said, lowering the bow and hoping he noticed that I wasn't impressed. "You haven't tried to deny any of the claims made against you in the rumors. By all the gods, I know I should appreciate what you've done for me, I know I should be more than grateful, but how can I be indebted to someone like you? How could I ever trust you again?"

"Because I know what it feels like . . ." Sam growled as he leaned in, grabbing the bow from my hands. "I know the fury."

"You know nothing of my feelings," I said.

"Don't I?" Samael asked, setting the bow to the side and picking up a crossbow leaning against the fence. "Don't *I* know how it feels when you enter a room and the others shrink away from you? Don't *I* know the stench of fear that emanates from everyone around us? You just don't want to admit how alike we are."

I snatched the crossbow from him with a scowl. "I still have others who love me!" I insisted, loading a bolt and taking aim. But Sam had successfully distracted me. I squeezed the trigger too soon, and the bolt hit the fence rail instead. I lowered the crossbow with a curse.

"For how long?" Sam asked, his arms crossed over his chest as he leaned against the railing. "How long until they realize that you have the power to break the world? People can never grow close to those they fear the most. Face it, Rowyn. You're alone. Your clan saw what you were and abandoned you. How much longer till the others see it too? How much longer do you think they'll stand by and watch you eclipse them?"

"I have friends at Solridge," I insisted, though I didn't know if I was trying to convince him or myself. "I have friends."

"Yes, you had friends," Samael said, his eyes somber. "But since you've become the most powerful sorcerer in the realm, where are those friends now?"

My breath caught in my throat. He was wrong. Destrian had seen what I'd become, and he hadn't abandoned me. It was I who left him. "Destrian—"

"A mere whelp of a boy," Samael grunted, grabbing the crossbow from me. "He may be a lord, Rowyn, but he's barely a man. How long will it take you to get over him? I promise that he's already gotten over you. Those born into nobility are all the same. They speak pretty verses and drip poison into a woman's ear long enough to bed them, then move on when the next pretty face catches their eye. Your lord Destrian is no different."

"You don't even know him," I hissed. How dare he throw Destrian's name in the dirt. "What would a monster like you know of love?"

Sam raised himself up, his eyes flashing. "What does your little lord know of sacrifice?" he asked. "I've bled for this empire. I've been to battle in service to our land. That boy hasn't once stepped on a full battlefield, yet I'm the one deemed without honor?" His voice grew louder as he gestured to himself. As though he wasn't simply trying to convince me of the injustice of my feelings, but the world. "The nobility shun my company as though I'm a pariah, but I won the war for them! You, of all people, should know what it's like to have others question every move you make from their silk cushions of comfort. We are the same, you and me. We have done the worst for our people and would continue to do the worst in the name of duty."

"You're wrong about me," I said, but my voice faltered, and I was filled with a sinking feeling. How many times had I watched the noblemen of Solridge enjoy their comforts while thinking of how hard it was growing up at home? The ladies at Solridge had never smelled the rot and decay of a plague-ridden sickroom. The noblemen had never actually felt the fear of a battle they were sure they would lose. The world seemed to have been sculpted for the likes of Marc and Ingrid, and even Destrian, while the rest of us rejoiced at the mere scraps we were able to fight for. By all the gods, the Butcher of Bruin was right.

Chapter 15

"HOW WAS WEAPONS WORK?" Ena asked when I returned, rubbing my arms.

"I'm already regretting making such a stink about it," I admitted, eying the large meal of dried meat, fruit, and fresh vegetables cut in the shape of animals that was set out on the table in the receiving room. Agramon would be absent for dinner, which meant I could skip the emperor's banquet. I leaped at the opportunity to have an evening to myself, away from the stares and whispers of strangers.

"You'll eat with me, won't you?" I asked, noticing the way Ena eyed the food.

"I couldn't possibly," Ena said. "If Agramon sees, he'll surely be angry I stepped out of my place."

I frowned. "Nonsense, I'm ordering you to eat with me. Besides, we can always take some to my room and shut the door. Here, help me with these dishes."

Ena took the platter from my hand and walked it to my bedroom. While she was gone, I turned and whispered, "Echo, warn me if Agramon comes in, will you?"

"*Yes*," Echo hissed in my ear. I smiled. The shadow soul was proving to be far more useful in the capital than

I'd initially thought. I wondered about her missing her home in the Nightlands, though, or her clan. I would have to ask her next time I was alone.

When the feast had been set up on my bed, I lay on my side, snagging bites from the different plates. Ena perched herself on the edge of the mattress as though she were ready to spring up at a moment's notice.

"Eat!" I demanded, shoving the meat toward her.

Ena obediently took a bite. "I heard you met with the empress the other day," she said, plucking a piece of fruit from a plate. "What did you think of her?"

I took my time answering. I'd have to be far more careful with Ena than I was used to. I wouldn't put it past Agramon to pore through her thoughts just to see if I was up to anything. If I were to make a bid for freedom, surely he knew I would take her with me.

"It was good," I said, chewing slowly. "She seemed serious, like she wanted to be a good ruler."

Ena smiled. "She's well-loved at the palace. The servants talk about her quite a bit, more so than the emperor."

"What do they say?" I asked. Ena had mentioned before that the easiest way to know a nobleman was to ask their servants. Nobles never bothered to hide anything from them.

"She's kind. There is always food in the kitchens for us. Leftovers from the fancy dinners and her luncheons. I was eating with the others one evening when she came into the dining area to ask after one of her handmaids who'd twisted her foot in a fall. The woman who's always with her, though, she's a fright and a half."

"Oh, Mem?" I asked, surprised Ena would be cowed by her.

"Yes, the others whisper that she and the family nurse-maid do witchcraft."

"Witchcraft? What do you mean, witchcraft?" It wasn't like Ena to be so superstitious. "Is it like sorcery?"

Ena shook her head. "No, the others are familiar with sorcery. They've seen the great ones here at the palace practicing, healing wounds and whatnot. One handmaid swears she walked in on the old nurse mumbling some nonsense under her breath, and then one of the birds became hysterical, squawking and flapping about and making the most awful fuss."

I almost laughed at such a ridiculous tale. "What of Mem? You say she does witchcraft too?"

Ena nodded. "One of the emperor's footmen swears he saw her talking to her blades as she was sharpening them. He thinks she's trapped human souls within them, and they're the reason that she never misses from drawing blood in a fight."

"Well," I said, unable to hide my smile, "I can tell you that I've met both Nini and Mem, and both seemed perfectly fine."

"Just be wary of them, Rowyn," Ena whispered. "There have been strange tales about Ember Innes. You should be on your guard in case they try to enchant you to do something wicked."

I laughed outright at that. "Because if I were to do something wicked, it would surely be the empress's fault."

Ena smacked me on the arm. "You know what I mean."

I lay back against the pillows, enjoying Ena's suspicious tales. "Tell me of the emperor. You say they don't speak of him much?"

"He's not a very nice man," Ena said, drawing her knees toward her chest and peeling another piece of fruit. "Given how the servants talk, he shares his bed with half the kingdom. It's shameful behavior, if you ask me, especially toward the empress. I've never understood such men. You have the most beautiful woman in five kingdoms, and you're going to flit around lesser women's bedchambers? It makes no sense!"

"You won't hear argument from me," I agreed. "What does he do all day, besides spending too much time on his knees?"

"Nico, his footman, says that he plays at ruling when he feels like it. Otherwise, he lets his councils do all the work for him. The Council of Five deals with the sorcerers' matters, while the emperor's council handles the issues of state. Most of the time, the emperor just goes out into the city with his friends, visiting the taverns and flirting with women."

I remembered back to the council room that morning. "Do you know who makes up the emperor's council?" I asked.

Ena looked up, counting off on her fingers. "There's Captain Diardo, head of the royal guard; the Baron of Bruin, imperial commander of the Lyrican Army; Solston Gowther, who heads the temple of Sol at the palace and within the city; Bald Walden sometimes joins as head of the city guard, and then of course, there is Agramon, who represents the sorcerers. There are others, like the Sage of the Treasury, and Edmund the Bright, head of the university, but Agramon, Diardo, and the Butcher make most of the decisions."

"By Imor's name, most who make up his council are military in some capacity. No wonder we've been involved in endless wars. Is there any voice of the common people present?"

Ena's eyebrows rose. "That's not how it's done, Rowyn. Though the idea is a good one."

A squawk came at the window. Ena and I shot up, almost upsetting the plate of sweet rolls. The shadow falcon stood on the sill, eying our feast with longing.

"You're back, Arden," Ena said with a smile. Grabbing a few pieces of meat, she went to the falcon and held out her hand. The bird, Arden, I supposed, carefully lifted the meat from her fingers and gulped it down.

"Is she a friend now?" I asked with a smile, approaching the bird with caution. Shadow falcons were known to be vicious, and it was important to be wary of their razor-sharp claws. I pulled off a piece of meat and held out my hand.

The bird snatched the meat, then jumped onto my arm, flapping her great wings to steady herself. I was nearly startled out of my skin.

"She likes you, my lady," Ena said with a smile. "I think she recognizes that you're from her homeland. She comes to the window while I'm cleaning your room and looks around, as though she's looking for you. Sometimes she settles down and keeps me company while I work."

"I wonder what she's doing so far from Morgania," I said, tentatively brushing my fingers along her head. Arden held very still and simply watched me.

"Some nobles like to collect rare birds," Ena said, starting to clear the dishes off my bed. "I'll bet a lord got her for hunting and she escaped."

I thought back to the golden cages in the empress's room. Stroking the shadow falcon's gray feathers, I found myself thankful that she'd gotten away. "You named her

Arden?"

Ena blushed. "I hope you don't mind. It means 'loyal friend' in Old Mor Tongue."

"I think it's perfect," I agreed.

Chapter 16

"I SEE THE EMPRESS IS TAKING you under her wing," Captain Diardo said as I joined the ladies who would accompany the empress to the city.

I nodded noncommittally but was not in the best of moods, having just endured the tortuous routine of curt-sying, dancing, and serving tea with Princess Willene. As I'd left, the woman thrust the lute back into my hands and assigned me taskwork to learn a *different* song during my free time. I grumbled the whole way back to my rooms.

At least I had my sword. Agramon wasn't there when I arrived, so I took that opportunity to arm myself as much as I dared. After all, I was heading into the city. Agramon wouldn't want me to venture in completely unprotected, would he?

As I looked around the ward of the palace, I was struck that it hadn't been that long ago when Destrian and I rode back into Helena, greeted by crowds of Morganians shout-ing for our attention. He'd looked back to me, with that handsome smile of his, as we rode toward his home. What was he doing now? I imagined he would be busy learning how to rule Morgania. He'd been away at Solridge for so long that it must've been a shock to gain the consulship so quickly. Who was helping him now that his father was gone? Was he continuing the feud with my clan? Did he dare to go against the land deal the Morganites made with the empire? Had he forgiven me yet? Would he ever?

Mem helped the empress into a carriage before leaping onto the back where a footman normally rode. The other ladies climbed into the royal wagons, but I dallied. I wasn't in the mood to feign interest in talk. It had been a long time since I'd been able to enjoy a ride, and I was itching to climb into my own saddle. "Can I have a horse?" I asked, squinting up at Diardo through the sunlight.

"It's easier for us to offer protection if you join the others in the carriage, Lady Rowyn," Captain Diardo said, leaning forward on the pommel of his saddle.

I furrowed my brows. "Please, I'd much rather ride if it's not too much trouble."

Captain Diardo looked at me for a moment, then whistled to another soldier nearby. Soon enough, another horse was led out to the ward, and I mounted, sweeping my voluminous skirt over the back and adjusting Iranoct.

I shot Captain Diardo a genuine smile.

Diardo directed me to ride between the carriages and wagon loaded with sacks and kegs, while his soldiers fanned out on either side. It was hard to shake the feeling that I was surrounded by enemies. Captain Diardo and his men all wore the snow-white color of Somme, with large golden sunbursts stitched onto their capes, signifying them as men who served the imperial crown. There was more than one instance in Espiria when we encountered the emperor's men in their white capes, and more than once, the altercation ended in blood. It was hard not to think of them as enemies. More than once I had to suppress a shudder as we trotted through the winding streets of the capital toward the sea.

The buildings rising on either side of the road were getting grimier and more run-down the closer to the wharves we got. It wasn't long before the beggars began to crowd the streets, their threadbare robes revealing skin and bones as they reached toward the carriage and shouted. Captain Diardo and his men rode closer to the carriages, watching the windows and alleyways for potential dangers.

"Be wary," Captain Diardo called to his men while adjusting his shield. "Bald Walden said the Shadow Rogue struck again last night. It won't be long till he tries to pick fights in daylight, going after richer earnings." Mem scowled at the news as she gripped one of her curved blades tightly.

After a long ride, the carriages stopped outside a warehouse bustling with all manner of people. Agramon had mentioned Scantytown before in one of his rants. Apparently, that was where the poorest of the poor lived in squalor. In the shadows of the building crouched women whose children clutched at their skirts, watching the gilt carriages with eyes wide in wonderment. One man stamped about with a wooden leg and a cane, directing the people inside while hailing the empress's carriage with a wave and a smile.

Captain Diardo dismounted and went to the carriage, opening the door and offering his hand to the ladies exiting. The other soldiers swept through the area, leaning into doorways and exchanging words with passersby. A majority of the soldiers entered the building, while the others asked those waiting outside to open their robes, presumably looking for hidden weapons. It was like a dance. No orders were shouted, no directions given. The soldiers knew their parts without being told, which meant the empress visited Scantytown as often as she said. Part of me had assumed she was playing a ruse, but the townspeople outside the poorhouse acted as if the empress's presence was barely noteworthy.

The empress was last to step from a carriage, Mem flanking her side. Captain Diardo bowed low, along with every denizen on the street. She wasn't adorned in the gold dust I'd seen her wear before, nor did heavy, gem-laden jewelry hang from her throat and ears. Even her dress, though vibrant in colors of yellow, black, and green, bore no expensive finishings. The only piece of finery was the bracelet I'd marked the day before, the one that distinguished her favored ladies.

"Good morning, Jon," the empress called to the man with the wooden leg.

"Your Eminence," the man said, taking her hand in his and kissing it. "We're thankful for the extra help this morning. There was a fire at one of the group homes on Cod Row, so our beds are overflowing."

The empress frowned. "Did everyone make it out safely?"

Jon shook his head. "Carl Brune's mother was killed from the smoke, but the others managed to escape with a few scrapes and bruises. The city guard is there now sorting through the rubble."

"I'll ask His Eminence what we are doing to assist in this tragedy," the empress said before turning to me. "Rowyn, can you come here for a moment? I want to introduce you to Jon. He organizes the poorhouses for me here in Scantytown." The empress smiled back at Jon. "Rowyn the Morganite is our new sorcerer from the western lands. She's the one who has brought the rain."

Jon bowed even lower than he had to the empress. "We are honored by your presence, my lady," he said. "Your performance was breathtaking. Is there a limit to how long your rain lasts? How far does your reach spread? Is it always a tempest that you call up, or can it be a light rain as well?"

I shifted my feet, uncomfortable with his questions in the presence of my betters. Luckily, the empress saved me from having to answer. "I know Rowyn and Duke Agramon are still studying the limits of her skills, and neither would wish to spread misinformation to the masses."

Jon's cheeks flooded with color. "By Sol above, I've forgotten myself. Quite right, Your Eminence, quite right. I can see why that would be a matter of privacy." He seemed to shake himself, then turned and hobbled into the warehouse. Mem went next, while Empress Lesedi grabbed my hand and pulled me after them. The rest of the ladies followed, and Captain Diardo brought up the rear.

We passed several people in the hall. They nodded to the empress as she passed but otherwise went on their way. Jon led us to an open room filled with wooden tables and benches. At one end was a large hearth filled with iron slabs and cauldrons of varying sizes.

The kitchen knaves had pulled the wrapped goods from the wagon onto several tables near the hearth. They began unwrapping them, revealing meats that I recognized from the emperor's dinner the night before.

"Is that . . ." I began.

The empress's eyes sparkled as she nodded. "Jon helped me come up with the scheme. He used to work in the palace kitchens, washing and polishing cutlery. They used to waste so much food after the royal dinners. Many at court would turn their nose up at eating the same meal twice. The leftover food would be thrown away, or the noblemen would feed the meat to their hunting dogs, until Jon came to me with his grand plan."

"So, you bring the food here?" I asked, looking over my shoulder at the children clustered around the tables, watching the preparations with wide, hungry eyes.

"Not just here," the empress said, motioning to the ladies behind her. They scurried to the hearth, wrapping aprons around their gowns and busying themselves with helping the kitchen knaves. I recognized Johane, the young mother who received her bracelet from the empress at the luncheon, laughing and chatting with one of the women from the poorhouse as they trimmed meat off the bone. Another group of ladies, much older than the empress, their silver hair plaited up and wrapped in linen coverings, heated water over the fire, scooping out cupfuls of dried legumes and adding them to the water.

Empress Lesedi walked toward the preparation area as Mem and I trailed behind her. She tied one of the aprons around herself before accepting two bowls from a kitchen boy and pulling back the piece of cloth on them. She motioned me to join her and tossed me an apron.

"I come here with food for the poorhouses twice a week. There is always enough for several days' worth of meals when we're finished preparing it. We also parcel out leftovers to the slaves and the city guards."

"That *is* an impressive scheme," I said, peeking into one of the bowls. It was filled with a floury sludge covered in bubbles.

The empress nodded and began spooning more flour into the mixture as Mem rooted herself to the table, her eyes on the rest of the room.

"The secret is how we prepare the food," Lesedi went on. "At home, on Ember Innes, we always ate meals with lots of sauce and beans and bread. Food lasts longer that way, and there is more to share. I've seen something similar here. I believe you people call it a stew?"

"We mostly ate stew in Espiria," I said.

Lesedi beamed. "In Ember Innes, we have so many different kinds of stew, with so many flavors. When we discussed how to make the food last longer, and reach more people, I began writing down what I remembered from preparing those dishes. Some of the spices are harder to find, but nobody has complained yet."

Lesedi began stirring her dough with a wooden spoon, then placed the bowl into my hands. I stirred obediently while she added flour to the other bowl, stirring and lifting the spoon, studying the dough as it fell.

"Your work here is admirable," I said, trying to mimic how Lesedi was stirring. "The emperor must be proud of your efforts."

At first, I didn't think the empress heard me, for she didn't answer right away. But after a moment, she gave me a tight smile. "His Eminence has so much to distract him that he doesn't really take an interest in my doings. The excess expenditures have been approved through council, but otherwise he leaves me to my own devices."

"Surely the townspeople are grateful," I said.

"But do you see what I mean? Why I need your help?" Lesedi urged, her voice pitched low.

Mem cleared her throat beside us.

"Please, Rowyn. If Agramon succeeds in his schemes, the emperor's family, *my* family, all of this, will be at an end. There is so much more we can do for the empire. Now that the war is over, I hoped to ask the council to build schools. Not just places for sorcerers or the nobles' children, but places where anyone and everyone can learn a trade."

"My lady," Mem hissed. "There are ears everywhere here."

"She has to know the stakes," Lesedi snapped back.

I looked down at the dough in my hands and hoped I wouldn't regret my next words. "I will help you, Your Eminence, in exchange for my freedom." By all the gods, I had a greater alliance with Mellan Lyon and the Empress of Lyrica than I did with my own clan. It was as though my life had turned completely upside down.

Lesedi grabbed my hand. "Really? You promise you will help?"

I drew my hand back and looked about the room, worried that we were being overheard, but everyone seemed too busy with their own tasks.

The empress had taken up her bowl once more and spoke with her eyes cast down to her dough. "You won't regret this, Rowyn. I won't fail you."

Lesedi smiled at me and faced the hearth. Scooping a dollop of thin dough out, she poured it over one of the iron slabs, spreading it out into a large circle. Another scoop went on another slab, and another, until the hearth was partway filled with the large ovals of bubbling bread.

In truth, I enjoyed myself that afternoon. The other ladies were good at cooking the stews of Lesedi's homeland. They would often call the empress over to taste their concoctions. She responded by nodding encouragement or grabbing a handful of spice and dumping it in the cauldron, explaining the mix of different flavors.

Suddenly, a wave of homesickness overwhelmed me, and I realized why I trusted Lesedi. She reminded me of my mother. Mother spent her days bent over boiling cauldrons, serving food to the rest of Espiria. The chieftain's wife, there at every birth to grab fresh linens, her smile welcoming the new babies into the clan with a blessing. I'd always admired my mother and regretted not striving to be more like her as I aged, but my father didn't have a son, and I felt it was my duty to fill that place for him, so I became what I was. I found myself wondering more and more, if I'd chosen my mother's path, would my clan have deserted me as they did?

Not only did the empress and her ladies cook the food, but they served it to the residents as well. We spooned the stews onto the empress's flatbreads, the people giving us a bow of thanks before going to enjoy their meal with their friends and neighbors.

BY THE TIME WE WERE FINISHED, it was late in the day. The entire house, and by all appearances, most of the residents on the row, had come and eaten the empress's meal.

It was with a full head that I mounted the horse and rode with the empress's procession back to the palace. In fact, it was only because I was absorbed in my own thoughts that I heard Echo's warning. We were riding in a wide lane, bordered by several tall buildings whose boarded-up windows gave the appearance that they were deserted. The only sign of life was a length of rope tied outside of one window, holding a billowing underskirt out to dry. A guard tower, several stories high, was farther down the road.

Instead of riding between the two carriages, I'd ridden in front, next to Captain Diardo. We'd exchanged pleasantries about the empress's work but otherwise kept to our thoughts. All of a sudden, Echo's voice hissed loudly in my ear, almost like a scream.

"Duck!"

I didn't question it. I threw myself against the horse's back, which meant the arrow hit Captain Diardo instead. He cursed at the arrow jutting out from his leg, then roared, "Circle the carriages!"

I turned my horse around to join the men. Mem was in front of the door to the empress's carriage, both blades unsheathed as she faced the direction from which the arrow had flown. I was about to kick my horse forward when I noticed odd movements beside me. Captain Diardo had turned a worrying shade of green and was slipping off his horse.

"The arrow was poisoned," he gasped, clutching the pommel with white knuckles.

"Hold on!" I shouted, dragging him onto my horse. I galloped into the circle of men, taking Diardo all the way to Mem, before dismounting and pulling him off. "Get him in the carriage!"

She glared at me. "My job is to protect the empress at

all costs. I take no orders that distract from that." She turned her attention back to the road, her stance unwavering.

"Fine!" I growled, flinging open the empress's door and shoving Diardo inside.

"Captain!" the empress gasped, her eyes widening when she saw the injury. I slammed the door to the carriage.

"Get the empress out of here!" I yelled to the driver. The men glanced at each other, obviously unsure about following my directive, but Mem leaped into action.

She whirled back behind the carriage and yelled at the driver, who whipped the horses forward. The mounted soldiers had no choice but to follow the rest of the carriages. The soldiers who had dismounted searched the abandoned buildings beside us.

"Where did the arrow come from?" I whispered.

Echo was in my ear in an instant. "*The red window.*"

To the south was a building several stories high. Most of the windows were covered in boards except one, out of which billowed a red curtain.

I grabbed Diardo's dropped shield, unsheathed Iranoct, and took off at a run.

Chapter 17

THE INSIDE OF THE BUILDING bore evidence of neglect and abandonment. Dust hung in the air, illuminated by the sunlight that managed to seep between the boards nailed to the windows. I held still, listening for movement, but heard nothing. I approached the wooden stairs. Studying the steps closely, I marked a set of fresh footprints in the dust leading up. There was no set of prints coming down, which meant the archer was either still up there or had found another means of escape.

I stepped up as quietly as I could, trying to see in the dim light above. The footprints followed the stairs up another floor, and another, until finally they stopped on the landing of the top floor. I waited and listened.

"Where is he?" I whispered, praying Echo could hear. Beside me, a new set of footprints stirred up little clouds of dust. After a moment, the footprints pattered back.

"*The roof,*" Echo whispered.

I nodded. Stepping into the room where Echo's prints came from, I found a ladder that looked as though it had been tossed. I leaned it against an opening in the ceiling, sheathed Iranoct, and looped the shield through my arm before climbing up.

As I reached the hole, I readjusted the shield. Poking it up through the hole, I stepped up higher, before the thump of an arrow slammed against the metal and my arm was jolted back.

At least the shield was facing the right way.

I scurried the rest of the way up the ladder as more arrows buried themselves in my shield, nearly knocking me back down the ladder.

"*Now!*" Echo hissed beside me.

I looked over the shield and saw a man in black throw away his bow and back up, before taking off toward the edge of the building.

I threw away the shield and unsheathed Iranoct. Raising the sword, the warmth of my gems screamed to life. Sparking blue energy threaded across my blade. I pointed the sword at the man, unleashing my power with a blast of thunder just as he leaped.

The bolt of lightning caught him in midair. His body catapulted so hard, he missed the next building altogether and disappeared over the ledge.

I cut off the power to my gems and realized my mistake.

What was I thinking? Agramon would be so angry when he found out.

"AND THE NEXT TIME the captain of the Royal Guard tells you to get in the carriage, I expect you to get in the carriage!" Agramon yelled, practically spitting his points at me.

I bowed my head and nodded. I wasn't in a position to argue, considering the circumstances. The arrow that hit Captain Diardo was surely meant for me, but so far, no one seemed to realize that. None of the soldiers were paying attention to us when we were moving down the street, so no one saw me duck. As far as anyone was concerned, the attack was on the empress. I couldn't let them know the attack was for me, otherwise I would give away Echo's presence, as well as my freedom. I was sure Agramon wouldn't allow me to leave the palace after an attack, even though the would-be assassin was now dead.

The soldiers had heard the thunder and seen the body go careening from the building. By the time they'd reached him, he was broken on the road, sporting a large burn that ran the length of his back. They'd draped his body over Captain Diardo's horse, and we'd ridden silently back to the palace, the men shooting me frightened looks the entire way.

"How is Captain Diardo?" I asked, my voice small. I had to get to him first. I had to tell him the alternate side of the story and hope he forgot the actual details of his poisoning. If he was still alive.

"He's been taken to the healing rooms. Tristam will take good care of him there," Agramon said, rubbing his fingers over his temples.

Behind us, I heard a shout and turned to find Del sprinting toward us. "I came as soon as I heard," Del said breathlessly, grabbing my arm and using it to hold herself up while she caught her breath. "First someone said you'd been shot, then someone said you killed someone, so finally I just decided to find out for myself," Del stammered before losing breath once more.

"She's fine," Agramon muttered, still obviously cross at me for taking matters into my own hands. I was sure if I could read his mind, he would be going over all of the precious investments he would've lost if something happened to me. It only made me more resolved to help the empress withstand his plots.

"Can you show me the way to the healing rooms?" I asked Del. "I want to make sure Captain Diardo will survive. I feel partway guilty that we didn't notice the archer in time."

Agramon scowled at me, but Del brightened.

"Of course!"

I turned to Agramon. "May I go see him, please?"

"Fine," Agramon said. "But I want you back in our

quarters within the hour. You still have your lesson with the precious Butcher, and he's a man you don't keep waiting."

I nodded. "We'll be back before then, I promise."

Del grabbed my arm and began tugging me through the halls. "I've been meaning to see you again. I looked for you at dinner last night, but you never showed up."

I raised my brows. "What is it?"

Del grinned. "Mellan has asked me to chaperone an excursion to the city for you. He was meaning to ask Agramon today at dinner, but that will probably have to wait. Either way, I wanted to check with you before I went to Agramon with the plan."

I plastered a false smile on my face. "That's kind of you to check with me, and I'd be happy to join you two on an excursion. It would be nice getting to know Mellan outside of court."

Del lowered her voice. "I confess I was utterly shocked when he asked. I would've thought there'd be no chance on Mother's earth that you would even consider him, given the amount of bad blood between you and his family, but court intrigues have always astounded me."

I shrugged. "Duke Agramon said I need to treat Mellan's advances seriously, so I intend to follow his orders." I cringed inwardly at my words, yet still hoped the duke would find that tidbit if he decided to rifle through Del's brain about me.

"See, he thought you would be trouble from the start, but that's the key to getting along with Agramon. Just do what he says, simple as that. Listening to him has only ever benefited me."

"You enjoyed his sponsorship?"

"Of course, I did," Del said. "My father is an earl of little note in the southern lands. Growing up, I knew nothing about court or the other nobles. When Duke Agramon offered to sponsor me, my father killed six hogs in celebration and still brags about it to this day."

"What is your power?" I asked, curious that she hadn't mentioned it before.

"I build things," Del said. "When Mellan and I take you out into the city, I'll show you some of the places I've put together."

Del led me into a part of the palace I'd never seen before. It was on the ground floor, with open arches forming a colonnade along a garden. But the garden wasn't the flower gardens the empress held her luncheon in every day. I recognized many of the same herbs that grew in Galena's stores at Solridge.

"Here we are," Del said, opening a door to the inside of a bright, airy room.

Lord Tristam stood at a large tome, wearing a simple tunic and breeches. He was scribbling furiously with a feather quill. I was struck by how much he looked like Lord Alexander. This man was leaner, with sharper features, and his beard was cut shorter, but the resemblance was unmistakable. He turned when we entered, and he smiled at Del.

"We've come to check on Captain Diardo," Del told him.

Tristam nodded. "He's in the first bed. The poison took hold much quicker than I would've wished. I'm hoping he won't lose the leg, but we'll have to wait and see. The empress is in there now."

Del led me to an arched door in the wall, but I pulled her back. "Can I go in alone?" I asked, doing my best to look upset. "It was just so frightening, and everything happened so fast. I want a chance to thank him for his bravery." Acting was another skill I was terrible at, but I was betting on her unwillingness to question me at such a time. Luckily, my bet paid off.

"Of course!" Del said, her brows knit with concern. "I'll just wait out here. I had a few questions for Tristam anyway about one of my workers who got injured last week. Just make sure you're finished in enough time to get back to Agramon's before your lesson."

I nodded, then waited for Del to flounce back to Tristam before cracking open the door.

Captain Diardo was propped up with several pillows on

a small pallet. Beside him was the empress, who clutched his hand with tears in her eyes. He lifted his other hand and swept it against the empress's cheek, murmuring something.

My eyes widened, and I tried to shut the door again, but the captain noticed me, and the empress whipped around.

"Rowyn!" she said, sweeping her hand across her eyes as though wiping away tears. "Thank the mother you're back. We were so worried for you!"

"Shut the door," Captain Diardo said, pushing himself up higher. His eyes followed me as I slipped in and closed the door quietly behind me.

I was resolved to say my piece as quickly as possible and leave them to their tender scene. I lifted my eyes, thanking the gods that Agramon couldn't read my thoughts. I wondered how Captain Diardo and the empress hid their feelings from Agramon. By Imor's name, how did they hide their feelings from the emperor?

"I just wanted to say that I'm sorry you were injured when the empress was attacked today. I hope that you are able to regain your full strength quickly," I said, all in a rush.

"That is very sweet of you, Rowyn," the empress said, but Captain Diardo just stared at me.

When he didn't say anything, I looked down, shifting my feet. "If there is anything you need, anything I can assist with to speed up your recovery, I hope that you will let me know," I stammered.

The empress was looking from Diardo to me with a frown.

Finally, the captain spoke, his voice heavy with weariness. "I will discuss the attack on the *empress* with the city watch. It could be that you caught the Shadow Rogue at last. They should know what happened."

I nodded. "Thank you," I said before I could stop myself. Lines in the empress's face deepened with her frown, but I was already ducking out of the room and speeding toward Del and Tristam, who were out in the garden studying one of the plants.

"I'd best be getting back to my rooms," I said, hastening past the two of them.

"Wait!" Del shouted after me. "Don't you need me to show you the way?"

I shook my head vigorously. "I remember!" I shouted over my shoulder and was out the door and rushing through the halls before she could stop me.

By all appearances, Captain Diardo had agreed to my story, though he seemed to remember more than I'd hoped. But I didn't want Agramon to confine me to the palace for fear of my safety. Gillius had done that at Solridge, and I'd hated it. Besides, I'd come into my own power and could defend myself far better than I could before. What was there for me to be afraid of? I supposed it was best not to think of that.

The nobles and servants traveling the halls shot me odd looks as I passed. I couldn't tell if it was because they'd heard the story of the attack on our party, or if it was the look on my face. I turned one corner, beginning to grow suspicious that I didn't, in fact, know the way back to my rooms, when I heard my name called behind me.

I turned and found Sam hurrying toward me, his expression as dark as a thundercloud. "Are you all right?" he asked. "I heard they got the jump on you in the city."

"I'm perfectly fine," I said. "It was Diardo who caught the arrow."

Sam's brows furrowed. "I was going to see him later, after I made sure that you were well."

I thanked the gods I'd managed to get to Diardo first. Though I wasn't sure how close he was to the Butcher of Bruin, I could only hope and pray that he kept to my story with everyone. Still, Sam looked at me as though I'd been beaten within an inch of my life.

"Really, I'm fine," I insisted, lowering my voice. "You didn't have anything to worry about."

Sam ran his fingers through his hair and glanced at those around us. "I know you're perfectly capable, it's just that . . ."

He paused as though not knowing how to finish, so I

finished for him. "It's just that I'm so valuable and all," I said, my heart sinking.

"That's not what I was going to say," Sam growled, his hand dropping to the hilt of his sword.

We stood awkwardly in the hall for a moment. Finally, I shrugged. "Do you still have time for me this evening?"

Sam seemed relieved by the change in subject. "Of course, I do, of course. After assessing your skills last night, I think we should focus on hand-to-hand combat along with some knife fighting and the like. You don't seem to know how to handle those who are bigger than you in close combat, so I figured we could start there."

My face twisted up, but I reminded myself that he intended to be helpful. "I learned some hand-to-hand in Espiria, but everyone was always afraid to practice with me, for fear of my father, being chief and all. At Solridge, it was expressly forbidden. Lord Alexander said that nobles don't fight with their fists."

Sam rolled his eyes. "Lord Alexander has also never really been in a battle. Everyone should know some close combat skills, even if they are the soft, doughy nobles the capital produces."

I smiled, happy we were back on safe footing and excited about my lesson. I'd always wanted to improve my fist-fighting. More than once I'd been overpowered by a stronger opponent when I lacked a weapon. Sam had chosen my skill work masterfully, especially if Agramon was going to continue insisting I waltz around the capital unarmed.

"I was just going to my room to change," I said, letting my smile deepen.

Sam looked confused. "Oh? I thought you were heading to the servants' quarters. Your rooms are on the other side of the citadel."

"Oh," I said, then shrugged. "I was wondering if I was lost."

Sam bowed. "Will you do me the honor of allowing me to show you the way?"

I checked his face for a hint of a smile, but there was none. As we walked, I wondered what joys Sam had in his life, then second-guessed myself. When it came to the Butcher of Bruin, I shouldn't care.

Chapter 18

GRAMON WAS IN LOW SPIRITS when he returned to our rooms later that evening. It didn't matter that I was already in my chemise, dousing the lights and readying for bed after a long day; he opened my bedroom door without knocking and said, "Put on a dressing gown. You're going to bring rain tonight."

"But . . ." I began. I was weary to the bone—from helping the empress, to the attack, to my sore arms, to Sam insisting I practice a throwing move to perfection. I couldn't fathom dredging up one more drop of energy.

"You know," Agramon said, his tone dangerously low, "I've had quite enough of the constant arguments when I request something of you." His voice rose. "The sole purpose of you being here is to gain control and use your powers, *not* trotting after the empress on her little whims, *not* batting wooden sticks around with broken men, and certainly *not* lazing about, eating food that I've provided, in clothes that I've bought, and arguing with me about every simple request!"

I froze. Agramon's heated gaze dared me to respond. But I didn't dare. Instead, I nodded. Opening my wardrobe, I pulled out my brilliant blue silk dressing gown and pulled it over myself before belting it tightly. Silver vines and flowers that looked like stars were embroidered on the collar. I supposed when Agramon chose a theme, he stuck with it. At least it was ornate enough that I wouldn't feel poorly dressed in the halls of the palace. There was no hope for pulling back my hair, as Duke Agramon was already holding the door open, tapping his foot impatiently.

He stormed through the halls, me following meekly behind, until we reached the massive balcony that the court had watched me on the day before. It was mercifully empty, with miniature globes hanging from the ceiling above, which offered a meager light to the ever-darkening sky.

"The emperor said that it's best that you practice your skills at night, so as not to disrupt the city markets and other goings-on of the people," Agramon said, settling onto a chair under the awning, facing the city. "He fears a dip in commerce will upset the townspeople."

"It may not be so helpful if I call the rain *every* night. I wouldn't want it to flood," I said, taking a deep breath and rubbing my hands together. I could do this. Duke Agramon didn't know my range yet, so I didn't need to reach as far as the day before.

"You won't," Agramon snapped. "There are many evenings that I'm fulfilling obligations here at the palace, or out in the city. But I don't care if I'm waking you up in the middle of the night while you're dreaming about your silly red lord—you will comply with my wishes, understood?"

"Yes," I grumbled.

"Good, now get started so that we can both get to bed," Agramon ordered, settling back into his chair with his staff across his lap. "And no more of your little tricks either. If I get so much as one drop of moisture on this robe, I'll lock you in your room for a week!"

I sighed and raised my hands, but the warmth from my power was slow to grow. I closed my eyes, following the magic's path and nudging the wellspring within, but still it moved sluggishly, without the burst of strength I needed.

Agramon cleared his throat behind me and tapped his fingers on his chair in a flurried beat.

I clenched my eyes shut and forced the wellspring up. It slipped through my mind, pooling back down into itself, unwilling to follow my lead. Angry, I gritted my teeth, putting as much pressure as I could onto it, driving the magic forward with all of my will.

The power shot out of me, but I didn't have the strength to send it up to the heavens. Instead, it surged around me in a great swell, whipping my robe and hair about and lifting my feet off the ground. I panicked, and the power slipped from my control, sending me whirling off the balcony and into the air with a scream.

The great wind kept twisting and turning me about,

making it impossible to keep my bearings. One moment I saw the lights of the palace, and the next moment, the lights of the city below. I threw my hands down, trying to regain control by sending more magic around me, but another gust of wind swept under me, sending me whirling farther into the city.

The roar in my ears made it impossible to think, but I had to get myself under control. In my panicked memory, I remembered that I'd done something similar before, controlling the wind when the bat I'd climbed onto was falling, and using it to soften my landing.

My next view almost sent me panicking anew. The small inland sea that bordered Somme was far closer than it should've been. I was heading toward the sea, and not even Imor could help me if I landed in it.

I had to try something different. Thinking back to the bat, I held my arms in alternate directions, sending power through both. My body slowed its momentum, but the wind sent me spinning more wildly to the point that I was sure I'd either be sick or ripped apart. Still holding my hands as best as I could, I slowed the power down, softening the release.

The spinning slowed, and I could discern the slanted rooftops beneath me. Looking up, the water was much closer. I couldn't panic, for that would mean certain death, drowning in the black waters beyond.

But when I slowed the magic even further, it was done with me. The power stopped altogether, and I plunged down, landing with a crunch on a clay tile roof.

Momentum sent me sliding down the tiles while I scrambled for purchase. The tiles that had cracked from my fall gave way, tumbling off the roof. I jammed my fingers and bare feet into the cracks, which stopped my descent with a jarring wrench.

I was spread-eagle atop someone's home in Somme, afraid to move. I took a moment to breathe and mentally assess my injuries. Remarkably, I didn't have any, if I didn't count my strained fingers and toes.

I sent a silent thank you to Imor, who was probably laughing himself sick at my expense. I took another deep breath and braced my feet, pulling myself up with the strength in my arms. It felt like ages, testing each tile with my fingers and toes before trusting it with extra weight, but I finally made it to the peak of the roof and sat with a leg draped over either side. The side I had climbed up was now in shambles. Broken tiles and open spots scattered there made it treacherous and unpredictable. My only hope was that the opposite side was in good enough condition to hold me. But even if I were able to make it down that side, what then?

I scooted along the ridge, trying to find a way off the roof. When I reached the end, I realized that the building was only two stories high, not a dire drop by any means, though the paving stones below would certainly make it a painful one. I crept down the tiles, again testing each to hold weight as I went, until I reached the edge of the roof. Peering over, I almost cried with relief when I noticed a small balcony below me. I lowered myself down until I dangled in the air. The roof crumbled under my fingertips, and I dropped onto the balcony.

The building was dark. I took that as a sign that either no one was home, or the building was abandoned. I climbed over the balcony and collapsed onto the paving stones, looking up between the buildings at the winking stars. I considered not moving from that spot for the rest of the night.

There was a moment when I was being buffeted through the air that I thought I wouldn't make it back to the ground alive. But now I had no idea where I was, in a massive city, in the middle of the night.

Despite my weariness, I knew that I had to find help. Surely there was a city guard somewhere who could take me back to the palace. I rose, and after orienting myself with the stars, I headed in the direction of the palace.

The streets were deserted. I began to run, wary of the dark buildings and shadowed alleyways. I turned a corner and ran into someone else who stumbled back with a curse before drawing a blade.

It was no wonder I'd run into the person. They were wearing all black, and a dark hood shadowed their features. From what I could see, a mask covered their nose and mouth. Four Ylirians in threadbare tunics stood behind the masked stranger. Two appeared only slightly older than I was, a man and a woman. Behind them were two older women, one clutching a bundle close to her chest. They shrank away from me, their black eyes widening in fear. One woman was gripping her robe at her throat, the sleeve of the garment pulled back to reveal a branded sun on her forearm. Slaves. But what were Ylirian slaves doing near the wharf in the middle of the night? The bundle began to shake, and a cry arose from the woman's arms. The shadowed figure with the blade stepped closer, drawing the weapon back as if to strike.

I held up my hands. "Please!" I said, backing away. "I'm lost. I'm trying to find my way back . . . home." At the last minute I opted against using the word *palace*.

The blade lowered. "Rowyn?"

I was sure my eyes nearly popped out of my head at the familiar voice. "Mellan?"

The figure swept back his hood and pulled down the black cloth, revealing none other than Mellan Lyon.

"By Sol above, Rowyn, what are you doing out here in the middle of the night? Is that a dressing gown?"

"I could just as easily ask you that same question. What

227

are you doing? Who are these people?" I stammered. Mellan shifted his feet. The younger man had stepped in front of the women, shielding them with his body. Realization dawned. "You're helping them escape."

"Rowyn . . ." It was as though his face revealed the inner workings of his mind. First lies, then denial, then panic, before finally he just grabbed my hand and pulled me toward him. "You need to forget," he urged. "If Agramon reads your mind and finds out what I'm doing, they'll execute me."

"Agramon can't read my mind," I assured him. I was still trying to wrap my brain around a Lyon embarking on such an honorable yet dangerous undertaking.

"He can't?" Mellan asked, his head tilting to the side. "You never mentioned that before!"

"It's a bit of a sore spot for Agramon, so I didn't want to spread it around," I admitted.

Shouts echoed in the distance and Mellan cursed, raising his blade once more. The women behind him whimpered.

"Who is that?" I hissed.

"The city guard. They discovered one of my launch points yesterday and have added extra security in this area. I'd already set up the escape, and we don't have a long window to get them to the boat."

"I'll distract them," I said, shoving Mellan away. "I was

looking for them anyway. Go, and get those people out of here!"

The last I saw of Mellan, he was pulling his hood back up and disappearing into the shadows with the others. I ran toward the sound of horses, and when I was far enough away from Mellan and sure that he was hidden, I shouted for help.

The city guard closed in around me. I raised my head high. "Who is in charge here?" I asked, using my best authoritative voice.

One of the guardsmen dismounted and lifted his helmet off. He was completely bald, with a scar running over one eyebrow, cutting it neatly in two. He put the helmet under his arm and stepped toward me.

"I am," the man said in a gravelly voice. His eyes seemed to take me in. "And what spells are you weaving out on the docks, sorceress?"

This had to be Bald Walden, the captain of the city guard. I'd heard of him, even as far as Morgania. He and his men had fingers in every purse in the city, legal and otherwise. "I was trying a new bit of magic and accidentally lost myself this way. I will need to be returned home, to the palace, immediately."

The man grunted, looking over his shoulder at the men behind him. "Was that what all that wind ruckus was about?"

"Yes," I said. "I apologize for any disruption it has caused to the city workings. As I said before, it was an accident."

"We received word that the Shadow Rogue would be working this wharf tonight. I can't spare any men to assist you. Can't your magic take you back?"

I drew myself up, trying to appear as intimidating as possible, given I was a full foot shorter than the man, and the rest had remained on horseback. "I'm afraid that's not possible, as I'm without the energy to recall my power. But you're free to go on your merry way and leave me to attempt to return to the palace in the middle of the night without a horse, weapons, or shoes. I'm sure the emperor would understand why capturing this petty criminal would be far more important than ensuring his favored weather sorcerer makes it back safely."

The captain grabbed my hand and held it up to the moonlight, then cursed quite colorfully. "It's the Morganite," he said, turning to his men. "Get her on a horse."

A guardsman dismounted and helped me onto the horse of another. I wrapped my arms around the guard's waist, thankful that I was finally going to head toward my bed at last. The men were conversing with each other in low voices, but the captain whistled them silent, placing his helmet back on his head. "We all go. After the empress's attack earlier today, we take no chances with this one."

I smiled as the men began trotting through the streets at a speedy clip. Looking up to Imor, I sent a prayer for Mellan and his runaways to find safe passage into the night.

ELGAR THE SWIFT MET MY escort when we were passing through the deserted market square. One minute, the road before us was empty, and the next, our way was blocked.

"Bald Walden," Elgar said, nodding to the captain.

The captain held up his fist to the men and reined in his horse. "We have one of yours, Swift," the captain said, motioning for the guard I was riding with to step forward. I peeked from behind him and waved at Elgar, who raised a single eyebrow at me.

"Are you hurt?" Elgar asked, helping me out of the saddle.

"No," I assured him. "Just exhausted."

"I'll have you back in a moment," Elgar said before turning back to the captain. "It's a good thing you found her. We were starting to worry that she'd been tossed into the sea."

Bald Walden reined his horse around. "We missed a

chance at catching the Shadow Rogue because of her. Tell Duke Agramon he needs to keep a better eye on his valuables." Without another word, the captain kicked his horse into a trot, followed by the other men of the city guard, until Elgar the Swift and I were left in the street alone.

"We'd better get you back before they expand the search," said Elgar from behind me. I stiffened as he wrapped his arms around my waist. Without warning, the air around us seemed to press into me, as though I were being sucked through time itself.

My ears popped, and my breath caught in my throat, the pressure sinking into my eyes until I thought they would burst from my skull. Suddenly, the feeling went away, and we were standing outside the palace gate. Elgar took my arm and guided me through the entrance and into utter chaos.

Apparently, women flying off balconies and into the night was an uncommon enough occurrence at the palace that it had caused a bit of a hubbub after I disappeared. Duke Agramon was shouting orders to a group of mounted castle guards, his staff emitting a rose-colored glow that bathed his face in light. Baron Samael was getting ready to mount his horse, wearing only a snow-white tunic and leather breeches, his hair mussed as though he'd just rolled out of bed. Owain and Tristam were talking animatedly to one another, gesticulating toward the city and having some sort of disagreement.

"She's here!" Elgar hollered, dragging me forward.

Talk ceased as all eyes shot to me. When Elgar released his hold on my arm, I dropped to my knees, leaned forward, and retched.

Chapter 19

AGRAMON WAS ABLE TO SUMMON a measure of kindness and allowed me almost an entire day's rest. I didn't have to endure a morning with Princess Willene, and Duke Agramon left me blissfully alone. I woke up late and ate from the plates left on my dressing table, then crawled right back into bed and slept some more.

Echo was hard at work while I slept. I followed her memory as she trailed Agramon to a richly decorated receiving room. The emperor was lounging on a low-lying couch, a crystal goblet filled with wine at his side. On his lap sat the young prince. Though they didn't share the same skin tone, nor hair color, the young prince had the emperor's strong bone structure and blue eyes. He would be handsome one day, as handsome as his father.

Across the room, Lesedi the Younger and Eledra played with blocks together, building a shining tower that resembled the palace. The girls whispered quietly as they worked, Lesedi showing her sister how to link the blocks together to gain height to the towers, while Eledra listened attentively.

Agramon wrinkled his nose at the sight of the young

royals as he took a seat across from the emperor. While Agramon and Emperor Arthello greeted each other, the young prince squirmed off his father's lap and ran to the girls, plowing straight into the tower they'd been constructing, knocking the pieces about in a great commotion. Eledra began crying, while Princess Lesedi stood and scolded Prince Artian, who also began to cry.

"Lesedi!" the emperor shouted, his eyes glinting. "Don't you dare speak to the heir in that way. Go to your rooms, both of you!"

"But Father," Lesedi began, her hand outstretched toward the broken remains of the tower.

"Now!" Arthello shouted before lifting his goblet to his lips. Lesedi's face fell, her look of defiance gone as she took Eledra's hand and led her from the room and into another, while Prince Artian sat and began beating the tower pieces together. Unable to figure out how to stack them on his own, he abandoned the game, going instead to a plant in the corner to pluck the leaves from its stem.

"The nobles are growing irritated," the emperor was saying, twisting his goblet. With his other hand, he pulled out a bundle of papers and tossed them onto the table. "I've received numerous queries to have Rowyn practice her arts in their fields, rather than here at the palace. They question what good it's doing the kingdom to have her here."

Agramon frowned. "I like having her here. The people in the city have been restless, especially since the war in Yliria has ended. The Morganite's presence has given them something new to gossip about, instead of why we began the war in the first place. Besides, I would've thought you'd want her to be here when the delegation from Lu Shen arrives. She would be a great show of power for you."

"Still," the emperor said, fanning the papers out, "the nobles do have a point. There is unrest throughout the kingdom, not just at Somme, and her presence could stem the tide of discontent if we use her appropriately. At least, that's what Samael and Diardo say."

"Who knows better what the locals are saying than I, Your Eminence?" Agramon asked. "The people of Somme demand strength of hand, especially in the presence of such a formidable power as Lu Shen. Rowyn will do far better good here, aiding in bolstering your power, then off in some count's field."

"Perhaps you're right," the emperor sighed.

Agramon smiled, leaning back in his chair. "I know I'm right, Your Eminence. Besides, I was planning to have Rowyn work on a welcoming performance for the ambassador. We'll go on our journey throughout the empire as soon as the delegation leaves. That will give me enough time to continue her studies and plan our route. We'll do our round throughout the empire and be back in time for the quinquennial celebration in the summer, I promise."

The emperor's face lit up. "Very good. Miyu has assured me that this will be the grandest quinquennial yet."

"Naturally," Agramon said, his eyes wrinkling in amusement before he glanced at the papers on the table. "If you would like, I can take over the communication of Rowyn's travel plans with the nobles for you. As emperor, you shouldn't have to deal with such pithy correspondence as a sorcerer's travel plans."

The emperor sagged in relief. "Please," he said, pushing the letters toward Agramon. "It would be a great burden off my mind if you handled it. You are her guardian, after all. Come to think of it, I wonder why they approached me at all. Don't they know I have more important things to do?"

"The nobles are trying to bully you, Your Eminence," Agramon said, rotating the staff in his hands. "You've acquired Rowyn as a gift to your people. How selfish of the nobles to fight over who gets her first. Naturally, the emperor and people of Somme should enjoy her before loaning her out to the rest of the empire. But don't worry, I'll handle the communications from now on."

"You're a good man," the emperor said, standing while Agramon gathered the letters. "Let me know when you've chosen your route."

"Of course, Your Eminence," Agramon said, sweeping his robes out beside him before striding from the room, tucking the letters into his pocket.

WHEN I AWOKE AGAIN, LATE IN THE afternoon, it was to a rustling at my window. I almost leaped out of bed and grabbed Iranoct, the memory of the golgeman assassin that plagued me at Solridge fresh in my mind, but it was only Arden, preening on the windowsill.

"Are you hungry?" I asked, stepping to my table. The plates had been freshened for lunch, though that was hours ago judging by Sol's position in the sky. Arden flapped her wings and ruffled her feathers before settling down on the sill. I grabbed several pieces of meat and let the meat dangle from my fingertips. Arden took it delicately in her beak and swallowed it down. I fed her a few more pieces until she stopped opening her beak to take it, then I stroked the soft feathers at her nape while I thought of the dream Echo had sent.

So, the nobles of the realm were restless, and a delegation from Lu Shen was due to arrive at some point. I wondered about Agramon's insistence that I remain at the capital longer. I'd thought that the whole purpose of me being shipped off to the East was to end the drought, but apparently it was simply to collect a token of power.

Since the empress had asked for any information I could give her, I pondered how to relay the dream. She'd mentioned using my mornings with High Princess Willene to pass information to Ledi the Younger. That was definitely the most convenient choice, though I loathed the idea of passing actual letters. What if they were found? What danger did that present to the young princess? Still, that was the option I was given, and I would have to work with it till a better opportunity arose.

The door outside slammed shut, startling Arden, who leaped from the window and took off into the sky. After a moment, my bedroom door opened, and Agramon came in, looking first to the bed, before finding me standing at the window in my chemise.

"Planning another escape?" he asked, his voice icy.

I frowned. "It wasn't my fault. I was tired, and it was harder to control my powers. I tried to tell you, but you didn't want to listen."

"And when were you going to tell me of your ability to fly?" Agramon asked, pulling the chair out from my dressing table to sit. "That was a juicy tidbit of information that I would've appreciated on the first day of our acquaintance."

"I can't fly," I said, looking away. "At least, not really.

I'd only used it once before, and it merely softened a fall."

Agramon glowered. "I'm sure that if you practiced enough, you could fly very well. You just need to control the direction and strength of the wind. The last sorcerer who had the ability was Matine Wind-Surfer. She died about ten years ago, but she worked at the university for a time, so they may have some knowledge of her powers and what she did to control them. Del will accompany you to the university library tomorrow before your lesson with the Butcher. Bring back any texts that you find may be useful, and we'll go over them together."

I nodded. When Agramon made it clear that he expected me to speak, I added, "Thank you."

I FELT THE LETTER BURNING a hole in my pocket as I walked to Princess Willene's chambers. Ever since I'd written it, I'd felt vulnerable, second-guessing each look that Agramon shot me that morning.

I threw worried glances over my shoulder at the guards and nobles I passed in the halls, sure that I was being spied on, positive that each person I passed knew about the damning letter in my pocket. I didn't breathe a sigh of relief until I finally made it to Willene's, yet even there I was not safe. What if Willene asked me to turn out my pockets? What if she saw me pass the letter to Lesedi the Younger? Would I even get the chance to exchange the information with her?

It was just my first official day spying on Agramon for the empress, and already I was regretting my decision. I was sure I would be found out at every turn.

When I entered the high princess's chamber, she greeted me as she normally did, with a scowl and a cold nod at my embroidery. I avoided her eye and took a seat beside Ledi instead of across from her, as I normally did.

Sure that my cheeks were ablaze, I picked up my embroidery round and began stabbing the needle through the fabric, peeking up at Princess Willene through my hair. She was sitting with her back to us, writing correspondence with a beautiful feather quill. Her slave girl, Anuta, faced us as she put a kettle to boil on the hearth.

Willene usually finished her morning correspondence before giving Ledi and me her full attention, which meant that the best time for me to pass information to the young princess was when I first arrived. I took a deep breath and pulled the letter from my pocket using my embroidery round like a shield, then pressed my letter to the back of it with one hand, while using the other to stab the needle down once more.

Ledi's eyes seemed to follow my movements. She glanced up at Willene, then checked Anuta's position before tilting her head to the side and examining my embroidery work.

"You've done it wrong," Ledi said calmly, pointing to the odd stitchings I'd made in my haste. She took the embroidery round from my hand, her fingers replacing mine on the letter, and undid the stitches before making new ones. "Here, like this," she said, carefully stitching the little *x*'s where they belonged.

I was so frightened, I couldn't register to do anything but nod. Willene shifted in her seat, as though she'd turned to watch Ledi correct my needlework, before the chair creaked and the high princess rose.

Ledi handed the embroidery round back to me. "There, now you try," she said with a smile.

I took the embroidery with trembling fingers, but the letter had disappeared. I looked up at Ledi, shocked by her sleight of hand, but she'd already returned to her own needlework, humming as she stitched around the outline of a blue bird, her stitches infinitesimally small and perfect. Clearly the young girl knew far more about being a spy than I did.

"Thank you," I murmured, trying to make my stitches as small as Ledi's. After *tsk*ing at my botched embroidery, Princess Willene sank onto the couch across from us. She pulled her own, much larger, embroidery stand toward herself and began stitching while Anuta served the tea.

"Tell me about your father," I whispered when my nerves had calmed.

Princess Ledi glanced at Princess Willene, who was having words with Anuta over the tea service. "What do you want to know about him?" she asked, her voice soft as she turned her eyes back to her work.

I made another stitch, then glanced up at Willene, making sure she was still occupied. "Is he kind to you?"

Princess Ledi bit her lip. "He's always busy on the empire's business. To be truthful, we don't spend much time with him."

"But your mother?" I asked. "She takes great pains in your education, does she not? Even more so than the princesses of the past, it would seem."

Ledi nodded. "It's in her culture. At Ember Innes, where she's from, rule is passed down to the eldest, no matter the gender. She's always viewed me as heir. Though . . ."

"Though what?" I asked when she didn't continue.

"It's not like it will do me any good," Ledi said, stabbing her needle through the fabric harder than was warranted. "The only one Father expects anything from is my brother."

"But hasn't your mother shown you how much power

can be had from behind the throne?" I asked.

Princess Willene turned her attention back to us. "I hope you're talking about the importance of small stitching and not gossiping, ladies," Princess Willene said. I swore her icy-blue gaze could cut through glass. "It seems there is a shortage of silphium at the capital. As I assume that none of us are engaged in child-bearing activities, I have agreed to serve the alternative until more can be procured." Her eyes were on me, almost questioning. I felt my face redden. Some might assume that of me and Agramon, but as much as I disliked the man, I had to be thankful that he never touched me.

"I didn't realize silphium was in lady's tea," I said instead of addressing Willene's silent question.

"It was a change my mother brought," Ledi said, brightening at the change in topic. "She told me when she first came to the capital, silphium was only reserved for the noble ladies, and it was a great secret that you had to buy from witches who practiced in dark alleyways or seedy taverns. So, Mother worked with an apothecary to create lady's tea. Once the recipe was perfected and tested, she distributed it to all the apothecaries in the city. Now anyone can buy it. Here at the palace, lady's tea is served to all the girls over the age of twelve. Women at Somme have made a thing of it, inviting their friends over for lady's tea and practicing their needlework or gossiping about their neighbors."

"Though, now that it's available to everyone, we have shortages at times," Princess Willene said, motioning the slave girl over to set the tea service on the table before us. "There was never a shortage before. The empress even allows the slaves to drink it, though it goes against all reason. We want them to be fruitful."

Ledi ignored Willene and went on, "Some ladies have even said it makes their courses run smoother, more predictably, and others have said that it lessens their cramps. Lady's tea changed many ladies' lives here at the capital, which is why Mother is so loved."

"Enough talk," Willene snapped at Ledi. "I wish to hear how you've progressed on the lute. Perhaps Rowyn would grace us with a newer, much more appropriate, song."

Chapter 20

"ARE YOU READY TO GO to the library?" Del asked, practically bouncing on her toes when she came upon me during the empress's luncheon.

I tried not to let my irritation show, especially since I could've done with a nice nap, but I plastered a smile on my face and nodded, motioning Del to lead the way. It wasn't Del's fault that Agramon was a tiresome bully. I didn't need to take out my irritation on her. Del wound her arm through mine and led me down the hall, chattering a mile a minute about a new building she was constructing in the temple district.

"Of course, the emperor said that cost is no object, but I still try to maintain the proper balance sheets, and I keep the workers paid well too. You'd be surprised how hard it is to find crystal sculptors. Agramon had to ask Solston Gowther to commission someone all the way out in Ember Innes. The man we found is a master at his craft, but strange mannerisms if you ask me."

On and on and on she went. I tried to make it seem like I was listening, but the girl didn't even stop to seek that affirmation.

She finally brought me to the library. It was grandiose and large, with gilt chandeliers hanging low over a large room of study tables. Several stories and balconies held the largest bookcases I'd ever seen. Alas, I was getting so used to the outlandish wonders of Somme that its sheer size didn't even amaze me anymore. It was the greatest library I'd ever seen. Given that it was the library of Somme, it was everything I expected it to be.

"Tell me more of Agramon," I said when Del paused to draw breath. She seemed to be on Agramon's good side, a side I had yet to see, and I had to get more information if I was to be any use to the empress, and in turn, any closer to gaining the freedom I craved. "He seems so influential at court, but where did he come from?"

Del appeared to be thinking my question over as she scanned the aisles of books. "Well, he wasn't born into nobility," she said, running her hand along one of the book's spines.

I wasn't even bothering to read the titles. Even though Agramon had told me to find more information on this Wind-Surfer character, I knew the only reason he'd want me to nurture that skill would be to make a spectacle of myself.

Del went on, "I heard that he grew up on the streets of Solin. The old duke hadn't any heirs or anything, so when Agramon got a job as an errand boy, he talked his way into the duke's good graces, so the duke adopted him. I don't even think Agramon is his real name."

"Did he attend university here?" I asked.

Del shook her head. "No, the old emperor wasn't too keen on mind readers. Even though the old duke petitioned for Agramon to be admitted to university here, they didn't accept him. Solin has a grand library itself, grander even than Somme's. Agramon studied sorcery there and learned how to mix the tonic for the Trial by Stone and embedded his gem himself. He became one of the most powerful sorcerers in the land without formal training, without a mentor, and without any support from the university or empire."

"So, he's used to being alone," I said, scratching my nose. "Is that why he has no servants?" I'd wondered about the absence of servants since my first day at the capital. It seemed normal on the road, but at the palace, I'd expected him to have someone serving him.

Del sighed. "I tried to convince him to get one once, but it didn't work. It seems that he finds out most of the other nobles' secrets through the minds of their servants, and he doesn't want that same weakness. Anytime he needs something cleaned, or food brought up, he just uses his mind to send the request to a passing slave or servant nearby. Otherwise, no one but his charges and their handmaids are allowed in without Agramon there. He is *very* particular about his privacy and prefers to do most things by himself."

I studied Del as she squinted through her spectacles, mouthing the words to a title. "I would think he'd have a bodyguard, at least, given his position on the emperor's council as well as the Council of Five."

"Anybody going after Agramon would be a fool. He may have more magical protections on him than the emperor. Besides, there are few who have protection stones against his mind reading. He would sense an attack a mile away and be prepared against it if needed. If that doesn't work, and the attacker is immune to his magic, then a ring he wears on his hand causes iron and steel to shy away from hitting him. He also wears a necklace that neutralizes poison in anything he's eaten."

By all the gods, the man was immortal.

"Like I said, a person would be a fool to go after him," Del said, correctly interpreting the look of amazement on my face.

"Is that why you admire him? Because he's had to do so much on his own?"

"Sure, I admire him, but I also owe him a great deal. I wouldn't be half the sorcerer I am today without him."

"Do you think he aspires even higher than his current position though? Do you think he would ever go so far as to reach for the crown?"

Del snorted, then threw her head back and laughed, holding her belly with her eyes clenched shut, as though I'd made some great joke. "I'm sorry," she said, wiping a tear from her eye. "It's just, who doesn't? I'm no mind reader like Agramon, but even I know that all the men at court are trying to position themselves closer to the crown. Most think they can do a better job than the emperor, and they all actively make moves to do so."

"The Baron of Bruin doesn't seem to be that way," I said, attempting to sound off-hand.

"He's different," Del admitted, her laugh tittering off. "Samael of Bruin is one of the few men at court who actually hate it. Did you know he's only ever wanted to be a farmer? Ugh, what a drab life that would be. Don't you think so?"

I shrugged. "I've known many farmers. Most seem happy in their work . . . when it's fruitful."

"I could never abide such boredom," Del said, letting out a gust of air.

I noticed bright-blue binding with stamped gold letters reading, *Matine Wind-Surfer: A History in Memories*. I pulled the book from the shelf and showed it to Del, who brightened.

"Agramon will be pleased we found it," she said, turning on her heels and leading me out of the aisle and toward the library exit. I ran to catch up since Del was quite a bit taller than me, and her stride longer.

When we returned to my rooms, I expected Del to leave me to my assigned studies, but she plopped onto Agramon's couch in his receiving room and helped herself to a fig from the fruit bowl. I gritted my teeth, annoyed by her presence. Even though maintaining the girl's friendship held strategic value for me, I couldn't help but admit that, though Del was considered one of the capital's favorites, I didn't entirely like her. She talked far too much and only listened if what I said was a juicy bit of gossip she could pass on to her other friends.

I stopped listening to her prattle as I feigned flipping through the book about flying and instead reassessed my other allies. The empress was the most surprising one I'd gained since entering the capital. As far as I knew, Ledi had given the empress the letter about my dream and Agramon taking over correspondence to the nobles across the Eastern Empire. If she was instrumental in helping Vianne flee Agramon's clutches, which I had no choice but to believe, then she was my best bet in escaping the capital unscathed.

Mellan Lyon was rapidly rising in my esteem, despite all my best wishes. I'd already decided to corner him at dinner that evening and find out more about his work helping slaves escape their bonds. I'd heard the guards speak of the Shadow Rogue in my brief time at the capital, but even though Mellan Lyon's moniker was *hero*, it seemed a stretch for him to claim the honored title for Ylirian slaves. He drank far too much and had a reputation for philandering as much as the emperor did. On top of all of that, he was a Lyon. In my experience, all seven of those brothers had been raised to be spoiled brats who treated women with disregard and had no interest in preserving, let alone saving, human life or doing the right thing. Each had only ever shown that they'd been raised to be as cruel as their father. But Mellan seemed different.

Finally, there was Sam. Out of all my allies at the palace, Sam was the most unlikely, as well as the most useful. I remembered hearing tales of the Butcher of Bruin and the rain of fire he poured over the Ylirian tribes. Even before the war, he'd been known to quash rebellions with brutal force and efficiency. By all accounts, he should be even lower on my ally list than Mellan Lyon, but for some reason, he seemed to take it upon himself to act as my protector against Agramon. But why? Who was I to him?

Remembering the look on his face when I'd returned from my brief flight from the capital the other night, I found myself even more confused as to his motives. He'd looked so stricken. When I was done retching, it was Sam who carried me up to my rooms, Agramon trailing behind us. Since I'd arrived at Somme, Sam seemed uncommonly concerned with my welfare. I thought back to our weapons training session. The one question Sam asked that I couldn't bring myself to answer.

Did I love Destrian?

Even if the answer was yes, why would Sam bring himself to care?

Sam had already proven to be useful more than once when it came to Agramon. I favored the Butcher more given the fact that he and Agramon seemed to be enemies in a way, and I was inclined to believe that Agramon's enemies were probably people I should count as friends. I had to keep Sam close as an ally, whatever the cost.

Chapter 21

I**T WAS NO SURPRISE** when I spotted Mellan by a barrel of wine at the banquet that evening. When he saw me coming toward him, he took a hurried drink and tried to slip away, but I proved to be much faster.

"Oh no you don't," I said, blocking his exit. "I want the story. The whole story."

Mellan glanced around us. "Not here," he whispered, leaning into my ear. "I give you my word, I'll ask Agramon if I can take you out into the city. I can't speak of it here. I can't even think about those things, or else one of the mind readers will catch me. Don't talk about it again at the palace." Mellan squeezed my arm. "Promise me you won't mention it again."

I nodded, realizing my foolishness. If I continued to carry on that way, I would surely get the young man killed, and I didn't want that . . . yet. "I promise, but you'd best take me out soon, or I'll have to corner you at the palace and rip the story from your throat."

Mellan waggled his eyebrows. "You make it sound far more titillating than it should be," he said. "I have to get out of here. You've already tainted my thoughts as it is. If Agramon listens in at this moment, I'm done for."

I grabbed his hand. "Did they make it out?" I whispered.

Mellan looked down at me in surprise. "They're sailing home as we speak."

I released him, and Mellan glanced at Agramon before heading in the opposite direction toward the exit.

"So, how's my little wind-screamer?" asked a voice behind me. I turned, about to offer a pert reply, when I recognized the emperor, flanked by a bodyguard I hadn't met.

I choked back my retort and instead lowered myself into the curtsy that Princess Willene drilled into me during my first lesson at the capital. "I am well, Your Eminence, and I thank you for your concern."

The emperor smiled as though me getting swept off the balcony was some great joke. "Where did you end up landing, anyway? They only told me that you'd made it back safely."

"A rooftop, Your Excellency, near the docks," I said, careful to keep my head bowed.

The emperor guffawed, slapping the bodyguard's shoulder as though he were in on a joke at my expense. "If that's not a Sol's surprise, I don't know what is. Tell me, my pet, is there anything you can't do?"

"Keep my temper?" I offered, raising an angry brow. "How's Captain Diardo? I haven't seen him since his injury. Was Lord Tristam able to heal him?"

The emperor glowered. "I'm not sure. I haven't had the time to go see him. I only know that he's still on the mend and hasn't been able to return to service."

I raised my brow higher in concern. "Aren't you two supposed to be great friends or something?"

Now the emperor was downright angry. I could tell by the way his eyes grew icy, much like his sister's did when they studied me. "I don't much like your tone, girl. Do you know to whom you speak?"

The empress appeared beside the emperor, her hand on his chest. "Your Eminence," she said, shooting me a wink, "Lord Ramin has the most entertaining idea for your birthday celebration this fall. I'm not sure it's Miyu's style, but it sounds like something you would enjoy."

The emperor perked up and smiled. "What is it this time?"

"You'll not hear it from me, my lord. It's far too improper." The empress laughed, sliding her arm through his and leading him to the other side of the hall.

I let out a sigh of relief. As I did so, I looked around the hall for a friendly face. Del had decided to stay in the city with her lover that evening, and Mellan had already left the hall. I shrank inwardly as I realized I was well without friends. I glanced at Agramon, trying to meet his eye and silently ask permission to leave, but he was lost in conversation with a nobleman. I was just about to make my way over to him when I was startled by someone staring daggers at me nearby.

He was an ancient man with pale skin covered in sunspots, and a crooked spine. He wore the white robes of Somme, though unlike the nobles, whose robes reached their knees, his fell all the way to his feet. A large golden sunburst and chalice, the symbol of a Solston, took up the front. I frowned. Why was a priest glaring at me? The man gripped his cane in his gnarled hands and began stamping toward me, his eyes narrowed as though angry, though for what I could only guess. I'd never met the man in my life.

"So, this is the great witch," the Solston said, speaking loudly enough that several nearby turned to see what the commotion was. "The child of darkness who will be the doom of Lyrica!" He pointed at me as I froze, shocked at his declaration. The Solston wasn't addressing me, but rather, the crowd of nobles around me whose attention he now held. "The black gods are using these children of shadows to tempt us away from the true light of Sol. Forgive yourself for being drawn in, for they come in pretty packages, revered as saviors to the weak, but our true dawn is approaching! Those who seek to drag us back into the shadows will be the first to feel the wrath of Sol!"

The Solston threw something at me, and I raised my arm instinctively. The vial was knocked away, but not before some of the liquid splashed onto my dress. My skirt ignited as screams and shouting filled the air. The vial rolled beneath the banquet table, erupting into a massive trail of fire. I tried to push through the crowd, ripping at my skirt as the flames licked my legs, and a searing pain erupted over my flesh.

Smoke choked the air as a massive surge of people tried to escape. I was knocked down but kept kicking at the fabric melting around my legs. Steps thundered around me, and I had a fleeting thought of either being trampled by the crowd or burned to death. A bloodcurdling scream pierced my ears, followed by the sounds of thrashing. The noise reached a crescendo of violence as people tripped over me, bruising my ribs and arms. I rolled on the ground, trying to get away from the stampede of feet, trying to put the fire out, trying to do everything I could to survive.

Suddenly, I was doused in a torrent of water. I coughed and sputtered, trying to catch my breath in the smoke-clogged air. My dress was no longer alight, but the pain in my legs had sweltered and intensified. I moaned, crying as every nerve seemed ablaze. I tried to move, but even the slightest twitch of muscle caused such immense pain that I froze in a pool of water, watching the smoke curl about me.

It took a moment for me to register the voices around me. The smoke began to thin, and an acrid smell filled the air. The scent of burnt flesh and wood mixed with the heaviness of water nearly choked my lungs as much as the smoke did. I looked around as much as I could without moving my head and realized I was lying in the middle of the room.

There was someone on the ground in front of me facing the wall on the far side of the room. Her dress was in tatters, with blackened fabric all along the back. A figure appeared, and a hand turned the woman over. Her throat and chest were black, the flesh seared almost to the bone. Lifeless eyes stared up at the ceiling, and I choked in terror, wracking my body in a new bout of pain. The figure moved toward me, their upper body hidden in the clouds of smoke that drifted about the room. Feet stepped beside me, and whoever it was kneeled, their hands on my shoulders, pushing me to my back.

I screamed. Agramon's eyes were fierce as they took me in, his brow furrowed as he surveyed the length of my body, his gaze lingering on my legs.

I grabbed his hand, the pain making each movement excruciating. "Please," I said, tears stinging my cheeks. "Make it go away!"

Agramon placed his hand on my forehead and closed his eyes. A rosy glow filled my eyesight, and my head dropped to the side as I floated away from the pain of Somme.

A GILDED CAGE

MY DREAMS CAME IN FLASHES. I watched myself being carried down to the healing rooms where Tristam the Miraculous barked orders and worked miracles on those injured in the fire. The empress and her noble ladies were busy assisting with the injured, along with a host of healers who seemed to appear out of nowhere.

Tristam stopped beside my bed, Agramon at his side with staff in hand as Tristam assessed my scarlet legs, the skin wrinkled and blistered.

"She will live," Tristam said simply, motioning the empress to his side. "Undress her as best you can and ready her for treatment. Once they are finished mixing the tonic, I will bless it. With Sol's help, we'll save her legs."

"She is to receive the first treatment," Agramon said, grabbing Tristam's arm as he began walking away. "The council wishes Rowyn to have priority in treatment, do you understand?"

Tristam glared at Agramon, pulling his arm from his grip. "We've already lost Lord Cassius. Though Rowyn is gravely injured, she *will* live, unlike some of the other souls down here. This is my healing house, Lord Agramon. You can't give me orders here."

"I will notify the emperor about this," Agramon

snapped, his voice hard. "You know that we share the same wishes in this case."

"Get him out of here," Tristam shouted. Sam appeared and stepped toward Agramon, who tried to puff himself up to greater size, glaring at Sam as though he were nothing more than the dirt on his shoe. Sam nodded toward the door.

"You will regret this," Agramon seethed, storming toward the door. "She'd better be back to normal, Tristam, or I will have your hands for this!"

Tristam turned away and went right back to work, walking among the beds and giving orders to the ladies and healers. Sam watched Agramon leave before returning to my side beside the empress.

"She will be all right?" he asked as the empress motioned someone to her. Ena appeared, her face drawn as she clutched a clean white sheet.

"She'll be fine," the empress said without pausing in her work. "If you want her to heal, you must give us space to do our jobs."

Sam nodded and stepped back, allowing Ena to lift the blanket to cover me from view as the empress took a pair of scissors and began cutting away the fabric to my clothes. At some point, I felt her dark hands at my waist, unfastening the Girdle of Ephema and slipping it into her pocket as she looked over her shoulder. Once I was naked, she helped Ena lay the clean sheet over me, and the empress smoothed back my hair and patted my hand before moving on to the next bed.

Chapter 22

I T TOOK THREE WEEKS for Tristam to decide I was well enough to leave the healing house. Ena was an excellent nurse, not just to me, but to others confined as well. Though the empress and her ladies would spend a few hours a day in the healing house, it was Ena who worked doggedly from morning until nightfall, changing bed linens, spooning soup to those who couldn't feed themselves, and mixing new tonic for the burns.

Agramon was barred from seeing me the first week of my stay in the healing house, while Sam visited every day at the time we would normally be training. He would stroll in with his favorite glass of amber liquor and sit beside me, leaning back in the chair and propping his feet on the side of my bed. Some days he would tell stories of the battle-field, while others he would teach me songs the soldiers would sing around the fire. I was pleasantly surprised to find that Sam was a gifted singer. Mellan would often come down to the healing house during Sam's visits, even joining him in song if the mood took him, adding verses far dirtier than the baron's.

Del would visit as well, though I didn't look forward to it. She would sit and go into excruciating detail about the court gossip that I couldn't care less about. The only interesting news she brought was that the emperor publicly flayed the Solston who had started the fire before hanging his body in the doorway of the great Temple of Sol.

"Weren't the other Solstons upset?" I asked, scooching up in bed so that I could easily reach my water.

Del shrugged. "There has been a lot of arguing in the temples. Apparently, the Solston who tried to kill you was from one of the border cities. Agramon thinks the seer, Chassandre, had something to do with it."

"What did she say?"

Del pursed her lips. "She denied it, of course, but also warned that the Solston spoke the truth. Elgar says there have been whisperings in the border towns and even here in Somme that you aren't the hero the emperor has presented you to be. He says they've begun to call you Imor's fiend. Their story is that you're using your powers of darkness to turn everyone against Sol's light."

I raised my brows. The girl I was a year ago would've felt guilty for being the cause of the pain inflicted on others using my name, but I was past that now. I didn't start the fire. I wasn't Imor's fiend, and it wasn't my fault I was born with this power, nor that the emperor dragged me to Somme in the first place. If they didn't want me in the eastern lands, then it was just as well for me.

Perhaps their enmity would be the last straw, and it would force the emperor and Agramon to send me back. I considered that for a moment, my heart lifting, but deep down I knew it was false hope. Even if Agramon decided to send me back, the Solston made it clear that simply leaving Somme wouldn't be enough. They'd proven three times now that they wanted me dead, once with the golgeman, again with the assassin in the market, and a third time with the fire in the banquet hall.

I lay back in bed, ignoring Del who'd begun outlining the repairs to the banquet room. Given her talents, she was put in charge of bringing it back to its former glory, especially since there was a delegation from Lu Shen due to arrive in a month's time. She'd stopped all work on her crystal temple and relocated her employees to the palace so they could finish it faster.

Despite hating being confined to my bed, I had to admit that I needed the rest, not just for my body, but for my mind. I'd never had a chance to fully recover from my journey to the Nightlands before Agramon had whisked me away to the capital. I spent the days sleeping, letting the tonic rubbed into my legs work its magic. Though the empress was often nearby, she seemed careful not to pay more attention to me than what was warranted, but she did help me don a short tunic after a week.

"Agramon will be allowed to visit you tomorrow," Lesedi whispered as she leaned me forward, Ena waiting patiently behind her. I felt the heavy gems at my waist as she used the movement to disguise clasping the girdle back on. "I think the danger of Tristam discovering my gift has passed."

Once dressed, Lesedi winked at me, then went on to attend another while Ena stayed to tuck me into bed. "How are you feeling, my lady?" Ena asked, sitting beside me and grabbing a bowl of soup from the table. She began spooning it into my mouth since my hands were still burnt and sore from the ordeal. I took it gratefully, taking great swallows as I watched her face. The last time I'd seen her that subdued was our first night on the ship from Dark-port.

"What's wrong?" I asked.

Ena shook her head as she spooned another bite into my mouth.

"I won't eat any more until you tell me what's bothering you," I said, resting my hand on her arm.

Ena sighed as she lowered the bowl and spoon. "Some servants have begun talking," she whispered, looking over her shoulder. "They are sharing false stories about you . . . about us."

I raised my brows. "Oh?"

Ena nodded. "I don't think I can stay in the servants'

hall anymore, Rowyn. I don't feel safe there."

"Has anyone threatened you?" I asked, my voice dropping low so the lady in the bed beside mine couldn't hear.

Ena shook her head. "Not really . . . not yet anyway. It's just, I worry it's only a matter of time."

I sighed, lying back and doing my best to keep from clenching my fists. I was beginning to feel so angry at the world. Ena, sweet and innocent Ena, was being dragged into my problems. I cursed Imor for putting her in danger.

"I'll get us out of this," I said finally, knowing that I still had to be careful with what I said. "I'll get us out of this, and in the meantime, I want you to move your things to my room. My bed is big enough for both of us, so you can just stay there when I return as well."

Ena lowered her eyes. "I don't think Agramon will like that," she murmured. "I've been going up to feed Arden and tidy a bit, and every time he sees me, he shakes his head and rolls his eyes, as though my presence is some great burden."

I clenched my teeth. "I need to send you home, Ena."

Ena's hands began trembling so badly that she had to place the soup back onto the table. "No, my lady, that's not what I meant. I wasn't trying to return to Morgania. I wouldn't leave you here all alone."

I shook my head. "I'm going to speak to Agramon, and I'm going to have him send you back. I won't have you risk your life for me. I'm not worth it."

Ena's voice broke. "Please, my lady, that's not what I want. I'm proud to serve you, and I can't let you face this path alone."

"Ena . . ." I began, then stopped. If I was being honest with myself, I didn't have the heart to send her back. Hers was the one true friendship I had at the capital. Seeing Ena every day gave me strength. Besides, I couldn't break the girl's spirit by sending her back when her heart was set on staying. "I can't fight with you over this. If you wish to stay, then I will speak to Agramon about what we can do to keep you safe." Ena sniffed, then nodded, picking the bowl of soup up once more.

WHEN I WAS FINALLY RELEASED to return to my rooms, I felt as good as new. Tristam had worked diligently to heal the skin on my legs until I couldn't even tell I'd been injured. The sleep did wonders for my state of mind, especially since Echo had decided to leave my dreams alone during my convalescence.

So, I was practically skipping when Agramon took me back to my rooms, and my heart soared when I found two letters written in familiar scripts. I grabbed them from the table and immediately noticed the wax seals were broken. Shooting a glare at Agramon's back, I practically threw myself on the bed as I shuffled through the papers. My heart sank when I realized the absence of one letter I'd been dearly looking forward to reading. I'd sent three letters to Solridge. Three letters that I was sure I would receive an answer to. Yet, there were only two in my hand.

I swallowed hard as I opened the first.

> *Dearest Rowyn,*
>
> *I have made it back to Solridge and can assure you that Lord Obi is well and has regained his strength and normal grouchiness. This year's batch of ale was particularly good (so he says) and has kept him in fine spirits during our evening visits. I've also begun playing chess with a new student in the library here. Pat doesn't let me win nearly as much as you did, but it's still fun, and Lord Obi has taken quite a shine to his sense of humor.*
>
> *We heard a troubling account from a bard during a visit to Seaport that had us all scratching our heads. It was about your and Destrian's journey to the Nightlands, and how you played him false in love. The new students were very diverted by the tale, but I assured as many as I could that it couldn't be true and that you would never betray someone in that way. I don't know how many I convinced,*

considering Ingrid was working against me the entire time. But I figure you could've probably guessed that.

There is something that I must tell you that I know will upset you greatly. Fin has disappeared.

Though I heard that Fin and Master Haris had returned from Horan together, Fin was missing by the time I reached Solridge from Livian. There is also a rumor that Fin never returned at all, and that whoever came back with Master Haris was a changeling who ran away and that Fin could still be trapped in Horan, whether it be willingly or not.

I'm sorry I must be the one to tell you this. I know how much her friendship means to you and I know that it will only make you worry, but you have a right to know.

I miss you and can't wait to see you at the quinquennial. (You'll be there won't you? Everyone who's anyone will be there.)

Your forever friend,
Pedr Tore of Livian

I couldn't comprehend what Pedr wrote. My heart pounded wildly, and my power pulsed beneath my skin. A blast of lightning crashed outside the window. My hands shook uncontrollably as I stilled the glow of the stones.

Agramon appeared in the doorway. "I'm sorry about your friend," he said, though his tone hinted that he felt I was overreacting. "Wasn't that one General Ivar's illegitimate daughter?"

"She was more than just an illegitimate daughter," I snapped, running my sleeve over my eye as I opened the other letter in the vain hope that it would contain happier news. It didn't. Araceli went into much more detail. She stated that she'd seen Fin return, and that she didn't seem to be herself. She kept riding out of the school grounds alone until one day, she rode out and didn't come back.

Araceli went on.

> *She spoke of you, Rowyn. She said that she couldn't wait to see you again, and that your destinies would forever be intertwined.*

I broke into sobs. Heavy footsteps left the room, then lighter ones returned. The bed bowed, and Ena's cool hand ran down my forehead as I wept into a pillow.

Scratching on my dresser drew my attention to Arden, who tilted her head at me worriedly, the rain outside my window drumming a steady rhythm of sorrow that I felt in my bones.

Fin, my truest friend, the one who made Solridge feel like it could be home to me, was gone. Was she hurt? Did she need my help? Had she gone willingly, or had she been taken? Perhaps her father had requested her back to his household after learning of her gaining her stone. Perhaps I would see her at the university. Could Horan have been her downfall? I'd heard of changelings before, little creatures that could morph into the forms of men and deceive everyone, even the men's wives. It was a common tale on the borders of Horan. The Woltari, or the Others, as they were commonly known in the West, had always been mischievous creatures whose magic rivaled that of any sorcerer.

"I'm sorry," Ena said while she hugged me close. The tears flowed freely, making my pillow damp. I wanted to find my friend. I wanted to leave and launch a search. I wanted to look in every nook and cranny for the girl who could speak with animals. But Agramon would never let me leave, especially since we had our big journey approaching. I had yet to fulfill my obligation to the empire, one that I doubted would ever end.

"I know you love her, and I know you want to help find her, but she has her stone now. Your gems changed you a great deal, so perhaps Fin's stone changed her as well."

I nodded, trying to see the truth in Ena's words. Still, I couldn't help but weep for the friend who seemed to have lost her way, or maybe she had even lost her life.

Chapter 23

"ARE YOU GOING TO ATTEND dinner this evening?" Agramon asked when I returned from visiting with Del a few days later. After the first day of grief for Fin's disappearance, Agramon had come into my room and announced that my time wallowing in bed was over, then promptly ordered me back into my routine.

I visited Willene's in the morning and told stories of Fin and me to Ledi, who listened with rapt attention. At the empress's luncheon, I would exchange small talk with Del, slipping in tidbits about how much I appreciated Agramon's taking care of my welfare and how I adored my wardrobe, hoping they would find their way back to his ears. My evenings, on the other hand, were left free. Agramon used my recent injury as an excuse to take a break from weapons training with Sam, and the emperor's banquets were postponed until Del finished repairing the hall. So, I hadn't seen Sam in several days except in passing.

Echo's dreams also returned. I learned that the emperor was sending out Bald Walden to ferret out any more assassination plots. He was also tasked with bringing the

Shadow Rogue to justice but had yet to have any luck capturing him. I learned that Miyu was assisting with the Lu Shen trade talks, and though the emperor was advertising that he wanted a Lyrican port in Lu Shen in exchange for a Lu Shen port in Lyrica, what he really desired was better access to their explosive black powder so that Berinon could figure out their secret recipe.

All the information I wrote in my secret letters to the empress. Echo was not only the perfect spy but also the perfect sentry, and could easily alert me when either Agramon or Ena returned unannounced.

"Del finished with the repairs to the hall," Agramon continued, looking up from his desk where he was writing a letter with a peacock quill. "Which means the emperor's banquet is tonight. There is a noble who's been asking to meet you."

Not seeing any way out of it, I nodded. "Was there something in particular you wanted me to wear?" I'd learned in my short time here that Agramon was far more amenable when I consulted him on things, no matter how small the question, or how little I really cared about his response.

Agramon glared at me with suspicion. I gave him a hopeful smile, and he shook his head while setting his quill in his inkpot and rising to stride to my bedroom. Opening the wardrobe, he flipped through the dresses before pulling out a rose-colored gown the exact hue as his gem. The skirt was made of gauzy fabric that draped over the shoulders and had a low bodice, which flowed down into a skirt that would billow as I walked. He held it out to me, as though daring me to challenge him.

I took the gown from his hands. "Thank you," I said, "I'll tell Ena."

Agramon left without another word.

"ARE YOU SURE YOU'RE READY to go socializing so soon?" Ena asked as she arranged my hair in voluminous curls, held up by a small braid that wrapped around the back of my head.

"I'm afraid of what the duke will say if I don't," I admitted as she shoved in another pin.

Ena turned my head this way and that, examining her most elaborate style yet. "I know what it's missing," she said with a sly smile. She left, and I listened to her rummage around the receiving room while I stroked Arden's head. The falcon had to have been someone's pet at some point, for she didn't have the fierce reputation shadow falcons were known for in the wilds of Morgania. I had to admit, I enjoyed the company of the bird, and Arden always managed to lift Ena's spirits.

When Ena returned, she held out four pink roses. "Hold still. They still have thorns," she said as she began to fasten them in my hair.

"Where did those come from?" Agramon didn't keep fresh flowers in the receiving room as far as I was aware, but I'd seen them earlier when I passed through.

Ena shrugged. "I've no idea. They were just sitting in a bunch on the back table when I came in."

I wondered about their presence, but I couldn't deny Ena that the flowers did look well with the dress. Perhaps Agramon left them himself in honor of the dress he chose. It wouldn't surprise me if he had.

The duke came as soon as Ena had pinned the last rose in place. Standing at the door to my room, he crossed his arms, his staff resting against his shoulder as he studied me.

"You learn quickly, Ena," Agramon said.

Ena blushed, unable to contain the glow of pride that illuminated her face.

"She's certainly outdone herself," I agreed, rising and joining Agramon at the door.

ELLIOTT VANDRUFF

THE GREAT HALL WAS BUSTLING as everyone admired Del's renovations. She'd finished in record time considering the damage. Miyu directed a troupe of musicians to one corner where they took their seats and began to play.

I sighed as I surveyed the room beside Agramon. I spotted Mellan by the university students. Though he waved, he didn't approach, likely due to my proximity to Agramon. Mellan had made a point to visit me a handful of times at the healing house, but I could never be too sure if it was because he was supposed to be courting me, or if he genuinely enjoyed my company.

"Where is this noble of yours that you wanted me to meet?" I asked, looking at the sea of faces around the room.

A servant appeared holding a tray of drinks. Agramon took two glasses and placed them on the sill of the arched window beside us.

"Do you see that man, over there," Agramon said, pointing to an older lord lounging on a low couch, his fingers swollen and dripping with gold rings crusted with gems. Gray peppered his otherwise-dark hair, and his lips were drawn into tight lines as he eyed the largesse around him, his eyes resting on the young ladies decked out in their finery.

"Yes," I said, watching the old man with growing distaste. There was a young lady beside him, her ochre skin overly rouged, and her smile empty.

"That's Count Balthazo of Gryse and his daughter, Jamilla," Agramon said as he thrust one of the glasses in my hand. "He wishes to meet you."

I wrinkled my nose. "He seems horrid," I replied, sipping the dark wine. It was strong and overly sweet, the syrupy taste sticking to my tongue as I swallowed it.

"He *is* horrid," Agramon agreed. "But you will meet with him, nonetheless. He's one of the wealthiest men in the realm."

"Isn't Gryse where the Morganian crops are sent?"

"Indeed, it is," Agramon said, though he didn't seem particularly happy that I knew that. "You look lovely in that gown by the way."

"Thank you for the compliment." Perhaps Duke Agramon wouldn't be so bad if all I had to do was smile and agree with him. I supposed it could be worse.

"Here, finish your drink and come with me," Agramon said, tipping his glass of wine back and downing it before setting it back on the sill.

I took a final gulp, clenching my eyes in distaste, before setting my glass next to his and following him out of the alcove and onto the main floor.

"Duke Agramon!" Count Balthazo said upon our approach. "I see you've finally brought your beautiful young charge to meet me!"

His daughter, Lady Jamilla, turned her sharp eyes to me, traveling from my face down to the dress. She wrinkled her nose, and I laughed, given that it was the same expression I'd worn not minutes earlier.

Count Balthazo whispered into his daughter's ear, and she sniffed before rising from the couch and disappearing into the crowd.

Duke Agramon pushed me down into Lady Jamilla's empty spot, while he settled into a chair nearby.

"Balthazo," Agramon said, sweeping his arm to me, "may I present, Rowyn the Morganite."

Balthazo turned to me with a vile smirk, his eyes on my chest. "I've heard so much about you, my girl. Of course, the rumors of your beauty don't hold a candle to the goddess beside me." The count ran his arm across the back of the couch, forcing me to lean forward lest he touch me.

I glared at Agramon, who seemed to be purposely avoiding my eye. Since nothing Balthazo said required a response, I didn't give any.

"Smile for me," Balthazo continued. "Tell me of your adventures with monsters."

"There isn't much to tell," I said, leaning away from him, "except the monsters of the Nightlands are incomparable to the beings of Somme."

"Yes," the count said, leaning closer, "and you went to the Nightlands with that young lord of Morgania, didn't you? Tell me, is he as soft as everyone claims?"

"That depends," I said sweetly, feeling a rising swell of indignation. "How soft must one be to conquer the land of lost heroes?"

I didn't know what I expected, but it wasn't for Count Balthazo to laugh like he did, his hand finding my shoulder. "What spirit," he said to Agramon, who was rising.

"Entertain the count until I return," Agramon ordered before sweeping into the crowd of courtiers.

The count settled back onto the couch, gripping my bare shoulder and drawing me toward him. I tried to hold my ground but found myself to be far weaker than I realized and couldn't pull away. "Tell me all of Consul Destrian's secrets, or yours. I'd be content with either."

I wanted nothing more than to follow Agramon away from the odious count, but my legs tingled oddly, and my arms felt heavy.

"Did you hear me?" Count Balthazo asked, his lips close to my ear.

Startled, I turned toward him and watched his mouth move, his jowls quivering as beady eyes darted around us.

"I heard you," I said, trying to push down my panic. Something about the count seemed gentler, and I wasn't pleased with the realization that my hatred for him felt trivial now. "But if you want to know Consul Destrian's secrets, perhaps you should be cozying up to him instead of me." My legs were being wretched creatures. I tried to rise, then cursed inwardly at the lack of response from my limbs. Had Tristam's healing worn off? Was it merely temporary?

Balthazo laughed. "Tell me, how did those savages breed such a charming and lovely young girl?" He leaned toward me conspiratorially, his eyes on my neckline. The count's fingers ran down my arm, gooseflesh rising in their wake.

My ears grew hot as a fuzzy warmth filled behind my eyes. Count Balthazo passed a bowl of grapes to me, and I took one. Popping it gratefully into my mouth, the fruit burst over my tongue, and my senses flooded with pleasure at the refreshing flavor.

Despite my initial revulsion of the count, I was finding myself perfectly content in his presence within moments. In fact, I was beaming. I sank into the soft couch, not even caring when his arm cradled me to him. I remembered detesting the man, but I didn't care why.

"My lady." A voice floated down from above. Sam, his face dreamy in the brilliant light of the great hall, looked down on me, his hand outstretched. "You look as though you need some air. Would you like to accompany me to the garden?"

"Come now, man, can't you see we're busy?" Balthazo grunted at the same time that I said, "I would be delighted to."

Sam's eyebrows rose as I took his hand and he helped me rise. The feeling of euphoria heightened the farther I stepped from the count.

Sam led me through the crowd while I admired the splendor of the newly decorated hall. I hadn't noticed before how the lanterns dangling from the ceiling glowed with a rosy haze. I breathed deeply, relishing the smells drifting from the tables. We passed a lady in a silk gown with a skirt so voluminous, she looked like a flower. I ran my hand lightly on a fold in the fabric, the silk as soft as butter. She shot me a curious look as Sam pulled me to the balcony doors.

"I wouldn't wish the company of Count Balthazo on an enemy," Sam grunted as he shut the doors behind us. "He's the worst of men. It needles me when others speak ill of my misdeeds, yet never seem to mind the company of such a wretched excuse of a creature."

"He wasn't as awful as all that," I admonished blissfully, breathing in the fresh air, the jasmine scent sending me soaring. My head was clearing now that I was away from the noisy hall. The stars twinkled above us, and I was brought back to the Nightlands, with Destrian. The stars had seemed like friends, constant companions on our journey.

Sam frowned. "He's incredibly wealthy. All the

Morganian produce sent from the West goes through Gryse before it's dispatched to the rest of the Eastern Empire. The man charges outrageous taxes on the food, nearly beggaring the army and forcing my men to go hungry. I would hang the man if I could."

"Couldn't the emperor stop him?" I asked, trying to shake the warmth spreading through my mind. It was coming back like a cloud. Perhaps Duke Agramon could enchant me after all. Perhaps the Girdle of Ephema no longer worked.

"He gets his cut, of course," Sam grumbled, palming the hilt of his sword. "But I don't want to speak of this anymore." His gleaming eyes rested on me. "I was worried about you."

"How did you know to come?" I asked, tearing my eyes away to avoid the intensity of his gaze.

"You seemed to be repulsed by him. But when I saw how he was looking at you, just the thought of it . . ." Sam's grip on his sword tightened. "It isn't often that the Count of Gryse is denied. Especially when most of the court is indebted to him."

I raised my eyebrows and leaned forward. "So, you were watching me?" I asked with a hint of a joke.

Sam didn't answer for a moment. He reached out and touched one of the roses in my hair. "I noticed you'd received the gift I left for you. I thought Agramon would've tossed them from the window, so imagine my surprise to see you wearing them tonight." Sam met my eyes, then looked away, dropping his hand back down to his side. "The truth is, I'm always watching you." He looked out over the city as though to avoid my eye. "I can't seem to tear my eyes away."

My breath caught in my throat, and I was filled with a sense of excitement. Excitement and longing. The music from inside rose to a crescendo, and the fuzziness behind my eyes grew. My legs felt as though they were melting, and I stumbled when trying to reach the balustrade.

Sam caught me, his forehead wrinkling. "Are you feeling all right?" he asked.

"I think so," I said, gripping the front of Sam's jerkin. My head was growing heavier, and the warmth in my cheeks had become a roaring furnace, but the leather was welcome and cool as I rested my cheek against it, breathing in the smell of sweat and jasmine. Sam's arms wrapped around me, holding me up as a delicious tingling crawled over my skin. I brushed my nose against the soft flesh at the crook of his neck. He was close, so close that I could tell he was holding his breath. Elation swelled within. I wanted to touch him. I wanted his fingers dancing across my skin. I wanted to feel his breath mingling with mine.

One of Sam's hands shakily cupped my cheek, his fingers brushing against it. Pleasure coursed through me, spinning and leaping below my skin until it felt as though I were floating, flying through the night.

Giddiness frolicked through my veins, and I pulled Sam closer. He groaned, gripping my waist, letting me feel the strength in his hands. I sucked in a breath, lifting my chin and rubbing my cheek against his. Sam's nose brushed mine, his mouth so close that I could feel the heat of his breath. I leaned forward, my lips desperate for his, but he kept away, and his whole body stiffened.

"What is it?" I whispered, trying to reach his lips.

Sam leaned forward, but not to kiss me. Was he sniffing?

Suddenly, his hands were at my shoulders, holding me away. I reached out, seeking his warmth, but he shook his head.

His hand on my chin, he turned my face toward the light, studying my eyes as he sniffed my mouth once more. "You've been drugged," he said gruffly, his eyes searching mine. "Someone has given you sweet delight."

"What?" I sighed, nuzzling into his hand. "You're so warm."

"Rowyn, stop it," Sam ordered, dropping his hands and stepping back. "What did you drink tonight? What did you eat?"

"I haven't eaten anything," I said. The fuzziness was taking over my mind. "Wine . . . Agramon got me some wine from a servant, but I didn't like it. It was too sweet."

"Agramon did this?" Sam asked darkly, stepping back to the glass door and peering down the hall. "He gave you sweet delight, then sent you into the company of Count Balthazo?"

I could barely hear him over the ringing in my ears. I clutched the balcony, the city swimming over my eyes. Despite my gasping breaths, I couldn't seem to stop the feeling of floating. My legs failed me, and I slumped against the balcony railing. The marble felt cool against my cheek, so I leaned my face against it.

"Rowyn!" Sam said, dropping to his knees in front of me, his hands on my face.

I smiled at him. "You have such beautiful eyes."

Sam's expression darkened. "It's taken hold of you now. I dare not take you into the hall. Agramon's probably looking for you, and if he finds you with the drug in full effect, he could do whatever he likes."

"I hated Balthazo," I said, nodding vigorously in agreement.

"I'm more worried about the duke. He's not known to turn away from dandling with pretty women. He could've done this for himself as well, you know. Maybe he was hoping you would throw yourself at him."

Sam stood and glanced at the door, then shook his head. "There's too many people." He turned back to the balcony, running his fingers through his dark hair and standing it on end. "If Agramon intercepts us before we get out, I'd have no choice but to hand you over or make a scene. Neither is appealing."

I giggled again, simultaneously hating and adoring the euphoria. Sam leaned against the balcony and looked down.

"It's the only way," he murmured before crouching in front of me. "Rowyn, I'm going to climb down. When I call, I want you to jump over."

"You want me to jump off the balcony?" I asked, the smile still plastered to my face as I sat up. What an absurdity. "Did you know I fell out of a window once?"

"Rowyn, I need you to focus. Whatever you do, don't go back into the hall. When I get down, I will call, and you will need to jump."

"I wouldn't call it falling, really. I was pushed out of a window," I amended.

Sam let out a gust of air. He was adorable when he was frustrated. I reached up and tweaked his nose. "All right. I'll jump if you call."

Sam's eyes softened. "Good. Don't move until I tell you."

I closed my eyes, nodding as I leaned my face against the balustrade. When I opened my eyes again, he was gone. I wondered if I'd even be able to stand. My legs tingled as though they were both asleep. I reached up and grabbed the balcony railing, pulling myself up with great effort. Something was in my way, not letting me rise fully. I looked down and giggled when I realized I'd stepped on my gown. Lifting my foot slowly, I straightened, then fixated on the glass door to the hall. The most beautiful song was playing within. It was a delicious melody, and I began to sway to the music, stepping toward the door to listen closer. Inside, the lovely men and women of Somme were laughing, eating what looked to be the most stunning array of food I'd ever seen. My mouth watered, and I reached toward the door handle.

"Rowyn!" a voice called.

I turned. "Yes?" I called into the night, but there was no one there.

"Rowyn! You need to jump."

Oh, right. I'd forgotten. I leaned over the balcony. Sam stood a story below, his belt and sword tossed in the grass beside him.

"You want me to try to climb down?" I asked, grinning into the wind.

"No!" Sam shouted. "It will be easier if I just catch you. Jump away from the wall."

"I'm an experienced climber," I shouted back. "I climbed trees at home."

Sam's frown deepened. "Rowyn, listen to me this

instant. I don't trust you to use your skills right now. Please, before someone comes to inspect what all the shouting is about, I demand you to jump!"

I blew the hair out of my face theatrically. "Oh, all right," I shouted back, then giggled again. I sat on the balcony railing and pulled my legs over, then I felt a warm gust of air from within the hall dance around me.

"Who's out here?" someone asked as the glass doors creaked open.

In my hurriedness to jump, I didn't push away as much as I had intended, but in the moment, I didn't care. The first time I'd fallen such a long way, I'd been frightened out of my wits, but now, feeling the burst of air around me, my arms outstretched, it felt as though I were flying.

Suddenly, strong arms stole my breath with the impact, and we went tumbling into the dewy grass.

"I was sure I heard something," someone said above us.

I was lifted and carried into the shadows beneath the balcony where the jasmine was thickest.

"Where have they gone?" the person from above asked.

Sam had encased me in his arms, leaning me into the jasmine as he blocked us with his body, his eyes turned upward. He smelled so good. I rested my head in the crook of his neck and rubbed my nose into his beard. "Stop,"

Sam scolded gruffly. "I can't concentrate when you do that."

He set me on my feet, but a shooting pain cut through my haze of elation. I cried out, throwing all my weight on my leg.

"You're injured," Sam said, leaning down and feeling my ankle. "By Sol above, I'll kill him for this business."

I teetered as I gripped Sam's shoulder. He lifted me into his arms as though I were a mere child, then walked along the stone wall of the palace, keeping to the shadows until we reached the end.

Sam peered around the corner. "There's a door just over there," he said. "These halls are usually only frequented by servants, so we should be able to get to my rooms quickly."

"Why aren't you taking me to my room?" I murmured in his ear. "I have a lovely bed, with the softest sheets you could possibly imagine."

Sam looked down on me, his eyes bright. "I'm not putting you anywhere near Agramon until you're back to your senses. We'll hide you in my room for the night and find a way to sneak you out in the morning."

I grinned. "I would adore seeing your room."

Sam actually smiled. "Well, then tonight is your lucky night, my little fiend."

We were moving again. Sam was surprisingly light on

his feet despite being hampered by my weight. The night seemed to swim by, for a moment later we were in the darkened halls of the palace. I closed my eyes, feeling the energy seep from my skin as a great weariness settled in my bones. I might have fallen asleep, for in the next moment, I was gently placed on a soft bed that smelled of sweat and man. I turned over. As the hands pulled away, I grabbed one.

"What if I want you with me?" I asked, trying to pull him into the bed.

"Rowyn," Sam said firmly, his hand stopping mine. "Please . . . I can't. Not like this."

"Where will you be?" I asked, squinting into the darkness.

"The couch in my receiving room. I won't let anyone disturb you, I promise."

"Thank you, Sam," I whispered, letting my arm fall back to the blankets and humming at their softness.

"Sleep well, little fiend," Sam whispered, drawing a thicker blanket over my shoulders.

I smiled into the pillow before the drug and night lifted me away.

Chapter 24

I T WAS STILL DARK when I awoke to a pounding head-
ache. I groaned, turning over in bed and nuzzling the
pillow, my nose filling with the smell of roses. The
feeling of the sheets against my skin, the rose petals litter-
ing the pillow, and the white ceiling came as a wave of for-
eignness, assaulting my senses and sending me upright.

I'd managed to twist myself into the linen sheets at
some point during the night. I disentangled myself from
their clutches and rose, using the bed for support as a
piercing spasm shot through my leg. The room could've
been grand if anything had been done to it. The windows
were as fine as those in Agramon's suite of rooms, but the
walls had been left a stark white, empty except for the wall
at the head of the bed, which had mounted weapons arranged across it. At the other end of the room was a small
mirror with a standing table and basin mounted below it.

I approached the mirror and blanched at what I saw.
Dark circles made my eyes look sunken, as though I'd not
slept for days. Roses and petals caught within the curls of
my tangled hair. I pulled out the pins and remnants of
flowers, letting them fall to the floor as I ran my fingers
through the locks, untangling them as best I could. I

swished some of the mint water beside the basin in my mouth to get the thick feeling off my tongue while straining to remember the night before.

I remembered Sam. Agramon had done something terrible, and Sam had taken me away. A memory surfaced, me pulling Sam into the bed, trying to kiss him. I nearly choked on the mint water.

I slapped my forehead. What had I done? Agramon had turned me into an utter fool. More memories began to surface. By all the gods, how would I bear to look at Sam again? I certainly couldn't just sit on his bed, waiting for him to check on me. It was far too personal, too . . . suggestive.

I looked wearily around the room, and my eyes fell upon a tiny portrait propped up next to the washbasin. Curious, I picked it up and peered closer, then gasped, recognizing the face in the moonlight.

It was me, etched in perfect detail. The brushstrokes captured every tattoo, each curl of my hair, the exact blue of my eyes. I grabbed the tiny frame and held it closer. I was wearing a dress I wore often at Solridge. It was lavender with black lacing. It had been returned with my other clothes, but Agramon had dismissed most of my Solridge gowns as being too simple—not fancy enough. I'd never worn that dress at Somme.

My hands shook. I couldn't fathom why this piece of

me existed or why it was in the hands of the Butcher of Bruin.

I limped to the door, using the bed and walls to steady myself. I opened it to find Sam's receiving room to be just as stark and simple as his bedroom. A large table adorned with maps sat to the side, while a few mismatched wooden chairs were set before the fireplace. Sam sat in one of them, his eyes on the fire, a dagger spinning in his fingers.

When I stepped out, he looked up and stood, letting the dagger clatter to the ground. He'd donned a different tunic and breeches but wasn't yet wearing the leather jerkin I was used to seeing him in. The tunic was unlaced at the collar, revealing a smattering of chest hair. I gripped the doorframe and looked at my feet, sure I would burst into flames from shame.

"How are you feeling?" Sam asked, stepping toward me.

"I feel much better, thank you," I said, still avoiding his eye. A tear escaped and I turned away. "I'm so embarrassed," I whispered.

"It wasn't you," Sam said gruffly. "None of this was your fault."

"The things I said, the things we did . . ." I shuddered. "Please, can you just forget this all happened? I . . . I said so many things that . . ."

"We'll forget it," Sam said. He cleared his throat. I

couldn't bring myself to look at his face. "I know you didn't mean any of them."

Hurt and anger filled his eyes. When he noticed me looking, his face erased of emotion, and he was back to the hard man I was used to. I almost reached out, closing the distance between us to assure him that wasn't what I meant, but something held me back. I'd never felt so lost than in that moment. I was drifting away from myself, from everything that made me a Morganite, and I was frightened by who I was becoming.

"What's this?" I asked, holding the little painting up to the light so Sam could see. His eyes widened before he dropped his head as though ashamed. "Where did this come from?"

He was silent for a moment, but I wouldn't leave until I heard the truth. It had to have been painted at Solridge because of what I wore. And my brow bore no stone in the image.

"Agramon received it in some correspondence with Gillius. One of the young sages at the school painted it for him so the council could see what you looked like, in case you went missing. I took it from the council chamber."

"Why?" I asked, barely holding myself together. "Why did you keep this?"

Sam's chivalry the night before was forgotten. All I wanted now were answers. Why in the world did Sam have a painting of me, created before I'd even known he truly existed?

"I couldn't bear to let Agramon keep the painting for himself," Sam said finally. "He already had so much power over you and would be given so much more when you came to the eastern shore. I couldn't let him have this one little painting, so I took it when the others were distracted and hid it in my room."

"But why?" I repeated, my voice hard. "Why would the likes of you care about me?"

Sam looked up at me. "It was your eyes. I recognized the look in them."

"What look?" I scoffed.

Sam bowed his head. "You were haunted. I knew then that we were kindred, you and I, both plagued by deeds of the past."

It hit me all at once. The reason he sought to mentor me with weapons training. Him interceding with the emperor and Agramon on my behalf. His insistence that we were alike.

Sam had feelings for me.

I hadn't seen it before because I hadn't been looking, but now that it crossed my mind, it was all I could see. The way he watched me during the emperor's banquets. His and Agramon's constant bickering. I hadn't ever considered him that way. After all, though he was handsome, in a rough sort of way, he was still more than a dozen years my senior. I chastised myself. That age difference was more common than not, and more gracious than many. There'd been many a noble lady spoken of at Solridge who married men twice that age difference. For nobility, it appeared age didn't matter as much as rank or fortune.

Still Sam refused to look at me. I couldn't bring myself to admit my new realization, and I certainly wasn't going to ask. Not now, in his rooms, in the middle of the night. "We won't speak of it, then," I said softly, feeling my cheeks flush with embarrassment.

"I'll kill him for this," Sam said, breaking the silence and pulling his leather jerkin on. "It's still early. We should be able to get you back unseen." He belted his sword to his waist, then went to the door and peered out. "Come, not even the servants are up at this hour."

I hesitated at the doorway as Sam checked the hall. Not knowing why, I placed the picture back on a chest of drawers. Looking up, I noticed Sam waving me forward, so I hurried to him, wincing with every step on my injured foot. We walked swiftly through the halls, me lumbering behind him. I ignored the pain in my foot, trying to stay silent when Sam stopped us at each corner and peered around. We made it to my quarters within a few moments. The door was ajar, and the light was on in our receiving room.

Sam shoved the door open and strode in with me behind him.

"So that's where the little minx ran off to. I should've known," Agramon said, smiling at us from his couch. "Did you enjoy her?"

"If I hear of you drugging her again, I will report you to the emperor," Sam said, his hand on his sword. "Sweet delight is illegal when forced on someone."

"What I do with my ward is absolutely none of your business, Baron, no matter how much interest you take in her."

"That's the thing, isn't it though," Sam replied, his voice hard. "She isn't really your ward. She's the ward of the empire. The emperor merely assigned you arbiter of his will. What would he say if the others found out that you were actively trying to turn his most prized property into a whore?"

"Do you really think the emperor cares what Rowyn is up to during the day? As long as she brings the rain, he will be happy."

"You're probably right," Sam agreed. "You also serve on the Council of Five, which defers to you in most cases as well, given how spineless the lot of them are. But I am on the Council of Lords, and there are many there who can't abide your sorcery and are looking for any excuse to censure you. If I hear of you drugging her again, I will personally bring a case against you. Who do you think the emperor would side with then?"

Agramon scowled. "Go to your room," he ordered me.

Sam didn't even glance my way as I stepped from his shadow and limped to my door. I glanced at the two of them scowling at each other before opening my door and collapsing on the bed beside Ena.

A few moments later, the door to my room opened, and Agramon stepped in, yanking me up.

"What did he do to you last night?" Agramon hissed, peering into my eyes. "What did he say?"

Ena groaned beside me, then rolled over. "Nothing," I whispered. "He refused to touch me when he found out."

My fear of Agramon heightened when a broad smile broke over his face.

"Oh, my dear girl, it seems that I have finally found the baron's weak spot. You're far cleverer than I gave you credit for."

"I don't know what you're talking about," I hissed, yanking my arm from his grasp. "How could he have feelings for me when you forced me to make such a fool of myself?"

"That poor, suffering beau of yours holds the loyalty of the entire armed force of Lyrica. His success is partly because he holds nothing dear and takes orders to a fault. I've been trying to crack that man for years, and now I've finally been given the means to do it."

"I won't be part of such a despicable scheme," I hissed. Though Sam's feelings were still a shock, I wouldn't go out of my way to hurt him, not after he'd shown me nothing but kindness. My stomach sank, and the horrific stories I'd heard about him disappeared from the forefront of my mind, to be replaced by his brooding look as he sipped his favorite drink in the moonlight, or the way his hands softened as he corrected my stance during weapons training.

Agramon cupped my cheek. "Oh, my dear, you won't even be able to help yourself."

Chapter 25

A S SOON AS I FELL ASLEEP, I came upon a scene within the palace. Echo was following Sam through the corridors until he came to a hall that I recognized from my visit with Empress Lesedi. It was the royal quarters. Sam stopped at a paneled wall, then knocked, gripping his sword as he waited. After a moment, a hidden door opened, and Sam slipped in, followed by Echo.

The room was small but neatly furnished like Sam's. Weapons adorned one wall while several suits of armor hung along another, their golden plates gleaming in the early morning light.

"I was hoping you'd be up this early," Sam was saying to the room's occupant.

Captain Diardo shrugged, shuffling across the room while leaning against his crutch and pulling the curtains back on the windows. My heart skipped when I realized he wasn't fully healing from his altercation with the poisoned arrow. It had to have been a strong poison to have stymied the power of Tristam.

"To what do I owe the pleasure of this call?" Captain Diardo asked, sitting on the bed with a groan and propping his leg up. Sam took a seat at a small table, leaning forward onto his knees as he took in the state of the captain.

"I'm surprised Tristam isn't able to return you to a better condition," Sam said, his concern evident as he took in the wrappings still covering Diardo's leg.

Diardo shrugged again, tilting his head back and resting it on a pile of pillows. "Tristam said the poison was too quick. By the time he'd gotten a look, it had done enough damage to my leg that I nearly lost the whole damn thing."

Sam grimaced, studying his hands. "I'm sorry, old friend, I didn't realize it was so bad."

Diardo studied Sam a moment, then readjusted himself. "So, what's on your mind? I presume this isn't just a social well-wishing call."

Sam looked up from his fingers, his expression solemn. "No, as much as it should've been." Sam looked back down. "I'm worried about Agramon. He's acting even more suspicious than usual. Last night he drugged Rowyn and put her in the way of Count Balthazo. Sol only knows what he was hoping to gain from it. He's going to go too far and really hurt the girl."

Diardo sighed. "I figured this would be about her. Let me guess, the count was being a bit too handsy?"

Sam shook his head. "I grabbed her before any damage could be done."

"Gods, so much worry over one girl," Diardo said,

looking toward the window. "Do you know what my men reported to me when they returned from the market that day I got shot? They were on the ground when they saw the assassin jump from a building, and she blasted him out of the air with a bolt of lightning. The man was dead before he even hit the street. Then we find out the girl has been hiding the ability to fly. Moreover, rumors are beginning to reach us about the battle for Espiria. She ran down an entire squadron of men in plate armor with this lightning business before the Espirians slaughtered the rest. The girl has been using her powers as battle magic, and I don't think any of us are prepared for what will happen if we truly anger her. I get that you're worried, Samael, but at this point, I'm more concerned about us. She's as good as a war dog! She's never held any loyalty to the empire, and yet we're forcing her here, under duress, to perform for us whenever we please, putting up the charade that we can bridle her. You all are fools, if you ask me, and Agramon is the worst of them. Did you know he can't even read her mind?"

Sam looked startled. "What? How do you know this?"

"Agramon and the girl told us themselves."

"He can't control it either?" Sam asked, leaning back in his seat. "He can't get in at all?"

Diardo shook his head. "No, which is probably why he had to resort to drugging her to get what he wanted."

"She never told me," Sam said with a frown.

"Baron," Diardo said, his voice dripping with warning, "I hope to Sol above you're not considering getting close to this girl. We've let the enemy loose within the gates, and we'll all pay the price for this folly, sooner or later. The only person with the right idea in how to deal with the Morganite is Chassandre. The fact that she failed should serve as a warning to us all."

Sam rose, gripping his sword. "You're wrong. The enemy here is Agramon. We've let him plan and bide his time and move his pieces into place, gaining more and more power, and now he has Rowyn. It will only be a matter of time before he strikes and reaches for the crown. It's what we've suspected for years."

Diardo sighed. "The emperor has never listened to us about Agramon. Les . . . the empress is highly concerned, but Arthello doesn't listen to her as much as he should."

"There is already discontent that the empress oversteps her bounds," Sam said. "It wouldn't do to expand her influence when people already distrust her as a foreigner."

"Pah!" Diardo said, tossing his hand up. "Discontent from who? The common people in the street love her!"

"You know Solston Gowther isn't a fan," Sam said with a frown. "The Solstons at the temples have been hinting that listening to her influence will make Lyrica weak. They speak out against her as much as they do Rowyn."

"What power do the Solstons have anymore?" Diardo asked.

"Normally, I would agree with you," Sam said, "but the nobility and merchants still seek their guidance in most things. If the Solstons are speaking out against the empress, she may be in more danger than you realize."

WHEN I RETURNED FROM lunch the following day, I barely recognized Agramon and Miyu sitting on the receiving room couch. They were dressed like commoners, Agramon with a dark tunic and simple breeches, while Miyu wore a linen dress and cape. I quirked my eyebrow when they both turned to me, their conversation silenced upon my entrance.

"Rowyn," Agramon said, rising from his seat. "We're going to train outside the city this afternoon, with Miyu to assist us. Please change into an outfit that will attract less attention."

Surprised, I nodded and hurried into my room, my eyes on Miyu as she flattened her skirt. I ripped the expensive dress off my body and donned my tunic and breeches.

I practically ran back out, excitement building at the

opportunity to leave the palace, pulling my boots on as I went, before being stopped by Agramon who was standing near my door. He looked me up and down. "A cloak and gloves would be wise," Agramon said, "to cover your gems."

I turned to go back into my room.

"And Rowyn?" Agramon called after me as I flung open my wardrobe door. "Bring your sword, and whatever other weapons you can handle, just in case."

We rode out a few minutes later, and I felt more like myself than I had in weeks. My daggers were hidden along my body while Iranoct was slung at my waist. All of us had our cloaks pulled up to hide our gems, though Miyu's was more to cover her distinctive Lu Shen features. We rode quickly through the city, weaving through the bustling streets as the midday sun crawled across the sky. Before long, we were outside the northern gates and riding through farmland.

About an hour outside the city, Agramon reined his horse off the road and through a field, leading Miyu and me away from other travelers.

When the road was out of sight behind us, Agramon dismounted and helped Miyu off her horse. I leaped down, looking for any dwellings or farming fields nearby, but finding none.

"What are we doing all the way out here?" I asked,

kicking the dust into a cloud.

"We have a delegation coming that we wish you to impress," Agramon said, sweeping his cloak off his shoulders and wiping away the sweat collected on his brow. "I've spoken with Miyu, and we feel that you should train a bit on the artistic side of your powers."

"You want me to put on another show," I said, gripping Iranoct's hilt. "What's wrong with what I did last time? Couldn't I just do that again?"

Miyu shook her head. "It is not impressive, being shown something that you have already seen. All of us have seen thunderstorms before, and though yours are louder and more violent than what we are used to, the presentation we wish to put on for Lu Shen should be quieter, more beautiful."

Agramon nodded. "I don't want you to think this is silly work either. You know how to use great amounts of power at one time—that much is clear—but you need more practice in delicate and detailed nuances. You don't always need a violent tempest when a light rainstorm will do. You don't need to blanket three leagues in fog if you wish to merely disguise yourself. This might be why you had so much trouble when you were flying. You have to practice more control. Sometimes, less is more."

My blood quickened. I'd practiced some control in the Nightlands, but I'd been woefully without a teacher there, and I regrettably had little imagination with what I allowed myself to do with my powers. In some ways, I had to admit that I needed Agramon, or anyone really, to help me. "What would you have me do?" I asked, my eyes on Miyu.

"There is a poem in my land, about the rainbow after the storm," Miyu said, pulling her hood off her face. "That is the theme of our welcome to the Lu Shen delegation. The invitations will be sent in a few days, directing the court to dress according to this theme. Meanwhile, Agramon has assured me that you can provide some entertainment in the form of a show. Have you ever tried to make a rainbow, Rowyn?"

I shook my head, turning my attention to the sky. "We used to get them all the time, though, out in Espiria. They would arc over the side of the mountain, or above the trees."

"To start with," Agramon said, "call up some clouds, but don't cover the entire sky."

I raised my hands and went to work. Even with the sky partially covered, it was hot.

Miyu directed me to trim the clusters of clouds into smaller and smaller lines. Sweat began to bead on my brow, but Miyu and Agramon acted like it didn't bother them, so I didn't say anything. We worked for hours, and when they were satisfied, Agramon gave me the signal to let the rain loose, but we were all disappointed when nothing happened.

"I think there still needs to be more substance to them," I said when we mounted, exhausted.

"Instead of building them out, like you're used to, next time let's try building them up, and giving them more height," Agramon said, leading Miyu and me back to the main road.

"That just might work," Miyu agreed before dropping her voice a bit lower. "You did well today," she whispered, pulling her cloak back up over her features. "Agramon may not have remarked on it, but he thought so too."

"But I failed," I said, unwilling to meet her eye. "It didn't work."

I couldn't tell because her face was shadowed, but I could've sworn Miyu was frowning. "Nobody sees success on the first try. It might be many more days of practice till we get this right. We have several more weeks until Ambassador Liu Da arrives. We will have something when the time comes, I'm sure of it."

I pondered Miyu's assurances. All I'd wanted once was to control my powers, and today I'd taken another step toward it. I'd achieved much in controlling the clouds and rain, but even knowing that, I couldn't help but think, to what end?

It wasn't long before we were back in the city, making our way through the streets. Lamps had been lit in the shops and homes along the way, and the taverns were much busier than they'd been when we left. Townspeople rushed past us, eager to be in their homes before darkness fell, their eyes watching the rising moon with earnest.

We turned a corner and saw a band of revelers, richly dressed men with goblets, staggering through the streets. One had his arm around a woman who tried to pull away, and I was reminded of my encounter with the Lyons. Seeing the look on the woman's face, I sat straighter on the horse and pulled the dagger from my waist, but Miyu grabbed my hand and shook her head.

As the group passed a lit window, and I saw the face of the man, I froze.

It was the emperor.

Frightened, I released the hold on my dagger and shrank into my cloak, while Agramon and Miyu did the same. The raucous group moved past us. I heard the tinkling of glass as a window broke and a loud shout filled the streets. Peeking over my shoulder, I saw a man leap out of a door, brandishing a walking staff.

"How dare you!" he said, gesturing to the broken window. "You unruly ruffians!"

The emperor stepped forward, his arm falling away from the woman who shrank into the shadows.

"You must build your dwellings with sturdier materials! It was but an elbow that caused that window to cave, nothing more."

"Your Excellency!" the man gasped, falling to his knees. "I'm sorry, I just thought . . ."

"Please, think nothing of it," the emperor said, nodding to his friends with a smirk. "Apologize to these good men at once for your callous behavior."

"Yes, apologies good sirs, apologies. I should've taken better care of the house."

The emperor smiled. "Kiss their boots, so they know you really mean it."

The man paused, but the emperor took the man's walking cane and rapped him in the face with it. Falling to the ground, the man got to his knees and began kissing the boots of the emperor's friends while they laughed.

I started forward when I was stopped by Miyu reining her horse before mine and blocking the way.

"Come," Miyu hissed at me. "We don't want to be around when he gets like this."

"But," I began, then stopped. A memory flashed before my eyes, of the swinging bodies hanging from the walls of Ayastaren. I'd interfered then, and that family had lost their lives. Though the emperor was clearly belittling the man, at least he was alive.

Agramon was already turning the corner ahead, so I kicked my horse to follow. We rode the rest of the way to the palace in silence, my mind roving over the emperor's unseemly behavior, and my growing shame for leaving the man to his fate.

As we wound through the palace grounds, I noticed a solitary figure at one of the fighting fields lining up an arrow. Sam's stocky build was unmistakable as he shot the arrow, sending it to the center of the target, before grabbing another from the quiver on his back.

It was well past the time I was supposed to begin practice with him, but it saddened me that he'd been out in the field anyway, as though waiting for me to appear. I slowed my horse and dismounted, handing the reins to Miyu while Agramon waited farther ahead.

"I'll have dinner in our rooms later!" I shouted to him. I couldn't read his face, shadowed as it was from the cloak, but he nodded and turned away, followed by Miyu, leaving me to run to the practice field and climb the fence.

Upon seeing my approach, Sam leaned against the fence with his bow beside him. "I was beginning to think you were done with me for good," he grunted, his eyes returning to Agramon's and Miyu's retreating figures. "Where have you been?"

"Agramon took me to practice my sorcery," I said, pulling the cloak back and sitting on top of the fence. "It was actually a lot better than it has been. There was no one else there to see except Miyu, and I didn't feel so worried about making a mistake."

"Do you often worry about the safety of others when you use your skills?" Sam asked.

I began fiddling with the dagger in my sleeve instead of meeting his eye. "I've made many mistakes in the past and caused quite a few accidents with my skills. I prefer to practice alone, when I don't have to worry about the safety of others."

Sam didn't say anything for a long time. Finally, I looked up and noticed he was watching me. "I hope you're not embarrassed about the other night," he said. "I've already forgotten it."

I looked away again. It wasn't just about the other night. It was the dream too. It was how Sam continued to go out of his way to be kind to me.

"Not anymore, I guess. I just wish things hadn't gone as far as they did," I muttered.

"I'm sorry for that too," Sam said. "But I hope you will still join me for weapons training."

I thought back to the dream. "Can Agramon read your mind?"

Sam's eyebrows quirked in consideration. "No," he said after a moment. "I have a stone that protects me. It wouldn't do for a spy to sneak in and steal plans straight from the high commander's mind."

"Where do you keep this stone?" I asked, curious knowing there were more like the girdle.

"My sword," Sam said, pointing to the large gem embedded in the hilt. "Some others have them too. Diardo, the emperor, some of the other sorcerers and noblemen if they can pay the exorbitant price for them. They are rarer than one would think."

That made me feel better. At least I could speak freely with Sam without worrying that Agramon would find out. Perhaps that was why Agramon avoided him. But Agramon had made it clear that he wouldn't avoid Sam anymore, which meant that Sam was in danger.

"Sam," I began, then stopped, not knowing how to go on.

"What is it?" he asked, his brow creased.

"As much as I appreciate you taking the time to train me, I don't think we should meet like this anymore."

Sam stiffened. "And why is that?" he murmured, his voice dangerously low.

I took a deep breath, then looked over my shoulder to make sure there was no one nearby. "Agramon has said things, like he would try to use me to hurt you, or something of that nature. I don't think it's safe for us to be friends anymore. Not for you anyway."

Sam seemed to visibly relax. "Is that all that is? You think I'm afraid of the sorcerer? Trust me, Rowyn, Agramon's been trying for years to expel me from court, and he hasn't yet succeeded. I'm in no danger from the man."

"But . . ." I began, but Sam shook his head.

"We will speak no more about this. It isn't I who needs protecting. Now, how come I've never seen you wear these?" Sam asked, pointing to the bulge from the dagger up my sleeve. "They do no good if they aren't worn."

I sighed, realizing that my words had made no mark on the baron. At least I tried to warn him. "I don't see how women can conceal daggers in those fashionable Lyrican gowns," I complained, "so I can't wear them without Agramon finding out."

He nodded. "Many have found a way to conceal them. I'll show you as long as you promise to come to the weapons field tomorrow evening, on time. Your skills will go fallow if you don't keep practicing."

I gritted my teeth at the order but nodded. At least he didn't seem angry at me, or awkward. He was more amused than anything.

"Come," he said, straightening. "Let's see if you are as good with those blades as I suspect you to be."

I grinned as I unclasped Iranoct from my side and let it fall to the ground, joining Sam in the middle of the field.

"HOW ARE THE IMPORTS COMING this year?" Agramon asked Count Balthazo in my dream from Echo that night. They were seated in a much smaller, though lavish, receiving room. Count Balthazo was buttering a piece of bread with the ornate dagger he'd pulled from his waist as a young slave girl served him.

"Ugh, by Sol above, Morgania's imports have been low for two years straight. I've a mind to petition the emperor to send that new young consul a warning that if he doesn't match the commodity amounts from years prior, then he will be personally fined. The man's going to beggar me, Agramon."

Agramon shrugged. "The young consul hasn't even taken his vows of loyalty yet. Maybe the emperor will deem him unsuitable, and the rule of Morgania will go to another."

Balthazo's eyes sparkled. "Do you know something I don't, Duke? You must tell me at once who you suspect will take Helena if the emperor does unseat that young Everett."

"You know I can't reach into his mind, Balt, but the boy will have trouble holding Morgania when there are so many experienced nobles vying for the job. I found him to be reckless and driven by emotions when I met him, and both traits will cause him to lose his seat if he's not careful."

"Come now. Duke Lyon made a claim for the seat and failed spectacularly, losing many men in the process. You can't think unseating an Everett, especially one versed in magic, can be so easy," Count Balthazo said, frowning as he took a swig from his goblet.

Agramon leaned back, his eyes measuring the count. "You forget, Balt. The only reason the Lyons were defeated was due to Rowyn and the Espirians. The Espirians hold no loyalty to the Everetts given what I could read in the chief's and the holy man's minds, and he doesn't have Rowyn. At least, not anymore."

"What if she petitions the emperor to go home though? What then? You can't hope to have her tied to you forever. Even Del was allowed to go her own way after a time."

Agramon twisted his staff, letting the gem catch the light and reflect in the count's eyes. "Let me worry about Rowyn's future, Balt. You just need to focus on making sure your allegiances are known when it's due."

I AWOKE TO A RUSTLING at the window, but it was only Arden, preening her gray feathers before settling down again to sleep. She'd been sleeping there most nights now, probably drawn by the promise of bacon for breakfast.

I wished I could simply turn over and return to sleep, but a cold sweat had broken out over my skin. Agramon was going to go after Destrian, even after I'd taken such care. I hadn't tried to write to Destrian once. I'd refused to even think about him as much as I could, for fear that the girdle wasn't working as well as I hoped. Did none of that matter? Was Agramon going to go after him anyway? What threat could Destrian pose to my mentor? Had he attempted to contact him about me? He'd mentioned petitioning the emperor when we were in the Nightlands, though I'd known that would be a futile effort. Had Destrian done it anyway, even after my warnings?

Thankful that Ena was asleep in the receiving room, I took Iranoct down from its hook and thought of Phyranox. The image of the sword's gold sheen filled my mind, with the sunburst carved into the hilt. Iranoct's blade lowered and nudged me toward the northwest, toward Morgania, toward Destrian.

A flood of wishes engulfed me, sending me to trembling knees. I wished we had more memories of happiness together. It seemed I'd been running from my feelings throughout the Nightlands, running from the inevitable. Destrian had believed so fervently that we belonged together. I wanted to believe it with him, but now that I was at the capital, it felt so far from reality. The nobles in the

East thought nothing of the Western Empire except for the goods they sent. Even Duke Lyon, the highest ranking noble in the West, was spoken of with contempt. My only hope was the empress helping me escape. Even then, I couldn't risk returning to Destrian, even if I truly wanted to. They would know to come for me there. That would be the first place they would look.

"Echo," I whispered to the darkness. Arden lifted her head and looked at me, probably wondering who I was speaking to.

"*I'm here*," Echo hissed in my ear.

I jumped, surprised that she was right at my shoulder. "Is there any way you can send a message to Destrian?"

"No."

I knew it would be a shot in the dark, but I had to ask. "Did no shadow souls follow Destrian like you followed me?"

Again, Echo was forceful in her response. "*No.*"

"But the shadow souls are able to communicate, aren't you? I know you've been talking to the souls in the Nightlands. Is there any way one of them can find Destrian and send him a dream?"

"*Not family, no stones*," Echo said, though her tone had softened.

I sat on the bed and sighed, setting Iranoct at my side. Arden hopped down from the sill and onto my bed. I stroked the feathers on her head. "How will I get a message to him? I can't ask Ena because I'm sure Agramon reads her mind."

"*Sam*," Echo said.

Echo was right. Agramon couldn't read Sam's mind, and it certainly wouldn't put him in danger, but still . . . "No," I said after I thought a moment. "I can't ask Sam."

"*Why?*" Echo asked. A portion of the bed bowed as though Echo perched herself there beside me. Arden squawked.

Since I knew where she was, I turned to her. "I don't think he would say yes. He would want more information first, like how I knew of Agramon's threat, and I wouldn't want to give you away. We're already in danger of that necromancer woman delving deeper into finding out why you follow me around."

"Speak of friendship, not danger," Echo insisted.

I sighed. "What if he reads the letter? Besides, I wonder if he's even less likely to send it if he knows I'm reaching out to Destrian as a friend."

"*Why?*" Echo asked again. "*You trust him.*"

"Not about that," I said, picking a stray thread from my bedspread. "I just get the feeling that Sam's feelings for me are not entirely rooted in friendship. I don't think he would take kindly to me asking him to send my old lover a letter."

"*The empress then*," Echo's voice began to fade as it normally did when she spoke too much.

I wrinkled my brow. "Can Agramon read her mind?"

"*No*," Echo replied before the indent on my bed rose.

I lay back in bed, contemplating my next move as I listened to Arden return to her spot on the windowsill. The empress was probably protected just like the emperor was, and she would surely want to know the contents of the conversation between Agramon and the Count of Gryse. I was also curious about the emperor's behavior in the city. Given the old man's reaction to his bullying, it seemed a common occurrence. What sort of man treated his subjects in such a way? Didn't he have more important business to attend to? Wasn't helping the empress keep hold of power the same as keeping the emperor on the throne?

I closed my eyes and decided to request an audience with the empress.

"No more memories tonight, Echo," I said, weariness tugging at the back of my eyes. "I have a big day tomorrow."

Echo didn't have a voice anymore to agree, but she granted my request, nonetheless.

Chapter 26

I DIDN'T GET A CHANCE to speak to Mem or the empress at the luncheon. Everyone was in an uproar about the invitations from Miyu that had arrived that morning, announcing the rainbow ball to be held in a fortnight to welcome the Lu Shen's ambassador and the rest of his delegation. All talk went to dresses and jewelry and other details that held no interest to me. I tried to catch the empress's eye more than once, but she was caught up in conversations about the big event.

I trudged back to my rooms where Agramon and Miyu waited for me. After changing into my breeches, I followed them outside of the city to practice my skills. It went better than the day before, though I could tell it wasn't even close to what Miyu and Agramon wanted yet, given their expressions.

I reminded Agramon about my weapons training, and he consented to return to the palace early so I wouldn't keep Sam waiting again. Secretly, I wished to be out of the city streets before dark. If I saw the emperor behaving so monstrously again, I wouldn't be able to help myself. I would interfere and do something ghastly, something that Agramon would surely punish me for, not to mention how the emperor might react.

Even though we left earlier than before, Sam was still waiting for me in the practice field when we returned. I waved off Agramon and Miyu, then climbed the fence to greet Sam. While Lord Alexander treated me joining weapons training as a chore, Sam seemed excited to teach me new skills. It was easy to get caught up in his excitement. And my own.

"How was your lesson?" Sam asked, waiting for Agramon to disappear over the hill before he unstrapped his sword and leaned it against the fence. "Were you successful in your performance?"

"Not nearly," I sighed. "I was never good at my sorcery lessons, even at Solridge. The only thing I've ever been good at is fighting."

"That's no small thing, Rowyn," Sam said. "It's how I make my living."

I smiled at him. "Maybe that's why we're kindred spirits."

"Maybe," Sam said slowly, his eyes sparkling as I rolled up my sleeves. "I brought you the gift I promised." He pulled out a parcel wrapped in paper and handed it to me. I smelled leather as I opened it, smiling shyly up at him. It was a small black holster, fitted with a silver buckle and five sheaths. Inside the sheaths were silver throwing knives, a field of stars etched on each blade.

My hands trembled as I inspected the knives, running my thumb along one and drawing blood. They were perfectly balanced, as I knew they would be. I looked up.

"I don't think I can accept this," I said, offering the holster back to Sam.

His eyes fell, and I knew that I'd hurt him. "I can return it if you don't like it."

"It's not that, Sam," I said, taking a deep breath to calm my shaky voice. "It's wonderful, but I don't feel right accepting such an expensive gift from you."

Good grief. I wished fervently that Vianne were there, or Ena, or anyone who could help me navigate the courtesies of gift-giving from men who had unreciprocated feelings for a woman. What did Sam mean by it? Was it just a friendly offering like he'd presented it to be? Or was it something more? If I accepted it, was there a hidden meaning involved? By all the gods, the knives were gorgeous. I wanted them . . . badly . . . but I felt that Sam had ulterior motives to his offering. After all, Destrian had given me a sword, and it damn near made me fall in love with him on the spot.

"They weren't costly at all," Sam was saying. "I have a friend on Steel Pass who I've bought weapons from before. He always cuts me a deal."

Sam was watching me closely, studying my face as the inner battle raged on, but greed won out. I'd sorely missed having weapons on me when I went out in my fancy dresses. It made me feel vulnerable and weak. I lifted the holster. "How does it work?"

Sam smiled. I realized then that I hadn't truly seen him smile before. It wasn't big—it wouldn't draw the attention of the room like Del's did—but its rarity made it seem almost precious. My grin spread wider when Sam took the holster from me.

"It goes around your thigh, opposite your sword, if you ever decide to wear them at the same time." He unbuckled it and handed it back to me while I wrapped it around the outside of my breeches. By Imor above, what a wonderful invention.

Sam set up a throwing ring while I practiced drawing the knives quickly. It would be tough in a dress. I would have to lift my skirt fairly high to get to them, but if I were in a situation that warranted a weapon and I had no other, I doubted I would care.

The rest of the evening was spent with me whipping the knives through the air, hitting target after target while Sam watched from the fence, occasionally correcting my stance or telling me to lift my arm more. It was wonderfully freeing.

A GILDED CAGE

I DIDN'T THINK THAT WHATEVER Agramon had planned for Destrian would be immediate, considering how calculating the man was. I'd also asked Echo to update me on anything new with Morgania, just in case, but Agramon didn't seem to be making any moves, or at least, not in conversation with others. Still, I knew I wouldn't be able to rest until I sent Destrian some word of warning. So, I endeavored to find a moment with the empress in the hope that she would know a way to deliver the message secretly.

Still, it took nearly a week for me to get Mem's attention while not arousing the suspicion of others. It was in a moment of panic that I found my opening, when a lady vomited up her lunch, simultaneously revealing that she was with child. With all the commotion of congratulations offered to the young woman, I was able to pull Mem aside.

"I need a moment with the empress," I whispered.

Mem frowned as her black eyes flicked over me. "What is this about?"

"I have some more information, and there is a message I wish to send to a friend. A message that no one can know about."

Mem looked over her shoulder at the empress, who was holding the sick girl's hand and wiping her brow with a damp cloth.

"She wants to limit the amount of time she sees you," Mem murmured. "We don't want anyone to grow suspicious, least of all the duke."

"I know, but it can't be helped."

Mem nodded and returned to her spot behind the empress. After the noble ladies stepped away, she leaned down and spoke into the empress's ear. Empress Lesedi glimpsed me only for a moment.

"Rowyn!" a voice said beside me, nearly startling the drink out of my hand. It was Del, dancing to me on her toes. "We still haven't taken that outing into the city you promised me."

The empress was already engaged with another. Frustrated, I turned back to Del and forced a smile. "Agramon asked me to train with Miyu in the afternoons, to practice the artistic side of my powers."

"Well, as much as I admire Miyu, she's getting in the way of my social goals, and we can't have that, now, can we?" Del said, wrapping her arm around mine and pulling me toward a table loaded down with food. "I will just have to kidnap you. There's nothing else for it."

I opened my mouth to speak, but Del put a finger over my lips. "Nope! I'll brook no argument. Mellan's already getting the horses ready, and we are going to have words with Agramon as soon as you've eaten."

I tried to make urgent eyes at the empress, but it was no use. As soon as I finished my plate, Del pulled me away from the other ladies and practically dragged me through the palace until we reached my rooms.

"Del!" Agramon said, opening the door to our arrival. "I wasn't expecting you today." Despite his words, the man was grinning at the expression on Del's face, a mix of adoration and coquettishness.

"Oh, you know you're always happy to see me," Del cooed, her freckles dancing when her cheeks rose.

"You won't hear me argue with you on that," Agramon agreed before a slight furrow wrinkled his brow. "What's this about you stealing my ward away?"

Del let out an exasperated noise and lightly smacked Agramon on the arm. "Come now, Your Grace, it's not fair for you to read my arguments before I present them."

"We have a lot of work to do before the rainbow ball," Agramon said. "You know the emperor is counting on us to make a good impression."

But Del wouldn't be denied. "Come now, Agramon, you've been working Rowyn to the bone since she got here. Let her have some fun! Let her be around young people her age. It will be good for her, I promise."

"Well . . ." Agramon said, his eyes on me. "What did you have planned? Just a trip to the city, right? Visiting your new temple?"

Del nodded. "And before you say anything, Mellan will be with us, so we'll be protected as well."

"His father did ask that I allow him the chance to court you," Agramon said, his eyes on me. "Is this your wish then?"

I nodded. I *could* use a break.

"Rowyn will meet you outside," Agramon told Del. "I would have words with her . . . *alone*."

Del grinned and flounced out of the room, shutting the door behind her while Agramon turned to me.

"This is a big moment, Rowyn," Agramon said, placing his hands on my shoulders. "It's taking a great deal to trust you, especially given our circumstances."

"If you think I'll try to escape, you have nothing to worry about," I insisted. "I have no wish to run from the empire for the rest of my life. Besides, I have nowhere else to go."

"That's the thing, isn't it," Agramon said, narrowing his eyes. "I have no way of knowing whether you're being truthful or not."

"And yet, that is what trust is, isn't it—to most men, at least?"

Agramon studied me a moment longer before releasing my shoulders. "Very well. You may go."

I couldn't help but grin at the opportunity for some excitement. Agramon followed me into my room and pulled

Iranoct down from the wall.

"Take your sword, just in case any more assassins are running about."

My excitement sparked at the command that, for once, I wholeheartedly wanted to obey. "Should I disguise myself?" I asked, opening my closet door. "Wear a cloak or something?"

"No," Agramon said, leaning against the doorframe. "The people should be able to see you every once in a while, otherwise they'd grow bored of you . . . and the dress you're wearing will suffice for a trip into the city." He said the last bit as I was pulling a pair of breeches from the cupboard. I sighed and put the breeches back. The dress I wore would be fine by palace standards, but it seemed too much considering I was going out to mingle with the common folk. I'd always hated to stand out, and given the number of tattoos and the style of dress I was wearing—a forest-green silk cut low in front, with sleeves falling off the shoulders and a narrowly tapered waist. It was exactly the type of dress Agramon loved to see me in, and the kind that I was most uncomfortable with.

Given that Agramon had already compromised with my schedule for the day, I decided against protesting my outfit. I buckled Iranoct around my waist and felt to make sure my new knife holster remained secured at my thigh.

Agramon nodded, satisfied with my appearance, and

led me out into the hall where Del was bouncing on her toes, waiting for us.

Agramon grabbed Del's hand. "Tell Mellan I am holding him personally responsible for Rowyn's welfare while she is out in the city. If she is injured, or fails to return, it will be he who pays the ultimate price."

Del nodded, her smile gone as Agramon seemed to press his will into her. Then, Agramon turned to me. "Take the afternoon for yourself. I'll tell the baron that you'll be absent from your evening lesson. Tomorrow, we will continue, with no more interruptions."

I nodded, and Agramon shut the door behind us. Del grabbed my hand and led me, practically running, through the golden halls as the early afternoon sun began to blaze through the arched windows. We skipped down the marble stairs and out into the ward where Mellan held the reins to three horses.

He bowed as we approached before helping Del onto her mount. I couldn't wait, impatient as I was to be away from the palace. I mounted, revealing more leg than I intended, and led the way through the palace gates.

Unlike before, where Agramon, Miyu, and I snuck through the city in disguise, we garnered a lot of attention from passersby. Del waved at the people while Mellan ignored them. I should've been used to the stares, the men and women whispering behind their hands as they pointed at my tattoos or gems, but still it bothered me. Perhaps it always would.

Most of the people in the streets watched us curiously, but several groups of young men looked downright hostile, almost challenging me when I met their eyes. On more than one, I recognized a marking on their arm that chilled my blood almost to the bone. It was the eye of Chassandre. The same mark that had been on the golgeman.

"Mellan," I said, interrupting his and Del's conversation. "Who are those men? The ones with the tattoos?"

Mellan followed my eyes. "Those are just zealots, calling themselves the sons of Sol. I would just ignore them if I were you."

"Why are they looking at me that way?" I asked, hating the way my hands started to shake on the reins. Perhaps it had been foolish to venture into the city, especially knowing that there hadn't been just one assassination attempt on my life, but rather two.

Mellan shrugged. "Could be any number of things, really. They hate foreigners, women who act outside of their station, and they can't abide magic. Considering you embody all three, I guess you can see why they might be trying to send you the evil eye." Mellan held my gaze, his brow furrowing. "Hey, I didn't mean that. You have nothing to worry about from them. They are just a bunch of crazies. Everybody knows that."

"I've seen that marking before," I said, nodding toward their tattoos. "I saw it on the creature the seer Chassandre sent after me."

"Well, she *is* kind of their leader," Mellan admitted. "She's been the biggest voice to regain the old ways and shun the changes that are being brought to the empire. Don't even get me started on what they say about the empress."

"What do they say?"

"You would get me started, wouldn't you," Mellan said with a laugh. "Fine, they hate lady's tea. They set fire to a couple of apothecaries that were selling it several months before you came to the city. They're angry that the emperor married a foreigner to begin with, saying there were plenty of eligible Lyrican ladies who would've been better suited for the task. It probably didn't help that the empress came from a land with far more advanced views of equality than we do."

"Are there many of them? These sons of Sol?"

Mellan shook his head. "Not really. Most of them are just young men who missed the war and were bored at home while the rest of us battled out our grievances in the east. I wouldn't give them another thought if I were you."

"We're here!" Del sang out in front of us. She'd reined in before a large frame. Shirtless men were hammering, directing horses and wagons, and lifting beams into place in what looked to be a series of triangles and tall spires.

"The crystal temple, where the majesty of Sol can be viewed no matter where you sit. Isn't it glorious?" Del asked, turning to me with bright eyes.

Mellan directed his horse to a side where the crystal was already inlaid into the frames. "It certainly is that," Mellan agreed.

"Does your magic help hold it up?" I asked, admiring the complexity of the spires.

"No, that's just good workmanship," Del replied with a grin. "My magic helps me see the different parts, how they fit together, and the best materials to use. It's even helped me come up with new building materials. The glass is held in place by a special glue that I made with Spark's help, strengthened by our powers, of course. Then, it's just a matter of putting all those pieces together."

Del was watching a group of men draw one of the frames into the air using a pulley and scaffolding. She let out an exasperated sigh. "You're putting it in the wrong way!" she shouted, storming off to direct the men to the correct orientation, leaving Mellan and me alone to watch.

Mellan threw glances at me out of the corner of his eye. I'd done as he asked, and not approached him about his secret identity as the Shadow Rogue during the emperor's evening banquets, but questions were still gnawing at my mind, namely, why him?

"You said you would give me the whole story when we were alone," I reminded him, careful to stay watchful of those around us. Luckily, Del's presence meant the men were busy with their work.

"There's not really much to tell," Mellan said. "I just kind of fell into it when I returned from Yliria last fall. I'd been planning to go home and get married, but when I heard of what my father had done, I opted to stay in the capital instead. Some of the men I'd fought with were staying also, and there are always plenty of women and drink to fill my time."

"So, how did you start dealing in slave rescues?" I asked, impatient for him to get to the point before Del returned.

Mellan patted his horse before meeting my eye. "There was a man I'd fought with in Yliria. He'd lived with one of the tribes that allied with Lyrica during the war and helped us translate. His sister was taken as a slave by another nobleman. He sent me a message at the capital, asking for my help to retrieve her and get her back home." Mellan shrugged. "The man saved my life during a battle, so I already owed him a blood debt. There was no way I could deny him the request and save face in the eye of Sol."

"So, you rescued her," I said, raising my brows.

Mellan nodded. "Her and four others, all young girls taken from that same village. Once I saw the condition they were in, there was no way I could leave any of them. I made inquiries into a small underground that helped slaves escape for a cost. So, I figured out how it worked and got the girls out. After that first time, word spread, and people have been approaching me ever since."

"How much do you charge these people? What cost do they pay for the freedom that was stolen from them?"

Mellan scowled. "You know, I'm a brilliant swordsman, the best many have seen. Unbeaten in duels, of which I've had many due to my bedroom habits. Out of all my brothers, I was the most skilled at battle. My father had such high hopes for me, but he couldn't abide my one weakness."

"Which is?" I asked, thinking of his wanton drunkenness or womanizing.

"I've a soft heart," Mellan said, winking at me. "It's an unforgivable failing if you ask my father. When these people plea to me, tell me of the horrors they endure at the nobles' hands, my heart just melts like butter. And if the women cry? By Sol above, I'm done for. So no, I'm not in it for a profit. I don't charge the slaves anything for their freedom, because as slaves they have nothing. Instead, I use the money my father sends me to pay off smugglers. Father thinks I have gambling problems, which is far from the truth. Money to me is too precious to waste on gambling when I could use it to save a life instead."

"That's why you were so worried about being cut off by your father? That's why you don't want to return home?" I asked, touched by his story. Before I'd been in danger of becoming friends with Mellan Lyon, but now, I was on the verge of admiring the man. If he were caught, he'd face the noose.

Mellan was nodding. "Yes, there's nothing for me at home except becoming my father's puppet and watching the love of my life waste away. At least here I'm free from his rule and can actually do some good with my life. I might even be able to make up for some of the evilness I've wrought on others during the war. Only Sol can know for sure."

"So why all the drunkenness? Why the women? You seem too noble for that."

Mellan laughed. "I needed to give myself a personality, something that would cause others to pass me over when they really began to look for the identity of the Shadow Rogue. So, I tried to be as roguish as I could so that no one would suspect, although the drinking has more to do with Agramon than anything."

"Really?"

"Oh yes. You don't have to worry about it because somehow you're immune from his powers, but the rest of us think about it often. I learned the trick from another soldier whose sister was a mind reader. Apparently, mind readers really struggle to follow a drunk person's thoughts. Because they're addled and difficult to follow, mind readers rarely try to figure out anything from them. I haven't shared that trick with anyone else for fear that Agramon would become suspicious, but so far it's served me well."

"I can't tell if you're the most noble man I've ever met, or the most brilliant," I admitted, still shaking my head at Mellan's story.

"Just make sure you keep my secret," Mellan said. "Nobody else knows, not even Del."

"You don't have to worry about me," I said as Del rode back toward us. "I wouldn't give up your secret for the world."

"Are you two lovebirds ready to go?" Del asked, reining in beside us.

Mellan lifted his eyebrow at me, and I couldn't help but laugh. The thought of keeping up the pretense of being courted by Mellan felt easier now that I knew what kind of man he was. "We are," I said. "I can't wait to see what this will look like when it's done."

Del looked over her shoulder. "It will be my most magnificent project yet. Even the emperor is excited about it. It should be done in time for the quinquennial, too, so it will be where everyone celebrates."

"Where were you ladies hoping to go next?" Mellan asked, turning his horse and heading back into the street.

"We could go visit Berinon's laboratory," Del offered.

"No!" Mellan said. "Berinon will have us there for hours talking about his work. Besides, you just want to see your lover."

"I did promise Sparks I would bring her lunch one of these days," Del admitted.

Mellan saw the look on my face and shook his head. "Not Berinon. I can abide anything but him."

"What did *you* have in mind?" Del asked, fluttering her eyelashes at Mellan. "Since you're being so picky."

"The pit fights are today. I heard there's a blood bath planned, but Mordog is set to battle. So, it will probably be good."

"Oooh, Mordog is fighting?" Del asked before turning to me. "You'll like him. He's a Morganite, like you, and so handsome."

Mellan rolled his eyes. "So, it's decided then?" he asked, already heading up the street to the large amphitheater that lay in the center of the entertainment district.

I wasn't interested in seeing the fighting pits, but I didn't have the heart to ruin Mellan and Del's fun. After all, they'd gotten me out of the castle and away from training with Agramon, and they truly seemed excited to go. Then again, Mellan and Del came from nobility, so they didn't have to worry about being forcefully conscripted like the lowest classes of Lyrica. Though Mellan had gone to war, he'd volunteered for the job and went his own way when the war was over. Such was not the case for the conscripted. The empire almost never sent those back. Instead, they sent them to farm the Fields of Forgotten Men in Bruin or forced them to battle in the fighting pits, where death was their only release. As Mellan and Del led the way through the crowds forming at the gates of the arena, a sinking feeling crept into my gut at what I would see within.

ELLIOTT VANDRUFF

Chapter 27

CHEERS ROSE THROUGH THE stands as we took our seats. The massive arena was dug into the ground, surrounded by a ten-foot wall. The seats nearest the wall appeared to be reserved for the nobles, for they were partitioned off differently than the others. The steps behind the noblemen's portion were already full of screaming denizens of Somme. Several people walked around with baskets, shouting about sweet treats or bread buns that they were selling for the fight.

My stomach felt as though it had knotted in on itself. I'd heard of Somme's fighting pits and what a draw they were for the people of Lyrica, but it was another thing altogether to see so many people screaming for blood.

Mellan smiled as he leaned over the railing. In the arena prowled a lion. It roared, and the noise reverberated through the stands. Women shrieked with giddy terror. Another roar shook the crowd, and I rose. Handlers wearing loincloths led a bear into the arena.

"What are they doing?" I asked.

"They're going to fight, of course," Mellan said, waving his hand to shush me.

I couldn't watch it. Not with the animals going after

each other. It seemed like such a waste to me. I only fought for survival. There was enough bloodshed in actual battles that it seemed cruel to tear those poor creatures from their homelands and have them ripped to pieces for entertainment. Instead, I turned and studied the people in the stands.

I didn't recognize any of the other nobles there, though there were many lounging in their seats as they watched the fight or chatted with those around them. Several ate on lavish spreads of food. I noticed a little boy, dirty from the city streets, reach out to pluck a piece of fruit from one of the tables. The nobleman's guard standing nearby smacked the boy soundly, the fruit flying out of the boy's hands and falling beneath the stands. I expected the young lad to cry, but he didn't. He merely glared at the guard and slunk away, his eyes on another, less guarded table. Disgusted, I continued my inspection of the crowd, surprised to find Sam leaning back and talking with several other men who sat around him.

"What is he doing here?" I asked, nodding in Sam's direction.

"The Butcher of Bruin?" Del said, following my eyes. "He usually watches the fights. It's his way of honoring the war dogs."

"There doesn't seem to be much honor in an event such as this," I snapped.

Mellan laughed, shaking his head. "Oh, you'd be surprised. The fighters who can make a name for themselves, like Mordog, get all sorts of advantages when they do well. Everyone loves to bet on a fight, and those with money will send the richest foods and most beautiful women to their fighters of choice in the hopes that it will give them an edge in battle."

"Even noblewomen have been known to romance the fighters," Del said, dropping her voice low. "I've heard it's common for ladies to sneak into the fighting cages to offer themselves to their heroes."

"That sounds mad," I said, shaking my head. "This whole thing is madness."

"Well, sure," Mellan said, wagging his eyebrows at me. "Why else would it be so fun?"

I let out a frustrated gust of air and turned my attention to the man in outlandishly colored robes who was shouting from a prominent seat at the center of the stands. The lion had lost the battle. The handlers dragged the bear and the lion's corpse out of the field and into a cage, where the bear was allowed to feast on the lion's remains while the games went on.

"And now, for the main event," the announcer was saying. "From the clans of the West, bearing the mark of Imor and kin to the great sorceress herself, Mordog and his pack remain undefeated!"

A GILDED CAGE

Gates at the end of the arena rose, and a crew of men appeared. The stands erupted into screams. Ladies were leaning over the railing, waving at the men on horseback carrying swords or maces. They wore breeches and leather guards over their shoulders, but their chests and backs remained bare. I groaned when I took in their unshaven faces, hair pulled into knots at the back of their heads, and markings covering their bodies. They were all Morganites.

"Mordog! Mordog!" the crowd chanted as the fighters circled the stadium in single file. They rode with surety, led by a man bearing an ax in one hand and a sword in the other. The man in front raised his sword, and the crowd went mad, screeching and throwing flowers into the ring. Markings covered his heavily muscled arms, the head of a howling wolf etched onto one side of his chest. Down his face, splitting one of his imorets, was a large scar.

I leaned forward, trying to make out more of his markings as if to assure myself. The way he moved, the angry way he eyed the crowd, made it seem as though their cheers meant nothing to him.

But that wasn't why I stared so wildly. I would know that face anywhere.

"Luc!" I whispered, thankful that Mellan and Del were distracted, chatting and remarking on the other fighters.

Though I'd known he was alive thanks to the seer, Arda, whom I met at the Last Dusk on the quest for my stones, I'd scarcely dared to hope that I would ever see him again. Yet there he was before me about to engage in a battle to the death. A swell of memories rose in my mind: Luc, laughing when he splashed water into my face as we played as children, my father and Luc discussing the logistics of a raid, Luc's eyes on me, sparkling from across the room, the feeling of his hand holding mine as we watched a shooting star streak across the sky. I almost choked, tears threatening my eyes as I gripped the railing in front of me, still not believing what I was seeing. Emotions flooded me, relief at seeing him at last, then joy, and finally, fear snaked in as I registered that the announcer had saluted the men about to fight to the death, and that Luc was in danger.

I turned my attention to the announcer, who had spun a great wheel with pictures painted into the slats. Luc and his men had returned to the side of the arena, standing in formation and watching the wheel slow as the crowd hushed.

I gripped Mellan's arm. "What's happening?" I pressed, my eyes darting between the wheel and Luc's face.

Mellan, too absorbed with the excitement to notice my panic, pointed to the wheel. "They are choosing the opponents."

My eyes went back to the dreaded wheel, which was ending its journey. The announcer grinned, spreading his arms wide. "Sol has made his decision. Mordog's Wolf

Pack will do battle with the Reapers of Dwi-Gemi!"

The crowd gasped, and Luc's face looked grimly reso-lute as he shouted out orders to the men around him. Fear filled the men's faces as they faced the other end of the arena, and gears began screeching from behind the gate.

"What is it?" I asked, seeing the look of nervous excite-ment on Del's face. "Who are the reapers?"

Del's eyes remained glued to the gate at the end of the arena. "They're from an island far south of Ember Innes. They're undefeated, too, and I fear this won't end well for Mordog. The reapers have too many advantages."

"What are the reapers?" I asked, nerves dancing be-neath my veins. The gears had stopped turning with a thud, and an unearthly shriek resounded from behind the gate.

"Them," Del said, pointing as five giant birds bearing riders on their backs thundered into the space. They had to have been ten feet tall, the tops of their heads nearly reaching the arena railings. Their yellow beaks were mas-sive, nearly as long as my arm, and tapered to a long, hooked point. I was worried the birds would start flying around the arena, but their wings were quite small com-pared to the rest of their body, making flight impossible. Their heads were red while the rest of their feathers varied in shades of gray and black. They sported two muscular legs, and at the end of each of their three toes were talons several inches long.

I would've thought the monstrous birds would've been enough of a foe for the battle, but each bird bore a rider, small men with dark arms and faces painted yellow, red, and black to mimic the birds. They carried nets and short spears that they brandished to the crowd who howled encouragement at them. The Dwi-Gemi turned to face Luc and his men, sticking out their tongues and contorting their faces while the birds shrieked their bloodcurdling cry.

Ice needled through my veins as Luc raised his arms and beat his ax and sword blade together. I sent prayer after prayer to Imor, asking him to protect Luc in the coming battle.

Suddenly, a trumpet sounded, and the birds and horses began thundering toward each other. I rose from my seat, clutching the railing as Luc led his men into battle, but disaster struck before they even collided. The giant predatory birds shrieked, spooking one of the horses. The horse reared, then kicked, colliding with the horse and rider beside it. Both fell, one trapped under his steed, the other rolling out of the way but losing his weapons. In a single breath, Luc and his men were put at a significant disadvantage.

Luc didn't seem to realize his men were down. He rode headlong into the line of birds, swinging his ax up and into the neck of one as it raised its head. Another bird slammed its hooked beak into the skull of the horse beside him with a crack that seemed to echo in the arena. The horse fell, and the rider became entangled in the Dwi-Gemi's net before being dragged to the ground where talons sliced him to ribbons within seconds, the man's cries barely heard over the groans and screams from the audience.

Luc fought well, despite the fact that his horse took a spear to the neck and was now being ripped apart by one of the reaper birds. Luc had leaped from the horse's back to take down one of the riders with his sword, but he was still grossly outmatched. Two birds had already felled the horses and riders who'd collided before the fray began and were feasting on their remains.

I gnawed away at my fingernails. The crowd was incessant, their jeers and screams filling the air and making my head ache. Luc called to the last living member of his party. The man grabbed a spear and hurled it into a bird that charged toward Luc. The bird crashed to the ground in a cloud of dust, its momentum carrying it forward as the Dwi-Gemi rider leaped from the creature's back, his spear at the ready. Luc was faster. He ran toward the man and gutted him before the spear could be thrown, sending his corpse sliding into the dirt.

I'd ignored the shouts and groans of Del and Mellan beside me, so engrossed was I in the battle. I kept telling myself that Luc was doing well. That he was an experienced fighter and that he would prevail, even against such narrow odds.

Luc's other rider, still seated on his horse, had already killed another Dwi-Gemi rider, but the giant bird was still very much alive as it darted around the far less agile horse and tried to deal a killing blow. The bird raised one of its legs and kicked at the horse's side. The horse crashed to the ground while a hooked beak stabbed the rider's back. The man's screams turned into gurgling as he was ripped to shreds while I screamed my frustration.

Luc was all alone in the arena, surrounded by three of the predatory birds, two still bearing riders. He was outmatched and I knew, deep in my gut, that he wouldn't survive this fight. But I refused to watch him die.

As if by instinct, I vaulted over the railing, my gems roaring to life as I fell and landed in the arena. Using my momentum, I rolled forward and back onto my feet. Unsheathing Iranoct, I aimed it at the bird and rider circling Luc, the rider getting ready to toss his deadly net while Luc brandished his sword.

Lightning screamed from the tip of Iranoct's blade, the light a brilliant flash as it roared across the arena, slamming both the bird and its rider into the wall in an explosion of feathers.

While the other birds and rider tried to find the source of the lightning, I used the confusion to unstrap Iranoct's sheath from my waist and tear through the green silk of my gown, shortening it so I could move unhampered. When I looked up, both birds were barreling toward me. The ground beneath my feet trembled. There was no way I could take them both at the same time. I didn't dare direct lightning to one just for the other to cut me down.

I readjusted my feet, trying to slow my heart, and noticed a small swirl of dust in the air. I looked back up at the birds and tightened my grip on Iranoct with one hand, while sweeping the other up, sending a gust of wind over the arena, drawing dust and dirt into the air in a massive cloud. The riderless bird that had run ahead of the other emerged, still shrieking as it thundered toward me.

I snatched a knife from the holster belted to my thigh and sent it flying into the bird's chest. I sent two more knives into the creature before darting to the side, narrowly missing the hooked beak while severing one of its legs in two. The bird went down with a squawk. I slammed my sword into the bird's neck, severing its windpipe, before turning to the cloud of dust that was beginning to settle.

The last of the Dwi-Gemi emerged from the dust cloud and dismounted from his bird. I gripped my sword tightly as they approached me from either side. The rider held his spear with one hand and twirled the net over his head with the other, sticking his tongue out as though trying to frighten me. Meanwhile, the bird had paused. It ruffled its feathers as it studied me, as though unsure it wanted to attack. I brandished my sword at it, which was a mistake, because it gave a great squawk and raced toward me. I was torn between the Dwi-Gemi fighter and the reaper bird, knowing full well that my defense of one would cost my life with the other.

It was then that Luc emerged, coughing, from the cloud. Unbeknownst to the Dwi-Gemi fighter, Luc ran toward him.

I turned and focused all my attention on the bird. As the creature charged, I darted to the side again, but this bird was much quicker than the last. It kicked me hard in the side, hurling me into the dirt where I rolled, losing my sword in the process. I came to my feet as quickly as I could, holding my aching side, sure that several of my ribs were broken. I grabbed a knife from my holster and flung it with as much strength as I could. Still, it was not enough.

The bird had wheeled around, ruffling its feathers once more as though contemplating another charge. I grabbed the last of the knives and let my power surround me as the bird took off toward me.

With a blast, I pushed myself into the air, flying up a good fifteen feet before I panicked at the thought of rising too high. I cut off my power when the bird stopped below me, squawking its confusion that I was above it. I dropped onto the bird's back and felt the creature's legs buckle slightly. I took that moment to stab it in the back of the neck as hard as I could with my last remaining knife.

The bird fell back, shrieking and writhing. I pulled the knife out and stabbed it over and over again until the creature stilled. Breathing a sigh of relief, I rose from the carnage of feathers and bodies and blood and turned to find Luc standing over the body of the Dwi-Gemi, beheaded at his feet.

Luc looked up and his eyes met mine. I walked toward him. Recognition flitted across his face, then hope, and finally, disbelief.

"If this is death," Luc said when I stood before him, his sword dangling at his side, "I welcome it with every fiber of my being."

"You're not dead," I said. Tears coursed down my cheeks at the reality that he was alive and in front of me. "I'm real, as real as that sword in your hand."

Luc dropped the weapon and sank to his knees, looking up at me. "By all the gods, don't toy with me. I've dreamed of this moment for so long."

"I'm real," I repeated, stepping closer and running my fingers over his imorets.

Luc's hazel eyes bore into mine. He leaned forward and laid his head against my stomach, clutching me around my middle. Tears flowed freely down my face as I leaned down and kissed the top of his head, scarcely believing it myself. Scarcely believing that we'd managed to find our way to each other at last.

Chapter 28

THE ROAR FROM THE STANDS interrupted Luc and my reunion when I finally registered the noise. I glanced around the arena and saw that many of the spectators were as coated with dust as we were. The stands now held piles of dirt that still twirled as those watching clamored against the railing, shouting at the announcer who was shrugging in confusion.

Dimly, I recognized the sound of the gears turning and gripped Luc's hair, raising his face to mine. "They are coming for you," I said before pulling away from him and finding Iranoct. I grabbed the sword and stood beside Luc, who'd reclaimed his own weapon as the gate opened and out marched a squadron of armed men in two rows. The guards parted, revealing two men dressed in lavish robes, their eyes on Luc and me as we faced them, our swords aloft.

"Mordog," one of the men said, his hands held out to Luc as if in friendship, "I'm glad to see that you were spared the slaughter of your pack given how valuable you've been, but I must admit, the circumstances of your win are most unusual."

The other man had crossed his arms, his brows

furrowed. "We're unable to honor any of the bets made at the pits today," he snapped, his eyes on me. "There's a reason sorcerers aren't allowed in the arena. It gives the other side an unfair advantage."

"Unfair advantage?" I shouted, motioning to the birds. "You put Luc and his men on horses, creatures with no offensive capabilities, and set them against those birds who could deal a death blow three different ways!"

The cross man drew himself up as though to cow me. "Mordog and his men had a perfectly fair opportunity to win the fight. They were all stronger, more seasoned in battle, and carried superior weapons!"

"Now Lunn," the other man said, resting his hand on his partner's arm. "Let's be reasonable here. We all know that the sight of blood can be quite startling for young ladies. I'm guessing this was the girl's first time at the games, wasn't it?" the man asked, turning to me.

I opened my mouth to give an angry retort when Luc squeezed my hand tightly. I gritted my teeth and nodded.

"See? It must've been such a shock to see her country-men at such a disadvantage so early on."

"We should throw you in jail for this," Lunn snapped.

"No," Luc said, drawing himself to his full height. "Rowyn and I were friends from home. She was protecting me because she knew me."

The nicer man raised his brows. "Oh, I didn't think the

two of you would've known each other. I was given to understand that you came from Morganite royalty, my dear."

Luc turned to me questioningly, but I was saved a response by three other figures hurrying into the arena. Sam strode in, followed by Del and Mellan.

"Men," Sam said, nodding at the guards as he passed.

I used the distraction to pull Luc down and whisper in his ear, "I will find a way to release you from this." Luc nodded just as Sam reached us and pulled me out of Luc's grip, thrusting me behind him where Del took my arm, and Mellan palmed his sword beside us.

"Good sirs," Sam said, nodding at the two well-dressed men. "I understand that Rowyn's presence may have been an inconvenience to the fights today, but I'm sure that we can resolve matters with an air toward forgiveness."

Lunn's eyes narrowed. "We lost almost all of our best fighters today, as well as an entire day's worth of bets."

Sam raised one brow, appraising Lunn with the air of someone assessing a slug that was making its way over their boot. "I'm sure you will recover swiftly from this loss, as the games are sure to be even more popular after today's events. The people in the stands paid for a spectacle, and they certainly received that today, wouldn't you agree, gentlemen?"

"I'm sure we can put this behind us, given who she is," the nicer man said hurriedly, as if he was trying to agree before Lunn could speak. "Especially if we can all agree that Rowyn the Morganite is no longer allowed to attend the games."

Sam nodded. "So agreed," he said, then turned and motioned Del and Mellan to lead me toward the gate while he remained with the men.

Del darted glances at me. Mellan was shaking, as though he was trying to stifle laughter.

"It wasn't funny," I growled, gripping Iranoct tightly.

"By Sol above, Rowyn, you must have balls as big as temple bells," Mellan said, shaking his head.

Del glared at him. "I don't see what's so funny. You know Agramon is going to be angry about this when we return."

Mellan held up his hands in mock defense. "He only said she had to be returned alive and safe. He never said anything about barring her from a sojourn through the fighting pits to go hunting for taloned chickens, and I absolutely intend to argue that point if he brings it up."

Del let out an exasperated gust of air as we reached the gate and waited for Sam. "Why, for the love of Sol, did you jump into the pit, Rowyn? You could have been injured or killed!"

I felt Mellan watching me as I battled with how to answer. There was no way Agramon could find out about Luc. Given his reduced circumstances, if Agramon heard about my relationship to the famed fighter, Mordog, he would dangle his life over my head to make me more docile. I met Del's eyes. "He was a Morganite, like me. How could you expect me to watch him die?"

Del shook her head and looked away, clearly irritated with me. Mellan never broke his gaze, but Sam was finally approaching. When he reached us, he held out my belt and knives. I slipped the knives into their places and buckled the belt onto my waist before following the others out of the arena and into the busy street. Del and Mellan led the way back to our horses while Sam pulled on my arm to stop me.

"What happened in there . . ." Sam began, his hands gripping my shoulders.

"I know, I'm sorry, I didn't mean to inconvenience you," I said hurriedly. I truly didn't want Sam and the others to be troubled by my interference, no matter how little I regretted it.

"That's not what I was going to say," Sam said, the corner of his mouth twitching.

"Oh," I said lamely. "I'm sorry, what were you going to say then?"

"I was going to say that you fought well," he finished, releasing my arms.

"Thank you," I said, unable to help the grin from spreading across my features. Lord Alexander had never complimented my fighting skills. Neither had Uncle Bay-lin.

Sam leaned closer to my ear. "Not a day goes by that I'm not impressed by you," he murmured as he placed a hand on my back and led into the street.

A blush spread over my cheeks at his words, but my attention was already flitting elsewhere. Luc was alive and in Somme, and I knew just the way to free him. I narrowed my eyes as Mellan's figure continued through the street ahead of us, my mind already concocting a plan.

Chapter 29

I SAT ACROSS FROM AGRAMON, who studied me, the gem at the end of his staff gleaming in the fading light from the open window.

"I would like to believe that you couldn't help yourself, that some great force propelled you over that balcony and caused you to make a spectacle of yourself in front of the city, bringing dishonor to my name, but I just can't dismiss your actions so easily," Agramon said.

"Your Grace," I began, opting for the utmost formality given how white his knuckles were around his staff. "The games were barbaric, truly, and I couldn't stand by and watch one more Morganite be slaughtered for the entertainment of Somme. How could you expect me to abide such cruelty?"

Agramon tilted his head to the side. "I am not so much a fan of the games myself considering the mad thoughts that run through people's minds during the battles. I've been once or twice, but it's been very tiring each time I've made the effort."

He looked back to his staff, his brow furrowed. "What of the boy, the Morganite you saved . . . What was his name?"

Here it was. Agramon was going to pry into my relationship with Luc, and I would have to take the utmost care. I couldn't let him know how deep our bond ran. I couldn't let him know that I loved him once. That, in a way, I loved him still.

"The crowd called him Mordog," I said, meeting Agramon's eyes while at the same time leaning back in my chair lazily. "I don't know much past that, other than he was a Morganite, and he'd been conscripted, just like many of the boys back home had been."

Agramon harrumphed, mirroring my movements as he slouched and leaned his staff against the wall. "You understand that this means Mellan will no longer be allowed to escort you out into the city, and certainly no more fighting pits."

"I suppose, if that is your wish," I said, picking at the arm of the chair beside me.

"It is my demand," Agramon snapped.

I met his eye and froze at the enmity I saw there. "Your Grace," I said, keeping my voice calm and even, "I know what people have said about me here, and what you fear they will say about me after word gets out about my interference in the games. That I'm a barbarian, a heathen from the wild, who is unable to be tamed—despite her master's wishes—but please understand. It was *my* people in the pit today, being slaughtered by a foe that they were outmatched against. Though I may have been cast out, I *am* still a Morganite. Additionally, given the nature of the fighting pits, I would argue that, though there were hundreds of barbarians in the stadium today, I was not one of them."

Agramon just rolled his eyes and shook his head. I stood and went to my room. Agramon had already told me that he would have my dinner sent up since he didn't want me at the emperor's banquet retelling my story, as though the attention would encourage me to act out more. In truth, I was glad of it, for I needed time to think.

I greeted Arden at the window. I hung Iranoct up on the wall and unbelted my knife holster, laying it on the table beside my bed before collapsing onto the soft sheets. Arden flew onto a pillow and settled down beside me while I absentmindedly stroked her feathers.

I was determined to free Luc and send him home. I just had to convince Mellan to help me. After all, he helped other slaves escape—why not someone forced into the fighting pits? Wasn't conscription just another form of slavery? Granted, the way Mellan told it, he mostly rescued women and the elderly, and Luc was as able-bodied as they came, but still. I felt the need to send him home to Morgania gnawing at me. I could grant one of my only wishes still available to me. I couldn't bring my parents back from the dead, I couldn't take back the mistakes I'd made when

I was in Espiria, and I had little control over my power, but I could send Luc home, where he belonged.

Ena came into my room carrying a tray of food. When she saw Arden, she grinned and grabbed a piece of meat, bringing it over to the bird and dropping it into her waiting mouth. I was on the verge of telling her I'd found Luc, the story on the tip of my tongue, but I stopped myself just in time. Agramon was sure to find out if Ena knew of my plans. I sighed, turning my attention back to the ceiling.

"I heard there was some excitement in the city today," Ena said, her voice soft.

I laughed. "Agramon is right not to employ any servants. Word gets around fast with you lot."

Ena chuckled as she lifted what was left of my skirt and shook her head at the slashed fabric. "They do love to talk," she admitted, pulling my hands and forcing me to stand while she lifted the tattered dress from my shoulders. "Did you recognize any of the boys who were fighting?"

I shook my head, my eyes on my feet as Ena untied my corset and pulled a chemise over me. It was one thing to lie to Agramon, but I felt rotten to the core not telling Ena the truth. I waited for her lecture, but it never came. Instead, she brought the tray of food to the bed and continued to feed Arden, who rubbed her head against Ena's hand.

"Aren't you going to tell me that I should've been more

careful?" I asked Ena as she inspected Arden's talons.

Ena laughed. "At this point, why bother? Besides, how I heard the story, it seems it's the rest of us who should be more wary of your temper."

I couldn't help but laugh with her as I joined her on the bed, hugging my knees to my chest as she uncoiled my hair.

"How are the other servants with you?" I asked, soothed by her touch. "I spoke to Agramon, and he said he would look into it."

Ena didn't speak for a long time. "He spoke to them, or must have done something, for they now look on me with fear instead of disgust. I don't know which is worse."

I rested my chin on my knees. "I've found that I much prefer fear, if that helps."

I thought back to Luc and how I yearned to send him home again. For the first time since I'd reached Somme, I felt a sense of hope. Luc and I had dreamed of a shared future in Espiria, ruling side by side, protecting our people, making our home greater than it had ever been before. Those dreams were ripped from us when Luc was taken, but now, I had a chance to resurrect at least some of them. I knew the Espirians would never let me return to Espiria—they didn't want my protection—but they needed Luc.

"What do you dream of, Ena?" I asked, running my

hands down the fabric of my chemise as Ena brushed my hair out.

"My lady?"

"What do you wish for in this life? If you had as much money as you needed, what would you do with it?"

"I don't know," Ena said. "I suppose . . . Well, it's silly, really."

"No, please go on," I urged.

"Well, I'd thought when I earned enough after my service, that I might get a parcel of land and farm it. Somewhere off in the wilderness, with not but my own family about. Away from the wars and consuls, away from soldiers. It's a silly dream."

"That sounds wonderful," I said with sincerity. "It's a beautiful dream."

"No, 'tis small. I've not much of an imagination."

"Sometimes, I feel I can't dream anymore."

Ena gently laid her hands on my shoulders. "My lady, don't give up hope yet. You will be free of here. I can feel it in my bones."

I grabbed one of her hands and met her eyes over my shoulder. "If I ever *am* free of here, then I will make sure to help you fulfill your dream. This I promise you, Ena."

"If ever the world is as you see it, then I know you will do me right in the end, Rowyn. I've always admired you so. You've always been so strong."

Tears fell as I turned away. "Ena, it is you who gives me strength. You're my only true friend here. The only person in this whole empire who I trust. I *will* do right by you, I promise."

"We have each other, m'lady," Ena said, wiping my tears with a corner of her crisp linen apron.

MY PLAN TO FREE LUC plagued my mind for the next few days while I tried to find a time to corner Mellan. It was out of the question that we would plan it during the emperor's banquet, for that was the time Mellan's mind was most vulnerable to being read. Instead, I would have to figure out a way to meet him alone.

So, I bided my time, following Agramon's every order. I dutifully listened to Princess Willene during her morning lessons, then followed Agramon and Miyu out of the city and practiced my powers away from the masses. Even Agramon was pleased with the progress I was making, and Miyu was nearly beside herself with excitement.

"The ambassador is sure to be impressed," I overheard her telling Agramon as we rode back through the city. "He may even try to purchase time to bring Rowyn to Lu Shen, to present her powers there."

Agramon had laughed at that. "She won't be leaving Lyrica anytime soon," he said, shaking his head. "She still has to end the drought."

Despite using my powers with Agramon every day, it was the evening lessons with Sam that sent me groaning to bed every night. Once he saw what I could do in a life-or-death fight, he worked me harder than ever. The next lesson we had, he'd stopped holding back. His blows came harder, he moved faster, and he wasn't afraid to bruise me as we each tried our damnedest to strike each other.

The opportunity finally came to speak to Mellan one morning as I made my way to Princess Willene's quarters. Princess Ledi stopped me at the door.

"Mother said you wished to speak to her," Princess Ledi said, taking me by the hand and leading me to a deserted hallway. "She's ready to see you now."

"What about our lesson with Willene?"

"The high princess was called away suddenly this morning and won't return until much later. She may have sent word to Agramon about her absence, but the servant could've been informed that the task had already been accomplished."

"*Princess*," I said warningly, a smile breaking over my face as Ledi's dark eyes sparkled with mischief.

"The empress didn't want anyone to know that you were meeting, so this was the only way to keep it secret,"

Ledi said, opening a door and leading me in to where the empress was seated at a table with Mem at her back.

Lesedi was dressed in her normal day clothes, rich, jewel-toned fabrics with intricate designs folded around her body and belted in place by a golden sash heavy with gems. Her ears and nose were pierced with several gold rings, but her dark skin was not yet painted gold like it usually was at the evening banquet. Her hair was wrapped in fabric and fashioned into a tall headdress, giving her height despite her relatively short frame.

"You wished to speak with me?" the empress asked, motioning me to sit across from her. "You understand that it's best that we communicate using Mem or Ledi instead of meeting in person, yes?"

I nodded. "Of course, Your Eminence, but the matter is urgent."

Empress Lesedi spoke to Princess Ledi in a language I didn't understand. The princess glanced at me, then nodded and left the room, shutting the door quietly behind her.

"Go on then. What is this important matter?" the empress asked.

I took a deep breath, then launched into my latest dreams and the fear that Destrian would somehow be displaced as consul at Agramon's whim. The empress listened respectfully, her hands folded over the table as I recounted additional dreams I'd had, of Agramon making sly comments to other nobles, hinting at loyalties, and my concerns for why he would take control of communication with the other nobles about how my powers would be used for the betterment of the empire.

When I finished, Mem crossed her arms. "How do you come by all of this information? I don't think the duke would be so foolish as to reveal it to you himself."

The empress quirked an eyebrow. "A fair question," she said, nodding at me to answer.

I bit my lip, though I was unsurprised that they would ask for my source. "Agramon can't reach into your mind, can he?" I asked the empress, who shook her head. "What of you?" I asked Mem, whose frown deepened.

"Why else would I be standing here?" Mem asked simply.

I took a deep breath. "Have shadows ever spoken to you?" I asked, hoping Echo wouldn't mind me revealing her presence to the empress. In the end, I knew it was the only way she would trust me.

Mem's eyes widened. "You can speak to Unagi? I thought the only necromancer in the city was Pythia Golden-Eyes."

The empress leaned forward, her eyes flitting over me as I shrugged. "I've never heard of Unagi."

"They're called lost souls, or ghosts here in Lyrica," the

empress said. "There are two types of Unagi. The Unagi-May, or souls that have been lost by fortune, or accident, and then there are the Unagi-Dom, those who've been turned by magic. The Unagi-Dom tend to be more tied to the earth and those around them, some even able to communicate with those who are not necromancers."

I nodded. "Echo, or that's what I call her, she's the second one. She and the rest of her tribe were turned by magic hundreds of years ago in the Nightlands. When I quested there for my gem, Destrian and I met them, and Echo ended up following me home."

"I've never heard of an Unagi-Dom able to leave the land they were reborn in," Mem said, her eyes narrowing.

"I was surprised too," I insisted, holding up my hands. "But I think the gems allowed her to do it. Since they were so closely tied to the land, or are the land, it allowed one of them to follow me."

"Those touched by the Unagi are considered blessed where we're from," the empress said. "How does she speak to you of Agramon's doings? I assume you asked her to follow him."

I nodded. "She doesn't talk much when I'm awake—I think it takes too much strength—but she sends me dreams when I'm asleep, memories of where she's been during the day."

Mem's eyes nearly bugged out of her head. "She's able

to leave your side?"

I nodded. "I don't think she can go far. The dreams she's sent me have all been here at the palace. Most of the time she's by my side, so there will always be things that she misses."

"Still," the empress said, shooting Mem a significant look, "I couldn't have asked for a more perfect spy, and Agramon has no idea?"

I shook my head. "I want to be clear; you're the first people I've revealed this secret to. Nobody knows, not my handmaid, Ena, not Destrian, and certainly not Agramon, so I'm counting on you not to reveal her presence. The only other person who knows she's with me is Pythia, but I'll wager she hasn't said anything about Echo, and I intend to stay away from her so Agramon doesn't catch wind of her presence."

"A wise choice," the empress said, nodding. "Could your Echo assist in keeping our agreement secret as well? Could she send dreams to myself or Mem?"

"Echo?" I asked, sure that she was in the room with us given the fact that we'd been speaking of her for several minutes.

"*I'm here,*" Echo hissed, loudly enough for even Mem and the empress to hear. The empress jumped in her seat, startled by the unearthly voice. Mem's hand had shot to her weapon, her eyes darting around the room.

"Are you able to send the same information you send to me, to them in dreams?"

"*Some*," Echo whispered.

The empress glanced at me and I explained. "Echo is weakened the farther away she is from me. She may not be able to give you the entire memory with all of the details, but she could send the most important points."

The empress nodded, her eyes on the table. "This changes everything," she said, speaking to Mem. Looking up at me, she added, "I knew Vianne spoke the truth, and I was right to trust you."

"Oh?" I asked, surprised that Vianne had anything nice to say about me. "When I was at Solridge, Vianne and I were not particularly close, and she deceived me multiple times."

"Vianne and I have worked together for many years. She saw early on that you shared the same goals that we do."

"Which are?" I asked, my brows raised.

"Creating a better world," the empress said simply.

I didn't have much to say about that. Instead, I opted to remind the empress of the task at hand. "We have to warn Destrian that Agramon may try to take Helena from him."

"You wish to send him a message?" the empress asked.

I nodded.

"That shouldn't be difficult, though a discreet messenger may be hard to find."

"I've already found a messenger," I said.

The empress's lips twitched to the side. "So then, what do you need me for?"

"I will need gold, lots of it, and Agramon doesn't ever give me money."

Mem and the empress exchanged glances. "I'm assuming this gold, should it fall into the wrong hands, or be inspected, should be untraceable to the palace?" the empress asked, tapping her finger on the tabletop.

I nodded. The empress looked up at Mem and waved toward the door. Mem nodded and strode out of the room, leaving the empress and me alone.

"Aren't you going to ask me to explain myself?" I asked, surprised how quickly she agreed to my offer.

"No," the empress said, shaking her head. "For two reasons: One, I don't really want to know, for I fear there is some danger involved, and the less I know, the less I will fret about it. The second is that an alliance with you is shaping up to be even more invaluable than I could've hoped. I feel indebted to you as it is, so such a simple request, so easily granted, is nothing compared to the information you've given me."

"Why do you care so much for the empire?" I asked, thinking back to what Mellan had said about the sons of

Sol decrying the empress's interference as a foreigner. "You aren't even from here."

The empress tilted her head to the side. "I'm not, but I have to do everything in my power to protect my children's thrones. You understand that, for them, this is life or death. If I'm able to hold their birthright and force the nobles to honor my husband's line for as long as possible, my children will be safe, but if someone wrests power from him, if it's taken by another, my children will be hunted and killed no matter where we run. Ember Innes wouldn't even be able to protect them from the assassins."

"I suppose I understand now," I said, frowning at the thought of murdering children, but it was exactly what Lyrica had done when it took over the Western Empire. The first move the emperor at the time made was to wipe out the ruling family, from old men to children still in swaddling clothes.

The empress looked out the window. "The empire is weak from the plagues of my husband's folly. Even the nobles loyal to him are unhappy. I'll need to work harder than ever to ensure that my family survives this."

The door opened behind me, and Mem stepped back in, holding a small, bulging bag. "Here," she said, setting the bag down before me.

I took it and smiled. "Thank you, Empress. Your kindness will not be forgotten."

"No," the empress said, rising from her seat. "Thank you, and thanks goes to you, too, Lady Echo. I look forward to meeting you in my dreams."

"Farewell," Echo hissed as the empress and Mem left me seated at the table, with more gold than I'd ever held in my life, and a blessed morning free from obligations.

I gave the empress and Mem time to get far enough away that no one would suspect anything. After some time had passed, I stood and hid the bag of gold in the folds of my skirt, anxious to get rid of it as soon as possible before Agramon found it and asked questions.

"Echo, do you know where Mellan's quarters are? Can you show them to me?" I asked when I was ready to leave.

"Follow," Echo said as I stepped into the hall. I smiled, feeling the surge of hope swell.

I KNOCKED AT THE DOOR that Echo whispered me to and waited outside, gripping the bag of gold and praying that no servants or nobles happened into the hall to see me standing outside the room of the court's resident lothario.

I knocked again, louder this time, and heard a moan inside, as though someone were in pain. Alarmed, I tried the handle and sent thanks to Imor that the door was unlocked. Slipping in, I found the room much darker than I anticipated, with the curtains drawn tight over the windows. It took a moment for my eyes to adjust, but when they did, I let out a sigh of relief.

An empty bottle lay near the couch where Mellan was sprawled. I lifted the glass and sniffed. The sour scent of liquor burned my nostrils, and I wrinkled my nose and set the bottle on the table next to the couch.

"Get up," I said, shaking Mellan's shoulder as he drooled into a heavily embroidered cushion.

He didn't move.

"Get up!" I said more forcefully, yanking his arm. I might have put too much strength in the yank, for he promptly rolled off the couch and onto the floor, letting out a startled yelp.

"By Sol above, what are you doing, woman?" Mellan said, glaring up at me as I crossed my arms over my chest.

"I need to speak with you, my love," I countered sweetly, batting my eyelashes and playing at demure. It was never truly effective when I played that hand, but what I had perfected were sarcasm and mockery. It was my only weapon at the capital, where honeyed words and darting eyes were the swords of choice.

"What do you want me for?" Mellan grumbled, picking himself up off the floor and wiping the dust off his gray breeches.

I shrugged as I walked around the couch, dropping the heavy bag of coins on a nearby table before heading to the windows. I pulled the curtains and tied them back, letting the early morning sunlight chase the shadows from the room, revealing Mellan to be a terrible clutterbug. A pile of clothes sat on top of the dining table, while stacks of books collected dust on the floor. Empty bottles had rolled under chairs, and a tray of old food had a veritable cloud of flies gorging on it. I wrinkled my nose in disgust.

"Do you not have a manservant?" I asked, eying the grime with distaste.

"No," Mellan said, running his hands through his hair. "The man got fed up and left after a month, which is just as well. I didn't really want to waste money paying somebody."

"By all the gods, if you aren't going to pay a manservant, the least you could do is clean up yourself," I admonished, shoving a pile of clothes from a chair and taking a seat.

"Did you just come here to mother me?" Mellan snapped. "We aren't married yet, Rowyn."

"No," I admitted. "I have a proposition for you, and I mean for you to hear me out."

"Fine, just give me a moment," Mellan said, walking through the doorway that led to his bedroom, or what I assumed was his bedroom, given the fact that I could barely see a bed. He stood at a washbasin and splashed water on his face before grabbing a bottle of mint water and taking a swig. He tilted his head back and gargled, then walked back into the receiving room and spit the mixture straight out his open window. "All right," he said, wiping his mouth with his sleeve before collapsing on the couch and propping his feet onto the pillows. "What brings you to my room besides the hope for a tumble in the sheets? If you can find them, of course."

"You are foul," I said, unable to help myself. "I have a job I need you to help me with." I nodded to the bag of gold that Mellan hadn't bothered noticing.

He leaned forward and snatched the bag from the table, whistling with respect as he peeked inside and jostled the contents about. "Is this to convince me? Already you know the language of my heart."

"No, it's not for you, it's to pay others. I need you to help me sneak someone out of the city using your team of smugglers."

Mellan drew his arm behind his head and studied me. "Oh, of course, and who, pray tell, are we going to be smuggling?"

"That's the difficult part," I said, smoothing my skirt with my hand. "It's Mordog, the Morganite from the fighting pits."

Mellan tossed the bag of money at me. "Get out."

"You're my only hope," I said through gritted teeth. "Please, there is no one else I can turn to for this. Besides, how is this any different than you rescuing slaves? Luc . . . Mordog . . . is a slave, too, you know."

Mellan scowled, as angry as I'd ever seen him. "You're going to get me killed. Mordog is the most famous pit fighter in the city, which means he will be the most heavily guarded. They live in cells, Rowyn, locked cells with armed guards. It's impossible."

Remembering Mellan's words from earlier, I thought back to how it felt when Luc had been taken and all my dreams had been crushed. I willed tears to my eyes, but I was too annoyed for the tears to come. I only managed to sniff a couple of times.

Mellan was watching me with narrowed eyes. "Are you trying to cry?" he asked. When I didn't answer, he shook his head. "Stop embarrassing yourself."

"Fine," I said, exasperated. "You're right, I can't cry right now, but I still need you to help me, and if I have to force you to, I will."

"And how do you plan to force me?"

"I plan to march straight to Sam and tell him exactly who the Shadow Rogue is." I wished it hadn't come to threats, but I refused to give up hope in rescuing Luc. In my mind, I had no choice.

"You wouldn't," Mellan said, narrowing his eyes once

more. "You would really risk the freedom of the other slaves I've helped, or could help in the future, all to get your way?"

"For Luc I would," I admitted.

Mellan shook his head. "So, you do know him?"

I nodded. "I didn't want Del to reveal anything to Agramon, but yes, I do know him. He's from Espiria, and we were betrothed before he was taken to war."

Mellan smiled. "Well, this just got juicier. If you want me to help you, I want to hear the story."

So, I told him. There really wasn't much to tell, but Mellan nodded as I talked, watching the ceiling as though deep in thought.

"Fine," Mellan said when I finished. "I'll help you, but unlike my other jobs, I won't be able to break him out on my own."

"Do you know of someone else?" I asked, trying to hide the excitement in my voice.

"Of course, who better than you? The girl who defeated the fighting pits."

I glared at him. "How do you plan to break me out of my rooms? Assuming this will be a night venture, of course."

Mellan waved his hand lazily. "That's actually the easiest part. Del already told me how she used to sneak out of Agramon's quarters at night. I'm just surprised she didn't tell you. I'm even more surprised that Agramon never found out." Mellan looked as though he was considering for a moment. "Actually, I'm betting Agramon did know and just didn't care. He's always had a soft spot for Del."

"So, how did she do it?"

"She snuck out her window and climbed into the rooms next to hers. Nobody likes to live near Agramon, so the rooms on either side of you all are normally empty, unless there's a visiting dignitary the emperor wants to keep an eye on."

"Brilliant," I said, slumping back into the chair. I'd never wondered about our hall being empty most of the time. It hadn't crossed my mind that there would be meaning behind it, or that it was something that I could take advantage of. "I wish you'd told me this sooner."

"Honestly, I thought you would've figured it out on your own by now and been halfway across the Ballerian back to Morgania. I'm surprised you've stuck around."

I shook my head. "I can't risk escaping, not when Destrian has such a tenuous hold on Morgania. Besides, where would I go? My family certainly doesn't want me back, and I'm not going to risk Agramon or the emperor hurting anyone I love to entice me back. I've hurt enough people as it is with my mistakes from the past. I'll not knowingly put people in danger again unless I'm forced to."

"You're so noble," Mellan said, though how he said it

came off like it was a flaw. "I would be careful with that mentality here in Somme. Rigid morals and a noble heart mean you're predictable. Me?" Mellan let out a sigh and stretched out. "I prefer to keep people guessing. They're less likely to count on you in any meaningful way, and nobody asks you to do anything or makes you a part of their plans."

"Except my plan, of course," I reminded him.

"Yes, well, you've only proven yourself to be simpleminded. Pinning all your hopes on me helping you succeed in this foolish endeavor is woefully misplaced, but since you insist, I will take payment in gold and a favor."

"A favor?" I asked, furrowing my brows. "What kind of favor?"

"I don't know yet," Mellan said. "But I like the idea of the most powerful sorcerer in the land owing me a favor, so I'll settle for that."

"Consider it done," I agreed.

Mellan and I sat for almost two hours creating tentative plans for getting Luc out of the fighting pits. Since Mellan could move far more freely than I, he was going to do some initial work trying to sneak into the fighting kennels, learning the guards' routines, and setting up a ship to take Luc back to Morgania.

Mellan assured me that he could sneak me out of my room, and I could go with him once he found where Luc was housed.

The thought of seeing Luc again, speaking to him again, seemed to fill my thoughts until I could think of nothing else. A few days went by in a blur while I waited for word from Mellan. I went through the motions of my routines mindlessly. If anyone noticed it, they didn't remark on it, probably because I'd also stopped fighting Agramon's orders, or shooting Willene rude retorts when she irked me. The only one who seemed to care was Sam. He asked me about it one evening after he'd sent me sprawling to the ground. I just told him that I was nervous about the Lu Shen welcoming performance, and to pay me no mind, but Sam wasn't convinced. Still, I had too much crowding my thoughts to give Sam much notice.

I was going to see Luc again, and I was finally going to send him home.

Chapter 30

I FOUND MYSELF AT THE EMPEROR'S banquet the night before the Lu Shen were to arrive. Agramon had let me take dinner in my room for a time, but with the imminent approach of the delegation, he said I had to return to dinners and fancy dresses. So, I found myself stuffed into a red silk gown with the V-shaped bodice that Agramon was so fond of.

When the Count of Gryse began to approach me, I skirted away, disappearing into the crowd and looking for a friendly face. I hadn't seen Del yet, nor Sam, but I spied Mellan standing by himself, oddly somber, with a glass of wine in his hand.

I approached, a smile brightening my face as I grabbed a glass of wine from a nearby slave and stood beside Mellan, who was watching couples spin around the room.

"How goes it?" I asked, taking a drink of wine and turning my eyes to the crowd. Thankfully, Agramon was dining with Princess Willene at a table in the corner of the room, which would distract him, at least for a time.

"Preparations are well underway," Mellan said under his breath. "Be ready for me to come to you tonight. I want you to see the layout of the fighting kennels on the inside."

"Have you found a way in?" I asked, raising my eyes to him.

Mellan nodded. "It will require you to do some acting, but I think it will suffice. We can even test out my theory tonight, and you can warn Mordog of his impending escape."

"I'll get to see him?" I asked, turning to Mellan in surprise. "I'll get to speak with him?"

Mellan nodded, then his eyes went past me and into the crowd beyond. He cursed and turned, setting his glass on the table behind him. "Agramon's spotted us. Come on, we need to distract ourselves."

I placed my glass beside Mellan's as he bowed, holding his hand out to me. "My lady," Mellan said, his voice loud and commanding.

"Good sir," I quipped with mock haughtiness.

Mellan's eyes sparkled as he pulled me onto the ballroom floor. Couples were swirling in unison around us, but Mellan began flinging me about, his feet moving fast as we careened across the hall.

I laughed as Mellan spun me with exceptional vigor. I added a flourish as I stepped out, dancing with such exuberance that the thin fabric on my bodice gave way at the merest tug, and one of my breasts popped out. I realized the slip when the Count of Gryse's mouth fell open. Mellan pulled me back in and, ever the gentleman, tucked my breast back behind the silk fabric while laughing.

Agramon's face was scarlet, but I supposed it was his fault. I'd always detested the gowns he stuffed me into. It was a miracle it hadn't happened sooner.

Mellan grabbed my waist and lifted me, spinning about. There was no denying it. Mellan was simply fun.

The song ended, and though Mellan pulled me to continue, I yanked my hand out of his grip.

"Please sir, give me a moment to catch my breath," I said, holding my side while gasping.

"I can't believe you're winded after a single dance," Mellan said with a glower. "You went to the Nightlands. Aren't you in better shape?"

"The Nightlands weakened me!" I said, feeling a rising swell of indignation. Agramon was still moving toward us. "Besides, *I* was the one with all the extra steps. You barely moved!"

Mellan grinned. "I will say, it was a very *revealing* dance. I may be rethinking what I said earlier. I could possibly tie myself to those breasts, for a few years, at least."

I raised my brows. "I thought they were too small for you."

Mellan let out a long-suffering sigh. "Quite right you are, my dove, quite right. But it's hard to tell in these dresses you wear. Perhaps if you let me dandle them a bit, I'd be able to make up my mind."

"If you touch me, you will find yourself on the long end of a blade."

"Alas," Mellan said, grabbing our wine from the table, "I still have my memory. It will keep me warm at night, even if you do not."

I chuckled, accepting the goblet he thrust into my hand.

Mellan looked over my shoulder and his eyebrows rose. I followed his gaze and saw Agramon standing menacingly behind me.

"Duke!" Mellan said, his hands wide. "What a pleasure to see you enjoying the festivities!"

Agramon raised his brow as Mellan took another deep swig of wine. "Rowyn," Agramon said, turning to me. "I hope this exhibition is not a preview for when the Lu Shen ambassador arrives."

Mellan shifted at my side. I refused to put Mellan, and my plan, in jeopardy so soon. So, I wrapped my arm through Agramon's and led him away from Mellan. "Don't be cross," I said, trying to mimic Del's flippant way of addressing the duke. "We were just having a bit of fun. You know I'll be on my best behavior when the delegation gets here."

Agramon looked down at my arm entwined in his, his brow furrowed. "I'm afraid you'll be the talk of court once again, Rowyn. You're beginning to make that a habit."

"I thought that was how you preferred it," I said, trying

to sound innocent.

Agramon wasn't fooled. "Not in the ways you've found."

"Don't worry," I said, patting Agramon's arm. "When it comes time for the Lu Shens' welcome, everyone will be so blown away by my performance that they will forgive me for all manner of foolishness."

"Let us hope," Agramon said, pulling his arm from mine. "In the meantime, return to your room and try to get some sleep. We have a big day tomorrow."

I nodded. "As you wish, Your Grace."

I was making my way toward the exit when strong hands grabbed me, pulling me into an alcove where I faced Sam. I frowned at his rough handling since we'd parted from weapons training on good terms.

"What was that?" Sam growled, pulling me away from the crowd, the muscle in Sam's cheek spasming.

His eyes raked over me, but I crossed my arms defiantly. "Was there something you wanted to say?"

Sam glanced over at Mellan, who was talking animatedly with one of the pretty university students. "I would've thought you'd be wary of associating with the Lyons, especially that rake. By Sol above, he had his hands all over you."

"I can choose my own friends, thank you very much," I snapped. "And we were merely dancing."

"You made your relationship out to be all for show," Sam growled. "You told me yourself that you were merely trying to appease Agramon, but then you put on this . . . demonstration. What's really going on between the two of you? There's something more to your friendship, I just know it."

I glared at him. "I am not your property, nor Agramon's, nor anyone else's. I'm so tired of being constantly watched and ordered about. Despite what you and Agramon think, neither of you is my father!"

Sam stepped back, his nostrils flaring. "Of course I'm not trying to be your father, Rowyn, I'm . . ." He never finished. His face bloomed red, and he looked away, but I was already in a temper, and there was no cooling down from it.

"What do you want from me?" I asked, this time a hint of desperation creeping into my voice.

Sam's eyes rose, meeting mine. "I would've thought that to be obvious," he said. The corner of Sam's lip twitched. "Forgive me, it was just . . . I expected better behavior from the *hero* of Ayastaren."

The way he said Mellan's moniker sounded more like an insult than a compliment, but there was also no mistaking the tinge of hurt in Sam's voice, nor the look he gave me as he turned and disappeared back into the crowd. It was one filled with disappointment.

A GILDED CAGE

It took everything I had not to go after him.

I LISTENED TO AGRAMON RETURN from the banquet about an hour after I'd lain down. He opened my door, leaned into my room, and said good night before retiring to his own chambers.

I'd left the window open, so Arden came in a while later and nestled on the bed beside me while I patted her absentmindedly. Ena had been commanded back to the servants' sleeping quarters, but she hadn't complained since about being afraid.

Thankfully, I didn't have much longer to wait. I heard shuffling, then a voice whispered, "Rowyn!"

I was off the bed and at the window in a thrice, meeting Mellan as he peered inside. I scrambled onto the ledge that he was standing on. I didn't realize that the stone forming the outside of the castle had rivets and creases deep enough for handholds. Sneaking out didn't even seem dangerous at that point, for it was simple climbing along the ledge and then into the window of the room next door.

Mellan led me out the door and into the hall. Given that not many people lived near us to begin with, and the fact that it was the middle of the night, meant that the hall was deserted. We snuck down the stairs and out a side door of the palace. I pulled down my hood and slipped on my gloves before following Mellan through the shadows. After slipping a coin to the guard at the gate, Mellan led me out into the city. I did my best to keep track of his steps, and soon enough, he came upon a door in a shadowed alley that he knocked upon.

The door opened, and Mellan pulled me inside where another man waited. Mellan pulled his hood down, motioning me to do the same, and shook the man's hand.

"Rowyn," Mellan said, motioning to the older fellow, "this is Gray. If people want a job done, they go to him, and he coordinates with me and the smugglers."

The man ran his fingers through his silver-black hair, his dark eyes assessing me as I nodded. One of his legs ended in a wooden peg from the knee down.

"Master Gray," I said, shifting my cloak over my shoulder. "I am Rowyn the Morganite."

Gray's nostrils flared. "I'm no one's master, but you're a welcome addition to our cause."

Gray motioned us to a table cluttered with papers as he thumped over. I sat next to Mellan, who picked up one of the papers that looked to be a drawing of a building, and began looking it over.

"So, I hear you want to rescue the famed Mordog," Gray said to me. "I confess, we've never tried to bust anyone out of the kennels before."

"Mordog is an old friend from home, and I would like to see him returned to his rightful people," I said, but Gray seemed to be inspecting my gems and markings, rather than listening.

"Gray found us a way in," Mellan said, pulling another paper toward him. "But you're going to have to be the one to scope it out."

Gray nodded. "The biggest threat to the kennels is an uprising. So, to make the fighters more content, the masters allow guards to sneak in women, foods, and other favors for the fighters. Mordog has had a few women visit him, so you'll masquerade as an infatuated fan, gain entry to the kennels, and have a look inside. Count the number of guards, where they are placed, and any other operations or notes you notice from the inside. You won't have long, maybe half an hour if we're lucky, but notice as much as you can while you're inside."

"Where will you two be?" I asked.

"Gray will be here," Mellan said. "He's our eyes and ears in the daylight, when he looks less conspicuous. I'll be exploring the outside of the kennels, looking for hidden exits and whatnot, waiting for you to return."

"Very well," I agreed. "Will we rescue him tonight?"

"No," Gray said. "The ship is due to depart the night after tomorrow. We have no place to stash him till then.

It's always best to smuggle slaves out of the city the same night they are broken free."

I stood. "Well then, what are we waiting for?"

MELLAN SNUCK ME THROUGH the shadows toward the fighting arena. The kennels was a low building nearby, built in a large circle. The fighters' quarters made up the outside of the circle where straight walls of stone with no windows rose before us. As we followed the curve of the kennels, Mellan whispered that the other side held barred windows that allowed in air, and on the inside of the circle was an open arena where the fighters rehearsed for the shows and practiced their weapons work.

When we reached the gate that made up the entrance, Mellan pressed several gold coins into my hand before melting back into the shadows and leaving me standing alone. I pulled my hood low over my face and my gloves tight before straightening and striding over to two guards, who played dice at the entrance. When they saw me approach, one elbowed the other and nodded, a slow grin crawling across his face. The other guard stood and crossed his arms.

"What business do you have here, little one?" The

sitting guard asked, leaning back against the wall as he looked me over.

"I would like to see Mordog," I said, revealing the gold pieces.

The standing guard shook his head. "Why are you dressed like a man?"

"How else would a lady make her way through the streets of Somme at night without issue?" I asked.

"She has a point," the sitting guard said, looking at his partner. "What does it matter anyway? Maybe that's Mordog's thing now."

The standing guard studied me for a moment. "Please," I added as an afterthought.

"I suppose you won't tell us who you are," the sitting guard said, shaking the dice in his hand as though bored. I shook my head and he grinned. "They never do, but I know all's your secrets. You just don't want your husbands to find out!"

I began to lose patience. "Will you allow me to see Mordog or not?" I asked, flicking a gold coin into the air before catching it again. "Otherwise, I'll stop wasting both your time, and mine."

"You can go in," the sitting guard said, holding his hand out for the money. He nodded to the standing guard who rolled his eyes but motioned for me to follow him as he unlocked the gate and went inside.

"We can give you thirty minutes, tops," the guard said, leading me across the open arena. All the cells along the outside were dark. I counted the metal doors from the left to the right of the gate in my head, marking which one I was being led to. There weren't as many guards as I thought there would be. Two outside the gate and four sitting inside the arena, drinking at a table and playing cards by torchlight. They all studied me as I passed, shooting each other knowing glances.

"She's one for Mordog," my guard said to the group at the table.

The other guards laughed. "I wish I were as popular as he," one said before turning back to his game. The guard leading me on stopped at a cell door across the way. I peered through the bars and saw the back of Luc's head, his hair pulled up into a knot, just as it would be back home.

The guard pulled out a key and fitted it into the lock, turning it with a great grunt of effort before swinging the heavy door open. "You have a guest," the guard said as his keys clinked back into his pocket.

Luc's cell wasn't as decrepit as I imagined. There was a large bureau on the far wall, the doors hanging open to reveal a wine decanter, two glasses, and a few articles of clothing. Luc sat on a low-slung sofa, his arms on his knees with his back to me.

"You certainly have become a popular fellow with the ladies," the guard said, motioning me inside as he lit a few candles.

Luc didn't even turn around.

My heart plummeted.

I stepped closer as the guard closed the door behind me with a loud clang.

"I'll leave you two lovebirds to it then," the guard said with a chuckle, then his footsteps died away. I watched through the bars as he made his way across the arena to where the other guards were laughing as they passed a jug around the table.

"You shouldn't have come," Luc said, still not turning around. "I've already told you, Freida, I'm done with this."

"Who's Freida?" I asked, pulling my hood down as I stepped toward him.

"Rowyn?" Luc exclaimed, spinning around on his couch before rising. He held his arms out, and I rushed into them. He breathed deep into my hair as he lifted me from the ground, kissing the top of my head. I let the moment go on for far longer than was probably prudent. In Luc's arms I felt the comfort of home again. It felt as though nothing terrible had happened to us, and we were back in Espiria, together once more.

But we weren't in Espiria. We were in Somme, with danger on all sides, and I didn't have much time. One of the guards' raucous laughter broke the moment and we parted, Luc holding my hands as he sank onto the couch, pulling me with him.

"Tell me," I said, reaching out and brushing a strand of hair out of his eyes. "What happened to you?"

"You know I was taken, me and the others. Well, we were already out at sea when we woke up. Hunt didn't make the sea voyage," Luc said, speaking of a friend who had disappeared with him. "They took us straight to Yliria, and we fought. As you can probably imagine, I was good at war, though even that wouldn't ensure a war dog's survival. Still, instead of dying, like the others, I lived. I kept hoping that if I was good enough, if I fought hard enough, or if I was ruthless enough, they might let me return home, but you know the rest. After the emperor ended the war, they brought me back here and sold me to the pits for entertainment."

I nodded, knowing his story before he even uttered it. It was an all-too-common fate for those whose lives were expendable to the empire.

"What of Mother and Father?" Luc murmured. "Are they well?"

I froze, unsure of what to say. I didn't want to tell him about my last words with Conal. How he'd left me to Duke Agramon because of Destrian. There was so much to say, and yet, I was fearful of revealing it all.

Luc was frowning. "You must tell me everything, Rowyn."

I lowered my eyes. "After you were taken, the plague found its way to Morgania. It took many lives. Both our mothers passed from it. Grandmother too. Father died soon afterward." I went on, revealing as much as I could without outlining the extent of Destrian and my relationship. Luc's face seemed to tighten the further into my story I got, and I became afraid of what he would say, or what he would think, if I told him the whole story. So, I skirted around the details, never telling him the full truth of my time at Solridge or in the Nightlands.

When I was finished with my tale, Luc took my hands in his and inspected them, then leaned to the gem in my brow and ran his fingers over the smooth stone. "I always knew," he muttered, then smiled. "I always knew you would rise above the rest of us."

"We don't have much time left," I said, pulling my hands from his. "I came here to tell you, we're going to get you out. We're going to free you and send you back home to Morgania."

"How can that be possible?" Luc asked. "I know my master, and he makes good money off of me. I can't imagine him willing to sell me."

"I don't intend to buy you. I intend to free you. I know someone who smuggles slaves out of the city, and they've already agreed to help send you home, night after next."

Luc gripped my hands in his. "You're a prisoner here as much as I. Are you going to come with me? Will we return home together?"

I shook my head. "No, Luc, Agramon and the emperor would never let me escape so easily. Espiria would be the first place they would look to find me, and it would put the clan and the rest of Morgania in danger if I did something so foolish."

"Then we can go somewhere else," Luc insisted. "Shea Innes, Yliria, Lu Shen, Horan even. Someplace where Lyrica can't touch you."

"No, Luc," I said. "You must return home alone. I have nothing left in Espiria, but you do. Your father is there. The people will need you to protect them, especially now that my father is gone and Baylin is in charge."

"I won't go without you," Luc said, his hazel eyes on mine. "I won't consent unless you agree to come with me."

I rose, taking a deep breath. "It isn't going to work like that. You'll go to Espiria, and I will stay here whether you like it or not. By dawn the day after tomorrow, you will be on a boat to Morgania, even if I have to drug you and toss you on board myself. Am I understood?"

Luc frowned. "You've changed since Espiria. You would never have spoken to me this way back home. We always worked together on everything."

A GILDED CAGE

"I had to change, Luc, as I'm sure you've had to change as well. I refuse to lose another friend to my foolishness. So, tell me everything you know about the guards' movements at night and the best way to break you out."

Luc seemed to sense that I would brook no argument, so we spent the rest of my remaining minutes fleshing out the guards' schedules until we were interrupted by the clanking of keys. I hastily pulled on my gloves and the hood of my cloak while Luc rose to face the door, readjusting his clothes while blocking me from the guards' view.

"All right then, time's up," the guards said, unlocking the door and opening it with a loud creak.

"Farewell, my sweet," Luc said as I followed the guards out of the cell with my head bowed. I squeezed his hand as I passed, then sped across the arena and out of the gate as fast as my tired feet could carry me.

Chapter 31

MELLAN, GRAY, AND I stayed up till almost dawn that night, going over the details I learned about the inside and finalizing our plans on freeing Luc.

I wondered about rescuing the other fighters in the kennels, but Mellan shook his head. "The more who go free, the more you risk pursuit. The masters would take a loss of one man, even one so well-known as Mordog, without venturing too far out of the city to track him down. If the entire host of fighters went missing . . . well . . . they'd be far easier to track down, for one, and two, the masters would send soldiers to fetch them back. They wouldn't be able to shoulder the loss otherwise."

Light was just peeking over the horizon when Mellan helped me sneak back into the palace and through the windows into my room. I tore my clothes off and mussed the bed, ignoring the growing pangs of weariness at the corners of my eyes as I tossed my clothes to the back of the wardrobe and chose something else to throw on. I was just beginning to tighten the laces when Ena thrust the door open, carrying a package, and she jumped when she saw I'd already risen.

"By Imor above, Rowyn, what are you doing up so early?" Ena asked as she laid the package on the bed.

"I couldn't sleep," I lied, sitting at the looking glass and rubbing at the dark circles under my eyes.

"It must be the excitement for today," Ena said as she began opening the package. "The delegation from Lu Shen is due to arrive sometime this afternoon, then there is the welcome ceremony, and the rainbow ball. It's a busy day, Rowyn, even for you."

"Is she awake?" Agramon asked from the receiving room.

Ena shot me an apologetic smile before calling, "Indeed, Your Grace, she's awake and decent."

"Good," Agramon said before sweeping in. "By Sol above, Rowyn, you look awful. Are you well?"

"I'm fine, Your Grace, just a bit tired," I said, watching Agramon open the package in the mirror. The folds of a dress fell upon the bed as Agramon held the garment up.

"Everyone will be busy with preparations today," Agramon said, handing the dress to Ena and nodding to me. "I wish for you to stay in your rooms until the welcoming ceremony. Remember all that we practiced with Miyu, and prepare yourself for the performance this afternoon."

I thanked Imor I would be saved from a tortuous morning with Willene.

"Oh, and Rowyn?" Agramon said, pausing at my door-frame. I turned. "Get some more rest."

"Yes, Your Grace," I said, trying to hide the flood of relief rushing through me. Ena hung the dress on one of the hooks, and I collapsed on my bed. The last thing I remembered before fading off was a flash of gray feathers as Arden swooped into my room and nestled down beside me.

THE LU SHEN DELEGATION was as grand as everyone was expecting. Instead of greeting the ambassador in the throne room, Miyu had convinced the emperor to relocate to the grand balcony they'd used to show off my power to the city.

Miyu and I were mirrors of each other, her standing on the empress's left hand with Owain creating a striking vision behind her, while I stood at the emperor's right, Agramon looking far less intimidating behind me.

Though I knew Miyu to be nervous, she appeared calm and welcoming. Her Lu Shen robe, embroidered with a flowering vine bearing multi-colored blooms, was a piece of artwork unto itself. She'd set her black hair into an intricate design, accenting it with jade combs. I barely saw a hint of the orange gem embedded in her chest.

I looked down at my gown, a dark twin of Agramon's, for he insisted we dress alike at the important functions of state, no matter how silly I thought it. The top of my gown was black, with long sleeves and a tight bodice. The black fabric gave way to ribbons of red, green, blue, and orange, streaks of color that mirrored the patterns of my gems. Agramon's robes were much the same, though his were white with muted ribbons of color. The rest of the court was a visual symphony. Some of the nobles had opted for wearing a single bright color, while others wore a multitude of shades, making the court look like a garden of hues. Miyu had even decorated the balcony with the theme. Different-colored glass lanterns hung from the balcony's ceiling, casting multi-colored light on those below.

Despite all my trials at the hand of Lyrica, a swell of pride rose within as I looked over the court. It was a wondrous sight, and I hoped the delegation of Lu Shen was honored by it. Agramon had drilled into me repeatedly how important it was that we make a good impression, after all, Lu Shen was nearly as large as Lyrica, and their universities were renown for advancements in medicine that Lyrica wanted to study.

Lu Shen's party was all men in robes of varying colors of silk with embroidered designs of fantastical creatures and beautiful flowers. Their dark eyes seemed to measure the room somberly, picking out the sorcerers and appraising them. Pythia garnered quite a few stares, whether it be from her red-brown skin and golden eyes, or the blood-red jewel at the center of her brow, I couldn't tell. Miyu was next. One of the men even leaned over and whispered into the ear of another member in the ambassador's party, nodding toward Miyu who straightened under their gazes. The other member's eyes narrowed as if appraising Miyu to find fault. Owain stepped closer to her, and I felt a shift in his warding.

The emperor and empress stood as the ambassador approached. Unlike the other members of his party, he wore a tall black hat fitted close to his head, with golden accents threaded throughout. Everyone, including Miyu and me, bowed low. I peeked up at the ambassador's party and noticed that, though they bowed, it was much higher at the waist than the rest of us, and wasn't the low deference that Princess Willene had preached into me my first week in Lyrica. Princess Willene wrinkled her nose in irritation at the slight from her place in the crowd.

"Welcome to Lyrica, Ambassador Liu Da," the emperor said, his arms spread wide. Immediately, Miyu began speaking in her home language, mimicking the emperor's movements as she translated his welcome speech. The ambassador smiled and nodded a thank you to Miyu when she asked the party to take their seats toward the front of the balcony.

I took a deep breath, ignoring the rest of the welcoming and preparing myself for the work to come. The sky was clear and empty, perfect conditions for what Miyu wanted for the performance. At her signal, I walked beside her to the balcony's edge, then curtsied deep to the emperor just as Miyu and I rehearsed. Turning to face the city, I called up the wellspring of my power and let it flow to the sky, darkening it to an ominous black. The wind picked up, sweeping through the crowd of nobles and the clusters of common folk who'd gathered in the city. Behind me, Miyu began to play her pi-pa, singing the rainbow poem in Lyrican and Lu Shen, alternating between the two languages as though in a dance.

I concentrated hard on remembering my cues as lightning tore through the sky and thunder rumbled ominously overhead. The wind whipped through my skirts, sending a swirl of color around me, a glimpse of what was to come. Within a moment, a torrent of rain began to fall, soaking those watching outside. It was but a minute later that I used the wind to push the dark clouds away, bullying them to reform into a spiral, allowing the sun to cascade through the droplets still falling, lighter now, in a gentle shower. I moved my hands in time to Miyu's music. I hadn't needed to move my hands at all, but Miyu insisted it looked more dramatic that way, so I complied, attempting to mimic the beats of her song. I pushed the clouds farther away from each other, allowing the dance of rainbows to begin.

A woman gasped behind me as rainbows appeared in shuddering waves over the sky. They started small, a glimpse of color darting through the mist, followed by another, and another, and another. Soon there were many streaks of color, chasing each other overhead like deer frolicking through an open field.

Miyu's song grew louder, more intense. I shifted again, making the streaks of color larger, the clouds smaller, overtaken by the brilliant swell. Before long, the final chords of Miyu's song were rising. I changed the light rain into a mist, the sky filling with color as the clouds disappeared entirely.

I let out a breath, closing my eyes for a moment as my heart steadied its beat. Despite my weariness and lack of sleep from the night before, the performance had gone exactly as Miyu and I had practiced. It felt like such a big moment. Despite my enmity toward Agramon and the capital, I'd found something I'd been seeking for years. Control. It felt as though I'd finally learned to harness what was within me. The feeling was so freeing. I would never be a slave to my power again. I would never fear myself.

I turned, unable to help the smile stretched across my

face as Miyu motioned me forward. I curtsied, and the nobles applauded, the emperor and empress even rising from their seats as they clapped, the empress shooting me a wink. I looked at Agramon. He was studying the faces of the other nobles, then the ambassador and his party, who had stood with the emperor and were clapping politely with the rest of the court.

Miyu held up both her hands and announced the ball's beginning. Slaves carried out great platters of food, some I recognized while others were completely foreign. A musician's troupe filed in and struck up music that sounded similar to Miyu's song, though far more lively. Miyu pulled me forward as the nobles began eating or dancing depending on their moods.

Owain met us halfway to the ambassador's party, his hand on his sword as we approached. The party stood, speaking animatedly in their language, though they stopped when they noticed Miyu and me before them.

"Chen Miyu, it's been a long time since I was graced with your beauty," the ambassador said, bowing to us with a smile. "I see you have made a home for yourself in this distant land, though you are very much missed at home."

"Ambassador Liu," Miyu said with a curtsy, "I would like you to meet our resident weather sorceress, Lady Rowyn the Morganite."

The ambassador glanced at me and nodded. "It was a

pleasure to watch you perform," he said, his dark eyes on my gems. "I see the land has blessed you thrice over."

I didn't know what to do other than curtsy awkwardly. The emperor's blond hair and golden crown bobbed toward us through the crowd, and I wanted to be away from them before the true diplomacy started. I was sure that my tongue would get the better of me, and I would mess up the trade agreement the emperor was hoping to make.

Miyu smiled, though it didn't reach her eyes. She darted nervous glances at the Lu Shen man who'd marked her presence before.

The ambassador turned back to Miyu and waved the other man forward. "You remember Huang Bo? He has often wondered about the life you've made for yourself on these foreign shores. The emperor thought it right for him to come and see you for himself, to give you a chance to make amends."

Miyu bowed to the man who sneered at his introduction. I searched for some way to escape. Obviously Miyu and the ambassador's friend knew each other, and judging from the way Owain was standing, this meeting was going to be far from pleasant.

Miyu's smile dropped as she rose from her bow. "What a lovely surprise to see you, Huang Bo. We hadn't known to expect the arrival of the emperor's most esteemed brother, but we're honored that you deigned to visit these foreign shores."

There was definitely bad blood between Miyu and the angry man. Even though it was rude, I tried to mimic Miyu's bow, said "Excuse me," and hurried away, dodging the emperor before finding a large, lovely pillar to hide behind. It was near the food, too, which was even better.

Sam found me there, eating my way through a plate of honeyed delicacies and congratulating myself on my mastery.

"I'm sorry about yesterday," Sam said, his voice contrite. "I overstepped my bounds."

I raised my eyebrows. "You all need to realize I'm still my own person, trapped in Somme or no."

Sam ran his hand through his dark hair. "I know that, I just . . . I wasn't thinking."

I nodded, taking another bite off my plate.

"That was quite a performance," Sam said, his eyes dancing as I licked my fingers. Apparently, Sam hadn't received Miyu's formal invitation about the ball's theme. Either that, or he didn't care, which was more likely. He wore a black overcoat, its edging embroidered with golden suns. Though the material was fine, its bleakness stood out among the rainbow of colors. Still, I realized, not for the first time, that I found the Butcher of Bruin handsome.

"I'm just glad it's over," I admitted, turning back to the crowd where Del and Mellan spun across the dance floor.

Mellan and I agreed to stay away from each other until we could pull off Luc's escape. It wouldn't do for Agramon to happen across that tidbit in Mellan's mind, and he was sure to think of it around me. Seeing how the Count of Gryse was making eyes at me across the room, I decided Sam would be my best bet for companionship during the ball.

After all, I didn't have the heart to be angry at Sam. I abandoned my plate of sweets and looped my arm through his. He looked down at me in surprise as I led him from behind the pillar and into the crowd. But I didn't want to hide anymore. I wanted to celebrate. I wanted to sing from the highest turret. I wanted everyone to know that I wasn't afraid of myself.

A pang of sorrow hit me in the chest as Destrian's face swam into my mind, but I pushed it away. Destrian hadn't come to me that night in Darkport, he hadn't written to me at the capital, he hadn't tried the daring rescue he spoke about in the Nightlands when he insisted that we could be together. I could feel his rage through the absence of any communication from him. What I'd always feared had come to pass. Our family's mutual hatred had won out against our love. There wasn't anything for me to do but move on. Still, I was resolved to send a warning about Agramon's intentions through Luc. It would be my attempt at seeking forgiveness for the pain I'd undoubtedly caused.

"What do you know of the ambassador's party?" I asked, trying to change the direction of my thoughts.

Sam leaned toward me, speaking into my ear given the noise of those around us. "There are several sorcerers with him."

I glanced at the men from Lu Shen and realized that their robes went all the way up to their necks, concealing any gem embedded in their chests. "I heard Miyu say that one of the men was the emperor's brother."

Sam nodded. "After the ships docked, Miyu watched who departed and gave a briefing to the emperor's council. The ambassador is accompanied by four sorcerers, several nobles from their royal council, as well as the emperor's brother and brother-in-law. They sent extremely high-ranking officials to engage in these trade talks."

I frowned. "What does that mean?"

"Miyu said it's a classic disarming tactic, to catch us off guard," Sam said with a shrug. "Luckily, we had her help steering through those waters. She's been instrumental in setting up these negotiations, and if they succeed, all credit will go to her."

I glanced back at the group and noticed Owain openly scowling, hidden behind the emperor who was talking excitedly to the ambassador while Miyu stood by, offering translations when needed.

Sam watched the dancers. Their brilliant colors shifted and spun, dipping as the nobles stepped around the room, creating a vision that looked as if it had been lifted out of a fairy story. He shifted his feet and watched me out of the corner of his eye.

I raised a brow. "Is something wrong?"

Sam shook his head, opened his mouth to speak, then shut it again. Sighing and shaking his head, he turned to me. "Would you do me the honor of a dance?"

I had to remind myself to shut my gaping mouth. "I didn't think you danced, Sam." I didn't add that it was one of the more charming traits that I appreciated.

I could tell Sam was upset by the way the muscle in his jaw shifted. I put my hand in his, unsure of myself. "Of course," I said, trying not to meet anyone's eyes as Sam led me to the floor.

I faced him as he placed a hand on my waist, and I tried to conceal the trembling in my hands. He'd touched me before, mostly during weapons training to show me a move, but for some reason, this felt different.

Sam began to sweep me around the floor, weaving through the other dancers. He wasn't as good as Destrian, nor Mellan, but he was still far better than me.

Chapter 32

"TODAY, WE FREE LUC, my friend," I whispered to Arden the next morning as the first rays of the sun peeked through the window. I'd stayed up late that night, lying in bed, a host of thoughts on my mind. I would free Luc and send my warning to Destrian through him, saving both men from imminent danger. Excitement drummed through my fingers as I chose a blue dress for the day and listened to Agramon moving around the receiving room.

Ena slipped in, saw me awake, and smiled. "I heard you did well last night," she said, lifting the dress I'd chosen and helping me pull it over my head. She tied the stays tight and then motioned for me to sit at the dressing table while she coiled my hair.

"Can you put it all up?" I asked, thinking of the task that night.

Ena nodded and began to wind the coil around my head, pinning it tightly. She made another coil, and another, and after weaving each, she wound them over my head in a sort of crown. It was much the same style my mother would do for me at home.

Agramon came in and shook his head at my

appearance. Walking to my closet, he pulled out a black dress with severe angles around the chest and no sleeves to speak of. "I want to show off her markings," he told Ena, who hesitated. She began unlacing the dress I was wearing.

"Do you mind?" I asked, motioning to the fact that I was about to change.

"Not at all," Agramon replied, inspecting his fingernails and not moving an inch. "The trade negotiations begin today, and the emperor has requested the presence of his council for the talks, which means you and I will be there for most of the day."

My heart fell. I would be under Agramon's thumb the entire day. "I'm not part of the emperor's council. Why would he want me there?"

"As one of the most powerful sorcerers in the world, the emperor thinks your presence will possibly sway Lu Shen's hand in some matters. It adds power to the emperor's side, especially because Lu Shen is under the impression that their sorcerers are far more disciplined than Lyricans."

"So, I have to participate in the trade talks their entire visit?" I asked as Ena pulled the dress I'd originally chosen over my head.

"You won't participate in the talks at all," Agramon said. "You will simply sit there looking dangerous and not opening your mouth unless I say so. Now, tell me, what is that?"

Blood froze in my veins. My first thought was that he'd somehow seen the Girdle of Ephema. I met Agramon's eyes, unable to conceal my fear, then saw where Agramon was pointing. My chemise had ridden up when Ena pulled my dress off, revealing the knife holster strapped to my thigh.

"It's for my knives," I said hurriedly, shoving my chemise back down.

"And where did that come from?" Agramon asked, his voice icy. "I don't remember you having it when we left Morgania."

Ena pulled the black dress over my shoulders and quickly began lacing it, as if concealing the knives would cause Agramon to forget what he'd seen.

"Sam gave it to me," I admitted. "He saw no reason for me not to have some weapons. My powers won't protect me from everything, now, will they?"

Agramon glowered. "I suppose you weren't planning on telling me that little tidbit, were you? Did he put it on you himself?"

I scowled. "Of course not! Unlike some, Sam has been entirely honorable."

"Oh please, I haven't ever touched you," Agramon scoffed. "Don't you ever get tired of playing the martyr,

Rowyn? It must be hard keeping up the act in all your fancy dresses, banquets every evening, weapons work with one of the most famed swordsmen in the empire. Life must be so hard for poor you. By Sol above, at your age I was scrubbing chamber pots and lighting fires at the crack of dawn for the Duke of Solin, all while staying up late into the night with the one candle I was allowed for the week, studying books and theories on magic *by myself* since I wasn't allowed into university."

I froze as Ena adjusted the dress. His words, so startlingly close to things Gillius and Pria had accused me of, cowed me into submission. I glanced down at Ena, but she'd schooled her face into neutrality. What must she think of me? Constantly complaining about my station, yet grossly above her own. If given the choice, would Ena trade places with me, given all of the comforts I was offered? Had I become the spoiled girl Agramon made me out to be? "I didn't mean to sound ungrateful," I said. "My apologies, Your Grace."

Agramon circled me, his cold eyes inspecting me as though I were a market horse he was thinking of purchasing. Yet, I said nothing, my head bowed low. "The hair looks well with it," Agramon said, speaking to Ena. "I wish for you to darken her lids with kohl, as dark as you can make them. Line them with that mineral paint I showed you as well."

Agramon stayed to monitor Ena's work and give her further directions. While Ena painted my face using one of Arden's cleaned feathers, Agramon wandered around my room, inspecting what few possessions I had. He came first to Iranoct. Unsheathing the sword, he noticed the necklace with Fin's timepiece, Pedr's chess piece, and Araceli's key. After inspecting those, he bent to look closer at the designs Destrian had etched on the blade.

"Are you looking for something in particular, Your Grace?" I asked, watching from the vanity mirror.

"I'm just admiring Everett's handiwork," Agramon said, running his hand along the sword. "Did you know his family have been well-known blacksmiths for generations? One of his grandfather's swords is kept in the emperor's personal armory. A great beast of a blade it is, nearly too heavy to be much use to anyone."

"Destrian mentioned that the skill ran in their family," I said as gooseflesh rose over my arms. Agramon had barely mentioned Destrian to me before, and now, when I'd finally found a way to send a message to him, Agramon was talking about him. Was it merely a coincidence or was the Girdle of Ephema slipping? Could he read my thoughts? Did he know I was planning to help Luc escape?

"I heard they're good at the anvil, but not much else. Your Destrian's father was a shit ruler, and the only thing that saved his seat was the fact that Morgania was already wealthy to begin with, so the emperor didn't interrupt the flow of goods."

I didn't know what to say. I'd always hated Consul Colman myself, and I'd be damned if I defended him now. "I don't know your measure of effectiveness at ruling a consulship, nor the emperor's, but he seemed to create further divisions among the Morganites and Lyricans."

Agramon rolled his eyes and brought Iranoct to me. "The Lu Shen are proud of their steel craft, and an Everett blade is a way to show that we are not without our own experts. Wear this to the meeting today."

I stood and belted Iranoct on. Gazing into the mirror, I had to admit, I liked my appearance. The dark shadows and lines, along with the imorets tattooed around my eyes, made me appear fearsome. The gems glowed deep against the black of my gown and hair. Even the Morganian rose vine on my neck and the ten-pointed star on my chest stood out more.

"Come on, we don't want to be late," Agramon said, leading me out of my room. I mentally reviewed Lady Vianne's training as we walked a familiar path through the halls of the palace.

Guards opened the door when we reached the council room, revealing the great table inside to be half-full. The men stood when they saw me trailing Agramon. Agramon took the seat directly beside the emperor's empty chair, while I sat on Agramon's other side. When I was seated, the other men sat as well. Sam nodded to me from his place across Agramon, directly to the emperor's left.

I didn't know most of the noblemen, though I'd seen their faces at the emperor's banquets. Some wore robes and appeared to be sages, wise men from the university, while others were far more richly dressed. I'd just had a chance to glance around the chamber when the door opened again to the emperor, Miyu, and Captain Diardo escorting the Lu Shen ambassador's party to the meeting.

We all rose as the noblemen from Lu Shen chose their places at the other end of the great table. The emperor waited for their shuffling to cease before taking his seat with Diardo heading to the shadows behind him, his limp still somewhat pronounced. Miyu sat beside Sam and shot me a smile before turning her attention to the emperor.

The entire morning was spent on a dance of welcome speeches, introductions, and compliments, with nothing of any importance said whatsoever. It seemed like an eternity, but eventually they decided to break, the emperor leading us to a luncheon out in the gardens.

Agramon abandoned me to have words with Huang Bo, the Lu Shen emperor's brother, as soon as we'd filled our plates. I stood awkwardly, trying to stay away from the clusters of men having their own conversations.

"Did you rest well?"

I turned to find Sam at my side, a glass of his favorite liquor in his hand.

"I did," I said, then nodded to his glass. "Are you not concerned that you're hindering your ability to negotiate?"

Sam shrugged. "I don't negotiate. As commander of the military, I'm just as needed in that room as you are. We're shows of strength, Rowyn, nothing more."

"You don't think he'll include me the entire time, do you?" I asked, unable to hide the dread in my voice.

Sam glanced at the emperor, who was already on his second glass of wine. "Who knows what Emperor Arthello will decide from one day to the next? We're all at his mercy." He took a drink, his eyes moving from the emperor to Agramon, who was now deep in conversation with three of the Lu Shen party.

Turning to me, he held out his arm. "Walk with me. There's nothing that says you have to spend the *entire* day with the delegations."

I didn't know what to do. It seemed I had set a precedent the night before by taking his arm, and now it was an expectation. I set my empty plate with the others and placed my arm on top of his instead of winding it through, letting him lead me into the hedge maze.

I couldn't help myself. My mind went back to Luc sitting in his cell in the kennels. I went over every detail of my plan with Mellan, of the letter I still needed to write to

Destrian. I hoped Agramon would release me from my duties early so I could get some rest before the trials of the night. Would he expect me to attend dinner that evening as well?

"You seem to be deep in thought today," Sam said, breaking the silence.

"There has been a lot on my mind lately, with my training and this Lu Shen business," I lied.

Sam nodded as though he knew what I spoke of. He left me in silence, casually sipping his drink. Eventually, we made our way to the center of the maze. Great rose bushes bloomed around the center, with climbing vines of roses creeping over an arch that gave shelter to a stone bench in the middle of the circle where Sam set his drink. The flowers' perfume filled the air in fragrant clouds that wafted over me as I inspected the blooms.

I turned to Sam, smiling with unexpected delight. "I had no idea this was at the center," I said. "Did you?"

"Not at all," Sam said, but he wasn't looking at the flowers. His eyes were on the rose marking on my neck.

His fingers reached out, lightly tracing the vine. A tingle rose over my skin at the lightness of his touch. I caught my breath, frozen as warmth bloomed within. I didn't know what to do or say.

"Remember that night that you spent in my room?" Sam whispered, his green eyes brighter in the light of midday.

"Please don't speak of it," I said, sure my cheeks were reddening. Why would he bring up *that* embarrassing moment? To make me feel foolish? To disarm me?

"You'd worn roses in your hair that night. When I went into my room later, the pillow was covered with petals. I couldn't bring myself to discard them." Sam's fingertips had stopped their journey around my marking. Instead, he ran his thumb along my jaw ever so slowly. "The scent lingered for days after, smelling just like this, roses after a new rain. I couldn't get it out of my mind."

His thumb found my mouth, lightly pressing into my lips as Sam leaned closer, then placed his lips gently on mine. I gasped, and Sam took advantage of my shock by nipping at my bottom lip before exploring my mouth with his. I couldn't stop trembling as the taste of his favorite drink met my tongue, its sharp, oaky flavor faint on his breath. He cupped my cheeks and pulled me closer.

I barely registered the voices that traveled up the path of the hedge maze, but Sam pulled away sharply. My cheeks were on fire as I smoothed my skirt and turned away from Sam as the voices made their way into the clearing.

It was several members of the delegation including Agramon. They continued their conversations despite Sam and my presence, though Agramon shot me an odd look, glancing from Sam to me. I covered my burning cheeks with my hands, sure the guilt was written clear as day over my face. Agramon's eyes narrowed when they met mine, as though all my secrets were laid bare before him.

Chapter 33

I COULDN'T CONCENTRATE on the negotiations for the rest of the day. I barely caught the Lu Shen ambassador's request for two ports, one on the eastern shore and one on the west, to use for trade and resupply. I nearly missed the emperor's insistence that some black powder that Berinon the alchemist used for his experiments be included as part of the deal. Instead, my mind looped through the memory of the kiss, how Sam's lips had felt on mine, the strength of his grip, the way he'd tasted. More than once my eyes traveled to Sam, who was doing a far better job of looking interested in the conversation than I was, though he gripped his sword the entire time, as if knowing that Agramon would try to weasel his way into Sam's mind.

Agramon hadn't remarked on my odd behavior in the rose garden, nor asked why I was there with Sam. Nervous energy flitted through my fingertips as the men debated back and forth for hours.

I tried to dredge up the memory of Destrian's kisses. The heat emanating from him, the fire that seemed to lurk just beneath his flesh. Sam's kiss had been so different. There was no magic simmering beneath the surface, only the look in his eyes. I couldn't help but admit that I'd liked it. By all the gods, what was I doing?

Finally, the talks were over, and they dismissed to ready for dinner. As soon as I was able, I hurried from the council room before Sam could rise from his seat. I heard Agramon behind me, so I slowed, trying to pretend as though nothing were amiss.

"I would hazard a guess that you don't wish to attend the emperor's banquet tonight," Agramon said as though trying to sound offhand. "However, you must know that your presence will be required."

"I dislike being a mere decoration," I grumbled, not meeting Agramon's eye.

Agramon grabbed my arm and swept me inside our rooms, slamming the door behind him. It took everything I had not to grab Iranoct.

Agramon leaned in, his gem casting a rosy glow on my face. His eyes, so muddy in color, were sharp as they tried to pierce through me. The scent he splashed on himself in the mornings flooded my senses, a mixture of vanilla and mint, deceptively pure. "I've been a patient man and put up with the Butcher's interference these past few weeks because, despite what you may think, I wanted you to be happy, but this has gone on long enough." Agramon grabbed my shoulders and shoved me into the wall, cracking my head against the wood. "What information are you giving him? Why does he have you spying on me?"

"Your Grace?" I stammered, stunned by his behavior. "He asks me nothing about you."

"Don't lie to me," Agramon said, his eyes refusing to leave mine. I met them willingly, trying to convince him of the half-truth. I wasn't spying for Sam; I was spying for the empress.

"He asks nothing of me," I insisted, shoving his hands off and twisting away. I was loath to touch my sword or the knives at my thigh, any weapon that Agramon could take away from me. I raised my hands instead. "Sam has never asked me anything about you, Your Grace."

"Then what was that business in the garden?" Agramon roared, pointing an accusatory finger at me. "I saw you together! I saw the look on your face when we came upon you. You're hiding something from me!"

"That's not what was happening!" I shouted back. "We weren't speaking of you at all. He was . . ." I hated what I was about say, but I couldn't let Agramon think that I was spying for Sam. It put both Sam and me in danger and threatened to reveal everything I'd done for the empress, not to mention Echo's very existence. "He kissed me," I said finally, lowering my voice in case anyone was in the hall. "It was just a kiss."

Agramon hauled himself up short. "A kiss," he repeated. Silence descended on the room. I could see the thoughts spinning behind his eyes, but it was impossible to tell what they were.

Finally, he faced the window, watching the sun disappear behind the western sky. "By Sol above, you look at me with absolute contempt, and yet you would let someone like the Butcher of Bruin put his hands on you? The man is the embodiment of death and ruination, yet you would encourage him to pursue you."

Then, he did something that caused my stomach to somersault, freezing the blood in my veins.

He threw his head back and laughed.

"DO YOU THINK THIS PLACE has changed me?" I asked Ena as she busied herself with unplaiting my hair. She'd brought in another new gown that Agramon had given her to press, and she'd lit a small fire in my bedroom, placing a round iron near the embers that she could use to curl my hair.

Already I was weary of the Lu Shen diplomacy. I had to stuff myself into a new gown every hour only to be paraded about like one of Empress Lesedi's colorful birds, a decoration for others to ogle at and to show off the power and might of my handlers.

Arden squawked from the windowsill where she'd been eating meat we left for her. I worried Agramon would find the gouges on the frame from her claws and figure out some way to punish me, but the bird seemed to know to remain hidden when Agramon was about. She was just as reliable as Echo in alerting me of his presence, for her head would swivel to my door before she took off, sometimes seconds before Agramon swept in.

Ena hadn't answered. I almost thought she hadn't heard me, except I noticed that she avoided my eyes. I looked down to my hands. "Was what Agramon said this morning true? Am I nothing more than a spoiled brat?" I whispered, fearing her answer.

"He's spoiling you, but that doesn't make you spoiled," Ena said, her voice hard.

"Then why won't you answer me?" I asked, grabbing Ena's hand to still her. I looked up and found tears in her eyes. "What is it?"

"I feel him in my mind, Rowyn," Ena gasped, then emitted a great, shuddering sob. "I'm sorry, I tried to keep him out, but it's like he's always there, snaking through my thoughts. He's planted things in my head, ideas I'd never considered before, things I'd never believe about you. I'm afraid to say anything because I don't know what my true thoughts are. Sometimes, I even wonder if what I see is real, if my memories of you are true. I feel as though I'm being driven mad!"

I rose, shocked at seeing Ena so distraught. "Why didn't you tell me of your fears? Of what Agramon is doing to you?"

"Because he wanted me to," Ena cried. "He was insistent with that thought. He *wanted* me to tell you, so I resisted."

I grabbed her shoulders and crushed her to me, holding her trembling body while my mind raced. Mellan and I were freeing Luc this very night. Should I send Ena with him? I immediately dismissed that thought. There was no way Luc and my handmaid could disappear without others suspecting my involvement, and that would put Mellan in danger. Besides, Ena was no slave. Presumably, she should be able to return whenever she wished. No, I would simply have to find some way to pay her passage back to Morgania. I didn't dare share that information with Agramon. I didn't know why he wanted Ena to tell me of her fears. Perhaps he wished I would send her away. He probably just wanted me to be further alone, separated from those who loved me. It didn't matter. I had to protect Ena—it was my duty—and I *would* find a way to get her out of the city and on a ship back to Morgania.

"Give me till the end of the week, Ena. Stay away from Agramon till then, and I'll find some way to pay your passage home."

Ena fell to her knees, pulling me with her as she wept into my shoulder. "I'm so sorry I haven't been brave enough," Ena gasped.

I grabbed her shoulders and forced her to look into my eyes. "Don't you dare speak that way about yourself. Of all my friends on the western shore, of all the people who said they loved me, you were the only one who chose to take this journey with me. That was no small deed, Ena. You are one of the bravest people I know."

I used the sleeve of my violet evening gown to wipe the tears from her eyes, not caring a jot for the silk fabric. After a while, Ena was able to compose herself, and finished curling my hair. Thankfully, she was gone by the time Agramon returned to escort me to the banquet.

It took everything I had to remain normal in his presence. I prayed to Imor that he thought nothing of my silence as I trailed behind him in the hall, stewing over his treatment of Ena. I couldn't afford to rebuke him as I wished to. Luc's and Ena's lives were on the line now, and it was up to me to rescue them.

A GILDED CAGE

THE EMPEROR TOOK ANOTHER drag of his goblet, talking loudly with the council members around him. Beside me, the Lu Shen delegation were talking among themselves, none drinking to excess like the Lyricans. Suddenly, I heard a boisterous laugh. It was the emperor, flinging his arm around Diardo who seemed to be attempting to quiet him.

"And why should they not agree to our terms?" the emperor proclaimed loudly enough for the entire hall to hear. "We have the only weather sorcerer of the age. If they wish to use her, they *must* agree."

"We have no need for a weather sorcerer," the ambassador said coldly. "The gods have blessed us these past hundred years, and our land remains as fertile as ever."

Emperor Arthello's eyes narrowed. "And how long do you think that would last if you displeased us by not accepting our generous offer? If my advisers have told me correctly, what Rowyn the Morganite can bring, she can just as easily take away."

The entire court turned to look at me. Sam's gaze darkened on the other side of the Lu Shen delegation, as if his expression alone could silence the emperor.

I knew the emperor intended to use me to bring fruitfulness back to his empire, but I hadn't even considered the thought that he could use me to punish others. I supposed what he said was true. Though I'd never tried to end the rain in a place, I would be able to do it. It was simply a matter of using wind to blow the clouds elsewhere. How many thousands could I help with my powers, and how many thousands could I curse if the emperor put his mind to it? I wouldn't do it. He couldn't make me.

But the Lu Shen delegates didn't know that. One whispered frantically in their native tongue to the ambassador. Huang Bo glared stonily at Emperor Arthello, who smiled gleefully as he surveyed the room.

"You seem to place so much worth on a simple sorcerer. One who is still mortal and could be defeated with the wave of a Lu Shen sorcerer's hand," Huang Bo proclaimed, his fingers fluttering through the air.

The last thing I heard was Owain cursing at the emperor's side. Searing pain ripped through my middle, and I bent double, screaming my horror as my insides were being seared. I lost all sense of time and place. The only thing I knew was a deep, unrelenting pain.

Chapter 34

I AWOKE IN MELLAN'S ARMS as he carried me through the halls. Voices rose around me, footsteps rushed about, and I made out the shouts of guardsmen giving orders. I gripped Mellan's tunic and raised my head.

He looked down. "Hold on a moment," he hissed. "I'm taking you to my rooms."

Mellan ducked down another hallway and put me down outside his door. He pulled a key from a pocket in his tunic and ushered me inside as he looked over his shoulder.

Mellan turned to me with a wide grin. "This is just perfect," he said, walking over a pile of clothes and pulling out a darker pair of breeches. "I couldn't have planned it better myself."

I checked my stomach, sure that there would be a gaping wound given the pain, but apart from a light stinging still present in my gut, I was back to normal. "How is my near-death now such a great part of your plan?" I asked, catching a pair of breeches and a tunic he'd tossed at me. I sniffed them and wrinkled my nose. "These are dirty."

"Did you want to wait for them to be washed before we rescue your friend?" Mellan asked crossly, lifting his embroidered tunic off and pulling on a plain one. I refused to admire the muscles in his chest . . . too much. "This is perfect because the emperor counted the attack on you as an act of war and has ordered the Lu Shen back to their ships immediately. The entire court is going to be ensuring that the Lu Shen delegation makes it to the docks, including the army stationed here, and the city guards. Everyone is going to be so distracted that I think our plan will actually work."

I couldn't bring myself to tell him about Ena. He was already putting himself at significant risk helping me with Luc. After all, Luc wasn't a mere house slave, but rather a famous war dog who brought his owners significant profits from the fighting pits.

Nerves surged through me at the thrill of doing something useful, of making a difference, of having a true adventure. My hands shook as I turned to the wall, yanking the sleeves of the gown down and pulling the tunic over it. I stepped out of the gown, slipping my feet into the black leggings and tugging on the boots. I turned and saw Mellan watching me.

"You couldn't have given me the least bit of privacy?" I asked crossly, lifting the gown and rolling it over my arm. Mellan tossed me a satchel that I shoved my gown and delicate shoes into, smiling.

"I'm a Lyon, remember? Never presume I'll make the honorable choice. It's in our blood."

I pulled out my daggers, belting them on the outside of my person so they'd be easier to grab. Mellan tossed me a simple sword, and I frowned at its short blade.

"I could've brought my own sword," I said.

"No," Mellan said, strapping another simple blade to his side. "Iranoct has specific designs that could easily be traced back to you. If you're going to be dastardly, you must ensure that everything points to anonymity."

He had a point.

"Are you sure Agramon's not going to search for me?" I asked. "How do you know he won't be worried sick?"

Mellan gave me an exasperated look. "I told Agramon I was going to take you back to your room, then I told Del I would take you to see Tristam instead. It will take them a while to unwind that story, and I can always trump it up to the chaos. Miyu had said herself that Huang Bo can only inflict pain in the moment, and that there wouldn't be any lasting damage. She said he'd done that to her loads of times over the years to teach her lessons and hadn't come to lasting harm from it, at least not bodily harm anyway."

"What an awful man," I said, shaking my head as I adjusted my belt.

Mellan nodded. "The Butcher, Agramon, Bald Walden, and everyone who is anyone is heading down to the docks to ensure that the Lu Shen haven't snuck their secret fighting crews into the city to mount an assault. They'll be gone all night unless I miss my guess, so a little trade ship out of the city carrying an escaped war dog will be the least of their worries. They probably won't even make it back before we do."

I slung the satchel over my back and faced Mellan. He tossed one more small bundle to me. I unfolded it, finding leather gloves, a hood, and a face wrap.

"To hide our features," Mellan said, pulling a hood over his head. "Some of us are more conspicuous than others."

When we were finally ready, Mellan rested his hands on his hips. "The boat will be in Scantytown's southern dock. There is an outlet in the city's sewer system near the fighting arena. If we can get him into it, we can lead him under the city and out to the other side, near the dock."

I nodded, trying to still my trembling fingers. "So, how do we get out of the palace?" I asked, looking over Mellan's shoulder to the alley.

I heard the smile in Mellan's voice as he looked out of his window. "That's easy, my dove. We simply climb down."

He hopped onto his windowsill and lowered out of view. My smile was hidden behind the black mask as I leveraged myself after him. I realized why Mellan used his window to escape. The side of the castle was hidden with vines of jasmine and ivy, and overlooked a portion of the wall that went unmanned, as it was farthest from the gate and facing a steep drop-off down a rough-looking cliff. We scrambled down, and upon reaching the top of the wall, Mellan took off at a run and leaped onto the roof of a building that had been built far too close to the wall. I followed, landing easily beside him. We leaped from roof to roof, making our way down the slope of the city and toward the entertainment district where the fighting arena lay.

The stars above me, the moon watching as I made my way over the buildings, the feeling of a sword at my waist, and a mission under my feet. It was as though I were in Espiria again.

Mellan slowed when we finally reached the kennels.

"Why is the Shadow Rogue so well-known?" I whispered as we climbed down an abandoned building into a dank alleyway. "I would think that with all the work it takes to free slaves, there would be far more of you helping." Though Gray was his partner-in-arms, so to speak, he could be hardly counted on in a fight. Other than the merchant ships that could be paid off, I wondered about so small an operation. Surely more people felt for the Ylirian slaves' plight.

"Sadly, do-gooders in this city are few and far between, and have a limited set of skills. They tend to be very nice, somewhat intelligent, and without a murderous bone in their bodies. That's where I come in. I have little enough scruples that I'll get the slaves out in a pinch, even with an assault or two, and I'm not in enough need for money that I would be bought over by the criminal element. It gives me the sense of adventure I crave, without the pesky guilt that I felt in the war. It's a win-win for all."

"Maybe I crave adventure too," I said, enjoying the thrill of breathing the night air and feeling the wind on my face without the stuffiness of the palace.

"I know you do. Trust me, I fought beside many a Morganite in Yliria. I had to take small jobs because it was just me, but if I have you by my side, a second rogue, then we could nab the bigger catches."

I couldn't help but get caught up in the giddiness of the moment.

Mellan crept around the side of the building and peeked out into the street. It was lucky that there were no taverns and whorehouses by the kennels, or else there would've been more travelers out in the street. As it was, the street was deserted except for the guards sitting outside the kennel gate. The sound of loud snoring could be heard, as both men were sitting with their backs to the wall, their heads slumped against their shoulders.

"Are they . . ."

"Sleeping," Mellan finished, holding the hilt of his sword before darting across the street to another shadowed corner. I took a breath and followed, bringing us closer to the gate.

Mellan crouched to watch the men and study the street. "Gray found out where and when they bought their booze. Turns out the men outside go to a different tavern than the men who guard the inside, so he had a hell of a time drugging their bottles, but he managed it. Lucky for us, they all enjoy their drink even more than I do."

"When do we go in?" I asked.

"Well . . . now, of course. Were you thinking we'd wait till they woke up?"

I punched him in the arm, and he steadied himself against the wall, chuckling.

"Come on," he ordered, "we still want to get you back before the court returns."

I followed Mellan as he crept toward the guard with keys hanging from his belt. Mellan kneeled and lightly tapped the man on the arm. His only response was to snort, then he turned his head and began snoring anew.

Mellan carefully pulled the key ring from the man's belt and handed it to me. I rose and placed the key in the lock. The tumblers fell into place, and the door to the kennels swung open with a loud creak.

I froze, my hand on the door, fearing to turn around. Mellan was up beside me in a moment and shoved me inside before pulling the door shut.

"Next time we plan an escape like this, let's be sure to

bring some oil for the hinges," Mellan said, studying the arena from the shadows. The men inside were still asleep. Two rested their heads on each other, their arms crossed over their chests as they breathed soft and even. Another had his head on the table, while another looked as though he'd fallen from his chair.

"Are you sure that one's not dead?" I asked, pointing to the body on the ground.

Mellan shrugged. "I'm not going to waste time to check. You go and find your Luc, while I get the keys to the cells."

I nodded and slipped along the outside of the cells, counting until I came upon Luc's from before. I stood on my tiptoes and peered inside.

"Luc!" I hissed through the bars.

Hands came into view and gripped mine. "Rowyn," Luc said, his fingers exploring mine. "Is tonight the night?"

"Yes, we're getting the keys now," I assured him before another voice butted in.

"What's this business?" someone shouted from the cell beside Luc's. "Are you escaping, Mordog?"

"Shhh!" Luc and I hissed at the same time.

"Take me with you!" the man begged, his voice far too loud. "Don't leave without me. They're putting me in with a bear tomorrow!"

"We can't," I whispered, trying to quiet him. "It will be too dangerous."

The man only grew louder. "Let me take my chances," he said. "Don't abandon the rest of us to this death!"

Another voice from the cells joined in, and another, each begging to be freed as well. By the time Mellan made it to my side, it seemed as though the entirety of the kennels was awake.

"Silence!" Mellan commanded. The voices hushed, their owners listening intently from behind their bars. "The court is at the docks making sure the foreign dignitaries leave. That's where the city guard is, as well as some soldiers from the army. We can let you out of the cells, but you all will have to scatter, each man for themselves. Nobody can follow my partner and me, save this one."

"We promise," one of the men said.

"Just give us a chance," yelled another.

I looked over my shoulder. It looked as though the guards were stirring from all the commotion. I shook Mellan's arm. "Hurry up," I hissed. "We don't have much time."

Mellan growled a curse at me as he fumbled with the keys, trying different ones on Luc's door until the key turned and the door swung open. Luc stepped out wearing a ragged tunic and breeches, his feet covered in a broken pair of leather sandals. I clenched my teeth, wishing I'd thought to bring him some clothes.

"Come," I said, taking Luc's hand. "My partner has a ship ready to take you to Morgania."

I pulled him toward the gate as Mellan released the man in the cage beside Luc's. He then released another, and another, before handing the keys off to one of the men and racing toward me. Two of the men headed toward the guards as soon as they left their cells, pulling the swords from the sleeping guardsmen's sides and systematically butchering them. I gripped Luc's hand harder when I realized what we'd done.

"Go!" Mellan said, shoving Luc and me toward the gate. The screams of dying men and the clanking of dropped chains filled the air as Mellan, Luc, and I ran out into the night.

Chapter 35

AIR TORE THROUGH MY CHEST as we bolted down one alleyway and up another. Mellan led the way, stopping at each corner to peer out into the darkness before motioning us on. Soon enough, we came to a large rock that seemed to be out of place on the side of the street.

"Help me lift it," Mellan said, grabbing Luc's hand and motioning to the rock. It took all three of us to shift the stone, but when we did, it revealed a tunnel into the ground.

"Come on," Mellan said when I hesitated. I glanced over my shoulder at Luc who looked at me with such trust. I couldn't fail him this time. We traveled through the tunnel, darkness swallowing us whole as we moved further into the earth. Soon enough, the sound of rushing water found our ears, and Mellan lit a small torch he'd stashed in his satchel. We kept going, now with light to see by, though it hardly made the going less scary. I stepped on animal bones that littered the way and listened to the scurry of little feet that brought me back to the Nightlands.

The sound of rushing water grew closer, and we finally came upon the source. The sewer tunnel was lined with rock, some built up on the side, creating a sort of walkway along the water's edge. The stench filling the air was unbearable, but I pulled my face cloth tighter and gritted my teeth, determined to see this through. Luc never once complained. He followed Mellan's orders without a word, yet I'd not even given Luc his name.

After walking several miles, we came upon an opening in the tunnel, the water rushing past us and down a rocky embankment where it poured into the sea.

We'd finally made it to the docks.

A figure waited by the opening of the sewers. Gray rose, using two paddles to help himself up. "Just in time," he said, holding his hand out to shake Luc's. "I'll warrant all went well?"

"As well as can be expected," Mellan agreed. "The rest of the fighters in the kennels insisted to go free, so now the city is filled with cutthroats and murderers, but what's new?"

Gray clenched his teeth. "Well, I'm glad you only brought the one with you. The merchant was already complaining that you paid him far more last time."

"Last time it was for four riders," Mellan growled, shaking his head. "Ungrateful chickensh—"

Luc pulled me away from the men as they talked. He led me down the embankment a bit and held my hands in his. "I don't like this," he murmured, pulling my hood and face-covering off. "I just found you again, and now you wish me to leave you?"

"We have no other choice," I whispered back. I reached down to my knife holster and pulled out a blade. Wrapped around it was a parchment of paper addressed to Destrian. "I need you to promise me something," I said, pushing the paper into his hands. "When you reach Morgania, I need you to deliver this to the new consul of Helena, Destrian Everett. Don't let anyone know you have this letter, and don't ask someone else to do the errand for you. Please make sure it reaches his hands yourself."

"Why are you writing to the consul's son?" Luc asked, his brows furrowed. "What do you owe him that you would risk your life to get him this information?"

I clenched my eyes shut, trying to keep my patience. When I opened them again, I realized that Luc was getting angrier the longer I dallied. "I owe him my life, Luc, and that's no small thing to me," I said. "Please promise that you will not fail me in this."

Luc lowered his eyes to the letter and nodded slowly. I reached up, my hand on his neck, pulling him down and kissing him on the cheek.

"Thank you," I whispered, resting my forehead against his. "I'll see you again soon, I promise."

Luc straightened, his eyes hard. "You shouldn't make promises you can't keep."

"Rowyn!" Mellan hissed from above us. "It's time."

I nodded. Gray was already making his way toward us, and below bobbed a little boat moored to the land with a small rock. I threw my arms around Luc, wishing I had more time to get to know the man he'd become, before giving him another kiss on the cheek. "Best of luck to you, Luc," I whispered, giving his hand one last squeeze.

"If I don't see you again," Luc said, then hesitated, "know that I've missed you."

I refused to let the tears fall as I watched him follow Gray down to the little boat. As soon as they reached it, Mellan was at my side, his hand on my arm. "We have to hurry you back. I think we can still make it before the court returns."

I nodded and let Mellan pull me back into the stinking sewer of Somme.

IT REALLY WAS FAR TOO EASY to break out of and into the palace. As soon as Mellan and I left the sewer, we made our way through the city, toward the palace at the center. We moved as fast as we dared, keeping to the shadows until the houses were packed so densely together that we could clamber up to their roofs and make the rest of our way from above. It was short work climbing the wall back up the palace and into Mellan's room where I changed back into my gown.

"Good luck," Mellan said as I slipped from his rooms and into the hall where I made my way back to my chambers. The halls were dimly lit given the hour, and strangely quiet. Usually there were at least servants moving about.

I slowed as I reached Agramon and my chambers. Light bled from under the door.

I froze, not knowing what to expect. Did I run? Did I dare go in? I almost turned heel but denied myself the cowardly act when I thought of Ena. I couldn't desert her to Agramon. Not when she'd shown me nothing but loyalty.

Taking a deep breath, I opened the door to our receiving room and stepped inside.

Agramon was seated on the couch, his staff twisting in his hand.

"So, you've returned," he said. His nose wrinkled as the stench of sewer filled the air, an inevitability that I didn't think about when I was tramping through the underground waterway for an hour. "Pray tell, where have you been, my dear Rowyn?"

I gritted my teeth. "I was down with Tristam in the healing house first, then lost my way on the way back to my rooms." I knew it was a weak excuse, but I had to tell him something. "I only now just found my way back."

Agramon canted his head to the side. "*Tsk, tsk*, my dear. It doesn't take a mind reader to know that you are spewing utter bullshit. So, I will ask you again. Where have you been?"

"What does it matter?" I said finally, walking toward my room. "I'm back now, aren't I? Who cares where I've been as long as your precious sorcerer has returned."

"It matters," Duke Agramon said, leaning calmly back in his chair, "because you have been deceiving me, and your lies will come at a cost."

I turned, resting my hand on the wall and never letting my eyes waver from his. "Your paltry parlor tricks do not work on me, my lord, so what then? You and I both know how valuable I am to your cause. But you have no control here, not in my mind. So, what will you do?"

Agramon laughed. "And what, my dear Rowyn, does this matter? Who do you think wields control in this realm? Who do the spies of the emperor bow to in the end? Whose very whim bends the ear of the emperor? You're foolish to think that a mere mountain girl from the West can come here and claim control over me."

"Of course, it's already known that the Duke of Solin will stoop to the lowest levels to gain control of the empire," I snapped. "If you want my help, if you want me to continue bowing and scraping at your every wish, then I suggest you drop the issue and let me go to bed."

The duke smiled. "My dear, I'm afraid I can't just do that. You act like you following my orders is a personal choice on your part. I'm surprised it's taken this long for you to realize that any freedom you feel you have is an illusion. You will do what I say whether you are willing or not, but I will *not* abide the lies." Agramon angled his head toward my bedroom door. "You may come out now," he ordered, the gem on his staff glowing as my bedroom door opened. Out stepped Ena, her eyes glassy. My breath caught. I was praying she was safe in the servants' quarters, fast asleep, but I was foolish to believe that was the case. Of course, Agramon would go after Ena.

But Ena was followed by another figure, and my heart fell straight to my knees. Luc stepped in from the shadows of my room, his pained eyes on me.

Chapter 36

"YOU DIDN'T THINK I wouldn't find out about your old lover here in the city, did you?" Agramon asked, one eyebrow raised. Ice spread through my veins as I met Luc's hazel eyes, their light beginning to dim.

"How did you get him?" I gasped, pulling a blade from my knife belt.

"Elgar was kind enough to deliver him at my request. Now, I gave you a chance to be honest before, a chance to gain my trust, and all you did was seek to betray me." Agramon shook his head as though I were some young, willful child he would have to punish. "I asked if you knew this Mordog, and you told me no. I gave you that chance, and you threw it away."

Agramon threw up his hands theatrically, as though this were all some queer sort of game to him. As though we were all puppets, our hands connected with string.

Tears threatening the corners of my eyes, I faced Luc, feeling all hope for the future seep out of me. "Why didn't you get on the boat?" I asked, my voice plaintive. "Why did you come back?"

Luc looked at Agramon, who nodded. "Master told me

to come back," Luc said, his voice wooden. "He told me to kill the man and come back, so I did."

I sucked in a breath. Gray was dead. All those slaves he'd helped rescue, all those lives he'd saved, and now he was dead at the hands of the man I'd sought to free. I glared at Agramon. "Why couldn't you let him go? What use is he to you?"

Agramon smiled. "If I'd had my way, you were never meant to see your dear Luc in the fighting pits. My young Del never gave a hint that she was considering taking you there, and of course, your beau Mellan was wise and didn't come to ask permission. So, imagine my surprise when I find out that you discovered your young friend's whereabouts, especially after I'd worked so hard to orchestrate his demise so he wouldn't be in the way."

"You set it up so he would be fighting the Dwi-Gemi?" I asked, horrified.

Agramon rolled his eyes. "Of course! I couldn't very well have him so obvious in the city where you were. I knew it would give you false hope. So, as soon as I was told to give you more freedom to travel about the city, I arranged for your young friend to die a hero's death. I thought I was doing him a favor. They would've talked about his last great battle for years, but you robbed him of that."

Luc held up my letter to Destrian. It had been opened.

The icy feeling in my spine turned into white-hot fear.

"Now," Agramon said, tapping the tips of his fingers together. "I don't know where you came upon this information that you were trying to send to your lover across the sea, and frankly, I don't really care. It will never reach his eyes; I promise you that."

Luc ripped up the letter, letting the pieces flutter to the floor.

"You see, Rowyn, I could tell you were trying to play our little games that we enjoy here at the capital. I wanted to see if you would come to realize that I was the way toward strength, toward purpose, toward greatness. Yet, you disappointed me every step of the way. It's now time for you to learn your lesson about who is the real power in Lyrica."

I glared at Agramon as Luc and Ena went to stand like soldiers next to his chair, their bodies rigid, their eyes glassy.

"Ena, step forward," Agramon said, shooting me a sinister smile.

"Yes, Your Grace?" she asked, staring at me with a dazed expression.

"Your lady here seems to think that she doesn't have to follow my orders."

Ena paused, her face unreadable. "No, Your Grace. 'Tis not possible."

"But you will follow my orders, won't you, Ena?"

"Of course, Your Grace," Ena said automatically. But there was no life to her voice. The words were not hers.

"No matter what, isn't that right, my dear?"

"Yes, my lord. I am at your pleasure."

"So, if I tell you to . . . say . . . hop on one foot. You would do that for me, wouldn't you, Ena?"

Ena began hopping rhythmically on one foot.

"Stop it," I snapped. "Stop playing with her. She isn't your toy, *Master*," I said, trying to be firm.

"Stop, Ena," Agramon said. Ena stopped. "Now, Ena, I want you to walk over to the hearth."

When she reached the hearth, the fire blazing before her, she turned toward Agramon, awaiting her next order.

"Agramon, please," I said, unable to hide the quivering in my voice. "Agramon, don't hurt her."

"Ena," he said, ignoring me with a smile. "Put your hand in the fire. There's a dear."

"No!" I screamed, but she thrust her hand in, holding it above the red coals.

I could tell when the pain registered in her eyes. They looked on me with terror, but her hand stayed in the flames till the smell of burnt flesh filled the room.

"Stop it, Agramon! Stop!" I pleaded. Throwing myself at Ena, I tackled her, rolling us both away from the fire. Tears streamed down her face as we both examined her hand.

"Do you understand now, Rowyn?" Agramon's voice was cold. He still hadn't moved from his chair. His hands were clasped together, his stark-white-and-gold robes untainted by Ena's torture.

"Yes, Your Grace. I understand," I said, helping Ena up. We turned, her expression still blank, but when I tried to usher her out of the room, she wouldn't budge. "Just leave them alone!" I screamed, trying to pull Ena away. I glanced at my hands and realized that I was wasting time.

I let the power well up into my fingertips as the night sky turned into a frothing boil of clouds and wind.

Agramon's eyes darkened, and his smile grew more sinister. "Go stand at the windows," Agramon said, his eyes hard.

Ena wrenched herself from my grip despite the injured hand and went to stand by a window. Luc followed her. They both turned and faced the room, their eyes growing more vivid and alive, tainted with fear as they realized what was happening.

"What now?" Agramon asked me. "You and I both know that you can't summon the clouds in here. You could, of course, push raw power into the walls of the palace, but how many innocents would you kill with your order?"

I gritted my teeth, calming my power reluctantly. In a

fit of desperation, I raised my hand and let the knife fly toward him. I was only trying to hit his leg, but before the blade could reach him, it turned around, mid-flight, and soared toward me instead. I had to throw myself to the ground to get out of its way. Agramon laughed as I rose once more, completely out of options.

Agramon stood and took a step toward me. "Do you remember when we landed? Do you remember what I told you?"

"No." I sobbed. "Please don't do this."

He ignored my pleas, taking a step, and another until he was right in front of me. "I said that I would break you," he whispered.

"Not this," I repeated. "Please!" I couldn't think. I couldn't breathe. Raw fear blinded my every thought and emotion.

"I said that I would break you, and I meant it."

"I'll do whatever you want!" I screamed.

Agramon laughed, tapping the staff on the ground as he chortled. "My dear, you aren't in the position to make deals, let alone demands. You broke my trust, and that comes with a punishment to ensure that it won't happen again. Now, let's play a game, shall we? Here I have two Morganites from your homeland, each devoted to you in different ways. One you've known since childhood, yet who disappeared during some of your hardest trials in life."

"Just leave them alone!" I screamed, throwing my arm toward Luc. "What more do you want from me that you don't already have?"

Agramon ran his fingertips along the imorets around the corners of my eyes. "I want your complete and utter obedience, Rowyn. I made that clear from the very beginning. I tried to give you what you wanted. I tried to gain your loyalty through spoiling you, and being lenient, and bowing to your whims, no matter how misguided. It was the way that Gillius suggested, yet you still openly defied me at every turn."

"Please, I'll obey you," I whispered as Agramon caught a tear with his thumb and drew his finger to his mouth.

"It's too late, my dear. You've given me no choice but to show you what happens to those who defy my wishes. I demand your loyalty and allegiance. If you won't give it to me willingly, then I will have to take it through fear." He looked up at Luc and Ena.

Ena had tears rolling down her cheeks while Luc's eyes snapped with hatred. Agramon's new cruelty was being inflicted with knife-point precision.

"Why can't you just leave them alone," I whimpered, trying to go to them—to do what, I didn't know.

Agramon caught my arms and held me back. Leaning into my ear, he hissed, "Look at them. Your two loyal friends. Which one will you save, I wonder?"

I struggled in his grip, but Agramon was stronger than he looked. He laughed, my dress slipping from his fingers.

"Jump!" Agramon shouted.

I didn't think. I didn't know what I would've done if Agramon had given me half a second to consider, but as it was, I raced as fast as my legs could carry me toward the windows. My hand reached out, as if on instinct. I caught an arm and pulled, tripping Luc beneath me as Agramon cackled.

"Enough!" Agramon said, wiping his eyes.

I spun around to where Ena had been standing, but she was gone.

Chapter 37

I DIDN'T SLEEP AT ALL THAT NIGHT. Guardsmen came in later with the news that Ena had been found, broken, outside the palace walls. Agramon wouldn't permit me to speak while he declared that Ena must've ended her own life in despair, so they took her body away to be burned. I wept until there wasn't a drop of moisture left in my body, and still it wasn't enough. How could I have let it get that far? How could I have ignored her fears for so long? What had I done?

Arden flew in and stood as an odd sort of sentry at the window, watching me shake on the bed as fear and hatred overtook me. I didn't think I would ever recover from Ena's loss. Not the girl who greeted me with a smile every morning, whose soft hands and kind heart had kept me going when my friends and family abandoned me. Ena was the closest to family I'd had left, and I let her slip away.

At dawn I left my room. I was concerned about Luc but found him sitting in the receiving room and staring at his hands.

"What are you doing?" I sniffed, running my sleeve over my nose.

"He told me to guard his room," Luc said, his voice

gruff.

Agramon's door opened, and he stepped out, newly shaven and in clean robes.

"Ah, you're out," he said, clapping his hands together. "I must admit, I may come to like our new arrangement. I've always been told I should hire a personal guard, so I think this will work out nicely, don't you, my dear?"

I glared at him. "Why can't you just let him return home. Hasn't he done enough for you?" I couldn't fathom hating anyone more than I hated Agramon. I glared at him as I sank onto the couch, losing all ability to stand.

"No," Agramon said, "I think not. Given his past, I think he'll be much more useful here, in Somme. Perhaps he can even help me keep an eye on you."

"How did you know about him?" I demanded, turning away from the shell of the boy I once knew to face Agramon. "You can't read my mind, so how did you find out about him?"

Agramon clenched his teeth. "Ever the one to ask the wrong questions. Don't be such a simpleton. What you should be figuring out, right about now, is how did we find out about you?"

My eyes widened, and I turned to Luc, astounded at Agramon's proclamation.

"Yes, you're seeing it now, aren't you," Agramon quipped. "How did we know about the little girl hidden behind the shroud of Morgania, with the power to shake the heavens? Quite frankly, I'm surprised it took you this long to realize what you should've already guessed. Who else had traveled east from your clan? Who else would've known you best, and possibly spoken about you to others? It didn't take long for another mind reader to hear the rumblings of a girl with enough power to bring the downfall of the empire. My comrade sent me notice, and I went to investigate, and what do I find, to my surprise, but that all the rumblings were true!"

I stared at Luc, unable to form words. My childhood love met my gaze, his eyes filled with an emotion I recognized more than any other feeling, guilt.

"It was *you*?" I gasped. "You were the one who gave me away? *You* started all of this?"

Luc shrank within himself, his face stricken. "Rowyn, they stole it from my memories!"

Agramon laughed as though the memory was some great joke. "By then, of course, it had been spoken of enough that the seer, Chassandre, found out. It was only a matter of time before her creature found you and sent you back to the dirt. So, I had to send the closest person at my disposal to assist you. Gillius was handy and already well-known on the western shore among the sorcerers, so he was naturally the one I asked to make the journey. I would've gone myself, but that would've scared you off, and it would've been far harder to keep you tethered to the empire.

"No, Gillius, the poor farmer's son from the Western Empire, his family killed in a rebellion, was the perfect candidate to lure you under our sway, and it was only a matter of time until Vianne worked her magic to ensure that any information you *did* find out was omitted from your memories. I will admit, she removed far more than was probably wise, but you've gotten it back, haven't you?"

I couldn't breathe, I couldn't think, I could do nothing but stare at Luc as all my dreams fell away. It was as if my entire life had been nothing but a great lie ever since I'd stepped from the woods of Morgania.

"You should tell her of all the comforts you gained for your memories," Agramon said to Luc as he went to sit in a chair. "You see, my dear, he was too valuable to keep at the frontlines. He knew his memories were important, and he figured out a way to keep some hidden, so instead of us torturing him and pulling the information the hard way, he began to make deals."

"What did you do?" I asked, choking out the words.

"Should I tell her?" Agramon prodded, nudging Luc with his staff. "Should I detail the nights you spent enjoying the company of countless women while your comrades died on those battlefields far away? He even offered to show us where to find you."

I glared at Luc. "How could you do that to me?" I asked as I felt every wretched feeling from the past year.

A dark expression crossed Luc's face. "They weren't going to hurt you. Would you have rather me die? How many Morganites returned from the battles in Yliria, Rowyn? How many Morganite slaves do you see here at the capital? How many of us are in the Fields of Forgotten Men? Can you imagine me in those positions? How long would I have survived?"

"What of your honor?" I shouted, practically spitting at him. "Here I did my damnedest to save you, and you sold me to the wolves. You've lost so much self-respect, you couldn't even be bothered to save yourself! Now all of this was for nothing! My betrayal of Agramon, me trying to save your life, *Ena's life*, it was all for nothing! You were never worth saving!"

Luc's eyes widened, hurt crossing his features, and I remembered the boy I'd grown up loving. He was still there in Luc, still waiting to be saved while hating what he'd become. I could see it in his eyes. Luc thought that no matter what, no matter how much he'd sold me out, he thought that I would've forgiven him.

Chapter 38

EMPEROR ARTHELLO STOOD AT the window, looking out over the city. "So now we're at war," he said. I stiffened under Agramon's fingertips. The emperor turned, and I noticed black circles under his eyes.

"The empire is sure to be upset," Agramon said, investigating his fingertips. "If you wish to appease the people, Rowyn and I will need to leave on our expedition. It's time."

"That's a wonderful idea," the emperor said, motioning a slave to pour him a goblet of wine. "Distract the people while we regain our honor."

"Your Excellency, the people don't care a jot about the honor of those in a throne room. They will care about the war," I said, insistent that he end that folly. The emperor looked at me, perplexed that I spoke in his presence.

"We can't let Lu Shen's insult to you stand," the emperor said, his hands clasped behind his back as he turned back to the window. "I've made up my mind. We are going to war. Besides, their black powder recipe continues to elude Berinon, and I'll need to ensure that we're able to bring more to Lyrica so that we can become even more formidable a force."

Out of the corner of my eye, Sam rose from his seat at the table. The entire time, I'd ignored his presence. I didn't know how much he knew about Ena's death, nor the fact that the boy I'd saved from the fighting pits was now Agramon's prisoner, but he had to understand Agramon enough to guess. Yet he'd done nothing.

"If we're to go to war, Your Eminence, then I will need to call up arms once more," Sam said, his eyes narrowed at Agramon. "I might as well accompany them on their expedition and help with security since I'll have to raise the banners again."

Agramon scowled. "There's no need—"

"Of course, Baron," the emperor interjected. "That's an excellent idea. Two birds with one stone and all that."

"I would think you would want to plan your assault here at the capital, with the rest of the generals," Agramon hissed.

Sam glanced at me for a split second before meeting Agramon's eye. "If the men are to be called up again, it's better if I'm the one to do it. You would know such things, too, if you had a loyal bone in your body."

"Come now," the emperor said, his smile wide. "There's no need to bicker. It makes far more sense for Baron Samael to accompany you on this grand procession. I can just see it now, the greatest Lyrican sorcerers to ever live, riding at the head of our vast army, about to brave battle once more for their sovereign. It will be the perfect start to our quinquennial year, wouldn't you agree?"

A muscle in Agramon's cheek spasmed. "Of course, Your Eminence."

Sam said nothing.

"Very well," the emperor said, striding toward the door. "Make the preparations quickly. I want you all out of the capital by week's end."

The door shut ominously behind the emperor. I looked between Agramon and Sam, who continued to glare at each other. Without a word, I turned and left the men in the council chamber. Walking down the hall, I headed to my room to throw myself on the bed and weep.

The End

The story continues in Tempest Rising Book 4

Empire of Dust

Preorder today on Amazon.com.

Please be sure to leave an honest review of
A Gilded Cage
at Amazon.com or Goodreads.com.

Follow us online!

https://www.elliottvandruff.com

https://www.facebook.com/elliottvandruff/

https://twitter.com/EVandruff

—

Make sure to sign up for our newsletter to receive communications on new releases and special content!

A GILDED CAGE

Acknowledgments

I would like to take the time to acknowledge several individuals who made *A Gilded Cage* possible. The first being my husband, whose continued unwavering support gave me the time and means to write.

I would also like to thank my three beta readers, Galen Gould, Aureece Einfeld, and Patrick Wolfgang, who took the time to provide support and ideas. Additionally, I would like to thank my fan and friend, Dani Frank-Browning, whose enthusiasm for what I've written kept the story at the forefront of my mind.

Finally, I continue to appreciate my editor, Cayce Berryman, from Kingsman Editing, whose patience with me this time around was very much appreciated.